Missing

Mark Harrison

UKA PRESS

UKA Press, 55 Elmsdale Road, Walthamstow, London, E17 6PN, UK
UKA Press, Olympiaweg 102-hs, 1076 XG, Amsterdam, Holland
UKAPress, Anderson St, 108, 2-5-22 Shida, Shizuoka 426-0071, Japan

2 4 6 8 10 9 7 5 3 1

First published in Great Britain in 2006 by
UKA PRESS
55 Elmsdale Road
Walthamstow
London, E17 6PN

www.ukapress.com

A CIP catalogue record for this book is available from the British Library

ISBN: 978-1-905796-02-1 1-905796-02-1

Edit © DON MASTERS (A.St.) of UKA PRESS
Interior design by DON MASTERS
Cover photograph © Mark Harrison 2004
Cover design by Peter J. Merrigan
Printed and bound in Great Britain by Biddles Ltd., King's Lynn

for Vivien

With appreciation and gratitude to
DON MASTERS *of* UKA PRESS
for editing and creative work

Missing

Chapter One

'Ah, Fernandez, just the man.' Chief Superintendent Philip Bowater OBE, QPM, glanced up. 'Take a seat.' He went back to scribbling. 'With you in a moment.'

So this was the inner sanctum.

Detective Inspector Michael Fernandez sat down and looked around the office, noticing the commendation for bravery signed with a squiggle of blue ink above the words, "Home Secretary."

Michael crossed his legs, straightened his back and adjusted his tie. He should have left his jacket in the office. He glanced at the knife-edge creases in his grey woollen trousers, and brushed away a piece of fluff. At least his black brogues were shiny. The Chief Super's shoes protruded beneath the mahogany desk. The tasselled oxblood loafers glistened in the light, revealing a faint crease along the top of the toes. The hard leather soles were almost as polished as the uppers, from miles walked over carpets and tiles. Huge shoes, size 11 or 12, and in perfect proportion with the rest of Bowater's frame.

When asked to explain how it was that his first impressions, according to him, rarely let him down, Michael often said he could read a person from the shoes they wore, and these shoes, though old, exuded quality and style, if not a particular talent for the job.

But why had the Chief Super asked to see him personally?

He usually managed to keep out of trouble. Throughout his fourteen years in the Nottinghamshire Constabulary, Michael had taken the attitude that rules were to be followed to the letter, seeing them (and this was the part others didn't understand), as a chance to relax over mindless paperwork and do some thinking.

True, a few jokes cropped up in the Criminal Investigation Division over his so-called "conscientiousness" – but he got results.

Ten years in CID had given him intuition, or 'a nose for the job,' as some said – making it sound as if his nose twitched. No, if he were someone else who had to write a report on himself, he'd toss off something like, "he has a gift, which he uses in conjunction with the facts." Whatever the definition, the results gave him a kind of mystique, an aura, that more than outweighed any teasing he might have to endure in the office. Though it certainly could be infuriating...

Two pairs of eyes caught his attention. They seemed to be gazing adoringly out at him from their silver frame. Twin daughters, long blonde locks draped across their shoulders, they formed mirror images in mortarboards and gowns. Distinguished parents flanked them, pride epitomised by beaming smiles.

Afraid of staring, Michael looked away.

Bowater leaned over the pages, his pen hovering and his eyes flicking from side to side as he followed lines of text.

Michael noticed a bald patch on top of Bowater's head. He'd started combing his hair forward in the last few months, and colleagues had remarked on it. The colour had also changed, from brown to black, coinciding with the disappearance of grey hair from the temples. No such problems for Michael, whose hair was "uniformly thick, and naturally slippery," as he'd explained last week to Inspector Rawlinson who was asking round the office, "What's your ideal detective hair style, for this week's suggestion box joke?"

Now, anxiety began to turn to impatience. Was this a "mind game" from the hopelessly redundant Interrogation Techniques Course?

'That's done,' said Bowater, rising to his full six foot six inches to look down on the Inspector.

He buttoned the double-breasted jacket of his blue pinstriped suit, strode across the office and stepped out.

'There you go, Penny. Just a few changes. Then get one of the constables to run it over to HQ this afternoon, please. Oh, and make a pot of tea for Michael and me. Soon as you can. Thanks.'

Michael? The Chief had never used his first name before.

'Let's sit over here. More comfortable.' Bowater gestured toward the coffee table as he collected a blue folder from his desk.

'How's your Spanish these days?' he said. 'You do speak Spanish, don't you? It's on your file. How is it?'

'Fine. I mean, it's – it's all right.' Michael felt himself stutter. 'Pretty good, I suppose. Don't use it much.'

'But I'm right in thinking you're quite fluent, aren't I? We're not just talking schoolboy Spanish, are we?'

'No, sir.'

'That's what I thought. How would you like to get some practice?'

What the hell was he on about? Michael had better be careful how he answered, or he might volunteer for something he didn't want to do.

'Not sure I really need to practise. I mean, it would soon come back to me if the need arose.'

'Good, that's what I wanted to hear.'

Michael's heart sank. This had all the hallmarks of a set up.

'Tell me Michael, are you married?'

'Divorced.'

'Children?'

'No, sir.'

'Live alone?'

'Yes, sir.'

'So, no family ties?'

'Depends what you mean.' And what *did* he mean? Michael's suspicions were now fully roused.

'You know. No one you're responsible for. Ageing relative, sick auntie, crippled dog, that sort of thing?'

'Not exactly.'

Michael flushed and stiffened, as if to protect an imaginary aunt or dog. But it was difficult to be evasive, short of telling the Chief to mind his own damned business, and say he had plenty of friends and family, thanks.

However... 'Look, sir, do you mind telling me what this is about?'

'Sorry, Fernandez – Michael. You're right to be curious. I just wanted to know how things stood. Have you seen this?'

Bowater pulled a Nottingham Evening Post from the folder and slid it across the table. Michael caught it before it fell to the floor. He read the headline: "NOTTS COUPLE DISAPPEAR IN SPAIN".

'Know anything about it?'

'Only what I've seen in the papers.' Michael stopped reading, put down the newspaper and looked at the Chief Super. Was this a chance to impress? 'A local couple left for Alicante two or three months ago.

Retired in search of their dream home. Not been heard of for a few weeks. Relatives getting concerned. Money still being withdrawn from the bank. Hire car overdue. Spanish police suspect foul play.'

A knock sounded at the door; three gentle taps.

'Come in, Penny. Splendid, we'll have it over here, please. Just leave the tray. Thanks.'

Penny Edwardes wriggled demurely toward them, her tiny steps determined by the circumference of her tight skirt. She lent forward carefully, bending her knees to prevent showing more of her shapely legs. Sitting at the low table, the two men were in direct eye-line with her cleavage. Michael reached for the tray.

'Here, Penny. Let me take that.'

'Oh, thank you, Michael.'

Penny turned and tiptoed back toward the door, her high-heeled stilettos leaving pin-point imprints in the thick woollen carpet.

'I forgot, you two know each other, don't you? I mean, outside the office.' It was the Chief Superintendent's turn to stutter. 'Not much escapes my notice. Office gossip, I mean.' He reached for the milk jug.

Michael felt his cheeks glow as they reddened. He picked the newspaper up. 'That was over months ago. It never really got started.'

'Actually, it was almost four months ago,' said Bowater, to Michael's surprise. 'I mean, since the Harrington's left for Spain,' he added quickly. 'And twelve weeks since they were last in contact with anyone over here.'

Michael was silent. He began to realise where this was leading.

Bowater poured the tea from the stainless steel pot, careful not to overfill the Royal Worcester cups. The gold rims were a little worn, but they would still create exactly the right impression, Michael imagined, for the elite who crossed the threshold.

'Help yourself to milk and sugar.'

Michael usually took his tea with lemon, but thought better than to ask. He added a generous splash of milk.

'Any ideas?'

Michael paused for a moment.

'Sometimes people want to disappear, of course. Start a new life. Lose the baggage. That sort of thing.'

Bowater sat back in his chair, cradling the bone china saucer in his left hand and lifting the cup with his right. 'That's exactly what I thought. But we're both missing something.' He took a sip.

'What's that?'

'It's happened before.'

'What has?'

'Last year another British couple left for Spain. Roughly the same area. Disappeared for months. Then they were found dead. Tortured and murdered for their money by a gang of Venezuelans. The Spanish cops caught them, but took a lot of flack for not taking it seriously in the first place. So did the Foreign Secretary for not putting pressure on the Spanish authorities. The Foreign Sec's PPS has already been on to the Chief Constable. Wants things handled carefully at this end. Covering his back this time. You get the picture?'

Michael nodded.He knew what was coming next.

'So you're the obvious choice. What do you think?'

'I suppose I can take a look. See if there's anything I can suggest.'

'I don't think you've quite got my drift, Michael. The Foreign Secretary wants someone in Spain to work with the Spanish police. And the Spanish authorities are worried about the effect on tourism and property sales. The Guardia Civil think it's a good idea, as well. They're not daft. Having the British police involved will share the responsibility, and the blame, if anything goes wrong. We need someone who can deal with the relatives at this end, and also work with the police in Spain. The Guardia Civil isn't exactly flush with fluent English speakers, so they've asked for someone who can speak Spanish. So you see? You fit the bill perfectly. What do you think?'

Michael took a long draft of tea and nearly choked. How could anyone drink this lukewarm, creamy stuff? He returned the cup and saucer to the table. 'I have to make a decision, then?'

'Not exactly that. Let's just say the Chief Constable would be very disappointed if you refused. Anyway, what's the problem? I thought you'd jump at the chance of visiting your homeland, all expenses paid, get a bit of spring sunshine.'

'What makes you think Spain is my homeland?' Michael managed a tight smile.

'Well, I just thought with the Spanish, and a name like Fernandez.'

'The name comes from my father. He was Spanish, I'm English.'

'My mistake. Sorry, but all the same it'll be good to go back. See the relatives, perhaps.'

'I'm afraid I've never been to Spain. I speak Spanish because my father taught me, but that's as far as it goes.'

If it wasn't in the file, he wasn't going to mention he'd taken and taught the subject at university.

Bowater straightened, removed his rimless spectacles and tossed them onto the table.

'You're joking. I thought everybody had been to Spain, even if only on a package – to Benidorm, or Majorca.'

'No, I've never set foot in Spain and the fact is, I'm not sure I want to go now.'

'Is there something I'm missing here? Something I should know? You're not wanted by the Spanish police, are you? An illegal immigrant or something?'

'No, sir.'

'Look, cut the "sir" crap, now. Let's be straight with each other. Unless there's any good reason why you can't, you're going to Spain. There's too much at stake here for you as well as for me. Now, for the last time, what's the problem?'

Michael hesitated, to consider his options. There were none.

'I'll be frank with you. I'm just not personally interested in going to Spain, especially on a wild goose chase. I don't see that anything could come out of it. But if there's no alternative, I will go.'

'Course you will. That's the spirit. I knew you'd do this, Fernandez. You never know, it could be the making of you. After all, you've been an Inspector for how long, twelve years? That's a long time. I understand you've refused offers to go before the promotion board.'

'I prefer to be involved in direct investigative work, sir.'

'Quite.' Bowater turned a page without looking up. 'And with excellent results. But this will give you a little limelight, give you a feeling for managing a larger team. Lot to be said for it, you know.'

Michael sat back in his chair. A thousand thoughts ran through his mind, not one of them to do with David and Alison Harrington.

The Chief Superintendent slid the folder across the coffee table. 'Here's what we have so far. You're booked on the 15.25 ValuJet flight from East Midlands on Monday. That gives you the rest of this week, and the weekend if you need it.'

'ValuJet?'

'Short flight. We need to be seen to make economies. There are a few leads to follow up before you go. Couple of property companies contacted by the Harringtons before they went in search of their dream home. Oh, and you'll need to speak to the brother and sister-in-law. They raised the alarm. Well, it was the sister-in-law, Linda Harrington, who made the first contact. The brother didn't seem too concerned.'

'Well, I would have to say, if the immediate family doesn't seem too concerned, then surely – '

'No, that's not enough, Michael. This is a public issue. We need to respond. The Foreign Secretary, the Chief Constable, and I, for that matter, think there's enough evidence to give cause for concern. So I don't want it to be a half-hearted effort on anyone's part. If you're right, they'll turn up as soon as the word's out that a search party's on its way. Then everyone will be happy and you can come back home. Until then, I want one hundred percent from you and your Spanish counterpart. Did I tell you the Guardia Civil have assigned their own officer to work with you? Captain Josie somebody-or-other.'

'Jose?' Michael, stressed the 'H' sound.

'Yes, all right. The name's in the file. He's picking you up at Alicante airport. Make sure you're ready. We need to be careful. Can't afford to do anything to upset our Spanish colleagues.'

Michael opened the folder, and Bowater returned to his desk. He sat down in the high-backed leather chair.

'That's all for now, Fernandez, but I'd like to see you on Monday, before you leave.' He opened his diary. 'Ten-thirty. Just before the HQ briefing. You can bring me up to date and I can put the Chief Constable in the picture while you wing your way to sunny Spain.'

Michael stood up, tucked the folder under his arm, and headed for the door. 'Thank you, sir.'

'It's Miguel-Angel, isn't it?' Bowater said. He pronounced it *Migwel* Angel. 'Your original first name. It's on your file.'

Michael turned. 'Mig-el, sir. I've never used the angel.'

'Just wondered,' said Bowater closing the pink personnel file. 'You're very lucky, you know. Beautiful country, Spain. Alhambra Palace, Granada – Seville, with Gaudi's Cathedral... You don't paint ceilings in your spare time, do you?'

'I'd like to, sir.' Michael opened the door. 'But Michelangelo turned out to be Italian, and Gaudi's cathedral isn't in Seville.'

Bowater continued cheerfully, 'What part of Spain is your father from, then?'

Michael glared at the photograph of the Chief Superintendent's two daughters.

'My father was from Alicante. Is that all for now, sir?'

'Just one other thing. We need to fax a copy of your passport to the Guardia in Alicante so they can arrange some kind of ID for you when you arrive. Pop it in with Penny in the morning, and she'll do the rest. You do have a passport, don't you?'

'Yes, sir. I have a British passport.'

Michael shut the door sharply. Penny and the other two secretaries in the outer office looked at him. Silence replaced the usual chatter.

'Some people have all the luck,' said Penny. 'Don't suppose you get to take a partner on your Spanish siesta, do you?' She adopted a provocative pose, mimicking a flamenco dancer.

'Is nothing confidential?'

'Ooh, what's ruffled your collar?' Penny laughed. 'Sorry, Michael, only joking.' The other secretaries giggled.

Michael slammed the door and marched down the corridor to the lift. By the time he reached the office of the Criminal Investigation Division, he was concerned only with: Why did it take so long for the family to come forward? Could this be a copycat of the earlier case?

He strode toward his desk in the corner, without lifting his eyes from the file. A humming from his work mates gradually rose to a crescendo. 'Oh, yes, we're off to sunny Spain, y viiiiivah España.'

'Ah, get lost.' Michael picked up his bag. 'Gringo bastards.'

'Have a beer, you lucky bastard. How about a *San Miguel*?' someone shouted.

Michael marched out to the street.

Chapter Two

He almost missed the office of Saunders & Shaw, Spanish Property Agents. Looking for a shop window, he was surprised to find only a small plaque directing him to the first floor office above a hardware store in Nottingham's Broadway.

'Please sit down, Inspector. How can I help you?'

Susan Shaw sounded more excited than concerned about the presence of a detective.

'You look well. Been somewhere nice?'

'Sorry, Mrs. Shaw, but I haven't got much time, and there are other property agents I have to see before next week.'

'Please, call me Susan. I don't know what more I can tell you. I told everything I know to the sergeant last time.'

'I know it's a bit of a pain, but there are just a few questions.'

Susan Shaw flicked her wispy blonde fringe back from her eyes, but it returned to the same position. Prim and professional in lime green skirt and jacket, her cream silk blouse set off a double row of pearls. As she flicked her hair again Michael caught a glint from a ring on her left hand. Three enormous, brilliant diamonds stood proud of her finger and seemed to dwarf the plain gold wedding band. A diamond solitaire on the third finger of her right hand confirmed that this was a lady of substance who liked to show it ostentatiously.

'Not at all, Inspector. Only too glad to help.'

She flicked her head so that her hair fell behind her shoulders and revealed more of her powdered face and the wrinkles on her neck. Her heavy perfume was beginning to irritate. She pushed her chair away from the desk and crossed her legs. The suit skirt was a fraction too short and gave a hint of slightly bulky thighs above the hemline. They were carefully covered by sheer, skin-coloured tights. Or were they stockings? Michael's eyes were drawn to the peach-coloured sling-backs that adorned her feet. The elongated toes culminated in vicious points that made her feet appear much longer than they were.

Susan licked her lips lightly.

'How do you make your money, Mrs Shaw?'

'What?'

She stopped flirting.

'Well, I know you advertise property for sale in Spain, but you don't seem to have a shop window, just this office. And I can't see any photos or brochures of property for sale. I just wondered how you manage to sell anything, and where the money comes from.'

Susan relaxed. 'Ah, I understand. You're thinking of us like an English estate agent. The Spanish market doesn't work like that. We don't actually have any properties on our books, so to speak.'

Michael let her continue, despite his confusion.

'You see, anyone wanting to sell a house in Spain, new or resale, would appoint a Spanish agent. The Spanish agent does the usual stuff, valuations, brochures, that kind of thing, and most have a shop window somewhere. But they rely on other people in the UK, Holland, Germany, wherever. That's where we come in. We advertise extensively – Sunday Times, Mail on Sunday, property exhibitions and events. When we get a response, we ask people what kind of property they're looking for – size, price, location, etc. Then our man in the Costa Blanca contacts all the local agents, and sends us details of properties that might interest our clients. We used to do it all by fax until a couple of years ago. Now it's all done by e-mail. Sometimes we just download details from web sites and send them on. If the details we send clients are of interest, we arrange for our man to meet them in Spain and show them round. You see, we are really just an intermediary between the client and the Spanish agent.'

'But how do you make money?' Michael tried not to look perplexed.

'Ah, yes – well, Spanish agent's fees are much higher than is normal in the UK, sometimes as high as ten percent of the sale price. If we introduce a client and the sale goes ahead, we take a share of the fee. There's plenty to go around, even after we pay our man over there.'

Michael stood up.

'That's very helpful, Mrs Shaw. Thank you.'

'Is that all?' Her disappointment was obvious. 'Don't you want to know about the Harringtons? About the properties we offered them?'

'It's in the file, thanks. Sergeant Rawlinson made extensive notes. I can talk to your man – Brian Small, isn't it – in Spain. I've got his details.'

'Yes, of course. He's an interesting character, you know. Lived in Spain for years. Not your typical property salesman, but the clients like him and he knows the Costa Blanca like the back of his hand.'

'I just hope he can shed some light on where the Harringtons are, then, assuming they're still alive.'

Susan looked serious. 'I hope to God they are. Another murder would be very bad for business.'

'And for the Harringtons, poor devils.' Michael moved toward the door. 'Thanks for your help, Mrs Shaw.'

'By the way, are you Spanish or English, Inspector Fernandez?'

'Yes,' Michael replied. 'Good afternoon.'

He was already on his way out.

The Hilltops Estate was as drab and dreary as he remembered from childhood. Block after block of identical terraced houses lined narrow roads. The town planners of the 1950s had not anticipated the spread of cars to the working classes when they designed this patch of social housing. Pennine Way, Cotswold Road, Cheviot Avenue, gave a clue to the well-intentioned post-war dreams of Nottingham's city fathers.

It would be easy to get lost in the rabbit warren of culs de sac that were linked to the main roads like tributaries to a river, but Michael knew the way to Brecon Road. He passed the Harringtons' house on the left and drove by, in search of a parking space. With some reluctance, he left his car in a garage forecourt where he'd kicked tin cans as a kid.

Always a scruffy backwater, it had deteriorated into a dumping ground. Half the garage doors were missing, the others kicked-in or obliterated by graffiti. An old Ford Escort sat abandoned in the corner, its wheels removed and the hubs perched on four columns of bricks.

He walked back toward No.22, passing four blocks of red brick houses with grey slate roofs. Gone was the uniformity, when the colour of a front door was the only distinguishing feature on a house. The old standard-style doors and windows had been replaced, by residents anxious to display their new status as property owners.

He opened the rickety gate to No.22, and walked up the weed-lined path. Before he knocked, Linda Harrington opened the door.

'Come in, Inspector. Thank you for coming.'

'Not at all, Mrs Harrington. Sorry to disturb you on a Sunday, but it's important I speak to you and your husband before I go to Spain.'

'John, the Inspector's here – we're in the kitchen. Coffee, Inspector?'

'Yes – yes, thank you… '

Michael was still surprised by Linda Harrington's soft hair and pretty face. 'That would be very nice, thank you,' he went on, watching the pale blue, calf-length slacks turn right at the end of the hallway, noting Linda Harrington's slim figure. He'd conjured up hair curlers, headscarf and fag.

John Harrington, on the other hand, did not disappoint. He shuffled into the hall in grubby, lace-less trainers without socks, and a T-shirt stretched over the waistband of track-suit bottoms.

The only thing that surprised was that he didn't sport a beer gut.

Several photographs of David Harrington were in Michael's file, and in them all, David was tidily dressed, clean-shaven and carefully groomed. John looked an inch or two shorter than the 180cm recorded on David's file, but though David was perhaps more strongly built it wasn't hard to see a resemblance in the sleepy eyes, square jawline and low forehead. However, John's ruffled mop and recalcitrant expression were in complete contrast to David's precise parting and close-cropped sides, and his warm, somewhat shy smile. David was a handsome man.

'Pass us the fags, love.' John slumped into a chair opposite Michael at the formica table, and ran a hand over the grey stubble on his chin.

Michael leaned back to take the report pad out of his briefcase.

'I don't need to go over everything. The sergeant's put me in the picture, but there are a couple of things. According to the file, your brother and his wife left for Spain on 7th January.'

John lit a cigarette, pulled hard on it, and expelled a cloud of smoke. 'Something like that, can't remember exactly.'

'After buying a property, they were due back here on the 21st.'

'Not necessarily.'

'Sorry, I don't understand. What do you mean?'

'Well, they were booked for two weeks, right, but that doesn't mean they were coming back.'

'I'm still not sure what you mean, Mr Harrington.'

'They booked the hotel for a couple of weeks, but David said something about renting a place after that so they could have longer to look round if they needed it.'

'Why didn't you tell this to the sergeant?'

'He never asked.'

'Mr Harrington, is there any reason you know of, why your brother might want to disappear?'

'What, like he's robbed a bank or something? You must be joking. You don't know David, do you? Everything carefully planned, everything worked out. Good job, steady wage, bought his house, saved his money, didn't smoke or drink. Then the bugger drops lucky and gets a redundancy payout. Before you know it, he's off to Spain with the painted princess and doesn't give a shit about anyone else.'

'Painted princess?'

'That wife of his, Alison.'

Linda placed a cup and saucer in front of Michael. 'John, whatever you think, it's not like David and Alison not to be in touch. As you'll have gathered, Inspector, we're not always the closest of families, but even so it's over ten weeks since we heard from them. And now it seems a couple were murdered over there, only last year.'

Michael sipped his instant coffee, and coughed. 'I shouldn't be too alarmed, Mrs Harrington. There's probably some logical explanation, and they'll turn up before I get to Spain, wondering what all the fuss is about.'

'That'll spoil your holiday.' John snapped open The Sun.

Michael began a sigh, but left it. 'I've got details of properties they were interested in and I'm meeting agents out there. But I was wondering, where did the money come from? I mean, some houses viewed were over two hundred thousand pounds, and they'd need money to live off.'

He had John's full attention now.

'Two hundred grand? Jesus, I knew they had a bit tucked away and the money from the house, but two hundred grand?'

'Don't get me wrong, Mr Harrington, some properties were much more modestly priced, but a couple were in that bracket. I'll have a better idea when I get to Spain...You mentioned a redundancy payout?'

'Yes, my brother worked for the local Council, in the Printing Department. They were getting rid of people and David volunteered to go. Tell you the truth, I was gob-smacked. He'd been there about seventeen years, but they must have made it worth his while to leave.'

'Any idea how much?' Michael knew the answer to that one.

'Nope. Like I say. You don't know my brother, the secret squirrel.'

'And you mentioned selling up. What do you mean?'

Linda jumped in, as John returned his attention to the back page.

'They lived just round the corner, in Mendip Road, overlooking the playing fields. They decided to buy from the Council about ten years ago. Got the place for next to nothing, what with the discount and all that. They did it up, put in a new kitchen and built an extension with a dining room and extra bedroom. Sold it last October for almost ninety thousand, and no mortgage to pay off. Of course, we could have done the same thing, but John wouldn't have it. "Better to rent," he said...'

John slapped the newspaper down, stood up and left the room.

Seconds later, the television roared as someone didn't score in a football match.

'Sorry about that, Inspector – they're like chalk and cheese, David and John, but quite close really, and John's as worried as me, deep down. Oh, look! – your coffee's gone cold. Can I get you a fresh cup?'

The offer was politely declined.

'Tell me about Alison. John seems to have a critical opinion.'

'Bit of jealousy, I expect. You see, David was a bachelor until he was thirty-five. Never seemed interested in taking a chance on marriage. More of the serious type, set in his own ways. Then he met Alison at the amateur dramatic society and we were all shocked when they announced they were getting married. She's an attractive woman, eight years younger than David, outgoing, and she likes to dress – well, let's just say – a bit younger than her age. Mind you, she's got the figure for it. Not expensive stuff, you understand, couldn't see David paying for that, but fashionable. You know, the sort of stuff the kids wear.'

'Does – did she work?'

'Yes, she had a job in a trendy hairdressers in town, but only part-time for the last couple of years.'

'Did she have money of her own? Inheritance, anything like that?'

'Not that I know of. Her parents died, I think, some years ago. At least, so we understood. Put it this way, they weren't at the wedding.'

'Any children?'

'No. That's another sore point with John. Especially when our two boys start playing him up, and asking him for money.'

'Anyone else they were particularly friendly with?'

'They had a few friends from the dramatic society, but no one they palled out with on a regular basis. I've spoken to people from David's work and from the hairdressers, but no one's heard a thing.'

'Did they contact you regularly when they first left for Spain?'

'Well, they phoned three or four times in the first two weeks, while they were in the hotel, but after that there was nothing for a couple of weeks. Then they phoned in early February. I was out at bingo, and they spoke to John one Saturday evening. John was watching football and he'd had a few beers, and he said David hadn't had much to say, but they were still looking round. I asked if David mentioned where they were staying, but he said they didn't talk about it – or if they had, he didn't remember.'

'What about Alison? Have you talked to her at all since they left?'

'Oh, yes. David talked to John for a few minutes, then I had a quick word with Alison, but I was aware of the cost and didn't speak long.'

'Did she say much?'

'Not really. Just that the weather was great, and they'd looked at some very nice properties.'

'Did she seem different to you? Excited, appprehensive, anxious or anything like that?'

'No. Just the same old Alison, as I recall. It was almost as if they were just on holiday out there again.'

'Again?' Something else not in Sergeant Rawlinson's notes.

'Yes, they had a holiday in Benidorm last August. They really liked it, though there was no mention of going to live out there at that stage.'

'So when did they first mention the idea?'

'I think it was around September. Yes, that's right, David had been offered the redundancy and that seemed to spark things off. It all happened so quickly. Before we knew it, they'd sold the house and off they went looking for their dream home.'

'So they hadn't talked about Spain before?'

'No. Even going to Benidorm was unusual, because they'd always gone to France before that. David loved it. He was a bit of a wine buff. He liked touring, visiting vineyards, tasting wine, that kind of thing. Though I'm not really sure it was what Alison wanted.'

'Why do you say that?' Michael asked, wondering why Linda kept referring to David in the past tense.

'Well, sun, sea and sangria was more Alison's idea of a holiday. You should have heard her, when they came back from Benidorm. All tanned, and full of the nightlife, restaurants, and shows they'd seen.'

'And David?'

'That's the oddest thing of all. I don't think he enjoyed it much. That's why we were so surprised when they went to look at houses out there. We assumed that it was all Alison's idea.'

Michael raised an eyebrow, and Linda caught the question.

'Oh, David was the steady one.' She picked up her cup, took a sip of coffee and continued in her low, slightly husky voice. 'He liked to think he was in control, but Alison ruled the roost. She could twist him round her little finger when she wanted to. I told you, Alison was younger than David, and she wasn't always happy just to stay round the house. Dinner at home with a bottle of good wine was David's idea of a good Saturday night, and he liked to cook – he was a marvellous cook. But that wasn't for Alison, unless they had friends over. Music and dancing was more her idea of fun. David went along with it, but every now and then he'd put his foot down. Even so, Alison usually got her way in the end.'

'So you think moving to Spain was Alison's idea?'

'I expect so, but it still seemed strange... You see, Alison would pester and push for her own way, and, like I say, it worked most of the time. But not where money was concerned. David always had control of the purse strings. But he must have gone along with the Spanish idea, otherwise they wouldn't have gone, would they?'

Michael paused, trying to find a way of framing his next question.

'This is awkward, I know,' he finally began, 'but how were they together? Would you say they were happy?'

Linda stroked her blonde hair, and pulled it back from her face.

'Happy?' She gave a smile. 'Not many of us could say that, but – yes, actually, I think they were. They had different ideas, but they were close, a unit. They discussed everything together. And they seemed very happy about going to live in Spain. I was quite envious, and excited for them.'

Michael flicked through the sergeant's notes. 'They moved out of their old home on 20th October, I see. Where did they live after that?'

'They rented a furnished flat in Regents Park, where the students stay. Alison enjoyed it, but it was only short term, until they could go to Spain.'

'And what did they do with their own furniture?'

'In storage with Gleesons. They paid for six months, but that's up now and Gleesons have been on to us to ask what's happening. They want someone to pay for another three months, but John's refused.'

Michael made a note to make sure Gleesons held on to the stuff. There could be something useful in there.

Linda looked up slowly. 'Are you sure nothing's happened to them, Inspector?'

'Well, that's what I'm going over to Spain to investigate.'

'But that other couple last year – the couple who were killed?'

'The culprits in that case were apprehended, and they've been locked up in jail all this time, so they're not involved at all.'

'Yes, but what if it's a copycat case? You read about that sort of thing all the time. It's horrible. I just can't understand why they haven't phoned.' Linda's eyes looked moist. She pulled a tissue from the box on the shelf by the table.

Michael was tempted to comfort her, but thought better of it when he heard another roar from the football crowd.

'I really must go,' he said. 'Thank you again for seeing me on a Sunday. We're doing everything we can, so are the Spanish police. I'll know more when I get there tomorrow, and the station will keep you posted from this end. Thank you for the coffee – it was very nice.'

Chapter Three

The ValuJet flight from East Midlands Airport on 4th May was 45 minutes behind schedule, 'due to the late arrival of an incoming aircraft.' Michael had opted for a window seat.

He was now hemmed in by an overweight possessor of sleeveless vest, shorts, trainers with black socks, and white legs. Blue and red tattoos ran up and down the man's arms. He had a shaved head and a heavy gold earring. He was beginning to snore.

The man's wife occupied the aisle seat. She leaned back to tell three kids for the fourth or fifth time to stop kicking.

Michael put his head down. He wanted to take off his jacket, but settled for loosening his tie, before leaning toward the window and opening the file.

David Harrington, 48, and his wife, Alison, 43, had flown to Alicante on 7th Jan for a scheduled two-week stay, returning to East Midlands on 21st Jan.

They were booked at the Hotel San Marco on Benidorm's Levante beach. The hotel had been suggested, but not paid for, by Susan Shaw as a good base from which to view property in both south and north Costa Blanca.

They had an appointment with Brian Small on 9th Jan and Brian had set aside two days to show them round. Susan had warned that they seemed a little vague about requirements in terms of both location and price. This was not unusual, especially for people on a first time inspection trip, and Brian was well used to dealing with this. His purpose would be to give a feel for the area and the lifestyle. More importantly, he would build their trust and confidence so that, if they decided to buy at some time in the future, they would do so through Saunders and Shaw.

David Harrington hired a car at Alicante airport, reserved in advance through Aurega and collected the day they arrived. A cobalt blue Renault Clio, registration number 1004 BYZ, it was never returned.

Brian Small had kept the appointment, and spent the next two days driving the Harringtons around the Costa Blanca from as far south as Torrevieja, to Javea and Denia in the north.

He had taken them to three new developments with plots for sale, four newly built villas, two apartments and five resale properties. The prices varied from 100,000 to 350,000 euros. Most of the properties were close to the coast, but a couple were inland from Calpe/Moraira in the Jalon Valley.

Brian left the couple at the end of two days. They told him they planned to look at some more properties over the next week or so and would be in touch.

Another British property agent, Spanish Home Sales, had arranged for their contact, Matthew Summers, to meet the Harringtons at their hotel on 14th Jan.

He went to the Hotel San Marco, but they failed to show up at the appointed time. He checked with the receptionist, who said they were still staying there, but the concierge thought they had left in their car earlier in the day. Summers left a message asking them to contact him by telephone, but they had not been in touch.

Inquiries by the Guardia Civil had revealed that the Harringtons visited a property exhibition on 15th Jan at Hotel Perdiz in Benidorm.

They'd collected brochures and leaflets from a number of stands but, so far, no one had come forward to say they had made any further contact.

There were also a number of possible sightings between 15th Jan and 6th Feb at the offices of Spanish property agents spread right along the Costa Blanca. None of these had been verified.

A Dutch couple, Jacob and Helena Gessels, who'd advertised their villa in the Costa Blanca News, had contacted the Guardia to say a couple resembling the Harringtons had viewed their house after telephoning to make an appointment for the 23rd of January.

They'd been shown an old photograph of the Harringtons, the best that could be provided by the family, and confirmed a strong likeness, though they could not be absolutely sure.

The couple had given the name Johnson, and appeals by the Guardia for them to come forward had drawn a blank.

The Gessels' villa was on the outskirts of the village of Alcalalí at the western end of the Jalon Valley, known locally as the Val de Pop. It was on the market for 300,000 euros.

A head of close-cropped ginger bristle came to rest on Michael's shoulder and he nudged it gently, inducing it to flop to the other side. He resumed his focus on the file, turning to another section.

David Harrington had worked for Nottingham City Council for the last sixteen and a half years. He had joined them as Production Manager in the printing department, but for the past five years he had been Head of the Department. He was described as quiet and conscientious but reluctant to embrace change. The introduction of digital printing equipment and the outsourcing of much of the routine work had prompted a slimming-down of the workforce in the department and a call for volunteers for redundancy. Everyone was surprised when David came forward because, at forty-eight, he would not qualify for his pension straight away, but would have to wait until he was sixty. His salary was £38,000 a year and his redundancy payout came to £24,330. He had left Nottingham City Council on the 30th of November without much ceremony.

Inquiries at his bank in Nottingham showed a well managed account, never in the red and with regular withdrawals in the form of cheques made out in favour of the Midland and West Building Society. The Building Society confirmed a gradual accumulation of £16,788 over the past five years. No significant withdrawals until recently. On October 21st the account was boosted by a cheque for £87,541 from solicitors, Warren and Barton, who had handled the sale of the Harrington's house. There was a further addition of £24,330 on 1st December when the cheque from the council had been paid in. At this point the joint account stood at £128,659, but not for long. On the 17th of December David Harrington had arranged an international money transfer of 100,000 euros (£69,000) to an account that had been set up in October in his name with the Javea branch of the Banco de Bilbao. A week later, he had asked to withdraw a further £55,000 in cash from the building society account. He had collected the money on 5th January, leaving a balance of just under £5,000.

There had been two withdrawals from the Spanish account. The first, on 12th January was for 20,000 euros and the second, on 13th March, was for 75,000 euros, both in cash.

'Anything to drink, sir?' interrupted the flight attendant.

It took Michael a few seconds to gather his thoughts.

'A beer, a vodka tonic, three Cokes for the kids,' said Ginger.

Michael closed the file and put it by his side.

'Just a mineral water, please.'

'Fizzy?'

'Si, con gas.' Michael surprised himself, though he'd been mentally practising his Spanish for the past five days. 'Thank you.'

'De nada.' The attendant placed the glass on Michael's tray. She smiled, and Michael wondered, too late, whether and how to respond.

'Not on a holiday, then?' said Ginger.

'No.'

'Thought not. You don't look like a holidaymaker. And that file isn't exactly light reading, is it?'

Michael grabbed the file and covered it with his hands.

'We're off to Torrevieja for two weeks. My sister's got a place, we come over four times a year. Lovely place, right by the beach, close to the shops and bars, there's even a MacDonald's. I prefer a curry, myself. There's a little place in town does a lovely Chicken Madras. Whereabouts you going?'

'Alicante.'

'Nice place. Lots of people I know never go there. They think it's just the airport, see. But I like it. Lots of shops for the missus, nice marina – and there's a beach as well, you know.'

'Yes, I know.'

'Where you staying?'

'In the centre. It's a business trip. In fact, I've got quite a few business papers to catch up on – sorry about that.'

'Don't mind me, mate.'

Michael did his best to angle his body away from Ginger.

He opened the file, holding it up to block prying eyes, and turned to the inventory prepared by Sergeant Rawlinson when he examined items stored by the Harringtons at Gleesons Furniture Store.

The list contained a full range of household furniture: three piece suite 'of nice quality artificial leather, almost new'; television, video recorder, radio, dining table and chairs 'which could be pine'; coffee table, two double beds ('plus complete sets of bedding, one almost new'); kitchen equipment, crockery and cutlery.

There was also a collection of garden furniture: plastic table and chairs, a parasol, sun-beds and a gas-fired barbecue.

A plastic document folder contained an assortment of papers: bills, bank statements, 'nothing we don't already know about,' which Michael glanced through to confirm: insurance documents, letters about the sale of the house and some personal correspondence relating to David Harrington's redundancy.

A 'large but battered old' suitcase, the list stated, contained several pairs of shoes and a few clothes, a heavy winter coat, three jackets, three cardigans.

The sergeant had been very thorough, going through the pockets to turn up sixty-seven pence, a credit card slip from a garage in Nottingham, a receipt from Tesco's (also in Nottingham), an expired library card, an out-of-date lottery ticket, a business card from Saunders & Shaw, one used postage stamp, two ticket stubs from the Odeon in Nottingham, a restaurant bill from *La Farola* in Derby dated 21st August last year, and a punched railway ticket from Nottingham to Derby, return, dated the same day.

It was all routine stuff, and not very revealing, except perhaps for the restaurant bill and train ticket, Michael thought, but it confirmed that the Harringtons had left in storage some papers that people did not leave lying around – bank records; insurance documents; letters... And then there were household items. Surely they must have planned to return at some stage... Otherwise, why not sell the furniture?

Michael turned to another page, then another. It was no use. His concentration had slipped and he was just staring at the pages. He closed the file again, pushed his head against the back of his seat and shut his eyes, trying (pretending) to sleep... but his thoughts raced.

Why the rush to get to Spain?

Why not find the right place, and *then* sell the house in Nottingham?

Why had David Harrington opened a Spanish bank account in October?

How had he opened it?

Why was it only in his name and not in joint names, like the English building society?

Why the cash withdrawals – from the English account, as well as the one in Spain?

Where, why, who, when, how...?

A fog of facts, suppositions, possibilities and unanswered questions. And he felt as if his nose was twitching. But something was wrong, and it stemmed from the way the Harringtons had just upped and left England. Was this the behaviour of two normally careful and rational people? He wasn't sure, but then, he thought, half-asleep, he had never taken a risk in his life. Never been a dreamer...

Heat from the door of the plane blasted him awake, and he was soon herded onto a transit bus with a pack of excited tourists. Minutes later the tourists were rushing down a corridor, leaving Michael to trot at a sensible pace behind.

By the time he reached the baggage hall, Ginger and troop were barging toward the exit – five pairs of trainers jogging alongside an overpacked trolley of cases.

After picking up his bag, Michael pushed his trolley down the ramp to the arrivals hall of Alicante's El Altet airport. He had removed his jacket, and now placed it neatly over his case. His tie still hung loosely round the open neck of his shirt.

A sea of faces crammed the other side of the barrier. Excited relatives and friends called out, jumping and waving, then hugging and kissing. A more subdued group, mainly men, held cardboard placards up, with names written in large heavy letters. Michael scanned the line as he approached, looking for "Fernandez."

He pushed his trolley to the end of the line, more self-conscious with every step. As the crowd dispersed, his composure slipped. He'd just become a foreigner, out of place in a strange land. He stretched his arm to bring his watch up into view from under the cuff of his long-sleeved shirt

A voice rang out, in Spanish: 'Inspector Fernandez, sorry I'm late. Parking's terrible.' An immensely tall man took control of the trolley, ducked and picked up a bag. 'Been circling the car park for ages. Captain Jose Luis Perez. Here, let me help you with your bags. Car's outside. Gave up in the end and parked on the road, told the traffic cop I'd only be a minute, but I don't trust those bastards.'

Michael grabbed his jacket up, and hurried along behind.

'How did you know it was me?'

Jose Luis looked back, showing himself to be plump-cheeked and friendly-faced.

Another group of tourists poured past.

'You don't look like the average tourist.' Jose Luis nodded toward red and white soccer shirts. 'Manchester flight. Come on, I don't want to get a fine.' He strode ahead with the trolley.

Michael had to jog to keep up with the dusty, brown leather slip-ons clipping across the marble floor. Probably Italian. Small for such a large man. Though large men did sometimes wear surprisingly small-looking shoes, and it did depend upon make and style...

The wide glass doors slid open, and the trolley rattled over uneven paving up to a silver Seat. The traffic cop stood in attendance, and Jose Luis nodded his thanks. Michael's suitcases were deposited in the boot.

'Wrong side,' said Jose Luis to Michael, standing at the driver's side door waiting to get in. Michael smiled in embarrassment, and switched to the other side.

Inside the car, Jose Luis turned the air-conditioning to full blast. An icy draught hit them in the face.

'It is Michael, isn't it?' inquired Jose Luis.

'Why do you ask?'

'Well, the fax from England said Michael, which I'd pronounce as the Spanish equivalent, but the copy of your passport they sent had Miguel-Ángel as your first name. I just wondered which, or what.'

Michael fiddled with his seat belt strap. 'Michael, pronounced however you like, will do fine.'

'Well, Michael, have you eaten?'

'Not a bite. No food on ValuJet.'

'Me neither, so let's stop. Then I'll take you to the hotel.'

Driving away from the terminal and out toward the A7 motorway, Michael spotted a blue Ford Mondeo parked behind a green and white Guardia Civil car with blue lights flashing. The driver of the Ford stood anxiously as the Guardia officer clasped a sheaf of papers. Two tourists standing by the car gripped their hand luggage, watching.

'They never learn,' said Jose Luis. 'Easy pickings.'

'Sorry?'

'You must have seen them in the airport, holding up names, waiting for passengers. Mostly unlicensed taxi drivers charging to take people to their hotels. The Spanish taxi drivers hate them because they undercut the licensed fares. They complain like mad, so every now and again we pick up a few drivers, impound their cars, slap on a fine as a warning to others.'

'How do you catch them?'

'Easy. We have a couple of plainclothes officers in the terminal. They look out for people with name placards and follow them to the car park. Then they radio ahead the registration number and a description of the car, and someone waiting outside the airport picks them up.'

'But what if they say they're just collecting friends or relatives?'

'Most of them are stupid. They leave the name placard in the car. We search the car and if the placard matches the name of the passengers, we've got them. You wouldn't need a name placard if you were picking up your friends or family, would you?'

'Suppose not, but it doesn't seem like the crime of the century.'

'Of course, it's not. But we have to be seen to respond to legitimate complaints, even if they're not top priority. It's a game, but don't tell me it's different in the UK.'

'I know what you mean.'

Jose Luis collected the ticket from the toll machine, and they joined the A7 heading north for the city of Alicante. The car was icy cold, and he turned down the fan.

They'd been driving barely five minutes when Jose Luis pulled into a service area, and parked.

'Not brilliant, but we can get coffee and a bocadillo.'

Michael sat at a square plastic-topped table with hard seats, and Jose Luis returned with two tiny cups of café solo and a couple of bocadillo rolls containing cheese and jamon serrano ham. The place was almost empty, the nearest customers several tables away. Jose Luis clenched the bread between his teeth and tugged until a chunk broke away, scattering crumbs over the table. Michael tried to be more refined, grinding his teeth to sever the crunchy bread and chewy dry-cured ham. He finally tugged until something broke away, leaving stringy ham dangling from his mouth. He pushed it in, but the dry bread went round and round in his mouth until he sloshed it down with coffee to get rid of it. He left the rest on the plate.

Jose Luis had finished his sandwich. He lit a cigarette.

Michael glanced round, looking for a NO SMOKING sign. There was none.

An awkward silence fell. Jose Luis made the first move.

'Your Spanish is excellent. Where did you learn it?'

'University. And my father was Spanish.'

'Really? Where was he from?'

'He... I'd better explain. I'm British, here because I speak Spanish, and I'm a bit uncomfortable about it because I don't know Spain at all. This is my first visit. But I've got a job to do, the quicker the better, and then I have to return home at once. I'm afraid that's all I'm able to say.'

Jose Luis bristled.

'Well, let me tell you, I never asked for help. If two stupid English people come to Spain and get lost, that's their problem. But the powers that be are worried about the effect on tourism, and from what I gather your bosses are keen to avoid criticism if it all goes wrong. So we're stuck with each other. Like you say, the sooner it's sorted the better, and we can both get back to real work... Anyway, we'd better check you into your hotel. Busy day tomorrow.'

The Seat rejoined the A7, approaching the outskirts of Alicante. Michael became uneasy with the tension. He wished he'd not been so abrupt. He spotted a road sign with the word "Alicante" crudely painted out in black aerosol and replaced with "Alacant".

'I see that some people still want to stick with Valenciano?'

Jose Luis responded quickly, as if relieved the silence was broken.

'Yes, Valenciano's the first language of many in this region, especially in the more remote parts. Everyone speaks Castilian, of course, but a few are sensitive about losing their identity, so they demand road signs are in both languages. If only Castilian is used for the signs they get changed in black spray paint. Looks a mess, but to some people it's important.'

'Do you speak Valenciano?'

'I can, but I don't unless I need to.'

Jose Luis was suddenly distracted as the steering wheel began to judder violently and the car swerved toward the metal barrier separating the two carriageways.

He braked gently and wrestled with the steering wheel until he had the car under control.

Michael clasped the dashboard in front of him, but looked behind at the same time.

'It's all clear on the inside,' he said. 'You can move over.'

The car came slowly to a halt on the hard shoulder, accompanied by the sound of metal on tarmac. Jose Luis switched the engine off and released his seat belt, glancing in the rear view mirror.

'Are you all right?' he asked.

Michael tried to look calm.

'Fine, thanks. You did well to get us here in one piece.'

Jose Luis was still looking in the rear view mirror, watching a dark blue Toyota pull up behind them.

'Open the glove box, will you?'

Michael did as he was told.

'Pass me the pistol.'

Michael gripped the black leather holster and passed it to Jose Luis. It was heavier than he had expected. His eyes widened as Jose Luis removed the pistol from its sheath, leant forward and stuffed the barrel down the back of his trousers. Only the grip was protruding above his belt as he turned toward Michael.

'In a moment I want you to get out of the car and walk round the front to look at the off side wheel. I will do the same. Try to look as if you're rattled. Okay?'

'Okay.'

'Right, let's do it.'

Jose Luis slid awkwardly from the driver's door, careful not to expose his back to the two men approaching from the parked Toyota.

Michael stood by the wheel, examining the shredded tyre and puffing his cheeks.

One of the advancing men called out in heavily accented Spanish. 'That was a close thing. We saw the blow-out. You did well to keep it under control. Need any help? Where's the spare? In the boot?'

Jose Luis approached the back of the Seat and Michael followed, trying not to glance at the pistol.

'Er, yes, thanks for stopping.'

Michael looked at the two men. Both were dark-skinned; not black, but more than just suntanned. They were smartly dressed in tailored trousers and open-necked shirts; one a patterned blue, the other dazzling white. Both wore reflective dark glasses and had similar mops of almost jet-black hair. Then he noticed the shoes. Cheap, rubber soled, heavy, dusty and badly scuffed.

His intuition was just kicking in when he saw the knives, pulled in unison from behind their backs.

He was a fraction too late in realising what was going on and felt the cold touch of steel against his throat as the white-shirted attacker slipped behind him.

Jose Luis had stepped back. Even so, he was staring down the long blade of a kitchen knife being waved just in front of his face.

'Give us your money and the keys,' said blue shirt.

'Okay, take it easy,' replied Jose Luis. 'We don't want any trouble.'

He reached behind his back as if going for his wallet, then swiftly brought his right hand back and clamped it with his left, holding the pistol firm and pointing it straight in the face of blue shirt.

'Police!' he shouted, 'Now drop the knives.'

White shirt was temporarily distracted. Michael slammed his right elbow into the man's rib cage with all the force he could muster and grabbed the knife hand, pulling it away from his neck.

His assailant doubled-up in pain as Michael took the man's arm with both his hands and cracked it over his knee.

The knife fell to the ground and Michael followed up his move by ramming the man's arm up between his shoulder blades and pushing his face to the tarmac.

'Here, put these on,' called Jose Luis. He was still in a stand-off with blue shirt, who'd viewed his compatriot's fall, but he tossed Michael a pair of handcuffs, removed from his side pocket. 'Now give me the knife,' demanded Jose Luis.

Blue shirt stood frozen to the spot for a moment, then raised his arm and threw the knife toward Jose Luis who jerked to his left.

The man turned tail and started running toward the Toyota as Jose Luis recovered his balance and raised the pistol.

'Stop, or I shoot!'

'Don't shoot,' cried Michael, already in stride and gaining on the fleeing attacker.

Suddenly a shot rang out and blue shirt faltered and buckled at the knees, losing his momentum for a second.

Michael lunged forward and clasped the runner around the thighs with both arms before slipping his grip to the man's knees and bringing him crashing to the ground with an agonised yell as his elbow smashed into the tarmac.

Before he could recover, blue shirt found his head pressed against the road with the barrel of Jose Luis's pistol shoved in his ear.

Michael released his grip and dusted himself down.

One knee of his flannels was torn, and the toe-caps of his brogues were scoured where they'd dragged across the rough tarmac. He looked at Jose Luis, who pulled blue shirt to his feet, gun jammed against his neck.

'Jesus! What the hell were you shooting at? You scared the shit out of me,' said Michael.

'I fired in the air, but it worked, didn't it?'

'I would have got him, anyway.'

'So you say.'

A squad car and two sergeants arrived to take the villains into custody and the two detectives returned to the Seat.

'Sorry Michael, but we'll have to make a detour to the barracks to file a report. They'll need a statement from you, as well.'

'Barracks?'

'Sorry, of course you wouldn't understand. I mean the central police headquarters. We're likely to be there some time. You know, paperwork. I'll take you to your hotel later on.'

'Oh, I know all about paperwork.'

'That was pretty impressive back there, the way you brought him down,' said Jose Luis.

'I played scrum half for Notts Police until last year.'

'Scrum half?'

'You know, rugby union.'

'What's rugby union?'

'Never mind.'

'The Colonel will be delighted. We'll be heroes. We've been after those two for ages. They've turned over at least twenty cars in the last six months with four woundings. Always the same scam. They look out for cars pulling into a service station and watch the drivers go inside. Then they stick a knife in the tyre and follow until you pull over. Usually they pick on tourists, but this time they made a big mistake. This will do our promotion prospects no harm at all. Oh, sorry, I mean my promotion prospects. Even so, I'm sure your bosses in England will hear all about it.'

'What would you have done if I hadn't brought him down?'

'Shot him, of course.'

'In the back?'

'I wouldn't say that.'

'Can I claim for a new pair of shoes? Mind are scuffed.'

'What?'

By the time they'd finished at HQ and reached the Hotel Ramis on Alicante's sea front, it was past midnight. Jose Luis lifted the two cases from the boot of the Seat and set them at the side of the road.

'Don't mind if I don't come in, do you? I need to get home. I'm in trouble with my wife for too many late nights, and I hardly saw the children last week. You've got the file, so if anything occurs to you, give me a ring in the morning. Otherwise I'll see you on Wednesday.'

'Wednesday?'

'Yes – oh, and I've arranged for you to see Brian Small tomorrow morning. He's set the day aside to show you around. I suggest going to places he showed to the Harrington's, but it's up to you.'

'How will I know him?'

'You can't miss Brian Small. He'll see you in the bar at ten-thirty. By the way, thanks again for today. I mean it, I couldn't have done it without you. Anyway, I'll pick you up here on Wednesday at ten.'

He looked for a porter but no one was about, so Michael carried the bags through the doors and dropped them at reception. He looked around the gloom of the midnight lobby. Sets of armchairs sat poised in the semi-darkness around polished coffee tables, as if worshipping their heavy glass ashtrays, and at the far end of the lobby he could make out a bar which looked to be closed forever apart from a faint pinprick of red, like an eye. The reception desk was thinly illuminated by a row of chromium spotlights set into the ceiling.

Michael thumped the bell, perhaps too hard. He waited a few seconds, and was about to ring again, harder, when a light flickered in the back office and he heard the creak of bed springs followed by a shuffling sound. A night porter brushed down his crumpled shirt and rubbed his eyes as he emerged behind the desk.

'Fernandez. You have a reservation for me.'

'Ah, Señor Fernandez... We were expecting you this afternoon.'

Michael took his passport from his jacket, as the porter ran his finger down a computer printout.

'Here we are. Room 711.' The porter scanned the pigeonholes. 'You'll have to carry your own bags up, I'm afraid. I can't leave the desk. The elevator is in the corner.'

He picked up Michael's passport, and peered. 'But this is a British passport.'

'So!'

'Your Spanish is excellent.'

Michael didn't bother to say thank you, as he carried his bags wearily to the lift.

The night porter didn't bother to say good night.

Chapter Four

The bar was empty next morning, and Michael seated himself on one of a long row of stools to wait for Brian Small.

He'd breakfasted early, and to contend with the heat he'd opted for a short-sleeved shirt.

Now, just as he was thinking that he was ready for work and it was late, a man appeared at the entrance to the bar. Short, slim, bald, tanned – in pink polo shirt, green checked trousers, and white slip-on shoes that matched his belt. A heavy gold bracelet hung from his wrist, held up as he spoke into a mobile phone.

Michael walked up. 'Brian Small?'

'Sorry, mate.' The man flipped the phone shut. 'John Evans.'

'Oh, my mistake. I'm expecting a property agent, Brian Small.'

'I know him well, but you obviously don't, or you'd never have made the mistake. As it happens, we're both in the same business.' Evans glanced toward reception. 'Ah, here's my punters. Look, here's my card. If Brian can't help you, give me a call. Bye.'

Michael returned to the barstool and finished his café solo. He was about to look at his watch again when he heard a voice.

'Inspector Fernandez?'

'Yes.'

'Brian Small.'

They shook hands.

Looking to be in his fifties, Brian had thinning hair, whisked to one side. His checked shirt and beige corduroy trousers would not have been out of place at an English county show, and the knitted cardigan with chunky leather buttons looked as odd in this setting as the two pairs of spectacles dangling from cords round his neck. He wore light brown suede desert boots. The jumble of styles was baffling. Michael's impulse was to play it safe and distrust the man.

'Anything wrong?' said Brian. He sat down and ordered coffee.

'No – it's just... meeting a stranger. I'm never sure who to expect.'

'Neither am I. Your English is excellent.'

'Thank you. How's your Spanish?'

'Oh, I get by... To tell the truth, I didn't know whether to expect an English-speaking Spaniard, or a Spanish-speaking Englishman.'

'Definitely the latter – though now I'm in Spain, I'm not so sure.'

'So, Inspector, where do you want to start?'

'Please – call me Michael.'

'I'm Brian.' He sugared his coffee. 'A small property agent.'

'I wouldn't have said you look like a typical property agent.'

Brian smiled. 'Pretty soon you'll be right. I retire next year. I've never really liked the property business.'

'Money, you mean?'

'Lord, no.' He took a long sip. 'I could make money anywhere. The property business just means I can live in Spain. I love it here.'

'Well, many would agree with you, of course.'

'Right. Am I a suspect?' Brian asked.

After the confusion of the man's appearance, Michael wasn't going to let him off the hook too easily.

'I suppose, since you were one of the last to see the Harringtons, but I'm not planning to arrest you just yet.'

'How do you want to play this?' Brian drained his coffee. 'I've made a complete list of the properties I showed the Harringtons, and I can take you to each one if you want.'

'That would be fine – and I'd like to understand a bit more about the property market out here, and how it works. I'd also like to know about the Harringtons. How they struck you. We'll have to use your car, I'm afraid. The Guardia Civil haven't provided me with transport.'

'All part of the service,' Brian said. 'We've a lot of ground to cover. I suggest we start in Torrevieja, about half an hour south of here, then we can head north to somewhere a little more exclusive.'

'What do you mean?'

'You'll see.'

They were soon heading south in Brian's green, four-wheel-drive Renault Scenic with 'Saunders and Shaw' painted on the sides.

Just a few wispy clouds speckled the vivid blue sky.

After the urban sprawl of Alicante, the countryside flanking the motorway was arid and dusty. Great hollows seemed to have been gouged out of the rock, where stone had been extracted to fuel the construction boom. The few surviving trees were taking on the shape of skeletons as they shrivelled in the water-starved landscape.

Emerging from a short tunnel, they cruised round a long gentle curve, and a forest of building cranes rose from a sea of pastel-coloured properties, stretching as far as the eye could see.

'Welcome to Torrevieja,' Brian said.

'Jesus, this is monstrous.' Michael had seen urbanisations along the coast, but nothing on this scale.

'That's exactly what it is. From tiny fishing port to one of the biggest development sites in Europe in just fifteen years. Population in excess of fifty thousand. Takes some getting used to, doesn't it?'

'You can say that again.'

They left the motorway, and swung down to the outskirts of the town, passing a MacDonald's and a Lidl superstore. A dual carriageway led them closer to the coast, flanked by new car showrooms selling every make and model from Mercedes to Mitsubishi.

'I'll pull off and show you the place I viewed with the Harringtons,' said Brian. 'It's just along here, about ten minutes from the sea front.'

A huge hoarding marked the entrance to Vista Verde development, the giant letters surrounded by pictures of beaches, boats, parasols, surfboards, sandcastles and sun. At first they drove along tarmac roads, piles of rubble alongside. Then they turned left and Brian pulled up alongside a quadrangle of three-storey linked houses, painted white, with terracotta roof tiles. They were separated from an identical block by just forty metres of new-looking gardens.

A Pickford's International removal van stood by the entrance to one of the ground floor apartments, and two men were humping a settee through the doorway.

Brian climbed out of the car. 'This is phase three. I showed the Harringtons phase two, but that's sold. They're all pretty much the same. Wait a moment, I need to see the site agent and get the keys.'

Michael sat in the car, still cool from the air conditioning.

He'd pictured the dream life in Spain to be a pretty villa with carefully tended gardens and a view of the sea. Instead, he was reminded of Hilltops Estate as it gradually emerged from the green fields on the edge of Nottingham in the late 60s. The only difference was the sun.

Brian was returning from the office, rumbling along with a slight limp, as if to keep the weight off. 'Okay, let's take a look.'

Michael followed Brian through to a quadrangle next to an unfinished swimming pool, and up the stairs to the top floor.

'This show unit is roughly the same condominium I showed the Harringtons, only theirs was on the north side. More sun, but hot in summer. You pays your money and you makes your choice.'

'And what sort of money are we talking about?'

'They start at 100,000 euros for two bedrooms, one bathroom, fitted kitchen, balcony, air conditioning and central heating.'

'Central heating?'

'Yes, of course. It gets cold here in winter.'

'And what did the Harringtons think of it?'

'Difficult to say, at that stage. They looked round the place, but were non-committal. I guess they knew they had more to look at. Seen enough? Want to buy the place?'

'Yes, and no thanks. Where to next?'

'Lets head back north, and I'll to show you around some more exclusive properties.'

On the A7 again, they skirted Alicante before seeing the towers of Benidorm's high rise hotels with the Hotel Bali dominating the skyline. At a glance, it looked like Manhattan.

'Are we going there?' he asked.

'Can if you want to, but I didn't go there with the Harringtons. Would you like to look round?'

'Sometime, perhaps. What's it like?'

'Benidorm? Ask the thousands who come back year after year. It's really two resorts. In winter, it's like the Costa Geriatrica. The grey pound goes a long way, and some people come for months on end to escape the British winter. Cheap food and drink, tea dances every afternoon, and plenty of day trips. Around Easter, it changes. Families arrive, beaches are crammed, pubs are packed and so are the burger bars. But this isn't Ibiza or Ayia Napa – it's basically a bucket and spade holiday for the kids, and the beaches are wonderful for that.'

'Where to next, then?'

'Moraira first, then Javea. The house in Moraira is still on the market, so we can look around. I phoned the agent, and he'll meet us there. Do me a favour, though. When we get there, act as if you're a potential buyer. You know, act interested, ask a few questions. He's a busy man, and I don't think he'd take kindly to being dragged out solely for the benefit of the police.'

'Well...' This sounded like one of the ridiculous role-play sessions on the equal opportunity training courses. 'You'd better give me some help. For a start, how much are we talking about, for this place?'

'It's on the market for three hundred, twenty-five thousand euros, but we could probably shave a bit off that if you were interested.'

'How much?'

'Property on the coast is always a bit more expensive, and Moraira's a very popular area. The place has boomed in recent years, but it's all done very tastefully. There's a promenade and a new marina, posh restaurants, walkways, lots of chic little shops. I'm sure you'll like it.'

'Not at that price.'

A series of small signs appeared at the side of the road: Partida A, No's 1 to 57, Partida B, No's 58 to 103. They had just reached Partida E when Brian turned off the road.

'Here we are. Number 237, right at the top. Spectacular views.'

They climbed in a series of zigzags, passing gate after gate on both sides of the road until they reached the summit of the estate.

'Ah,' Brian said. 'Vinnie's here. Now remember what I said.'

'I'll try. But do me a favour, and don't drop in any Spanish when you speak to me. I should be totally English, don't you think?'

'Totally English it is.'

Vincent Roberts was leaning against the bonnet of a blue Mercedes Cabriolet; its roof dropped down to expose cream leather upholstery and burr walnut dashboard.

Approaching, Michael began to weigh him up.

Everything was casual but expensive: tailored blue shorts, Calvin Klein T-shirt, heavy gold necklace, and a Rolex watch that Michael doubted was fake, until he spotted the rubber flip-flops.

Vinnie pushed himself away from the Mercedes and walked up.

'Hi, Bri. Still rustling up the punters?'

He had a broad northern accent. Lancashire, maybe.

'Thought you'd have retired by now,' he said, 'with all the fees I've given you over the years.'

'Unfortunately, you're the one making all the money, by the looks.' Brian nodded toward the Mercedes.

'Who've we got this time?' asked Vinnie.

'This is Michael Fernandez.'

'Fernandez?' queried Vinnie. 'English or Spanish?'

'English,' Michael said brusquely.

'Hope you're not wasting my time like the last lot Brian showed round. Ever hear anything of them, Brian?'

'Not a thing.'

Vinnie led the way into the villa and rushed from room to room as if he was in a hurry, or had done this too many times and was fed up with having to explain things to half-witted punters.

'Built about six years ago. Just a holiday home, hardly been used. Nice kitchen, three bedrooms, two bathrooms, big naya. Air conditioning in the bedrooms. That's all you need, really. No central heating, but then you don't need it out here.' Vinnie pushed open double doors leading to the terrace and pool. 'Here's the best bit. Just look at that view, one of the best in Moraira. This is the thing I like.'

Vinnie walked across the terrace and around the pool He inserted a key in a small box on the side-wall and pressed a button. A wide roller shutter rose to reveal a large bar, with a row of optics on the back wall. A shiny chrome beer pump was clamped to the ledge, a steel barrel underneath, and a stacking hi-fi system rested on a shelf in the corner, wired to two large speakers at each end of the bar.

'What do you think, Michael? Impressive?'

Michael was looking over the far side of the terrace at the house about ten metres below. The villas on either side were separated by just a low, open-block wall and a few climbing plants.

Brian nudged him.

'Oh – yes, very impressive...'

'So what are you looking for, Michael? Holiday home, thinking of joining the exodus from the UK?'

'Well, just a holiday home right now. To start with. I mean, I may spend more time here later on.'

'You'd love it. Thousands of ex-pats – English, German, Dutch, some from France and Belgium. Weather's great, cost of living's cheap, and let's face it, Britain's going to the dogs. So what do you think?'

'Brian said it was three hundred, twenty-five thousand euros.'

'That's right. Snip at that. Prices have rocketed in the last couple of years. I'm telling you, you won't get a better bargain anywhere on the Costa Blanca.'

'Is the price negotiable at all?' Michael asked.

'Just leave that to Brian and me. We won't quibble over a few hundred euros. So you're interested, are you? The place is empty. You could be swimming in the pool in less than a month. What do you say?'

'I'd like to think about it.'

'That's what they all say. I'm telling you, it's a bargain. Don't think too long, or it will be snapped up. I've lost count of the number of punters who dither, then come back too late when their dream home has already been sold. Ain't that a fact, Brian?'

Brain wandered into the garden with his hands behind his back, as Vinnie went on. 'Cash, is it? Or do you need a loan? I can fix you up with a mortgage if you want. Interest rates have never been lower.'

This was just wasting time, and Vinnie was too irritating to stand.

'Did you ever see the Harringtons again, Mr Roberts?'

Vinnie was knocked off his stride.

He spluttered, 'No. I mean, what the fuck's going on here? Brian, who the hell is this?'

Roused from his reflections, Brian came rushing round the pool.

'Who the fuck is this, Brian?'

'Sorry, Brian, but this is a waste of time. Mr Roberts, my name is Michael Fernandez. I'm a British CID officer working with the Guardia Civil in the search for David and Alison Harrington. Now, did you see them again after Brian brought them to see this place?'

'Don't know who you're talking about.'

'Then why did you say "no" the first time I asked?'

'Look, everyone knows about the Harringtons. It's been splashed all over the Costa Blanca News. They've even got their own reporters on the case after those two were murdered last year. It's a bloody nuisance. People are saying it's not safe to come here any more. It's ruining business. Look, are you accusing me or something?'

'I'm just trying piece together their last movements and the people they met. I assume you have already contacted the Guardia?'

'No. Look, I only saw them for a couple of minutes. Brian's the one you should be talking to. I've had enough of this. I'm off. Brian, you bastard, don't bring any more punters to me. You're finished.'

Vinnie began striding toward the road.

Michael called, 'The Guardia may want to see you, Mr Roberts.'

The engine of the Mercedes was already revving.

'They can piss off,' yelled Vinnie, as the car screeched away.

Michael turned to Brian. 'I'm sorry about that, Brian, but I needed to ask the questions. I've put you in a bit of a spot.'

'Don't worry about it, Michael. He's an arsehole.'

'Couldn't have put it better.'

'Do you really suspect him?'

'Can't say as yet, but he seems a bit of a shady character. It wouldn't do any harm for the Guardia to have a little chat.'

'He'll love that.'

'My thoughts exactly. Where to, next?'

'Javea, that is Xabia in Valenciano. It's just along the coast heading north, but shall we stop for coffee first?'

'Sounds good to me.'

They parked on the outskirts of Moraira and walked along the seafront promenade. Brian led the way to a restaurant overlooking the sea.

'Sun or shade?' he asked.

'Shade please, if that's all right with you.'

They sat at a small table under a large green and white parasol, and Michael got back to business. 'Can you tell me, Brian, what did you make of the Harringtons, yourself? Just your impressions.'

'Well, it's hard to say, really. At the time they were just two more potential clients, and you meet all sorts in this game. I've stopped being surprised by anyone. But I suppose there was one thing...'

'Yes?'

'I only thought about it afterwards, but I never really got a feel for their budget.'

'What do you mean?'

'Well, normally I like to find out at an early stage what sort of money people are looking to spend. It's not that I'm nosy, but it saves a lot of time if I know they have an absolute limit. Sometimes I have to talk them up a bit. You'd be surprised how many people still come here expecting a nice villa for a hundred grand, but those days are long gone, at least in this part of Spain. So I talk them up to a realistic price level for the type of property they are looking for, then tell them how cheap it is to live here. If they are only looking for a holiday home I tell them how much they could expect to make from letting it out, if that's what they want to do.'

'And the Harringtons?'

'That's what I mean. I pushed, gently of course – that's usually enough – but they never gave anything away. Even when I showed them more expensive properties, they never seemed to be put off.'

'And yet they started in Torrevieja?'

'Not that surprising. They seemed to know a bit about the place, as if they'd been before. Perhaps it was just a starting point. You know, to see – well, let's just say – the cheaper end of the spectrum. But they definitely gave me the impression that they were looking for something a little more – shall we say – exclusive.'

'What made you think so? I mean, you said they didn't discuss their budget.'

'Just that they didn't linger for very long at the condominium in Torrevieja, but showed much more interest in some of the other places I took them to. As you will see later on, there's a vast difference.'

'What did you make of them as a couple?'

'They seemed nice enough, but they were very quiet. Never got to know them really, which again is quite unusual. I get to know something about most of the people I show round. Not that I pry, but it's inevitable when you spend two or three days with someone, in the car, over meals, they often open up. You'd be amazed at what some people are willing to tell me. I've had complete life histories and witnessed several blazing rows. But the Harringtons were different. They asked all the normal questions about prices, the cost of living, the process of buying a house, that kind of stuff. But they never opened up about themselves; never mentioned family or friends. It didn't bother me at the time. I just thought they were private people, and that's their privilege, of course.'

'Tell me about buying a house. How does it work?'

'You might be better speaking to an Asesoria lawyer, but basically, an informal contract is drawn up by the Asesoria and the buyer pays a deposit – usually ten percent of purchase price, but it's negotiable. Before completing, you need a Numero de Identificación de Extranjeros – NIE. It's a simple process, you just fill in a form with a few personal details and provide a copy of your passport. The form is taken to the local police station and stamped, and you're issued an NIE number.'

'Do you need a bank account in Spain?' Michael asked.

'You don't, but most people set one up. The Asesoria takes care of it. All you need is your NIE number and the copy of your passport.'

'I see. What next?'

'The Asesoria carries out a search on the property, mainly to establish the property's free from debt. It's important, because in Spain any debt is passed on to the new owners.

'Then an appointment is made with the Notario and everyone meets on the appointed day. The rest of the purchase price is handed over, and other things are sorted, like rates and local taxes.

'The Notario signs the escritura deeds, and the place is yours. You get a copy of the escritura there and then. The original goes off to the Central Registry in Madrid, and you get it back some weeks, or months, later. It's a bit more complicated if you're buying a plot of land to have a house built, because stage payments are made, but that's about it.'

'So how long does it take?' Michael asked.

'It varies. Sometimes the sellers want a long completion period, especially if they're looking to buy another house, but it can all be done in less than a month if everyone is happy.'

'And what does it cost?'

'You sound as if you're interested.'

'Just humour me.'

'Well, let's see. The asesoria's fee, Notario's fee, bits and pieces for paperwork. Let's say, a thousand euros. Then the purchase tax, seven percent of the declared value of the property. The buyer pays this.'

'You said, "declared" value?'

'The value's commonly under-declared on the escritura. It saves the buyer a slice of the purchase tax, and the seller avoids capital gains tax.'

'Is that legal?'

'Strictly speaking no, but everyone knows it happens. The declared value is usually paid by cheque in front of the Notario and the rest is handed over in cash – its called "black money".'

'Doesn't the Notario check?'

Brian smiled.

'Lord, no. You really don't know much about Spain, do you?'

'And what about your fee?'

'You mean the fee for Saunders and Shaw, don't you?'

'Whatever.'

'That comes later. We claim our share from the seller's agent when everything is done and dusted. It can take weeks, sometimes months, depending on the agent.'

'And what does it amount to?'

'That would be telling. It can vary, but it's usually a percentage of the sale price.'

'Is that the actual sale price or the declared value?'

'What do you think? Come on, time we were moving. We've still got a lot of ground to cover. We may not finish today, at this rate.'

They haggled over the bill, though it was just a few euros. Brian won when he said Saunders and Shaw would reimburse him for expenses. 'And now for something completely different. Let's skip Javea. We're off to the mountains, where the best people live.' Brian grinned. 'Guess where I live.'

They joined the N332, the old coast road, and headed south again through Gata de Gorgos to Benissa. Brian explained this wasn't the quickest route to the valley, but he wanted Michael to get his bearings by viewing it from the top of the slopes.

A moment later, a giant builders' yard appeared on the right. Stacks of concrete blocks, gravel and bricks gleamed in the dust. Fork-lifts buzzed around, feeding a fleet of lorries. A red brick and glass office building looked out of place, as did the cars – BMWs, Jaguars, a Porche – in the executive car park.

A cement wagon lurched round the corner in front of the Renault, almost forcing Brian into the ditch.

A few minutes later, they arrived at the tiny village of Lliber, and were halted by traffic lights.

'Could be a long wait,' Brian said.

'Why's that?'

'Most of these villages have main streets for two donkeys to pass, carrying panniers. They're gradually building by-passes, but not here. So there's a single track road through the village, with traffic lights at each end. We'll have to wait a while.'

After ten minutes, five cars came through from the other end of the village. The traffic lights changed to green, but Brian was prevented from moving off by a delivery truck rumbling toward him. When it had passed, the lights turned red again and the driver of a blue BMW behind Brian sounded the horn. Brian jumped the lights, followed by four cars.

'Bloody Germans – sorry, BMWs,' he said, 'always in such a hurry. We'll have to gun it, otherwise we'll meet the next lot coming through.'

Halfway through the run, the road widened at the side of a tiny square and this created a dogleg in the route. Brian slowed, but the BMW returned to his horn, so Brian pressed on. He'd cleared the bend when a frozen food van tore towards them, followed by three cars. The van driver joined the horn-thumping, and gestured to Brian to reverse.

Twenty minutes later, they escaped into open countryside.

'What was that?' Michael said. 'It's a wonder anything gets done.'

'Well,' said Brian. 'It's Spain. Works perfectly if you're Spanish, or if you like it here. And there's always mañana.'

'Wouldn't be allowed in England, by the traffic engineers.'

'Precisely! Anyway, here we are. Welcome to the Jalon Valley.'

Tiny buildings pepper-potted the landscape. The bed of the valley was about two kilometres wide; flat land lay in vine-planted plots, criss-crossed by tracks. A few grand villas rose above low growing vines. Jagged mountains tapered to a point in the distance.

'Jalon ahead,' said Brian. 'See the blue domed church? And beyond that Alcalalí, and then Parcent. Look, you can just about see the village on the hill, with the church spire sticking up.'

Michael stared straight ahead. His heart skipped a beat.

'Sorry, Brian. I have to get back.'

'But you haven't seen the houses I showed the Harrington's. There's a new development in Jalon and a resale villa just outside Alcalalí – and a very pretty town house in Parcent. We've got plenty of time.'

'Not today, though – sorry about this. Take me back, will you?'

'You're the boss.'

Brian reversed the car, and returned through Lliber, this time without incident. Michael broke the silence.

'You said you live in the mountains?'

'Yes, in a tiny settlement. Castell de Castells.'

'You didn't mention it – when we were looking up the valley?'

'No. We couldn't see it from there. It really is in the mountains, right at the top of the valley. Real Spain.'

'How long have you lived there?'

'Oh, about eighteen years.'

'You obviously like it.'

'Wouldn't want to be anywhere else in the world.'

Brian took a glance over at Michael, took a deep breath and said casually, 'Tell you what, it's a bit early, but how about stopping for a bite to eat. Do you like fish?'

Before he could think of an excuse, Michael had said, 'Yes'.

They left the N332 at Calpe and dropped to the coast.

Calpe was a bustling town, dominated by high rise buildings and overlooked by a gigantic rock that stretched far out into the sea. After rounding a lake where pink flamingos waded at the water's edge, they entered the old town and parked by a fish market. Brian led Michael across the street, where he paused at a display of fresh fish on platters, each with a price tag. A glass of sangria was thrust in Michael's hand by a waiter.

'Give it back,' Brian said. 'He's forcing you to sit down.'

They moved on.

'What's your poisson?' Brian grinned. 'Okay, sorry, I mean your pescado.'

Michael followed Brian to sunlit seats on a terrace, and agreed with the suggestion that they order a platter of fish and shellfish for two.

'How's the sangria?' Brian asked, after they'd been served.

Michael took a sip. 'Seems all right.'

'They usually water it down.'

'I've never tasted it before.'

'You're joking!'

'No. Never been to Spain. Never tasted sangria.' Best to anticipate the questions. 'My father was Spanish, but left here before I was born. I've never felt the need to come. I'm only here now, for a job.'

Brian took a sip. 'Your father taught you Spanish?'

'Mainly... At first.'

They looked about in silence for a moment, until Michael looked behind to see the waiter carrying their platter toward their table.

'That was quick. It looks good.'

'Smells good, too. They're quick because it's fresh, and lightly cooked.' Brian ladled a few scoops onto each plate. 'So your father didn't completely abandon his Spanish roots?'

'Why do you say that?'

'Well, the language and, of course, your name was kept. Fernandez isn't common in England, or the easiest name to pronounce. Some people would change it to Francis, something like that. '

'Never really thought about it that way.'

'So why did your father leave Spain?'

'It's a long story.'

'How's the fish?'

'Wonderful. In fact, I've never had anything like it.'

Bones and shells gradually mounted on the platter in the centre of the table. The waiter removed the empty wine bottle and replaced it.

'So how did you find your way to Spain?' Michael said.

'That's a long story, as well. I was divorced in 1973. No one's fault really, but it didn't end amicably. I travelled for a few years, had my share of adventures, but never really settled. Then I came to the Costa Blanca in 1984 to do some photography, and I fell in love with the place.'

'And the property business?'

'Just a means to an end. I knew John Saunders from way back and he was just setting up over here. He needed someone to deal with the customers at this end, so I said I'd take it on. Never looked back.'

'You still don't seem like a typical property agent to me.'

'I've never seen myself as a hard sell merchant, if that's what you mean. Don't get me wrong, I like to clinch a deal, I need the money. But mostly I see myself as the middleman, helping people to fulfil their dreams. The last thing I want is to put square pegs in round holes. I live here, remember, so I'm always bumping into old clients and it would be awful to find they weren't happy.'

'Does that happen?'

'Rarely used to, but things are changing.'

'What do you mean?'

'Until a couple of years ago, most people I met wanted to come to Spain. They knew something about the country, the people and the way of life. Many chose this part of the Costa Blanca because they'd been before, not just for a day trip. But it's changed. Half my buyers don't have a clue about Spain. It's sad, because Spain is magnificent, but you need to adapt. You need to *want* to adapt. If you come here to escape, you'll probably be disappointed. After all, Spain isn't paradise. Sorry... I'm rambling. And lecturing, and moralising.'

'Fascinating, though – to me, as someone who's also a bit ignorant about the country, and confused about what I'm doing here. Why, would you say, do you love the place so much?'

'You saw the mountains. How could you not be inspired? The climate's one of the healthiest in the world. But it's much more. The people are so... at times chaotic and disorganised – they're Spanish, after all – but astute, thoughtful, and warm. If you adapt, they make you welcome. You can't expect people to change for you, especially up in the mountains. The way of life is what's precious, though you'd have to live here a while to – well, it's impossible to explain. Sorry, I'm off again – you were telling me about your father, why he left.'

Michael sat forward. Whether it was the wine, or a sense of camaraderie, he felt like opening up.

'He was ill, and he had to go to England.'

'What part of Spain was your father from?'

Michael hesitated, and the waiter came up to ask if they wanted coffee. Michael ordered a café solo.

When it came, he emptied sugar into the tiny cup and stirred for a minute or more.

'Parcent.'

'What?'

'My father came from Parcent.'

'Christ! No wonder you looked so shocked – surprised – when I pointed it out. Of course, you've never been there. Never seen the place before.' He continued, as if allowing his enthusiasm to take over, 'It's a beautiful place. I've been there many a time. Even sold a few houses in the village. You'll love it.' Brian was now in full flow, and had obviously lost all sense of information-eliciting tactics as he posed the next question.

'Wait a minute. Your father wasn't a leper, was he?'

Michael looked up in horror.

'He suffered from leprosy. If that's what you mean.'

'No – sorry, I didn't mean to pry. It's just that when you mentioned Parcent... you know... when you said your father was ill.'

Michael had one question. 'What made you think of leprosy?'

'Well, there's a history of leprosy round here. In the nineteenth century it was almost an epidemic. Living in these parts, you get to know. There's even a sanatorium in the mountains which has patients to this day.'

'Fontilles?'

'You know about it?'

'Yes. I know all about the sanatorium at Fontilles.'

With that, Michael had said enough. He'd never told anyone, and now he'd talked about it to someone he barely knew.

'Better get the bill,' he said. 'And I really do need to get back to Alicante.'

Chapter Five

After going over his day with Brian Small, Michael focused on what might have happened to the Harringtons. He had to prepare for his meeting with Jose Luis in the morning, and tried to consider the steps he would have taken if he'd been running the investigation from the start.

It was nearly midnight. His concentration slipped, his mind took him back to the view of Parcent in the far distance, to Fontilles...

He wished he'd never met Brian, wished he'd kept his mouth shut, wished he'd told Brian not to say anything to anyone, wished he could sleep...

Jose Luis arrived at the hotel just as Michael was finishing breakfast. His outfit was the same as before, except the shirt was short-sleeved pyjama stripes – and he had sunglasses on top of his head.

'You look tired,' Jose Luis said cheerfully.

He pulled up a chair at the breakfast table and summoned the waiter to bring him a cup of coffee. The dining room was almost empty.

'Right, let's get down to business.' Jose Luis rummaged through a cardboard folder he'd taken from under his arm. 'Here's your ID. It's only a civilian ID card, we couldn't give you a proper warrant card and badge, but this will get you into most places you're likely to go.'

He slipped the card across the table and Michael picked it up.

'Where did you get the photo?'

'The wonders of e-mail. Your station sent it yesterday. Make sure you carry it when you're on duty. By the way, it doesn't give you police powers, so don't arrest anyone. We can't issue a gun, either, but then of course you wouldn't have a gun in England, would you? Can't understand that, in this day and age. I mean, with the crime in England I'd have thought you'd need all the help you could get.'

Michael didn't rise to the bait.

'Right,' said Jose Luis, 'so what would you like to do now?'

'You make it sound like I'm on holiday. But let's keep it straight. You're no happier having me here than I would be if this was my investigation in England, but I agree that we're stuck with each other, and the sooner we clear this up the better. So – why don't you start by bringing me up to date on what your team's been doing?'

Jose Luis smiled. 'Team? There's just me, I'm afraid. And I happen to have a full caseload already. If a couple of dreamers come to Spain and get lost, that's their business. The bosses are panicking because of heat from the Ministry for Tourism, but I've made all the usual inquiries and come to a dead end. As far as I'm concerned, it's now a question of wait and see.'

'Is that what you thought about the couple murdered last year?'

Jose Luis leaned forward so that his face was close to Michael's.

'For a start, that wasn't my case. And another thing, right from the start it was clear the couple had been abducted. This is a completely different case. There's no evidence at all to suggest anything other than that the Harringtons have just disappeared. Who knows, perhaps they don't want to be found. Anyway, we got the last lot and they're locked away in Alicante prison, so it's no use looking there for clues.'

'Sure you got the right people?'

'Dead sure. They confessed, didn't they?'

'I know, but I just wondered. The confessions weren't – let's say – "helped" in any way, were they?'

Jose Luis slammed the folder shut.

'For your information, Detective Inspector Michael Fernandez, the Spanish Inquisition ended in 1780.'

'And the last victim,' Michael said, folding his arms, 'was tortured until he confessed to carnal knowledge of the Devil, then burnt at the stake, but right now... How about a nice little chat?'

'If you put it that way.'

The waiters were re-setting tables for lunch, and Jose Luis suggested they move to the terrace by the pool. They found a table in a quiet corner, and sat in the shade. It was too early for sunbathers, but a grey- haired old man ploughed up and down the pool.

Michael said, 'I understand you need an NIE number before buying a house in Spain. Do you know whether the Harringtons ever applied?'

Jose Luis rolled his eyes. 'Yes, we checked that, and yes, Mr Harrington registered for his NIE number in October last year. You see, you also need a NIE number to open a bank account in Spain.'

'Harrington wasn't in Spain last October – so...?'

'It was handled by James Weeks Associates, asesorias in Javea. The forms were completed by post and James Weeks took them to the police station with a copy of Mr Harrington's passport. The forms were stamped and the NIE number issued on the spot. It's just routine. We have copies of the forms. They're in the file, if you want to see them.'

'Later, perhaps. I'm surprised to know that you can open a bank account by post.'

'Well, actually you can't, but the asesoria can do it for you and then you can transfer money into the account. Then you have to visit the bank and prove your identity – usually by showing your passport – before you can make any withdrawals. Like I say, it's all pretty standard stuff. Is this leading us somewhere?'

'No, I just want to understand the process. Would you need a NIE number to rent a house?

'No, thousands of people rent villas every week for holidays.'

'Is there any way to check whether the Harringtons rented a place, after they left the hotel?'

'We've trawled the main letting agencies, and drawn a blank. But there are a lot of small agents and ways to rent a place, especially if you have cash, and we know Harrington had plenty of that.'

'Yes,' said Michael. 'What was it? Fifty-five thousand pounds from the English bank and another twenty thousand euros from the Spanish bank in January while they were staying in Benidorm. Then seventy-five thousand euros in March. That's a lot of money to carry around, and that's what puzzles me. You see, if they'd been carrying the cash, then we might imagine they had been robbed, possibly by a gang like the ones we picked up on Monday. That would be straightforward and they'd surely have reported it. But why would someone abduct them if they'd already got their hands on so much money? It doesn't make sense.'

Jose Luis looked up as if interested for a second, then shrugged. 'Perhaps the abductors knew they had more money tucked away.'

Michael considered the suggestion.

'It's a possibility, but I still think a robbery for that sort of money would be enough for most people. Just take the cash and run. Why take the risk of abducting two people when you already have the best part of a hundred thousand euros in the bag? It doesn't add up. Have you checked to see if there are any other bank accounts in the Harringtons's name?'

Jose Luis raised his eyebrows at the continued probing – as if he was used to asking the questions, thanks, not answering them.

'Of course,' he said abruptly. 'Why do you think they looked at properties that seemed well outside their resources? Are you sure they don't have more money in the UK that no one knows about?'

'Sure as we can be. As for the houses, Brian Small says it's not that uncommon for time wasters to take a guided tour without ever intending to buy. You know, have a good look round, enjoy a free meal or two. It's better than a coach tour.'

Jose Luis looked smug. 'You English never cease to amaze. By the way, how did you get on with Brian Small yesterday?'

'Fine. Didn't really learn much, just went over the same ground as you three weeks ago – but then we didn't see all the properties the Harringtons looked at. Ran out of time. I'll meet him again at some point. By the way, I don't suppose the Guardia could provide me with a car? Only I feel a bit dependent, stuck here with no wheels.'

'I can recommend a cheap car hire company,' said Jose Luis. 'I'm sure the Nottingham County Constabulary can run to that.'

Michael didn't reply. He stared across the terrace, trying to pull threads together. 'That other agent, Summers, the one who says the Harringtons didn't show up. Have you checked him out?'

'Of course. His story holds up. The hotel receptionist remembers and confirms it. We're as sure as we can be that he never met them.'

'That reminds me,' Michael said casually. 'I came across another agent yesterday, who met the Harringtons in January but never came forward. His name's Vinnie Roberts. I think you should pull him in.'

Michael sat back, enjoying an image of Vinnie in shorts and flip-flops, sitting in a cold damp cell at Alicante police station.

Jose Luis seemed to read his mind.

'Look, I don't know how you operate in England, but we don't go arresting people just because they've been in contact with the missing couple. If you give me his details, I'll talk to him this week, but I don't expect anything to come of it.'

Michael considered telling Jose Luis what a shady character he had deduced Vinnie to be, but thought better of it.

Jose Luis continued to spar. 'You're really wasting your time looking at known property agents.' He leaned back, as if dragging out his spell of superiority. 'There are so many other ways,' he said, restraining a yawn, 'of buying houses in this part of Spain. It's highly unlikely any property agents would get involved in something as sordid as abduction.'

He paused, forcing Michael to ask the next question.

'What other ways?'

Jose Luis smiled. He'd retained the initiative.

'Houses change hands all the time, especially where there's cash involved. People do deals in bars on the shake of a hand. You know, "a friend of a friend has this place he wants to sell, strictly cash, no questions asked, no tax." Then there are property auctions, where a group of villains set up in a room somewhere, purporting to sell-off repossessed houses. It's a scam, of course, but you'd be surprised how gullible some people are, if they think they're getting a bargain. We have a saying here. "People in search of dream life often leave brains at border." Not just the British – the Germans and Dutch are just as bad. People come to Spain and do things they'd never dream of doing at home. I think it's the cheap booze. So you see, following up on contacts with property agents, at least bona fide property agents, is unlikely to lead you anywhere other than on an inspection tour of some very nice and very expensive houses.' He sat back again, triumphant.

'But what about the paperwork,' Michael said, 'and the escritura, the Notario, NIE numbers, all that sort of stuff?'

'My dear Michael.' Jose Luis tapped his companion on the shoulder. 'You really do have a lot to learn about Spain, and about human nature, come to that.'

'Well, a bit of study can't go wrong. Thanks for the tip.'

It was hot on the terrace, and Michael's head was spinning again –

as if, removed from familiar surroundings, he couldn't function. Perhaps it was lack of sleep. Or the heat. Perhaps it was just Spain.

'So where to, now?' he asked, trying to sound businesslike.

Jose Luis shrugged.

'It's up to you. I've exhausted all my leads. Like I said, I've got other crimes to solve. Here, you can have my file if you want it. You've seen most of it already, but there are notes in there of all my interviews. Perhaps you can come up with something. Feel free to ask around some more if you want, or just enjoy the sun.'

He slid his chair away from the table, and began to stand.

'Oh, I forgot to mention – there's a press conference at eleven-thirty Friday. We've reserved the business suite here at the hotel. All the local English press are invited, and the British papers are sending reporters. Apparently, the story's hit the headlines in Britain and everyone wants in. Spanish TV and radio will be there, and the BBC. John and Linda Harrington are flying in tomorrow. It's your boss's idea, what's his name – Bowater. He's been talking to my Colonel, and they set it up between them. Just a publicity stunt, I expect, to show how well the Guardia and the British police are working together. That's all right with you, isn't it?'

Jesus. Michael visualised the packed audience, John with fag and rolled-up newspaper, Linda weeping, reporters firing off questions, trying to trip him up, exposing gaps in the investigation.

'Ah – hmm, yes. Probably a good idea. Renew interest in the case, get some fresh coverage, and it's possible we might get some new witnesses to come forward, that sort of thing. But, ah... will there be a briefing beforehand?'

'What, to get our stories straight, you mean?'

'No, I mean... Well, sort out who – who does the introductions, that sort of thing. You can't go into these things cold, you know.'

'Of course not,' said Jose Luis. 'And what I mean by *that* is, of course there will be a briefing. My Colonel's running the show. His name's Cardells, Antonio Cardells, and for Christ's sake don't call him Antonio. Ever. He'll be here nine-thirty Friday morning and we can run through the details then. The Harringtons will be here at ten-thirty with someone from the British consulate. Don't worry, it's all arranged.'

'Who said I was worried?'

Jose Luis started toward the sliding doors of the hotel lobby. 'I've got things to do,' he said. 'See you on Friday. If you want me, just phone.' He added, 'Just think – you could get yourself into the papers, maybe even on TV.'

Michael didn't say goodbye. He stared out over the pool and the turquoise sea to the horizon for a while, then ordered a pot of coffee and a bottle of mineral water to be delivered up to his room.

He retired there for most of the afternoon, skipping lunch while he pored over the files again.

The Harringtons had checked out of their Benidorm hotel as scheduled on 21st January. They left in the hired blue Renault Clio, but didn't catch their flight home. The car had never been returned. Could they have been robbed on the way to the airport?... But the Gessels in Alcalalí said that a couple called Johnson (almost certainly the Harringtons?) viewed their house on 23rd January. If this was true, the Harringtons obviously never intended to catch their flight home.

They were moving around in January, so if they'd been abducted it was some time later. But where had they been staying? Another hotel, a rented villa, somewhere else? There had been a few more possible sightings over the following weeks, and the phone call home in early February. Then, on 13th March, David Harrington had visited his bank in Javea to withdraw seventy-five thousand euros in cash.

Michael turned the pages of Jose Luis' file to find the notes of the interview with the cashier. The money had been ordered three days in advance and David Harrington had been alone when he collected the cash. The cashier had confirmed his identity by asking to see his passport. He signed for the cash and left with a large bundle of five hundred euro notes. The signature had been confirmed as authentic. The cashier said it appeared to be a normal transaction (large cash withdrawals were not unusual for visits to the Notario) and Mr Harrington had seemed perfectly calm and relaxed, as far as anyone could remember. So, Michael surmised again, by 13th March, David Harrington was, seemingly, still around and doing business as usual.

But where was Mrs Harrington? Were abductors forcing Mr Harrington to withdraw the cash under threat of violence to his wife?

At this point the trail went cold.

Repeated appeals through the press had failed to turn up a single new sighting since the trip to the bank nearly two months ago. If the Harringtons were hiding, they'd been very careful and discreet otherwise someone would surely have spotted them. On the other hand... if they'd been abducted there was every reason for them to be well hidden. Indeed, Michael thought, with the Spanish bank account virtually cleared, there was very little reason to keep them alive, especially if they could identify their abductors.

Though he'd never admit it to anyone, he was at a dead end. He sympathised with Jose Luis's predicament. What could he do? There must be something he'd failed to notice, and he was still puzzled about why they'd viewed properties well beyond their means. Free inspection trips at an agent's expense was one thing, but what about their trip to the Gessels' place in Alcalalí? Assuming it was them, of course.

Bereft of other ideas, Michael decided to visit Jacob and Helena Gessels. He phoned and made an appointment for 11am the next morning, then arranged a hire car for a week, through the receptionist. It would be delivered to the hotel first thing in the morning.

He ate in the hotel dining room that evening, finishing with coffee, then a large brandy he hoped would help him sleep. The brandy was a Gran Solera from Jerez called Grand Duque d'Alba, and he thought for a second that the waiter looked surprised when Michael asked for it by name. Or disapproving. Or something.

After that, he lay on top of his bed staring up at the cracked white ceiling. The air conditioning unit rattled over the door and wafted barely chilled air over his near naked body. He fought for sleep, but his mind worked overtime. He tossed from side to side, trying to find a comfortable position as he wrestled with ideas. It was as if someone was flashing a series of photographs before his eyes.

As soon as he managed to delete one picture, another one came in to replace it, with increasing rapidity. It felt as if he was sitting in front of a computer, clicking the mouse to clear the screen only for another image to pop up in front of him. Click, click, click... only the computer was beginning to anticipate his moves.

And one image kept returning with escalating frequency until, suddenly, it stopped and the image remained fixed on the screen.

Click, click, click... but the image was frozen and could not be removed. He seemed to be able to view it in three dimensions, moving around to see it from different angles and perspectives and zooming in and out. But it could not be erased.

A higgledy-piggledy collection of colour-washed houses rose around a hill surrounded by much taller mountains. The roof lines of weathered terracotta tiles seemed to form steps as they climbed to the summit, punctuated by a few round green trees and pencil-thin pines. Irregular spaces marked the position of narrow streets, all appearing to culminate at the top of the hill. High above the rooftops a white church tower with a Moorish fretwork spire was silhouetted against a clear blue sky. Parcent. Michael had caught only a brief glimpse from his distant viewing point on the outskirts of Lliber, but it had left an impression seared into his mind like the patterns on a memory chip.

Early next morning, Michael rose feeling surprisingly fresh. Before breakfast he made another telephone call.

'Brian, it's Michael Fernandez. I'm coming to Alcalalí this morning and I wondered if we could meet, if you're free.'

If Brian was surprised, it didn't show. 'Delighted. I'm with some people this morning, but I can meet you for lunch, about one o'clock.'

They agreed to meet at Bar Porche in the centre of Alcalalí, near the church tower.

Michael set off. Approaching Jalon, following the directions to the Gessels' house, he found the road sign spray-painted to obliterate 'Jalon,' leaving only the Valenciano 'Xaló.' After bypassing the town centre, he drove past a row of bodegas on the left-hand side of the road, with tourists tumbling out of the Cooperativa. Laden with five-litre packs of wine, they headed back to a coach parked under riverbank trees. A sign on the coach announced: *Benidorm*. Between the bodegas, a new shopping arcade had a 'Hamiltons of London' window displaying hundreds of properties – and two doors along from that, a new-looking awning announced fish and chips. Up to the north, three or four large urbanisations were being developed on the slopes of the mountains.

After crossing the narrow bridge over the dried-up River Jalon, he could see Alcalalí about two kilometres away. The road twisted and turned, opening up new views toward the top of the valley as he wove his way through the gentle hills.

A glimpse was all he saw of the distant church tower, but it was enough for him to match it with the imprint etched on his mind from the previous sleepless night.

He continued following the directions he'd scribbled on a notepad the previous evening, when he'd spoken to the Gessels on the phone.

"Turn left just after the entrance to the Almazara urbanisation, cross the tiny bridge, then follow the road for about five hundred metres through the almond and olive groves."

They'd said the road was a little bumpy, and it was. He feared he might rip the sump from the engine as he steered between pot holes and rocks – and was forced to pull over at one point, to allow a small tractor and trailer to pass in the opposite direction. The trailer was laden with long bamboo canes bearing leaves, and it bounced up and down on the uneven surface. The driver, in a tattered straw hat, had the stub of a torpedo-shaped cigar clenched between his teeth. He gave a cheery wave as he passed by, and the scene looked so typically Spanish that Michael felt for a second that he must have seen it before, in a holiday brochure.

"Turn right at the fork in the road and keep straight on until you see a black, wrought iron gate on the left."

The road continued to deteriorate, with still no sign of a house. He was just concluding he was on the wrong road when he spotted it, and saw Jacob and Helena Gessels waiting at the gate.

They were both remarkably tall, about six foot six in Mr Gessels' case, his wife only a little shorter.

Helena Gessels' tightly permed hair was grey, dyed light brown. She wore a cotton top with teenager-ish calf-length slacks, and open-toed, pink mules.

Jacob, in a stiff-collared, pinstriped shirt, looked as if he'd seen time in an office. His neatly-laced shoes were made of interwoven strips of polished brown leather. They belonged with the shirt, Michael thought, and reflected a man of substance and good taste, though the effect was knocked off-balance by white sports socks and baggy shorts. They both looked to be mid- to late-seventies.

He followed them round the house, past a pool and into a garden like a tropical oasis, delineated by tall hedges of oleanders just coming into bud. The patch of green lawn could have come straight from suburban England – except that it was dotted with orange and lemon trees.

They led him to a glass-topped wicker table, in the shade of an open-arched naya.

The coffee was dark and syrupy, and Michael took a sip before going through the usual preamble, apologising for having to ask more questions, before getting down to the questions.

'How certain are you that the couple who viewed the house, the Johnsons, were in fact Mr and Mrs Harrington?'

Mrs Gessels answered, explaining that her husband did not speak much English. 'We were quite sure from the photographs the Guardia showed us, even though they weren't very good. We found the man in the photographs hard to be sure about, but the woman we recognised at once. Petite, very beautiful with long blonde hair, and she had very distinctive eyes. Like a doe's eyes, I mean – slightly sad.'

Michael continued, 'Did you talk to them much?'

'Quite a lot, yes. I remember they asked a lot of questions. They seemed very interested.'

'What sort of questions?'

'The usual, you know, about how old the house was, how far to shops and restaurants, if it was cold in winter. We don't have central heating, you see. Oh, and Mr Johnson also asked about neighbours. I thought it was a little strange because it's only too obvious when you drive out here. We told them that no one else lives nearby. Our closest neighbours are on the edge of the village, about one kilometre away.'

'Was that the answer he was looking for?'

'I'm sorry, I don't understand.'

'I mean, did he give you the impression that he was looking for somewhere so isolated?'

'He commented on how nice and quiet it was, so we guessed he liked the idea of being away from people. That's what attracted us, sixteen years ago when we bought the plot and had the house built.'

'Did they say anything else?'

'Not that I remember. We left them to wander on their own for most of the time. They looked round the garden. I remember Mrs Johnson said how lovely the garden was, but that was about it – wasn't it, Jacob?'

Mr Gessels responded grumpily in Dutch, and his wife interpreted. 'He's saying that they asked why we were selling. Jacob thought they were being nosy.'

Michael phrased his next question carefully, aware that Mr Gessels was following every word of the conversation.

'Did you give them an answer?'

Helena ignored a muttered comment from her husband.

'We love it, but the garden's hard, and it's a long way to the village. I don't drive, and if Jacob was ill I couldn't manage alone. We plan to buy in Calpe, close to the shops, with a terrace but no garden.'

'I can see why you fell in love with the place, it really is beautiful. By the way – is it still on the market?'

Mr Gessels sat up. 'Why? – Do you want to buy it?'

'Out of my league, I'm afraid. I only asked because it was the end of January when the Harringtons, if it was the Harringtons, came to see it. It's now May and I wondered why it hasn't sold.'

Before her husband could say anything, Mrs Gessels answered.

'Something to do with the euro, so they say. The English pound has gone up or down, so it's more expensive for English people. I told Jacob we should put the house with agents but he didn't want to pay their fees. So we advertised it in the Costa Blanca News. Anyway, we've put it with agents now, only I feel we've wasted three months.'

The answer hit Michael like a boxer's right hook.

'When you say you advertised in the Costa Blanca News, do you mean the English version? It's printed in Dutch as well, isn't it?'

'And German,' said Mrs Gessels, 'but we put it in the English version because all the houses round here seem to be bought by English people. Ten years ago it was mainly Dutch and Germans who came to the mountains, but now the place is gradually being taken over by the English. It seems they're the ones with the money now, especially since prices here have rocketed in the last couple of years.'

Remembering the fish and chip shop in Jalon, Michael understood what Mrs Gessels meant – but he was still missing something. He asked the next question to buy time, anticipating the reply.

'The German and Dutch versions of the Costa Blanca News, do they have advertisements for houses for sale?'

'Of course,' said Mrs Gessels, as if it was obvious.

Michael almost ignored the answer. He was still ruminating... pattern, process, procedure, deduction.

'Are the advertisements in Dutch and German, or English?'

'They're all in Dutch and German. Nobody English would read the foreign versions of the Costa Blanca News.'

'Oh, yes.' The coin dropped, and Michael gave a brief smile. 'Tell me Mrs Gessels, where did you hear about the Harringtons?'

'I read about them in the Costa Blanca News.'

'The English Costa Blanca News?'

'Yes. I don't usually buy it, of course, but I was buying it then to check that our advertisement was in.'

'Have you ever read anything about the Harringtons in the Dutch version?'

Mrs Gessels hesitated, and asked the question of her husband. The answer was clear from the shake of his head. 'Now you mention it, I don't think we've seen anything in the Dutch papers.'

Michael needed to make a phone call, and he thanked Mr and Mrs Gessels for their time and coffee, and wished them success in selling their house. He opened the door of the hire car, intending to make the call on his mobile phone. It was like an oven, so he set off back along the bumpy track with the air conditioning blasting on full power. By the time he reached the main road the car had cooled, but his back was wringing wet. He parked in a cart track and left the engine running while he made the call. Jose Luis was not too pleased with Michael's demand that Dutch and German reporters should be invited to tomorrow's press conference. Colonel Cardells would be furious at this last minute interference with his carefully laid plans, but Jose Luis agreed to put the suggestion to him.

At 12.45pm, Michael parked his car at the entrance to the village of Alcalalí. The church tower was in the distance. He headed off in that direction, passing a modern bank and a sign for the municipal library.

He walked beneath an impressive stone arch into the tiny square, and spotted Bar Porche. Nervous about entering a Spanish bar alone, he hesitated, then continued walking, pausing in front of the church to read an inscribed tablet which explained the origins of the village which dated back to Roman times, and mentioned the "Reconquest of the Moors by King Jaime I in 1238."

'Interesting, isn't it,' said Brian, appearing at Michael's side. 'Most of the villages round here were ruled by the Moors at one time or another, until the Reconquest. Moors and Christians lived side by side for centuries, but there was always distrust and the Moorish people were finally sent packing by the Decree of Expulsion in 1609.'

'Yes, and the valley was repopulated with Majorcan farmers.'

'You certainly know your history,' said Brian.

'Bits of it.'

They walked back to the bar, where a chalkboard with a menu for tapas hung on the wall, and sat down at a corner table.

Michael ordered quickly, but found himself sitting back to eat slowly, watching tiny dishes of tapas arrive, two at a time, all freshly cooked and served with crusty bread and alioli. The bar gradually began to fill with 'tradesmen looking for lunch at the start of their two-hour break before taking their siestas,' Brian explained.

Soon the place was a noisy, heaving mass of people, shouting orders, greeting friends, eating, drinking beer or wine and smoking. Almost everyone smoked and, despite the presence of ashtrays on the bar and tables, cigarette ends were invariably stubbed out on the floor to join empty sachets of sugar casually discarded in the same place.

He'd expected to feel uncomfortable, yet there was an air of conviviality about the place, and he felt curiously at ease. It was not until a waitress asked if he had enjoyed the tapas, and remarked on the excellence of his Spanish, that he felt like a foreigner again.

Brian had discarded his woollen cardigan in deference to the heat, but in all other respects his outfit was in the same style as before – country gentleman meets desert trekker.

'So what's it to be?' He wiped away a few morsels of tapas that had fallen onto the spectacles dangling on the cords around his neck.

'Sorry?'

'Well, I assume you didn't just want to meet me for lunch.'

'Oh, no. No, not at all. You mentioned some other properties the Harringtons had looked at.'

'You mean the town house in Parcent?'

'Well, yes, but you said something about...'

'Let's go, then.' Brian caught the waiter's eye, scribbled with his finger and mouthed the words, "la cuenta".'

They met at the edge of Alcalalí, and Michael followed Brian's Renault as it headed up the valley. A few minutes later they rounded a sharp bend and the village of Parcent came into view, every detail just as Michael had visualised it the night before.

Brian drove almost full circle around the base of the hilltop village, then turned sharp right into the settlement itself. They parked along a wide, tree-lined street.

'Follow me.' Brian headed off. 'It's a bit of a climb.' He strode up another tree-lined street, and into a steeper slope.

'Where are we going?' asked Michael, struggling to keep up as he tried to take in every detail of the surroundings.

'To the town house, of course. You can have a look round.'

Anxious again, having that feeling of being railroaded into something he was not sure he wanted to do, he thought about turning back, but curiosity overcame unease.

They turned into a two-donkey lane lined by pastel walls of varying textures. Carved doors opened onto the pavement, inches from the street. Behind window grills, the shutters were closed, and it was easy to imagine dark little rooms, starved of sun.

Most houses were two storeys, with two or three balconied windows hanging over the pavement. A few were taller, with more balconies at a higher level. The soffits had been colonised by swallows with two, three, or more mud nests clinging to the undersides of the eaves.

Halfway along the street an old lady, perhaps four and a half feet tall, was sweeping the pavement with a hand-crafted broom. She was in a black skirt, blouse, cardigan – and bedroom slippers, also black.

Brian stopped. He gestured for Michael to take a peek inside an open door.

'This is it,' he whispered. 'Shall I knock up the younger folk?'

'No.' Michael put his head quickly inside the door.

A waft of cool air hit him, as he adjusted his eyes to the dim light.

The flagstone floor of the entrance hall was dominated by a dark oak sideboard, and an enormous vase of flowers filled the air with scent. Leaning further in, he could see a large lounge with a high moulded ceiling and stone framed fireplace. The furniture was rustic, dark wood with a warm patina. Ornaments and framed photographs decorated shelves and mantelpiece. An expensive-looking Afghan rug covered the centre of the mosaic-tiled floor.

Beyond, a white-walled courtyard seemed ot stretch back almost as far again as the house, a collection of pots and tubs could be seen, overflowing with geraniums and petunias.

'Are they all like that?' he asked Brian, as they walked on. 'I'd imagined these places to be cramped and claustrophobic.'

'Claustrophobic houses?' Brian replied. 'We'd have to put them into cognitive therapy – but yes, some are bigger, and that one was particularly nice. I know other people in the village, as I said. We can go inside somewhere and look round, if you want?'

'No, not right now. I didn't want to intrude, and I just wanted to see, and think about the village itself. But how much would something like that – the house we just looked at – cost, approximately?'

'Just over two hundred thousand euros, give or take.'

'How much?'

'The ex-pat boom's arrived. Two years ago you could have picked up places like that for next to nothing, but prices have rocketed. The coastal towns are overcrowded, especially in the summer.'

'And what do the locals think of it?'

'Many put up with it, for the time being at least. You see, not so long ago, people here scratched a bit of a living off the land and foraged in the hills for wild plants and herbs. Many of the men hunted – still do, today – rabbits, birds, wild boar. The ex-pats have changed all that, though. Foreigners are welcomed for the money, and the value of property has soared. Whether this will all stay as it is, remains to be seen.'

'Thins are changing already, though?'

'Inevitably. Most of the elderly keep to the old ways, despite their wealth. But foreign influences impress the younger generation, and there's not a lot of money in a few hectares of olives or oranges.'

'I don't know,' Michael said, stopping to look back. 'But I think I rather resent the destruction of a decent way of life.' He turned to walk on. 'How far does the expat boom go, in the valley?' he asked.

'This is about the limit, for now at least. There are a few small urbanisations further up, around Benigembla, but after that they begin to peter out. A few intrepid ex-pats are in the more remote villages, even in Castell de Castells, and that's about sixteen kilometres away.'

'Castell de Castells, that's where you live, isn't it?'

'That's right, want to take a look?'

'I do, but I'll have to make it another time.'

They continued on up, passing narrower houses that seemed to cling to the slope, until the top of the street opened into a village square littered with parked cars and vans.

A tobacconist stood in one corner, near several grand, balconied houses. In another corner, red plastic tables and chairs sat under lace-curtained windows. A faded sign read, "Bar Moll."

The square was centred by a drinking fountain, and four trees protected by wrought iron rails. Opposite, a heavy, metal-studded wooden door straddled a stone archway.

Above, a clock face and a stone cross were pinned to a white tower.

Michael picked out lines of the fretwork spire against the blue sky, just as he had dreamed. An inscription below read, "1949."

'Come on,' said Brian, 'if you want to return before nightfall.'

At almost 7.30pm, Michael arrived back at his hotel.

From the reception counter, the concierge called out, walking over to thrust a note into Michael's hand.

A few minutes later, he was on the phone.

'Where the hell have you been, Fernandez? I've been trying to contact you all day. You're not on a bloody holiday jaunt, you know.'

'Sorry, Chief Superintendent,' Michael said, half-heartedly proceeding to explain some of his movements.

'And what's all this about wanting to invite the Dutch and the Germans to the press conference? I've had Colonel Cardells on the phone. He's livid. You'll want to involve Interpol, next.'

Chief Superintendent Bowater seemed just about satisfied with Michael's explanations, but still wanted the final word.

'Look, just don't go upsetting the Spanish Police. It's their show. Remember you're only there to lend a hand, not to take over the whole bloody shooting match. And keep in touch. Buy yourself a mobile phone and charge it to expenses. Let me know the number.'

Michael thought about mentioning the hire car, but decided to leave it for another occasion.

Chapter Six

Michael breakfasted early, having slept well again. He was thinking about the press conference when Jose Luis marched through the door, crisp in grey trousers and a dazzling white shirt. His shoes had been polished, and were without a trace of dust. He seemed edgy.

'Colonel Cardells should be here in ten minutes. Remember, he likes things on a formal footing so don't get familiar. And whatever you do, *don't* spring surprises. It's his show, let him run it his way.'

'You make him sound like an ogre.'

'I work for him, you don't. Here – he wants everyone to wear these.' Jose Luis handed Michael a name badge and clipped his own to the pocket of his shirt.

Michael looked at his badge: "Detective Inspector Michael Fernandez, Nottingham County Constabulary". The blue insignia was reproduced in the bottom right hand corner. He began to clip it to the lapel of his Prince of Wales checked jacket.

'Do yourself a favour, Michael, dispense with the jacket. This isn't England, you know, and it's likely to be hot in there.'

'If you're sure.' Michael slipped the jacket from his shoulders.

'And the tie isn't strictly necessary,' added Jose Luis.

'I'll keep it on, if you don't mind.'

'The Colonel asked if you'll interpret. He wants all questions to go through him, so if any British reporters ask questions in English you'll translate. Only answer yourself if he tells you it's okay.'

Jesus. Michael finished his coffee. *Right farce this could turn out to be.* He nodded, as if he thought it an entirely practical plan.

Jose Luis looked at his watch. 'Let's go, mustn't be late.'

In the hotel lobby, near the business suite, Jose Luis paused. 'By the way, I met Vincent Roberts yesterday. He didn't tell me anything new. I'm fairly sure he only met the Harringtons once, when Brian Small took them to Moraira. He was furious about you, though. Said something about acting under false pretences. He wanted to lay an official complaint, but I told him to speak to your Chief Constable.'

Jose Luis smirked.

Michael airily adjusted his name badge, straightened his tie, and took a quick look at his shoes. 'The hotel polishing machine did a great job, buffing the scuffs out. You should try it.'

Colonel Cardells stood by a coffee trolley in the corner of the ante-room, his vast frame casting a giant shadow on the stained beige carpet. A uniformed waiter fussed at his side.

Jose Luis waited for the Colonel to turn before introducing Michael. Perhaps it was the cup in the Colonel's right hand, but Michael's tentative offer of a handshake was brusquely ignored.

The two men gave each other the once-over.

A sparse covering of glossy jet-black hair was evenly spread across the top of the Colonel's head, carefully positioned to give maximum coverage, a la Chief Superintendent Bowater. A pencil-thin moustache, coloured to match the hair, sunk into flabby jowls beneath the Colonel's cheeks. The buttons of an epauletted white shirt just about managed to contain the Colonel's paunch, which drooped over the front of dark green trousers that looked to be part of a uniform, of sorts. The shoes were rubber soled, with dull black leather uppers and fraying laces... Augh!

Before Michael and Jose Luis could get coffee, the Colonel ushered them to a small table in the centre of the room.

They took their places, the Colonel sitting beside a fidgety young man shuffling files. He was introduced as Sergeant Ramirez, the Colonel's personal assistant.

As Jose Luis had anticipated, this was the Colonel's show.

He launched into commands as to how the press conference would be run. He stressed the key themes time and again: the British police and the Guardia were co-operating fully; everything possible was being done to find the Harringtons; no one should give the impression that they had come to any harm; this type of incident was very rare on the Costa Blanca, and it needed to be clear that tourists and potential homebuyers were visiting the Costa Blanca in complete safety.

Coming to an abrupt finish, he looked across at Michael as if to check that he understood.

Michael suspected the inquiry was not really about his grasp of the language, but replied, 'Yes, Colonel. I understand your Spanish perfectly.'

Cardells grunted. He continued to spill out directives, and finally asked if anyone had any questions as he rose from the table.

Jose Luis rolled his eyes when Michael, with a vaguely apologetic shrug in response to the Colonel's glare, began to speak.

'Just one thing Colonel,' said Michael.

Cardells resumed his seat.

'How are you going to handle John and Linda Harrington? I mean, it's going to be difficult to control what they say, isn't it?'

At once, Cardells was up and moving toward the door. 'I think you'll find that's been taken care of, Inspector Fernandez, but if there are any problems I expect you to deal with them.'

He left, with Sergeant Ramirez scurrying along behind.

John and Linda Harrington were in the adjacent room with Timothy Middleton, a British Consular Official from Alicante. He'd been chaperoning them since their arrival in Spain the previous afternoon.

Colonel Cardells introduced himself briefly, before heading for the coffee trolley, where the waiter stood holding out a fresh cup.

Michael greeted the Harringtons, expressing his regrets for the lack of positive news. They seemed to have made an effort for the occasion. Linda was in deep grey-lilac, and John was in a (tight-jacketed, ancient-looking) beige suit. They almost made a smart couple, right down to the shoes; John had come in trainers, but today they were neatly laced.

The consular official anxiously interrupted, handing Michael a sheet of paper. 'Chief Superintendent Bowater wants you to cast an eye over this before we start the press conference.'

Middleton hovering at his side, Michael moved away to look at the document. On official Nottingham Police stationery, it was headed: "Statement prepared by John and Linda Harrington."

This should have read: 'Statement prepared by Chief Superintendent Phillip Bowater, OBE QPM', but it was too late to do anything about that.

Colonel Cardells led the entourage into the Business Suite.

Two Guardia Civil officers flanked the doors and Michael nervously noted their black leather holsters, but his attention was then drawn by a platform at the end of the room, beyond the seats.

A giant logo of Nottingham County Constabulary hung onstage, alongside that of the Guardia Civil. He was contemplating the clash of designs when he was interrupted.

'Here you are, Michael.' Penny Edwardes thrust a plastic document wallet into his hand.

'Jesus, Penny – what the hell are you doing here?'

'The Chief Super sent me with all the public relations material. He wants to make sure this is seen as a joint operation, not just the Guardia Civil. Have you seen? The BBC are here.'

He was already struggling to retain equilibrium, and now butterflies converged. His palms were clammy and he felt beads of sweat on his forehead. Perhaps Jose Luis had been right about the tie.

Penny's sudden appearance was not going to help, and the sea of reporters and cameramen made him more nervous. He took his seat next to the Colonel, with John and Linda Harrington on his other side.

The chatter subsided as the Colonel made it obvious he was impatient to get proceedings underway; such was the air of authority he exuded.

He performed introductions and perfunctorily thanked the assembled gathering for attending. Then he launched into reading in Spanish from a script, in a re-run of the rehearsal he'd been through in the ante-room.

He thanked the Nottingham Police for sending Detective Inspector Fernandez to help with the investigation, and added that the Inspector was working closely with Captain Jose Luis Perez of the Guardia Civil to pursue a number of lines of inquiry.

He hoped the press would give widest possible coverage to the case. In particular, the police needed to hear from anyone who had seen, or thought they could have seen, the Harringtons or their hired car since January.

He gave the registration number of the blue Renault Clio and said photographs of the missing couple were in the press pack.

He ended by saying the pack contained a transcript of his statement, in Spanish as well as English.

A Spanish reporter rose, but the Colonel brushed him aside, saying questions would be taken at the end. He handed over to John Harrington, inviting him to read his statement.

John Harrington sat facing the assembled press corps and an array of microphones, squinting into the glare of camera lights. He failed to respond to the Colonel's invitation, not being able to follow the Spaniard's statement.

There was a brief pause, until Michael said quietly to John that it was his turn to speak.

John stood up, shuffled the papers in front of him, and spilled some onto the floor.

Michael retrieved them, whispering, 'Relax, take your time.'

With a pair of steel-rimmed spectacles perched on the end of his nose, and his hair flattened, John Harrington looked almost scholarly as he began to read the statement into the microphone. Only his shaking hands indicated his terror of showing himself up on television.

He gave each word equal weight, as if considering evidence.

'I would like to start by thanking the press and television for the interest they have shown so far in the search for my brother David and his wife Alison. I would also like to thank the Guardia Civil and the Nottingham Police for everything they have done to investigate the disappearance and follow up on the information they have received.'

He coughed twice. Michael passed him a glass of water.

John resumed. 'My wife and I are seriously concerned about David and Alison, as are family and friends in England. It is most un-char-ac-ter-ist-ic,' (pronounced syllable by syllable) 'of them not to be in touch for such a long time. However, if, as we hope, they are simply keeping out of contact for some reason, I urge them to get in touch with me or the police so we may know they are safe. Anyone who has seen or heard of them in the past few months, please contact the police. Any information, however insig-nifi-cant, could help solve the mystery of their whereabouts.'

John paused again, distracted by camera flashes, shutters clicking and the whirring of motors automatically winding film forward.

Colonel Cardells interjected abrasively to say, 'No photographs until the end.' Everyone complied.

'Our worst fear,' John said, 'is that David and Alison may have been abducted. If anyone is holding them against their will I appeal to them directly not to harm them, but return them safely to their family and friends. The continued uncertainty about what has happened is causing us enormous stress and worry, so please, if you are holding them, make some kind of contact if only to let us know they are safe.'

John's eyes glistened. He lifted his spectacles to rub his face.

Linda Harrington blew her nose softly and wiped her cheeks with a tissue. Camera flashes followed, several photographers risking the Colonel's wrath, knowing this was the picture their editors wanted.

John sat down, pushed the papers to one side, and looked toward Michael. No longer playing the careless, knowing lout with the fag, dressing down to prove he was a man of the world, his fear was exposed on his face.

Michael patted him on the forearm. 'That was fine.'

To everyone's surprise, Linda Harrington grabbed the microphone and the attention of the audience.

'David and Alison, if you're watching or you read about this, please get in touch. We need to know you're safe. We hope to God no one is holding you but if you are, please, please let them go. They have done you no harm. We just want them back safe and sound. This is destroying our family. I don't know how long we can go on like this. We just want it to end. It's a nightmare. Please let them go. Please, someone must know what's happened to them. Please... '

John Harrington halted Linda's rambling, placing an arm round her shoulder in an awkward display of affection. She sobbed uncontrollably, her shoulders bobbing up and down. An embarrassed-looking Timothy Middleton pulled a tissue from the box, and thrust it in front of Linda.

Colonell Cardells took command once more.

'We'll take questions now. Please bear in mind that this is very stressful for Mr and Mrs Harrington, and address all questions to me.'

At least half the audience failed to understand what he'd said, and Michael didn't think to interpret until someone stood up.

An impatient Spanish reporter was first off the mark, asking if there was a link between this case and the one last year. Cardells brushed aside the idea. A couple more questions from Spanish reporters received reassuring replies. Yes, everything possible was being done to find the missing couple. No, there was no firm evidence to suggest they had been abducted. Yes, it was perfectly safe to come to the Costa Blanca.

The Colonel stiffened, but regained composure as the team from Spanish television put him in the spotlight to pick up more platitudinous remarks.

A BBC reporter, John Lynes, was the first of the foreign contingent to enter the fray. His cameraman swivelled to get him into the frame. He had a smattering of Spanish and seemed to have understood most of what the Colonel had said. Even so, after his self introduction he framed his question in English for the benefit of viewers back home.

'Colonel Cardells, is there any truth in the rumour that the Guardia Civil failed to assign an officer to this case for three weeks after the Harringtons were reported missing?'

The camera swung toward Cardells who had a look of calm innocence on his face, oblivious to the reporter's accusation.

His expression changed profoundly when Michael interpreted without attempting to tone it down. In return, Michael received the Colonel's glower as his dark eyes turned to thunder. By the time he returned to the BBC, he'd regained composure and responded with a masterly side-step, ignoring the question and delivering a longwinded 'no stone left unturned' diatribe against time wasting.

Lynes' attempt to follow up was studiously avoided as the Colonel scanned the audience for a sympathetic questioner. He found the familiar face of the reporter from the Spanish equivalent of the Police Gazette and nodded for him to speak.

A reporter from the Spanish Daily, El Pais, was next, more by the force of his voice than any invitation on the part of the Colonel.

'Inspector Fernandez, since you joined the investigation in Spain, have you been satisfied with the steps taken by the Guardia Civil, and are they co-operating fully with your own inquiries now you're here?'

About to respond, Michael felt the force of the Colonel's stare, saying: You may answer, but you had better be very, very careful.

Michael made the right kind of noises, responding in Spanish.

A reporter from The Times posed a similar question in English and Michael gave a similar reply, noticing from the corner of his eye that Sergeant Ramirez was whispering in the Colonel's ear.

A Dutch reporter, Jan van Orterloo, posed the next question in perfect English. 'Colonel Cardells, why did you specifically invite Dutch and German reporters to this press conference?'

Again Michael interpreted the question for the Colonel's benefit, and in turn he was required to interpret the answer.

'As part of our investigations, information came to light suggesting the Harringtons may have been in contact with Dutch or German property owners or agents. There has been little coverage of the case in local Dutch and German newspapers and we' (Michael nearly said 'I', but was conscious of Sergeant Ramirez hanging onto his every word) 'thought it germane to extend the press coverage to include the Dutch and German media. A telephone number is in the press pack for people to call. The lines will be manned by Dutch and German speaking operators.'

The next questions were aimed at John and Linda, the British tabloids probing David's and Alison's personal lives.

A thinly disguised question from The Sun's reporter suggested they might be hiding from the British Police with the rest of the fugitives on the Costa del Crime.

This brought a resounding table-thump from John Harrington, as his wife blubbered at his side.

Timothy Middleton interceded to call for decorum and led the Harringtons away with muttered comments about, 'Understandably upset, distressed, all very traumatic.'

As he was ushered from the room, John Harrington turned and jabbed a finger in the general direction of the Sun reporter.

'I'll get you, you bastard,' he shouted.

Middleton's firm hand on his back finally saw John Harrington leave the scene; not before a myriad of flashlights popped in unison.

The Colonel allowed one more question as a sop.

The Daily Mail's Mark Slaughter grabbed the opportunity.

'Inspector Fernandez, is it true that you were instrumental in the capture and arrest of a notorious gang of motorway robbers on the day you arrived in Alicante?'

Ramirez whispered furiously to the Colonel, and Michael shrugged in response to the Colonel's piercing glare.

'We're here to discuss the disappearance of the Harringtons,' said the Colonel. 'This is not helpful.'

He slammed his folder shut, shoved it at Ramirez, descended from the platform, and marched out between the aisles of seats to the door, muttering to Ramirez and ignoring shouted questions from reporters.

Jose Luis gathered Michael by the elbow and propelled him forward. 'Come on, and for Christ's sake say nothing on the way out.'

Michael did as he was told.

Ramirez was waiting just outside the door of the Business suite.

'The Colonel wants to see you both in the ante-room.'

'That all went rather well, I thought,' said the Colonel, puffing himself up to even larger proportions. 'Pity about Harrington's outburst, but it will capture the headlines, if nothing else. We'll just have to wait and see if we get any new leads. Thank you all for your help. Now I must get back to the office. Keep me informed if anything turns up.'

As Ramirez hurried out, shadowing the Colonel, Michael called out in English, 'Thanks for your help, Sergeant Ramirez.'

'You're welcome,' he said in English, without a trace of accent.

Penny was in the lobby when Michael and Jose Luis came through. She'd been busy stacking the surplus press packs and rolling up the Nottingham Police banner, and now she crouched to cram it into a heavy cardboard tube. Jose Luis spotted her, and stopped, startled. Her tight-fitting skirt was stretched virtually to breaking point around her trim hips. As she bent on one knee, the soles of her white, ankle-strap stilettos appeared ready to split.

Michael had seen the shoes before and thought they were graceless, even vulgar. Hideous, in fact. But then, Penny's inclination to dress provocatively was just one of the things that made Michael feel less than comfortable in her presence. He had been, as he would put it, were he writing a report, "disconcerted on more than one occasion, during their brief and ultimately ill-fated relationship, by Penny's somewhat forward and flirty deportment." The idea of this report crossing Bowater's desk made him grin, and he turned away.

Behind him, a faltering, 'I help,' came from Jose Luis in English. He bent to clumsily help Penny slide the banner into the tube.

Michael had, he recalled, done much the same thing 'on many an occasion' even while recognising that she was not all that damned attractive – which probably explained why they'd broken up before they began.

'Ooh, that's a tight fit,' Penny exclaimed.

She rose to her feet, wriggling to straighten her skirt.

If the words were lost on Jose Luis, the innuendo couldn't have been, especially when reinforced by Penny's would-be alluring smile.

Jose Luis took a step backward.

'Now, which of you handsome men is taking me to lunch? I go back to England tomorrow, and it would be nice to look around today.'

'Sorry, I've got things to do,' Michael said, before Jose Luis had fully grasped the invitation, 'but I'm sure Jose Luis will be delighted.'

Jose Luis was finally up to speed with the conversation, or the word "lunch." 'I know nice restaurant.' He took another step backward.

Penny stooped again to pick up the folders and the cardboard tube. She dumped them on the reception desk.

'I'll collect these when I come back,' she said to the startled concierge before linking through Jose Luis's arm, looking back as she marched him to the door. 'And Michael, I will be having supper with you tonight!'

'You're staying at this hotel?'

She walked away with metal heel tips clicking on the marble floor like a stonemason's chisel.

'Of *course*,' she replied, half-closing her eyes at him over her shoulder without breaking her stride.

Jesus.

He'd got rid of her before, by claiming a fictitious relationship "had deepened" elsewhere – that could hardly apply in Spain.

Michael took a salad for lunch and returned to his room, channel-hopping on the small, wall-mounted television.

Only BBC News 24 offered any respite from the seemingly endless stream of commercials on the Spanish channels. But by five o'clock the news editors had sifted the day's events, and their morning press conference was second only to Prime Minister Zapatero attending a summit meeting in Rome to discuss the latest round of reforms to the constitution of the European Union.

Colonel Cardells featured prominently in the slot and Michael realised it was true what they said – television did make people look fatter. The Colonel's platitudes about efforts being made to find the Harringtons were heavily edited, but the message came through.

A brief snippet of John Harrington followed, with Spanish subtitles and a close up of the weeping Linda. They had tactfully omitted the outburst directed toward the Sun reporter.

On the news, a Nottingham Police logo now appeared in the background as the announcer spoke.

'... a measure of the concern by the British Police, they have sent one of their own policemen, Detective Inspector Michael Fernandez, to work alongside the Guardia Civil. Here's what he had to say.'

The camera zoomed in on Michael speaking in Spanish, then answering a question.

It was his first time on television, and he looked different to the image he was used to seeing in the mirror. Unsettlingly grim, in fact, though he did give a slight smile at the end, directed at someone or other. Perhaps Linda Harrington. He was satisfied with what he'd actually said, however.

The report ended with a still shot of David and Alison Harrington above the telephone number of the Alicante Police incident room.

It wasn't long before BBC News 24 caught up, though the item merited just a brief slot toward the end of the half-hourly news summary.

Michael featured again, this time answering in English, then a short clip showed John Harrington reading from his script.

In a statement that would not have pleased Colonel Cardells or his bosses, the correspondent added: 'This is the second incident of its kind, after another British couple were found tortured and murdered in the Costa Blanca last year. There are fears this might be a copycat crime, and there must be questions about the safety of Britons travelling to this part of Spain with a view to buying property.'

Five minutes later the phone rang in a long, high-pitched, electronic chirp that woke him from heat-induced drowsiness.

It was Chief Superintendent Bowater.

'Just seen it on the BBC. Good show, Michael, you came over well. The logo looked good, don't you think? All good publicity. Any coverage over there, yet?'

Michael put him in the picture and told him about the outburst by John Harrington, warning him to look out for the Sun in the morning.

Bowater seemed to think Michael should have prevented the incident. Michael didn't bother with excuses.

'So what's next?' Bowater enquired.

Michael had given this no thought, so said quickly that he had a couple of people to see in the morning before going to the Alicante police station to await responses to the news coverage. It sounded reasonable to him, and the Chief Superintendent had no better suggestions.

'Penny's not with you, by any chance?' said Bowater.

'No.' Michael bristled. 'What makes you think she might be?'

'Oh, er, it's just that I've tried calling her room and there's no answer. Any idea where she might be?'

'At lunch, sir. It's lunchtime here in Spain, and...' Bowater must have called Penny before calling him, perhaps hoping to get a report on proceedings from his spy. Michael was tempted to say she'd gone off with one of the Spanish policemen for a free lunch; but the gentleman in him, or the caution, led him to make excuses. 'After lunch, I expect she'll go shopping – probably buy a few trinkets for herself.'

'What!' Bowater's disapproval was clear in his voice. 'You let her go out on her own? Alicante's a very dangerous city, by all accounts. What on earth are you thinking of, letting her wander around a place like that? She could get lost, mugged – even abducted. I expected better of you, Fernandez. You'd better find her and make sure she's safe. And for Christ's sake, make sure you stay with her and get her on that plane tomorrow. We're going to look pretty stupid if anything happens to her.'

'I'm sure she'll be fine – she's not exactly the shy, retiring type.'

'You'd better bloody hope so. Now get off your arse and find her.'

The phone slammed down.

Michael shouted back at the receiver, 'Ef you, too!' though he could not quite say the word to Bowater.

After six or seven repeats of the same news broadcasts, the novelty of seeing himself on the television finally began to wear off and he switched off for a while, and sank back on the pillows.

When he woke later, after what he thought had been a short doze, he found it was past seven-thirty.

He telephoned reception at once to ask if Ms Edwardes was in her room but the receptionist was unable to help.

A call to room 318 failed to produce a response. With Bowater's words ringing in his ears about danger on the streets, even knowing better didn't prevent a flutter of anxiety.

His first timid tap on the door of room 318 would, he realised, have failed to disturb a slumbering dormouse let alone someone sleeping off a Penny-style shopping expedition and wine-soaked lunch – he knew from experience that Penny rarely said "no" when there was anything left in the bottle. In fact, she rarely said "no" to a meal or a cup of coffee – more like, "Couldn't you have parked nearer!"

So he rapped harder, surprising himself with the volume produced by knuckles on a hardwood door.

Finally, he heard movement.

'Just a moment.'

As he waited, he suddenly realised he could be recognised from television by anyone passing – and here he was, calling on a woman in her hotel bedroom.

The door opened, and Penny appeared in an oversized bathrobe.

From her tousled blonde hair, it was obvious she'd just had a shower.

His embarrassment increased when a door opened at the far end of the corridor and a couple walked toward him.

They both glanced directly into his face, then at Penny in the open doorway, as they passed.

His rehearsed lines deserted him, and he stuttered, 'Ah, Penny, er, is everything all right? Only the Chief Superintendent was worried, er, and I wondered if you wanted to have that supper tonight?'

Not wishing to stare at Penny's proudly displayed cleavage, he shifted his gaze to the background.

Penny had just begun her usual, 'Why, Michael, I didn't know you cared,' when he spotted brown leather size 7 slip-ons at the foot of the dishevelled bed.

He looked at her, then at the door, then at the floor, then toward the end of the corridor.

'Sorry... I see you're busy.'

He began to move away.

'Michael!' called Penny in a sing-song voice to the back of his head, 'Where do you think you're going, then? What about the Superintendent?'

'Don't worry, I've covered for you,' he said, without turning round.

Chapter Seven

No need to look up from his breakfast cup to know that Penny approached. She tip-tapped up to join him at the table, and caught the waiter's eye to ask for tea.

'So, Michael, are you going to run me to the airport?'

If Penny felt any embarrassment about the previous night's events, it was impossible to detect.

'I thought your Spanish consort would be taking you.'

'Don't be like that, Michael. It was only a bit of fun.'

'He is a married man, you know.'

Penny giggled girlishly, and patted his hand. 'Oh Michael, you're such an old prude. Anyway, what did you tell Bowater?'

'I told him you went shopping, but you'd better say we had dinner together last night. He thinks I should be looking after you.'

She giggled again, and squeezed his hand. 'You're sweet.'

Michael withdrew his hand. 'What time's your plane?'

He deposited Penny at the departure point of El Altet airport a comfortable two hours before her midday flight.

She pecked him on the cheek by way of farewell, and he was still wiping away bright red lip-gloss as he drove towards Javea, to meet James Weeks, Asesoria, who was free for lunch. They'd agreed to meet at the Christobal Colon Restaurant on Javea's Arenal beach.

Michael took a table under a striped canvas canopy that offered shade and a cool breeze.

He scanned the beach, trying not to stare at the topless sunbathers, and tried to conjure up an image of James Weeks, whom he'd spoken to only once on the phone – but it was difficult to untangle his image of the man from topless bathers, brown slip-on shoes, Penny's lip-gloss, and a feeling that he should have done something to protect Spain from Nottingham.

However, he was expecting, in James Weeks, to meet somebody with a bit of dignity for a change.

His quiet contemplation was disturbed by a rumble as a Harley Davidson swept into a narrow parking space at the side of the restaurant. A portly figure in a black helmet dismounted from the black and silver machine. The helmet was discarded and draped over the handlebars to reveal a mop of wispy brown hair, much of which was stuck to the man's forehead. Beads of sweat trickled down sideboards and disappeared into a thicket of whiskers. The man's generous frame was not flattered by a loose-fitting T-shirt, faded denim jeans, and open-toed canvas sandals.

James Weeks had obviously conjured up his own mental picture of Michael as he strode directly to the table and introduced himself.

'Let's sit inside,' he said, rolling his eyes. 'These stalls are for tourists, it's much cooler inside at the back.'

They relocated to the air conditioned rear of the restaurant, and took a table with a pink linen tablecloth, and napkins neatly folded inside polished wine goblets.

A frozen glass tankard filled with icy beer appeared in front of James Weeks as he sat down. Michael declined an offer of the same in favour of another mineral water.

An ashtray appeared next, placed alongside a packet of Mehari's cigars and a silver Dunhill lighter.

The beard made a guess difficult, but Michael put James Weeks at around 35. On the phone, he'd sounded a well-educated man...

'I'm an Air Force brat,' James said, 'in case you're wondering. Went to school here in Spain. Father was R.A.F. So I know this place well, but not much about your neck of the woods. Here, let's order the Menu del Dia.'

Michael accepted, and within seconds he was facing a glass of Rioja Reserva. 'You set up the bank account for John Harrington, I believe, and obtained his NIE registration?'

James took a gulp of his Rioja. 'Yes, it's standard practice. You see, people come over for a couple of weeks, without intending to buy. But they fall in love with a little villa, get back home to dreary old England and decide they can't wait. So they contact me, or another asesoria, and we set the whole thing up at this end. It's all done by phone, fax and post.'

'You need copies of their passports for that, I believe?'

'Yes, for the bank account, the NIE registration and also for the escritura. If the people are here at the time they usually pop into the office and one of the girls will take the copies. If not, I usually ask people to post me a photocopy from England. It would be impracticable to ask them to put their actual passports in the post.'

'Does anyone ever ask to see the originals? The actual passports?'

'They're usually produced at the Notario's before the escritura's signed. And the bank should of course see the passport, before they hand over any cash.'

'Does anyone ever check the details on photocopied passports?'

James frowned. 'What do you mean?'

'I mean, doesn't anyone ever check that the photocopied passport is valid? To see if the passport number tallies with the name?'

The frown turned to a scowl. 'No. Are you suggesting forgery? As I said, the originals have to be produced for the bank and the Notario.'

'I'm sorry.' Michael nodded. 'I didn't mean to imply anything about the way you conduct your business. I'm just trying to understand the process. Forgery is always a possibility of course – not necessarily to commit any fraud, but sometimes just to disguise someone's real identity.'

'But it can't be that easy to get hold of a forged passport, surely?'

'No, but it's easy to tamper with a photocopy,' Michael said, before changing the subject. 'So how's business at the moment?'

James smiled. 'These few years have been exceptional. I sometimes wonder if anyone wants to stay in England. But the last couple of months have been fraught with problems. The pound's weakened against the euro by something like fifteen percent. When you're buying a house for two hundred and fifty thousand euros, that's a lot of extra money to find. I've had at least half a dozen clients pull out in the last fortnight.'

'Really?' Michael sat back, as lunch arrived.

'It's a typical problem. People come over with a budget of, say, one hundred and fifty thousand, but these days that's not really enough in this part of the Costa Blanca. Some quick-talking agent persuades them to extend their budget with scares about rapidly rising prices, which is true enough. So they stretch to two hundred thousand. That gives them no leeway. Next minute, the pound sinks and they're in a mess. Of course the most cautious people reserve their euros in advance, to hedge against this kind of problem, but you'd be surprised how few think of it. If only Britain would join the euro, life would be much simpler, but these little Englanders think they're so different to the rest of Europe.'

James took another sip of wine and smiled across the table.

Michael reached for the mineral water.

They both laughed.

Michael looked out for a supermarket on the way back to Alicante. He wanted to find some of the same mineral water he'd had at lunch, to take back to his room at the hotel.

Passing through Benissa he noticed a sign for Mercadona, so he followed the directions to the car park.

On a Saturday afternoon, it was crowded; two laps round the fume-filled, grimy underground car park left him wishing he hadn't bothered.

About to leave, he spotted a car reversing from a space next to the exit ramp. He pulled into the tight – very tight – space between two concrete columns, and went in.

A few minutes later, he found his water. He placed half a dozen bottles in the trolley and was on the way out when he saw an offer of wine at 'almost give-away prices.'

He resisted this offer but weakened at a special promotion on Cardinal Mendoza Gran Solera Brandy de Jerez. This was 'like nectar' and 'knocked the spots off,' as he'd heard someone say on television, even the very best French Cognacs.

Just the thing to stand on the telephone table in his room, with a couple of (used) glasses, for Jose Luis to see next time he dropped in.

Coming out of the lift, pushing a trolley over the uneven car park, he had a sense of movement behind and turned to see two sharply dressed young men.

They turned to the left, heading for the far side of the car park. Fair enough, but the two men carried no shopping, had no trolley, basket or bags. Why were they walking away from the lift?

He deposited the brandy and bottles of water in the boot of the hire car and returned the trolley to the bay, recovering the euro coin from the slot. The car was stuffy and hot so he started the engine, turned on the air conditioning, and opened the passenger side window.

He engaged reverse gear and took a careful look in the wing mirrors to make sure he didn't take a further chunk out of the already gouged concrete columns. Over the revs of the engine a shrill cry came from the vicinity of the lift.

'Help! – they've taken my bag,' shrieked an English voice.

Almost immediately he heard loud revs from another motor, followed by a screech of tyres from the far side of the car park.

A black four-wheel drive lurched from a parking space and rounded a row of parked cars at speed, heading for the exit.

Michael slammed the accelerator to the floor. The hire car lunged back. He stamped hard on the brake pedal, bringing the car to a halt in the path of the on-coming jeep. By now he could see it was a Subaru.

The rest seemed to happen in slow motion. Blue smoke emerged from the Subaru's tyres before the sound of shredding rubber reached his ears. He braced for the collision, gripping the steering wheel and straightening his elbows, jamming his back against the seat. He screwed his eyes tight shut and tensed the whole of his body. 'Shit, no seat belt,' he realised, a fraction of a second before the impact.

The sound of crumpling metal was surprisingly quiet and soft, as seemed the force of the crash. But gradually it reached a crescendo of cracking, jangling, twisting, tearing, shattering metal and glass. Michael's head remained motionless as the rest of his body, braced against the back of the seat, lurched sideways once the metal had crumpled to its full extent.

The muscles in his neck stretched and tore as his right ear thumped against his shoulder.

Like the recoil of a gun, his head snapped back in the opposite direction, smashing his left ear against the driver's side window with a thud that echoed through his brain. The pain came slowly, rising and ebbing then rising again, each time to a new level of intensity. He waited for it to peak as he made a mental assessment of the extent of his injury.

The noise of the crash passed as abruptly as it had arrived, and the sound of tinkling pieces of metal and glass gradually subsided, like the last few drops of rain at the end of a cloudburst. Silence returned.

He gingerly turned his neck. The contour of a man's head bulged from the passenger side of the Subaru's crazed windscreen.

Despite the pain, Michael leaned against the door until it fell open. Still dazed, he walked around the front of his car to the driver's side of the Subaru.

The front seat had lurched forward and was pinning the young driver against the steering wheel. Even so, the man had managed to shove the twisted door open and, with his hand on the roof of the car, he was trying to lever himself out.

With all the force he could muster, Michael shoved his right hip against the partially open door.

The man let out an ear-piercing scream as his forearm crunched between the door and its frame. It signified the end of the struggle.

'Are you all right?' A woman's face leaned over Michael.

That was the last thing he remembered.

'You're a regular Superman. What are you trying to do? Solve the Costa Blanca crime wave single-handed?' said Jose Luis, bursting through the doors of the private room in Denia's General Hospital at eleven o'clock on Sunday morning. 'Nothing but the best for you, I see. We must look after our celebrity detective.'

Michael smiled weakly, but that sent a searing pain down his neck, now cocooned in a cushioned brace that restricted his head movement to little more than a nod. His left ear throbbed inside a padded bandage, and he didn't need to look in a mirror to know he had a black eye.

'What chaos you've caused,' said Jose Luis. 'Two villains in hospital, one with head injuries and the other with a broken arm that he insists was not caused by the crash. Two vehicles written off – I hope you had full insurance on the hire car, by the way – and a Mercadona supermarket closed for half a day. The Colonel will be delighted, especially as you have no jurisdiction over here. What on earth did you think you were doing?'

'I didn't think,' croaked Michael.

'I guess we'll have to call it a citizen's arrest, but there could be repercussions, especially if the two villains decide to sue.'

'Is that likely?'

'Only when they get out of jail, and with a bit of luck you'll be in England by then. By the way, they recovered this from the car.'

The Cardinal Mendoza was safe, protected by its soft cork box.

'You have excellent taste. Here, take a look at these.'

Jose Luis tossed the morning papers onto the bed.

Coverage in both the British and Spanish press showed John Harrington comforting his tearful wife, but The Sun opted for a close-up of finger-stabbing John, with his eyes bulging, mouth wide, face contorted with anger. Michael was mentioned in most articles and, in the British press, received more column inches than Colonel Cardells.

A couple of phone calls had come in, with possible sightings of the missing couple in Denia and Calpe. It was too soon for the weekly foreign language papers; Jose Luis thought these might provoke more interest in the case, but they'd have to wait until the middle of next week. In the meantime, he suggested Michael take a rest, especially since the doctors had said he should remain in bed for a couple of days at least.

'By the way, your Chief Superintendent has been trying to reach you. We told him you were alive and well, but he still wants to talk to you. Perhaps he wants you to go home.'

Michael thought he detected a hopeful note in Jose Luis's voice.

'Anyway, I must go now. If there's anything you need, just let me know. Take it easy, then, and don't go making any more citizen's arrests.'

Jose Luis eased himself off the bed and moved towards the door.

'Oh... almost forgot. We had a call. A woman wants you to call her. Says it's personal.' He withdrew a notepad from his pocket and turned the pages. 'Here you are, Rosana Ferrando Moll.' He tore the page from the pad and placed it on the bedside table. 'Anyone you know?'

Moll? Where had he heard that?

Cogs whirred but the accident seemed to have put them out of synchronisation. Output zero.

He stuttered, 'No – no, I don't think so.'

'Perhaps our intrepid hero has a fan,' said Jose Luis as he headed back to the door. 'Just stay out of trouble. If anything happens, we'll let you know. Take it easy. Bye.'

Michael stared at the paper.

Concentration deserted him, replaced by foreboding, which only relented when tiredness took over and he drifted into uneasy sleep.

He woke with a jolt ninety minutes later, when a dark-haired nurse, whose sturdy white shoes he'd noticed earlier, prodded him apologetically and whispered, 'Sorry, I have to take blood pressure and pulse. Head injuries, you know. Can't be too careful. Anyway, it'll soon be time for lunch.'

Michael complied meekly, dazed from broken sleep and disturbed dreams. Sleep hadn't alleviated the anxiety induced by the name on the paper that lay at his bedside, but gradually the mists rolled away as an image came into focus... Moll?

Bar Moll. The square in Parcent.

'Get me a phone, will you?' he snapped, before recognising the tone in his voice and adding, 'Please.'

'You're supposed to be resting,' the nurse protested, only to be persuaded by several repeats of "please" as Michael attempted charm.

He waited until the nurse had left before punching in the number. As the ringing tone chirped in his ear he almost hoped that no one would answer. His throat was dry, and though he sensed what was about to happen, he had no idea what he was going to say.

'Si, digame,' the woman responded in a quick, matter-of-fact voice. Michael was still getting used to the Spanish way of answering the telephone. Literally translated, it meant "tell me," but it was framed in the imperative and sounded more like an instruction than an invitation.

In response, Michael's reply was much more politely put. 'Please – may I speak to Rosana Ferrando Moll, please.'

'Speaking.'

'This is Michael Fernandez, you wanted to speak to me?'

Rosana's voice slowed. 'This is difficult, Señor Fernandez, I'm not sure where to start. Your full name is Miguel-Ángel Fernandez?'

'Yes.'

'Your father's name was Francisco?'

'Yes.'

'He came from Parcent?'

That seemed hard to deny, at this point. 'He did...'

'Then your grandmother's right. She saw you on the news last night and before they mentioned your name, she recognised you.'

'My grandmother?'

'Maria Carmen Fernandez. Her son was Francisco, your father. She wants to see you. She hasn't stopped talking about you since last night. You look exactly like your father, she says. She's so excited.'

Michael played for time. 'What's this to you?' he said, realising too late that this was tactless.

'My grandmother and yours are cousins. When Maria Carmen saw you on the television she asked me to call you. We tried to put her off, but she's adamant. Crying, joy, excitement – call it what you want, but she knew it was you. You have to see her. She's eighty-seven, you know, and very frail. It was a shock to her. If you didn't come, it would break her heart. She needs to see you urgently.'

He rarely refused a challenge. Though there were many things in his life he'd rather not have done, faced with the inevitable he'd got on with it. But this was not just a few minutes or hours he could write off, before returning to matters of more importance.

'Look, there are things you don't know, that happened years ago. My grandmother, if she is my grandmother, will understand this.'

'What do you mean? *If* she's your grandmother? There's no possible doubt. I know what happened with your father. That was almost fifty years ago. It broke your grandmother's heart, and – I'm sorry, but you can't do this. What kind of a man refuses to see his own grandmother...?' Her voice tightened. 'It's none of my business, but if you'd seen her elation when she saw your face, you'd understand.'

'And if you know about my father, you must know why I can't go back to Parcent.' As soon as he had said it, he realised his mistake.

'Back? What do you mean, back? Have you been here before?'

He needed a way out while he had the chance.

'Look, I'm in hospital at the moment, so it's out of the question, anyway.'

This sounded like a feeble excuse, since he'd been talking vigorously and obviously would not remain in hospital forever.

'I'll give it some thought,' he said. 'That's the best that I can say. I can't make promises. I have to go now. The doctor says I must rest.'

That excuse was as feeble as the last, but it produced hesitation.

'Goodbye,' he said. 'I will call you again.'

As he replaced the receiver he thought he heard a faint voice saying, 'But, Miguel-Ángel...' and it left a feeling of desperate ill-ease impossible to cast off. There was something in Rosana's voice, something in the words, 'But Miguel-Ángel,' that began to haunt him.

He wrestled with the stiff white bed linen for the rest of the afternoon. The pains in his head and neck reached an intensity that could not be subdued by painkillers. Every attempt to blank out his mind was frustrated by Parcent zooming in and out of focus.

This time, he also saw his father – an image that had once peered out from a silver picture frame on the cabinet at the side of his mother's favourite chair. Dark hair slicked down tight, precise parting on the left. The slight sharpness in the cheeks softened by the smile, a dimple on the right side. The boyish appearance of a closely shaved chin. The eyes, large, round and deep-set beneath thick eyebrows, that appeared to sparkle for the camera.

Another image flashed across Michael's mind.

An old woman with a deeply-lined complexion. She came closer. Her eyes stared back at Michael as if he were looking into a mirror.

By evening, Michael was still considering his next move.

It had been wretched, the way he'd handled the telephone call, but he despaired at the idea of acquainting himself with a part of his past that he knew he should never explore.

Perhaps his injuries provided the justification he needed... Yes, that was it – call Bowater, catch the next plane home, slip back into work.

Whether he could have taken this course, he would never know, because he was interrupted whilst debating with himself.

'You have a visitor, Señor Fernandez.'

The nurse bustled in, pulled him up, fluffed his pillows, and straightened the bed.

He flopped back – then sat up bolt upright to ask about his visitor.

Before he could get out a word, the nurse had departed with an unsubtle wink, and the visitor had appeared at the door.

Michael surveyed his guest with caution, starting with dainty cut-away pink leather sandals, moving up to a sylph-like, belted waistline, and on to a startling head of strong, dark auburn hair.

'Are you Rosana?' he asked, in what he hoped was an unknowing, invalidish tone.

'You sound as if you were expecting me.'

'I'm sorry... ' Michael continued weakly. 'Please... sit down.'

Rosana pulled the hard plastic chair closer to the bed and crossed her legs, straightening the creases in her figure-hugging cream trousers. There was a soft rustle from her white silk blouse as she settled back in the chair and tossed her wavy locks back behind her shoulders, like someone, it suddenly struck him, on the cover of a romance novel.

He wanted to laugh for a second, but was suddenly conscious that he was staring at her face, studying the harmony of her features.

An instant later, he became aware of his own pose, with the neck brace pushing his chin up and the heavy bandage clamped against his ear. He sat on the edge of the bed, his hospital gown tied at the back, ending just above his knees. His bare legs and feet dangled in mid-air.

He put his knees together and tugged at the gown.

'They told me about the accident,' Rosana said. 'Are you all right?'

Rosana's arrival had distracted him from the pain, at any rate.

'Oh, yes. As you can see, it's nothing really.' He tried to grin. 'I'll be running round in no time.'

'You don't seem too popular with the Guardia Civil,' she said.

'You noticed.' He continued, 'Look, about this afternoon, on the telephone, I behaved rather badly. It's just that...'

'No need to apologise. I don't think I handled things very well, myself. I know what a shock it must have been.'

'Actually, it wasn't a shock. I mean...'

'You expected a call?'

'No, but as soon as I got the message to ring you, I suspected what it might be about. Your name, Moll. I saw it outside the bar in the church square. It didn't take much to put two and two together.'

'Bar Moll, that's my uncle's place. It's been there for years. So I was right, you have been to Parcent before?'

'No – well, once, a couple of days ago. Part of my investigation.'

'So where do you go from here?'

'My grandmother, you mean? Of course I'll see her.'

Rosana's eyes widened. 'Oh, Miguel-Ángel,' she said.

'You don't need to call me Miguel-Ángel. Michael will do.'

'When will you come?'

'It's slightly difficult.' He had genuine excuses. 'I'm stuck here, in hospital right now, and of course I'm working, so I can't just swan off when I feel like it. And I have no car. Well I did, but I wrecked it.'

'You could, of course, get another.'

'What – another – car, you mean?'

'Miguel-Ángel Fernandez.'

She placed her hands on her hips, drawing attention to them, not quite in the way Penny did.

'I'll drive you there myself – and as for work, I'll speak to Captain Jose Luis Perez. I'm sure we can arrange a few days' sick leave. When are you coming?'

'No, don't speak to Captain Perez. Is tomorrow all right?'

'Tomorrow,' she said, as if she'd anticipated the answer. 'It's the start of Fiesta and all the family are having lunch at Restaurante L'Era.'

'Oh.' The whole lost tribe... 'Perhaps that's not – '

But she'd slipped out, leaving a trace of perfume to drift around the room. A sort of polished mahogany.

When Rosana returned at ten the next morning Michael was shaved, dressed and ready. In fact, he'd been getting up and sitting down for half an hour.

Deciding he could not face Parcent, he'd sent for his suitcase and some clothes from the hotel and dressed carefully in sports jacket, white shirt and tie, grey flannel trousers and freshly polished black brogues, so that he could go back to work. The neck brace had been discarded, despite protests from the nurse, and the wound on his ear was covered with Elastoplast.

He'd been thinking he could leave a note for Rosana, but had lingered, indecisive, for a moment too long. Here she was.

Today Rosana wore a short-sleeved, peach cotton two-piece suit with a skirt just above the knee. Her peach shoes, with low, oblong heels, had to have come from somewhere other than Parcent.

He stood up, and she greeted him with a stab of a kiss on both cheeks.

'Thank you.' He adjusted his tie.

'Perfect.' She grabbed the suitcase and linked her arm through his.

He tried to unthread himself, recalling Penny's armlinks, and imagining the nurses watching, but Rosana held fast.

On the journey to Parcent Rosana asked questions; casually, but with a glance across at him after each answer, as if to see if he was lying.

'Your accent,' she said after a while. 'I can't quite place it. Have you spent time in South America?'

'No.' His answer hung in the air. 'Well, my wife was Argentinean. I suppose it rubbed off.' He added, after a second, 'About my grandmother, she's very frail, you said?'

'I may have exaggerated a little. She suffers from diabetes and has a few aches and pains, but she does quite well for eighty-seven.'

'Where will I meet her?'

'Don't worry,' she replied. 'We're going straight to her house, where you can meet her alone. After half an hour, we'll go to lunch.'

'I'd prefer not to be alone, meeting her, if that's all right.'

'Of course... You've caused quite a stir turning up, you know – but it's nothing. Just don't let any anyone bother you.'

'All right. And you were saying there's a lunch?'

'At Parcent's famous paella restaurant, L'Era. You like paella?'

'I've never tasted paella.'

'Miguel-Ángel Fernandez,' she said in that now familiar psuedo-sisterly tone, 'you've never tasted paella?'

'Why do you call me Miguel-Ángel? I use the name Michael, I always have, from school on up. My father gave me a first Spanish name as a gesture, but all my qualifications, and my driving licence, belong to me as Michael. And I'm Inspector Michael Fernandez.'

'Miguel-Ángel is your proper name. And in Spain, amongst family, no one would shorten it. Besides, it's a lovely name, isn't it?'

He didn't answer.

Rosana parked in the Plaça del Poble, the square next to Bar Moll, and they walked the short distance to the home of Maria Carmen Fernandez. Rosana linked her arm through Michael's and strode purposefully down one of the streets. It wasn't clear whether she did this to support him or prevent him running away, and against a rising tide of nervousness he struggled to remember what he planned to say.

Halfway along the street, they stopped at an ancient wooden door centred between a pair of grilled and shuttered widows. Without thinking, he lifted his head skywards – to observe that there were two more storeys of balconied windows – and the pain in his neck made him wince. He took a deep breath, and felt his tie to check it was straight.

Rosana tapped on the door, and stepped into the cool, dark interior. 'Maria Carmen,' she called out, 'Miguel-Ángel is here.'

Through a short vestibule, he saw across a living room. His grandmother rose from a high-backed chair. She squinted as he walked up and reached to clasp his face between her hands. She pulled his head down, kissed him on both cheeks, and rested against his chest. He put his arms awkwardly around her.

'Thank God,' she whispered.

After a moment he eased her back into the chair. She raised her spectacles, wiped her eyes. 'You are so like your father.'

'Sit down.' Rosana moved a chair behind him. 'I'll make coffee.'

Michael lowered himself into the chair. 'Grandmother.' Now he half-remembered what he planned to say. 'I don't know what to say.'

'Say nothing,' she said. 'It's enough that you have come.'

She was silent for a few seconds. 'Your mother?'

'She died two years ago.'

'I'm sorry to hear that. What age...?'

'She was sixty-five.'

Maria Carmen shook her head slightly.

'The young English nurse... later, I recognised her courage. You must miss her. Miss both your parents.'

'I do.'

'Susan wrote to me when you were born. And occasionally, after that. They were very warm letters, translated by your father, so in his hand, and he always added a few words for me. I often wondered if I should...'

'There's no need to explain anything. I have no questions.'

He hadn't known there had been letters, but he didn't want to have to come up with explanations of his own.

'Coffee,' Rosana said, coming in with a tray. 'You like it black, don't you, Michael? The nurse told me. By the way, Miguel-Ángel says he's not used to his Spanish name, so we have to call him Michael, for the time being. I said we would, though it's ridiculous.'

Rosana placed the cups on a table next to Maria Carmen's chair.

'Now let's drink this quickly, then,' she said.

Maria Carmen caught Michael's eye and grinned, raising her cup in a gesture of full compliance with the law.

They left the house with Maria Carmen holding Michael's arm.

She stepped out with surprising vigour for someone so tiny and "frail." A stout black leather handbag hung over her left arm, and her low-heeled court shoes tapped smoothly along the road. Her deep blue outfit, with the broad-rimmed hat and soft coat, was reminiscent of the Queen, Michael thought. Her demeanour, too, had a regal air.

Several neighbours had appeared on the street and they looked up, seemingly casually, as if saying to themselves: 'Long lost grandson...'

'Bon dia, Maria Carmen,' they called out.

Maria Carmen smiled. Michael glanced back, to see faces at windows and doors – and Rosana, who clipped along behind Maria Carmen, looking neither right nor left, like a royal entourage.

But everyone else in the village seemed to have gathered at the Restaurante L'Era. They hovered by a round main table with seats for twelve. Maria Carmen sat down, Michael stood beside her, and introductions began. Uncle Jose Maria was first, offering a handshake that turned into a hug. He was Francisco's younger brother, he said, though a resemblance was hard to detect.

'They call me Pepito.' He introduced his wife, Lorena.

Pepito's eldest son, Pedro, was next. Well scrubbed and pressed, Pedro shook Michael's hand like a wet dog shaking its head until the ripple could reach its tail. One collar of Pedro's shirt turned up outside the lapel of a jacket with too-short sleeves. His crooked tie gleamed, and his brown hair went its own way, despite flattened areas proving an attempt had been made to bring it under control.

'Pleased to meet you, Michael,' he said in English.

Other introductions – dozens, it seemed – were quickly made.

The chairs filled. A boy and girl, children of Rosana's brother, wore outfits reminiscent of Michael's Sunday school days. Rosana's mother and grandmother sat nearby; her mother nursing a lifeless left arm, the after-effect of a stroke. There were just two vacant seats.

'Oh, well,' murmured Maria Carmen. 'God tries our patience.'

The gathering was completed with the arrival of a buxom, heavily made-up blonde in a short red leather skirt stretched over disturbingly bulky thighs. Her flimsy white heels tried but failed to compensate for lack of stature.

Her partner, in a pale grey suit and silk tie swaggered in. His dark hair was manicured to a predetermined profile that had defied the breeze outside. For a second, Michael thought there might be a family resemblance, but quickly dismissed the idea.

He didn't need to examine the man's shoes (chisel-toed grey slip-ons) to form an impression of the latest arrivals.

'Your cousin Julio, Pepito's youngest. And his wife, Teresa.'

'Hello, Grandma.' He kissed her on both cheeks.

As soon as they'd taken their seats at the main table, steaming paella was carried in, in black bottomed pans the size of cartwheels. Everyone lifted portions onto plates, using long-handled spoons.

'Wine next – From Pepito's bodega,' Maria Carmen said. It was delicious, though poured from dusty, scraped-looking bottles.

One by one, polite enquirers began to address him.

They were saddened to hear about his father and mother. How long was he staying?

The atmosphere implied questions unasked, and Julio's eyes flashed away when Michael looked toward him.

At last Maria Carmen scraped a large spoonful of burnt rice from the bottom of the giant pan. 'The best bit.' She tapped the sticky brown lump onto Michael's plate.

'It's called socarrat,' said Michael, glancing towards Rosana, to see on her face the anticipated look of surprise at his knowledge.

The meal ended with coffee and sweet Mistela wine made from dried muscatel grapes (again from Pepito's bodega).

A handful of strangers wandered up to speak. A few said they recalled Michael's father, though without effusing in his memory.

Julio watched each encounter, as if making mental notes. And it was Julio who felt it was time to bring proceedings to a close.

'Come along, Grandma, I'll walk you home.'

'No. Thank you, Julio, but I need to go back with Michael.'

She rose so awkwardly that Michael felt obliged to take her arm. Julio glowered as if regretting a decision to leave the daggers at home, and marched past Teresa, who was talking to her father-in-law.

'We're leaving,' he called.

Heads turned. Silence was followed by whispering.

Back at Maria Carmen's house, Pepito and Lorena, with Rosana, led Michael out onto the rear walled terrace, to sit with them in the fading light of a slowly sinking sun.

But Michael's neck ached, and the small talk had been tiring – as had the endless joyous remarks about his miraculous appearance, the whispering, and the unasked questions.

He leaned over. 'Time I started back,' he said quietly to Rosana.

She stood up, beckoned him to the kitchen, and closed the door.

'What are you talking about?'

'I have to leave now – I have to get back.'

'Don't be absurd.' Her fists went back on her hips. 'Leave? You think you can say hello, then turn around and just disappear?'

Michael leaned back against the sink bench.

'Look, I'm glad I came, and I intend to keep in touch with my grandmother, but I don't belong here. I never planned to come to Parcent, or Spain for that matter. I have work to do, I'm tired and ill, and I need to get back to my hotel.'

Rosana folded her arms. 'You want to slope back to your dark little closet, Miguel-Ángel Fernandez, with some theory about your father.'

'Not in the least. And it's not a theory at all. You have no idea what happened, or why my father rejected this place.'

'He did not – your father called you Miguel-Ángel, after your great-grandfather! – and you said yourself, he taught you Spanish. You've never been to Spain, but you know as much about Spain as most Spaniards. In fact, *you want people to know that you do*. You're *fascinated* by Spain, I saw that today. This big English gent act of yours, it's all a façade.'

'Let's just leave this, Rosana. Some things are best left alone.'

'No, they're not, and your grandmother needs you, and you need to talk to her so you don't spend your life full of anger and hatred.'

'I am *not* full of anger and hatred,' he said, glowering. 'I simply have my own opinions.'

He wouldn't be pushed around, but apart from that, he was right. This could only end in trouble.

'I'd like to talk to my grandmother, naturally, but it can't be arranged right now.'

Rosana's face lit up. 'You're saying you want to stay?'

'No, of course I'm not – and where on earth could I stay?'

'Here.' She led him back to the terrace. 'Maria Carmen, Michael has decided to stay to the end of the week.'

His grandmother bobbed to her feet. 'The bed's made up.'

'I'll get your bag from the car,' said Rosana, rushing into the house. 'Tell him about tonight, Maria Carmen,' she shouted back.

In one second, he'd been turned into a forlorn schoolboy on holiday with relatives, itinerary pre-arranged, every move mapped out.

'It's fiesta in the village,' Maria Carmen said enthusiastically, 'and tonight there's a mass for San Lorenzo. Then there's a procession, and fireworks. Come, I'll show you to your room. We need to get ready.'

This would be a nightmare. All the feelings he'd fought to suppress were being prised into the open. But still he failed to protest.

Completely out of place and uncomfortable, not just because of the hard wooden pews, Michael sat halfway down the church, grandmother on one side, Uncle Pepito on the other.

Embroidered, laced and cummerbunded villagers were still entering the tiny flower-adorned Church; latecomers sat near the door on picnic chairs, or red plastic chairs advertising Mahou Cerveza.

Aunt Lorena fussed over Pedro's collar. Cousin Julio was in his sharp suit. Teresa had changed into knee-high boots. Rosana sat in front, her long wavy hair lifted from her shoulders, held up either by magic or a comb.

Mass proceeded, the community practising the rituals of Christian belief. A community that had failed to find compassion for his father.

After mass, children in sailor suits, or long white, blue-sashed dresses and tall black mantles of lace, filed out first. The rest of the congregation followed. A procession formed, its centrepiece a plinth holding the statue of San Lorenzo. A clergyman in gold braided costume, a mitre perched on his head began the slow march; the village priest followed, and then the band, playing sombre music. Villagers, carrying candles, fell in behind.

For a few minutes a crowd lingered in the square, and Michael was standing with Maria Carmen, when Rosana came up. 'I know a better place,' she whispered. 'All right, Maria Carmen?'

Maria Carmen smiled as she'd been expecting this move.

Rosana led him down a narrow side street, and opened the door of an empty house. He followed her through the half-light up two flights of stairs, to a rooftop terrace with a view over the chimneys, and across the valley.

The jagged ridge of Carrascal mountain range formed a dark silhouette in the distance, framed against the sky and a full moon.

Across the valley floor, house lights flickered.

To the east, the outline of Alcalalí was dominated, like Parcent, by a church tower.

On the outskirts of the village, a crowd had gathered in the dusk.

A rocket soared, and exploded softly, with a glare that illuminated the whole of the valley in a fountain of colours and drifts of smoke.

Michael clutched the wrought iron balustrade at the edge of the terrace and watched in silence.

A breeze cooled the night air to a chill, and the faint scent of Rosana's perfume was overpowered by spent gunpowder.

Rainbow showers flared and faded, and the display seemed to be reaching a climax as the frequency of the flashes increased – until a moment of silence heralded one last giant sky rocket that shrieked heavenward, leaving a trail of smoke and sparks.

Rosana clasped Michael's arm. An ear-piercing boom split the atmosphere and resonated round the valley before bouncing back off Carrascal. The echoes faded, to a faint ripple of applause from the crowd. Rosana eased back and looked up into Michael's startled face. He returned her look, contemplating his next move.

'That was loud,' he said foolishly.

'That's the whole idea.' She smiled up.

He managed to return his gaze to the panorama in front of them.

'It's a spectacular spot,' he said. 'This house. Whose is it?'

Staring out over the valley towards the mountains in the far distance, she answered.

'I think you'll find it's yours.'

Michael spent a restless night in his father's old room. I own a house in Parcent. What am I supposed to do with it? My grandmother, what am I going to say to her? What will she say to me? Where is all this leading? How can I get out of this mess? I wish I'd never come.

This was his father's home. His father's room. He was a leper. This was his bed... He remembered when he had found out what a leper was. Cried in his room, stood stiff in his father's arms.

He saw his father's face... Saw himself take his father's arm, in the years when he was getting weaker, speaking Spanish...

Chapter Eight

Michael called Jose Luis first thing in the morning.

'Having a good holiday, Michael?'

'Not very.'

'Great news,' Jose Luis went on quickly. 'We've arrested a couple of Dutchmen. They're being questioned right now. 'A stroke of luck, really. We had a call from a Dutch couple in Holland, Mr and Mrs Ruiter. It seems your hunch was right about the Harringtons possibly contacting foreign agents. Anyway, the Ruiters were out in Spain in April and they contacted these two supposed agents through an advertisement in the Dutch edition of the Costa Blanca News.

'The agents took them to see an old finca near Orba. Well, they call it a farmhouse, but it's rundown. They were interested in the place, but got cold feet when the agents became very aggressive.

'They wanted to drive Mr Ruiter to his bank to withdraw ten thousand euros for a deposit. One of them bundled Mr Ruiter into their car and drove him to Denia while the other stayed with his wife.

'On the way to Denia, Mr Ruiter says the man made vague threats, saying he'd better not back out. Luckily, he had the sense to create a fuss inside the bank and the man ran off. Then he called his wife on her mobile. She managed to get to their car and drive away.

'They didn't report it at the time because they felt a bit stupid, but they've just read the story in a Dutch newspaper. We managed to track the men down through a mobile phone number the Ruiters gave us, and I posed as a potential buyer and set up a meeting. We picked them up last night in Orba – and here's the best.

'The mobile's a pre-paid line so there's no way to trace it. But we checked calls made from the hotel in Benidorm where the Harringtons stayed, and the number came up. This could be all over. All we have to do now is find out what happened to the Harringtons. We're searching the finca in Orba this morning; sniffer dogs, digging equipment, the lot.'

Michael listened intently, but something didn't ring quite true.

If these two had abducted the Harringtons, why were they so easy to track down? They'd have ditched the mobile phone, especially if they'd got their hands on the Harringtons' money.

'I'd better come over now, while you interview them.'

'No need, Michael. You've no jurisdiction over here and we don't want to foul things up by breaking rules. We'll handle it. You're on sick leave, remember. Make the most of it. You could be on your way home in a couple of days. I'll be in touch as soon as we have news.'

'Have you told Chief Superintendent Bowater?'

'The Colonel spoke to him first thing. Don't worry, we gave you the credit for bringing in the foreign press. We told him what a great help you've been, and he knows you're recovering after the accident.'

Michael would be more insistent if he thought this was a real breakthrough, and somehow he doubted it. He decided not to mention misgivings on the phone to Chief Superintendent Bowater, however.

'Well, Michael, looks like they've cracked it,' said Bowater, sounding smug, 'and it's all down to you. Well done. How are you, by the way?'

'My neck's still giving me a lot of pain, I think I may have whiplash.' He decided to lay it on a bit thick. 'But I should be well enough in a couple of days to stop relying on the crutches.'

'Well, take it easy, everything's under control. With a bit of luck, we'll have you back by the end of the week. By the way, where are you? I called your hotel last night, but they said you weren't there.'

Michael hesitated. 'Er... with my grandmother.'

'Oh, very nice – so you do have a family! It's turned out to be a bit of a holiday, after all?'

'Well, no sir... I simply thought I should perhaps...'

'Don't worry, only joking. Officially you're on sick leave, so you're probably in the right place, recuperating with family. Very nice. Take some rest, but keep in touch. *H*asta la Vista.'

'*A*sta Luego, sir.'

In the kitchen with his grandmother half an hour later, before he'd finished his coffee, Uncle Pepito, dressed in faded jeans, appeared at the door. 'Let's go, Michael –'

'Where?'

'We're going to the campo. All arranged, isn't it, Maria Carmen? I'm going to give you a tour.' Pepito folded his arms.

After leaving the house, he led Michael a few hundred metres to one of the steep streets leading down and out of the village.

'Hop on!' Pepito slid onto the hard metal bench-seat of a small open trailer, hitched to a kind of garden rotavator. 'Mula mecánica.'

Michael slid aboard, and Pepito set the rumbling, rattling machine in motion. They chugged down the hill, leaving a cloud of blue smoke.

'Watch your knees!' Pepito pushed the handlebars out wide to negotiate a bend. At nine-thirty, the sun was beating down. Pepito reached behind to the trailer for a frayed straw hat.

He plonked it onto Michael's head. 'You need this.'

'Thanks!' Michael took the hat off, and fanned himself with it.

They trundled onto a cart track, the trailer bounced up and down for fifty metres, and the engine spluttered to a halt.

Pepito dismounted, and waved his hand over a plot that resembled an English allotment. The rich red-brown earth was freshly tilled, and tomatoes, peppers, beans, onions, aubergines, courgettes, peas and pumpkins were lined up in neat rows.

'Well, now, how's this?' Pepito raised his hat, mopped his brow.

'It's all very nice.' Michael climbed down. 'I'm impressed.'

'There's *more*.' Pepito marched off along the long thin plot, leading Michael into a terraced olive grove at the far end. 'A lot more. Seventy-four trees at the last count,' he said. 'Good trees, as well, but there's no money in olives these days. The vineyard's over here.'

They crossed the olive grove and scrambled up a low stone wall.

Row after row of lush green vines stretched out before them. Michael made a quick calculation. Fifty rows of fifty vines – 2,500.

'Pepito,' said Michael, 'What is all this about?'

'It's yours, Michael. Yours and mine. And there's six plots like this on the other side of the village, with almonds and olives. And a big orange grove. Then there's mother's house, of course. That belongs to us, but Maria Carmen has the right to live there for life – and there's another house, but it's empty.'

Pepito took off his hat and twisted it thoughtfully. 'Oh, and there's an old riu rau, Michael. I'll show you that later.'

'But Pepito, how can it be mine? Did grandfather leave a will?'

'No will.' Pepito shrugged. 'We don't need one. Under Spanish law everything came to your father and me as the direct descendants. When Francisco died, his half automatically passed to you. So it's yours.'

'But – I don't want any of this.'

'No, no, it's yours, Michael. No one can do anything, without your say-so. They've been waiting. But come, let's have breakfast.'

At the side of the olive grove, a dry stone wall made a seat. Pepito brought out freshly baked bread, drizzled with olive oil and layered with wedges of hard goats' cheese and slices of tomato. He produced a chilled bottle of beer, and poured two glasses.

'A little early, isn't it?' Michael reached out a tentative hand.

'You English,' replied Pepito. 'Drink more than any other nationality, but pretend you don't. Beer isn't alcohol, its sustenance.'

Michael sipped the beer, and pictured Nottingham City centre at closing time. 'All right. You mentioned some things to be sorted.'

'It's hard to know where to start.' Pepito scratched his chin. 'Ten years ago, land here had no value, except for crops. But the development in the valley has gone crazy. Now it's reached Parcent. Plots like this are fetching more than sixty thousand euros, if you can get permission to build. And the houses in the village, some sell for two hundred thousand, or more. Crazy.'

'So – what's the problem? Sounds like you're onto a good thing.'

'Oh, some people can't wait to sell, especially the younger ones.'

'How do you feel?'

'I've worked this land all my life, so did your grandfather,' Pepito said slowly. 'I could sell, but then what? Watch the destruction?'

'Perhaps that's progress?' Michael said, looking around.

'Not to me. Land isn't a car, or a machine. You have land once. When it's gone, it's gone forever. This land has been in our family for generations. They shaped the landscape, cut the terraces, moved the rocks, planted trees and vines. The land is soaked with their sweat. Who am I to end all that?... No, this land should be there for the next generation, and the one after that... though not everyone agrees.'

'Julio, you mean? He doesn't work on the land?'

'He's not interested. It's too hard, and there's too little reward. He runs his own construction company instead. It's only small, but he's got big plans, and that's why he'd like to get hold of this land. He wants riches, but only so he can squander them – and what would that leave for his children and grandchildren?'

'My appearance has complicated things...'

'You can say that again. Julio's been pestering for years for some land for houses. He wanted to take over the empty house in the village, but I told him it wasn't mine. Until recently, the Mayor refused any new building around the village. But there's a new Mayor, backed by Julio and builders and speculators. He jumps to their tune.'

'And what about Pedro?'

Pepito paused, then spoke carefully. 'Pedro... He's a good son. He works the land every day. It's his life. He's never done anything else. When I go, my half will pass to Pedro and Julio. It wouldn't take Julio long to sell. But now you've appeared on the scene, they can't do a thing without your agreement. That's the law.'

Michael took another sip of beer.

'What do you think my father would do?'

Pepito looked surprised. 'Francisco? He'd keep it. He rushed here after school every day to help tie up tomatoes, prune vines, collect the olives. Father said he was a pest, but he loved having Francisco come over. They'd sit on that wall over there talking until dusk about the state of the olives, when to plant tomatoes, how to know when the grapes were ready for harvesting, and all that, but...'

'I'm sorry, Pepito. But I would like to know what happened.'

'I know.' Pepito blew his nose on a crumpled handkerchief. 'I'd like to tell you, if I knew. I was fifteen, Francisco nineteen. They said he had to go away for a while, then kids said my brother was a leper. At first I hated him. I hoped I'd never see him again, because of the shame. But I grew older, and missed him so much. Believe me, Michael, I often wondered about him. But mother and father suffered most. For years they cut themselves off from almost everyone. It suited some, mind you to keep away from the family. Some said the disease was hereditary.'

'But grandmother and grandfather?' Michael asked. 'Couldn't they have stood against the village, so he didn't have to leave?'

Pepito's chin dropped to his chest.

'Don't you think I've asked that question a thousand times? It's impossible to know what it was like back then. Talk to your grandmother, see if she'll explain... She will tell me nothing.'

At the riu rau on the edge of the village, carts and farm implements littered a yard as if they'd gathered dust for a hundred years.

Inside five arched vaults lay a vast collection of dusty wine bottles – neatly stacked, faded scraps of paper denoting the years. One shelf was labelled *1954*, and Michael recognised the value of the bottles.

After a few minutes, Pepito started back, and Michael declined the offer of a ride. He walked back through the village streets, head down.

Rosana's voice interrupted. 'Well, Michael,' she said cheerily, 'now you do look like a real Spaniard.'

'What?' He snatched Pepito's tattered straw hat off.

'Had an interesting morning?'

'Does everyone in this place know what's going on round here?'

'Pretty much. Village life, you know.'

'Well, this place is just a bit too prying. You can't move without everyone knowing what you're doing.' He continued along the street.

'Michael, I thought we might have dinner tonight.'

'I can't.' (He almost said sorry.) 'I'm tied up.'

The door to his grandmother's house was unlocked, so he stepped in. Maria Carmen was standing there, smiling, to greet him.

'I need to speak to you.'

He led her to the armchair, and pulled another chair over. 'Why did you allow father to be driven out?'

'I can't talk about that.' She turned her head to one side.

'No one understands. Father would never explain what happened, and Uncle Pepito doesn't know. I have to hear about it from you.'

'It's wonderful you're here, Miguel-Ángel, but please leave this.'

'I can't. I never wanted to come to this place, I know what it did to my father. But now I come, and find out I own half the village. How can I deal with it, if I don't understand what happened?'

'It's not half the village,' she snapped.

'Not quite. But neither of us is going anywhere, until you tell me.' Maria Carmen bowed her head. Michael clasped her hands in his.

'Grandma,' he said softly, 'I know this is painful, but don't you think it will help, if you talk to me? I understand guilt. I withdrew from father when I found out about the leprosy. I couldn't touch him.'

She stiffened. 'I never did that.'

'Then – you must tell me what happened. Please tell me.'

'I could try...' Maria Carmen sighed, and was still for a moment. 'Oh, but you see, Miguel-Àngel... Francisco was a beautiful boy. Not a day went by, I didn't thank God for the blessing He gave us when Francisco was born. Pepito too, but Francisco was our first and he would always be special. We watched him grow, always happy...'

She took a deep breath.

'He was nearly eighteen when a lesion appeared on his right arm. It was small, but red and sore looking, though it didn't itch. Francisco said it had no sense of feeling, but we didn't even go to the doctor.

'Four months later another appeared, on his shoulder. And he complained of numbness in one foot. The doctor prescribed antiseptic cream. It was my mother, who first knew. She was in her eighties, and she'd seen it before. Leprosy used to be quite common around here.

'In the last half of the nineteenth century there were sixty-five cases in this village, and the population was much smaller, then. That's why they built the sanatorium at Fontilles.'

'My father told me,' said Michael.

'Anyway, when my mother finally saw the lesions on Francisco, she recognised them straight away. There hadn't been a case in the village for almost forty years, but mother had seen the early signs before. She'd also seen the way the village dealt with the disease.

'Anyone suspected of having leprosy was driven out, the entire family shunned. She warned us to keep quiet. But this was 1951. Leprosy was treatable, and we hoped people would be more understanding, but we should have known better.

'We didn't dare go back to the doctor, because we knew it would get round the village. So we went to Fontilles. They knew immediately. It was the worst day of my life. Our beautiful Francisco was a leper. Nothing would ever be the same... Francisco refused to accept it. He kept saying, "Why has this happened to me?"'

'What did you do?'

'It got worse. Francisco had only a mild form, tuberculoid leprosy, but the doctors said it was contagious. It could be cured, though, and after three months treatment it would no longer be contagious.'

Maria Carmen stared at the floor, her mouth a tight line.

He had to get her to speak on. 'You have a good memory.'

Her eyes widened, and flashed. 'Do you think I could *ever forget*? Listen. At first, this was good news. Francisco could be treated and then return home, everything back to normal. How stupid we were...

'Francisco refused to accept it. He wanted to get out, but we stayed to talk to the doctors. They took Francisco out of the room. More tests, they said. Then they told us he couldn't leave. Your grandfather, Antonio, tried to fight, but they pinned him down. The doctors said Francisco must stay. For his own good, and the community, they said.

'Francisco needed to be in isolation for three months. Antonio refused. "We'll take him away from Parcent," he kept saying. 'But They showed us around. It was like a group of family homes. Everyone with a private bedroom, surrounded by open space. But a high stone wall encircled the area. The only way out was through the main gates. When we came back in, the doctors asked us to tell Francisco what needed to be done. Antonio said he couldn't, so it was left to me.

'He didn't want to listen, but I calmed him down, said he was in good hands, that he needed treatment or the disease would get worse. I explained he'd be there only a few months, then he'd be home.

'He broke down in tears and sobbed like a little boy. I held him in my arms, and felt his body shaking. He was still crying when he approached Antonio. But Antonio flinched. I know he regretted it for the rest of his life, but Francisco saw fear in his father's eyes, and it was as if he realised what living with leprosy was going to be like.'

Michael nodded, and Maria Carmen went on. 'Francisco walked off with the doctors, and the door closed. I told Antonio I would never forgive him, but he never forgave himself. As we left, we walked between two of the blocks towards the main gate. One of the assistants was trying to tell us everything would be all right. And then

I heard Francisco's voice. I looked round to see his face in a window opening, with his hands tugging the metal bars. "Don't leave me, mother," he screamed. I can hear it now. "Don't leave me, mother."'

Maria Carmen dropped her head in her hands, and wept uncontrollably. Michael put his arms around her.

After a few minutes, Maria Carmen's long, shuddering sobs slowed. She pulled herself upright.

'No, no, it's all right, really. I must – I must tell you.' She wiped her face with the handkerchief Michael held out. 'It's all right. I'll just catch my breath. You want the rest?'

Michael nodded, as she gasped.

'We visited often... ' she began slowly, gripping the handkerchief. 'Antonio came to start with, but he began to make excuses. Francisco was hostile – I think because of the way Antonio had reacted that first time... Anyway, we told people Francisco had gone to visit a cousin of mine in Galicia – it was summer, and he'd been there before.

'Francisco settled in at Fontilles. He was free to wander round once they trusted him not to run away, and he'd met Susan, a nurse with the Red Cross, but we never realised they were becoming close.

'After a few months, the treatment was going well, and the doctors were pleased. Then someone discovered he was there. At first I noticed people seemed anxious to get away if I stopped to talk. Then one night the village priest, Father Ramon, visited. He said he'd been approached by a group of villagers. He put it very politely, but made it clear these people would not accept Francisco back. He said there would be consequences if he returned, and it would be better for Francisco to stay in Fontilles, as others had in the past.

'Antonio was furious. He said that Father Ramon should persuade people to show compassion, instead of doing their dirty work. There was a dreadful scene. Father Ramon – he was in his seventies – said God had a purpose and we should look to ourselves for the reason He'd brought leprosy to our family. Antonio raised his fist, and if I hadn't stepped between them, he'd have killed him. The old man was knocked over – with me. Antonio picked me up, then picked up Father Ramon and threw him out of the house. Antonio never entered the church again, even after Father Ramon retired a few years later.

'I went and pleaded with Father Ramon to talk to the villagers. I told him the treatment was working, the disease wasn't contagious. I begged him to talk to the doctors at Fontilles. He could have helped. But he was from the old school. He'd seen leprosy before. I think he truly believed that the disease was a punishment from God and that the only way of dealing with it was to isolate lepers.

'He wanted me to persuade Francisco not to come back, but I said I couldn't. He was livid. He said, "Maria Carmen Fernandez, there will be dire consequences if Francisco ever sets foot in this village. He will be shunned, and so will you all. You are going against the will of God." And he left the village.'

'Called himself a man of God... *Jesus.*'

'A few days later, I went to see Francisco. I knew something was wrong at once. Father Ramon had been to see him and told him what he'd told me – worse, he'd told Francisco that for the sake of his family he must never return. I thought Francisco would be upset, but he just shrugged. "Don't worry, mother." I didn't know what to say. I cried, and he held me. For the first time, Francisco comforted me, not the other way round. Then he kissed me, and said, "You had better go." That was the last time I ever saw him.'

Maria Carmen pointed to a corner. 'Pass me that bible.'

A leather bound bible, worn gilt running along the edges of the pages, sat on a shelf. He handed it down to his grandmother, and she opened the cover and carefully took out a slip of yellowing paper.

'This was at Fontilles next time I went.'

Michael unfolded the note and read the familiar handwriting.

"Dear Mama, by the time you read this I will have left Fontilles and Spain for good. I've gone to England with Susan. Apart from you, she is the only one who accepts me for what I am, a leper. I'm sorry for all the pain to you. I think it best if we don't meet again, so please don't try to contact me. I will always, always love you. Francisco."

Michael looked up. 'Couldn't you *stop* him?'

'He'd left. And should I have forced him back to Fontilles?'

'Did you try to contact him?'

'I always went back to that letter. If he needed help, he would have asked. He knew I loved him and that I thought of him every day.

And then later, I had Susan's letters, and his notes. He knew that I would treasure them.'

'But how could you stay here in the village?'

'Antonio's family, and mine, had lived here for centuries. Antonio made his living off the land. Without it, there was no way to survive.'

'But how could you live with these people?'

'It was not simple. We did have a few real friends. And we didn't know who told Father Ramon to ban Francisco... Three years later, Father Ramon asked me to go and see him. He was very ill and close to death and he wanted me to know the truth. He told me he'd been visiting Fontilles when he saw Francisco. He talked to the doctors, and they told him Francisco would return to Parcent after treatment.

'He thought it was wrong and the village would not accept Francisco back, so he invented a story about a group of villagers pressing him to talk to us. I was deeply shocked. It was terrible to think it need never have happened. But Father Ramon was unrepentant.'

'That priest was evil.'

'Don't judge him too harshly,' said Maria Carmen.

'I believe in evil, and that priest was evil.'

'He was probably right. The village would never have accepted Francisco. Perhaps this way, we were spared the pain of finding out.'

If his grandmother had learnt to forgive the old priest, it would serve no purpose for Michael to express his feelings further.

He also sensed that Maria Carmen's story was at an end.

She sat quite calmly in her chair, her eyes fixed on the young man in the silver-framed photograph on the table beside her.

Chapter Nine

The mobile phone woke him. 'Good morning, Michael, you can book your flight home,' said Jose Luis with obvious glee.

'What?'

'It's all over, we've got them.'

'The Harringtons, you mean?'

'We haven't found the bodies yet, but it's only a matter of time.'

'Bodies? Will you tell me what's happened?'

'The Dutchmen, Hagemans and Van Doorn, we searched the old finca in Orba and found their fingerprints. We found bloodstains as well. The results came through overnight and we matched them to the Harringtons. There's no doubt about it.'

'Have they confessed?'

'No, but it's only a matter of time. It's not the ending we would have wanted but, like I say, the case is all but over. We'll be charging them later this morning.'

'Has anyone spoken to John and Linda Harrington yet?'

'I don't think so.'

'Well, don't. I'm coming over.'

'There's no need, there's nothing you can do.'

'I'm coming over,' repeated Michael, before ending the call.

He said goodbye to his grandmother, promising to be back, then headed down to Rosana's house.

'What do you want, Miguel-Ángel? – or is it *Michael*?'

Her dark tousled hair hung randomly about her face. In a baggy T-shirt over faded denims, and pale blue ballet pumps, she was beautiful.

'I need to borrow your car,' he said abruptly.

'What for?'

'To get to Alicante. Something's happened in the investigation.'

'What if I say *no*?'

'Just give me the keys.'

She returned a moment later with a bunch of keys, removed one from the ring, and slapped it into his open hand.

'You've got a nerve.'

'I know,' he replied. 'It's terrible – look, I'm sorry about yesterday. But at least you know I'll be coming back, to return the car.'

'Is that the only reason?' She placed her hands on her hips.

'Of course not.' He leaned forward to kiss her – very briefly – on the lips, and then took off before there was a reaction. 'Bye.'

At the Guardia Civil Headquarters in Alicante, Michael's civilian pass failed to get him past the front desk. He was told to wait until Colonel Cardells was free, and waited forty minutes in the public area while officers dealt with an assortment of villains and victims. Eventually a summons came and he was escorted into the Colonel's inner office. Jose Luis was there, looking nervous. The greeting was cordial enough.

'Good to see you again, Inspector. I hope you are fully recovered from your accident,' said Cardells.

'Yes, I'm fine, thank you.'

'Jose Luis says you insisted on coming, but there was no need. You see, we're convinced that Hagemans and Van Doorn abducted the Harringtons and probably murdered them. It's just a matter of time before we wrap it up. It's a tragic ending, not what we wanted, but they've been interrogated and we're searching the house in Orba and their apartment in Denia. There's nothing you can do at the moment.'

'Can I see the interview notes and the forensic evidence?'

'Of course you can, but there's not much point.'

'And then I will want to speak to Hagemans and Van Doorn.' Michael deliberately framed his remark as a statement, not a question.

Jose Luis looked uncomfortable, and Cardells stiffened. 'I'm sure I don't need to remind you, Inspector, that you have no jurisdiction here. You're here by invitation, and only because we thought it would be useful to have you. This is a Guardia Civil investigation, and now that the case is as good as solved I see little point in your continued involvement. In fact, you can make plans to return to Britain.'

'I need to remember that I was sent here to work alongside the Guardia Civil, Colonel, and not in a token position,' Michael said, in no mood to back down despite the Colonel's authoritarian tone. 'It is important that I'm useful. I will need to talk to John and Linda Harrington some time today, and I'd like to be able to satisfy them that everything possible has been done and that the real culprits have indeed been uncovered. What's more, when the news emerges, the media, at least the British contingent, will expect me to comment. I would find it very difficult to express my complete confidence in the investigation until I have seen the files and talked to the suspects.'

'Have you discussed this with Chief Superintendent Bowater?'

'I don't need to, at the moment, but can I see the files and notes?'

The Colonel's bloated face reddened.

'Give him the files, Perez, and arrange for him to see the prisoners, but I want you with him at all times. Is that understood?'

'Yes – yes, Colonel,' said Jose Luis, as if disconcerted not to have witnessed one of the Colonel's real rages. He raised an eyebrow at Michael, and nodded towards the door, indicating it was time to depart.

'Thank you, Colonel,' said Michael, as he stood leave.

'And Perez,' said Cardells, 'tell Ramirez to get Chief Superintendent Bowater on the phone right away.'

Outside the office, Jose Luis rolled his eyes.

'I've seen people shot for less.'

'I don't doubt it.'

For the next hour Michael worked through the files and interview notes in a back office, while Jose Luis stood by, answering Michael's questions, and occasionally popping out for coffee.

The finca in Orba, it turned out, was hidden away at the end of a dusty track, and barely visible from the nearest property over a kilometre away.

No one was sure who owned it, though it clearly did not belong to Hagemans or Van Doorn. A search of the two-roomed ruin had revealed several sets of fingerprints, including those of the two suspects as well as Alison and David Harrington's, and several others as yet unidentified. Both rooms turned up several small bloodstains, though most were in the second room, which contained an old bed. The stains were mainly on the floor, but a few specks in a spray pattern were found on one wall. The DNA tests identified the blood as belonging to both Mr and Mrs Harrington. Most, but not all, of the blood on the floor of the first room belonged to Alison Harrington, while the blood in the second room was mostly from David. There was no sign of a weapon.

The first room was a kitchen of sorts, with a stone sink (though no running water), a work surface, and a couple of cupboards containing a few old mugs and a collection of drinking glasses, none of which appeared to have been used recently. There was also an ancient two-ring gas hob (but no gas bottle) and a rusty old kettle, which showed no sign of recent use. The suspects' fingerprints had been lifted from doors and door handles, and the dusty work surface in the kitchen.

David Harrington's prints had been found on the floor of the bedroom, Alison's on the floor nearby.

Next, Michael turned to the interview notes.

The interviews were conducted by Colonel Cardells and Jose Luis. Both suspects spoke little Spanish but were reasonably fluent in English, so Sergeant Ramirez had acted as interpreter.

The Dutch consulate had provided an interpreter for the later interviews, and a Dutch lawyer had also been present.

The two men admitted they had tried to use the Orba property for a scam. They placed advertisements in the Dutch edition of the Costa Blanca News offering a finca for restoration together with a parcel of land. Their plan was to persuade prospective buyers to hand over a sizeable deposit, and then abscond with the money.

They'd found two other remote properties and planned to use them in a similar way in the future. They had shown three people around the finca in February and March, including Mr Carrington, but were getting nowhere because no one expressed any interest in the place, even when they reduced the price. Then the Ruiters came to see the property in April and seemed interested.

By this time they were getting desperate for cash, but Hagemans blew it when he made threats to Mr Ruiter on the way to the bank.

After that, they decided to back off because they were worried the Ruiters might report the incident. They claimed they had not been to the finca since the beginning of April.

The police had searched the two men's apartment in Denia, but found nothing to link them with the Harringtons.

'Is this a mistake?'

Michael turned the file towards Jose Luis.

'What?'

'In the notes of Van Doorn's interview, where he refers to Mr Carrington, not Harrington.'

Jose Luis studied the notes.

'Yes, a mistake, I expect. Something got lost in translation.'

'I'm ready to see them now,' said Michael.

'Together or separately?' asked Jose Luis.

'Together, I think. After all, I'm only satisfying my curiosity. You've already done the interviews.'

Up from their basement cells, the two men looked tired as they entered the room. V

Van Doorn was a surly man of considerable height and bulk. His face was wider at the bottom than at the top; an imbalance exaggerated by the dense, dark stubble on his chin and upper lip. The man's demeanour, size, and scuffed Doc Martins, laced above the ankles through metal clips, made it easy for Michael to imagine him kidnapping, or worse. In complete contrast, Hagemans was nervy, fidgety, thin. He had fair, wispy hair, and no more than a trace of blond bristle on his boyish face. Both were in their late twenties.

Michael emphasised that they were not obliged to talk to him, but he wanted to understand their stories. They could have a solicitor present if they wished, but this was not a formal interview. He presented himself as "a friend of human rights," and after his introduction they both seemed anxious to talk, preferably in English.

Jose Luis put a hand across his mouth and protested quietly. 'I'll have to get Sergeant Ramirez, if you're going to talk in English.'

'Relax Jose Luis, or we'll be here all day. I'll tell you what's said, if there's anything significant.'

'Just don't tell the Colonel, then.'

Before Michael could start, Hagemans burst out hysterically, 'You've got to help us, Inspector Fernandez. They're trying to pin murder on us.'

'I see... it's Wilhelm, isn't it?'

'Wil.'

'Like I said, Wil, we can all just relax. I've come here to get to the bottom of this, and if you're innocent you've got nothing to fear. First, you both agree you met David Harrington when he came to the finca on 27th January?'

'Yes,' said Hagemans, 'He called about a week before, but he said his name was Carrington.'

'Are you sure?'

'That's what it sounded like,' said Hagemans, looking towards Van Doorn, who nodded confirmation.

'But you are sure it was him?' asked Michael.

'Yes, they showed us his picture, but that was before they told us about the fingerprints and the bloodstains.'

'Did he come alone?'

'Yes,' said Hagemans.

'And you've never seen his wife?'

'No,' said Van Doorn, suddenly taking an interest. 'Look, what's the point of this? We've been through it all with the Spanish cops.'

'The point is, Johan, the Spanish cops have enough to charge you with murder. At the moment I'm your best hope of getting out of here, so it's in your interests to tell me as much as you know.'

Hagemans touched his partner on the arm.

'Please, Johan, let's try to help – tell him all about it.'

Van Doorn pulled his arm away and folded it across his chest, but leant back in his chair and slipped downward, stretching the Doc Martins out under the table.

'How did he meet you?' asked Michael.

'We met him at a bar in Orba, then he followed us in his car,' said Hagemans.

'What kind of car?'

'I don't know. Blue. Small Renault, I think.' Hagemans looked at Van Doorn but got only a shrug of the shoulders.

'What was he like?'

'What do you mean?'

'You must have talked to him. What did you talk about? Did he

122

seem interested in the place?'

Again it was Hagemans who answered.

'He seemed pretty interested. He asked about how much land was included, and we told him about forty thousand square metres – everything around the house. Then he asked about neighbours, and we said there weren't any. I remember he wanted to know how soon he could move in. Johan said he could have it straight away, but that he needed to make his mind up pretty quickly because we had other people interested. We said we'd accept a cash deposit to secure the sale and then draw up the papers. It could be his in a couple of weeks. I was convinced he wanted to buy the place. I really thought we were going to get a deposit.'

'He was never going to buy,' interrupted Van Doorn.

'Why do you say that?' asked Michael.

'Because he never asked the obvious questions about a water supply or electricity. One or two had seen the place and asked, but he just looked around. I tried to tell him things, but he just asked if the sixty-five thousand price included the access road, and the garage nearby, and I said yes. He never haggled or anything. He was just going through the motions.'

'What happened next?'

'He just said he'd think about it, and left,' said Van Doorn. 'I was pretty pissed off with him. He was bloody rude, to be honest. Just wasting our time. I thought about grabbing his wallet or something, but he didn't seem the sort to be carrying a lot of money.'

'Why do you say that?'

'Oh, there was just something about him. He was kind of putting on an act, pretending to have funds – but any budget he might have had was kept a complete secret. I doubted he had money to buy anywhere. Like I say, he was just a time waster.'

'Did he mention his wife?'

Van Doorn said no, and Hagemans nodded agreement.

'How did think you would get away with selling the land and the finca? What if the real owner had turned up?'

Hagemans was keen to answer. 'We looked for land that looked like it was unregistered. We got the idea from the newspapers.'

'Why did you keep the phone?'

'What?' said Van Doorn.

'After that business with the Ruiters, surely you must have realised you could be traced through the phone?'

'It was just a pay-as–you-go. I didn't think you could trace those.'

'You can't, but when Captain Perez here phoned you, didn't you realise it might be a set up?'

Van Doorn looked a little less confident, as he contemplated the question. 'Look it was a good plan. People come over here and do stupid things. I know, I've seen it. People buy houses like cars. Cash changes hands in bars and no one bothers about contracts or stuff like that. Sooner or later someone would give us money for that place.'

'And in the meantime, how do you make your living?'

'We sell stuff,' Hagemans replied, almost childlike in his anxiety to tell the truth. 'At the rastro markets in Jalon and Teulada on Saturdays and Sundays. It's mostly junk, but people buy anything out here.'

Michael noticed Van Doorn twitch uneasily, and flash a warning glance towards his partner, but Hagemans failed to pick it up.

'What sort of stuff?' Michael asked.

'Old china, copper and brass, bits of jewellery – just glass – a few books, even bits of furniture. Sometimes we go back to Holland to buy stuff there, and bring it back to sell in the markets.'

Hagemans jumped as Van Doorn kicked him under the table – which everyone could see – and shot him a glance.

But Hagemans was keen to continue.

'Look Johan, illegal importation of junk is a lot better than murder. Okay, so some of the stuff might be stolen. We buy it cheap in Holland, no questions asked, but I tell you most of it is worthless. Look for yourselves, it's all in a trailer locked in a garage near our apartment in Denia.'

Van Doorn reached across to pull Hagemans away from the table.

'Shut up, Wil, you've said enough.'

Michael spoke briefly to Jose Luis, then turned back to the men. 'You can tell the Captain where the garage is, and give him the keys.'

'Yes.' Hagemans obliged, despite Van Doorn's furious frown.

'How do you account for the blood stains at the finca?' said

Michael, watching the two men to gauge their reactions.

Van Doorn didn't flinch, but Hagemans was visibly unnerved. A look of panic crossed his face, his lower lip quivered and he started to babble as his eyes filled with tears.

'Mr Fernandez, I don't know how that blood got there. We've told you the truth. We met Harrington at the finca for just a few minutes and then he left. That's it, end of story. We're not murderers. Please help us, otherwise the Spanish police are going to fit us up. You know what they're like, don't you?' Tears rolled down his cheeks, and he reached out for Michael's hand.

It was a pity to scare the young man further, but this wasn't on. Michael pulled back.

'Tell me, Wil, has Johan ever been to the finca without you?'

Hagemans' expression changed as he pondered the question.

Before he could answer Van Doorn shot forward from his slouching position and banged his fist on the desk. Jose Luis started.

'Don't answer, Wil.' Van Doorn pulled Hagemans away from the table again, and forced him against the back of his chair. 'You can see what he's up to. Well, it's not going to work. The interview's over. We'd like to see our solicitor now.'

Hagemans was still looking confused when the door opened and Colonel Cardells strode in, with Ramirez at his tail.

'Thank you, Michael, that was most useful,' the Colonel said.

Van Doorn sprung up again and lunged at Michael. 'You bastard,' he shouted, as Jose Luis pinned him to the desk. 'You set us up.'

Hagemans cowered in his chair like a timid hamster, still not sure what was happening. Two uniformed policemen entered the room and took the suspects towards the door, but Cardells turned to Michael.

'You'd better tell these two that we've just found the Harringtons' car in an old garage about five hundred metres from the finca in Orba.'

Michael managed to restrain himself from swearing at the Colonel, and spoke to the two Dutchmen in English.

'It's a set up,' said Van Doorn, calmly. 'These bastards set us up.'

Hagemans was not so unperturbed. He twisted his head to look at Michael, straining the sinews in his neck as he spoke. 'Please, Mr Fernandez, can you help us?' he begged, as the policemen led him away.

The look of wide-eyed panic hit Michael like a bolt from a crossbow, but he could offer no more than a gentle nod.

'They weren't the only ones who were set up, were they?' Michael stared directly at the Colonel's grinning face.

'I think you'll find that your Chief Superintendent wants to talk to you,' he replied, ushering Ramirez and Jose Luis out of the room.

Jose Luis looked briefly back at Michael and shrugged, but Michael already knew that Jose Luis was not complicit in the deceit.

'What the hell are you playing at, Fernandez?' Bowater said as soon as Penny put the call through. 'Colonel Cardells is furious.'

'It was all a set up,' said Michael.

'What is, the case against the two Dutchmen?'

'No, Cardells. He set me up. He pretends to be indignant about my involvement, but he just used me to get to the suspects. He was listening to every word while I spoke to them. I was trying to be friendly, you know, someone they could trust. I think I was getting somewhere, with Hagemans at least. Then Cardells bursts in with news that they've found the Harringtons' car. I swear he knew it before I spoke to them. Now I've lost them. They'll never want to talk to me again, and who'd blame them.'

'I doubt you'd be talking to them again, in any event. Cardells wants you called back. He says it's an open and shut case and there's more than enough evidence to convict them.'

'Well, he's wrong. Van Doorn could be lying, but Hagemans is just his puppy. Even Van Doorn doesn't seem stupid enough to kill the Harringtons and hang round afterwards. There are too many unanswered questions. Besides, they haven't found the bodies yet.'

'So what do you want to do?'

'I'd like to stay around for a while, if that's all right, sir? I'll have to talk to John and Linda Harrington anyway. And I think I can keep in touch through Captain Perez. I don't think he believes the Dutchmen are guilty, but he's afraid to challenge Cardells.'

'I thought you didn't want to be in Spain, Michael.'

'I don't, but I don't like unfinished business, and I've got a few other matters to attend to.'

'Such as what?'

'It's personal, sir.'

'Tread carefully Michael, whatever it is you're up to.'

The meeting with John and Linda Harrington at their Benidorm hotel was bound to be difficult. If he shared Colonel Cardells' belief that the two Dutchmen were guilty of abduction and possibly murder, it was bad news. If he expressed doubts, it only prolonged their anxiety. And how could he explain the bloodstains, without leading them to fear the worst?

They met at three o'clock in a quiet corner of the hotel bar. Linda took a Coca-Cola in response to Michael's invitation. John asked for beer and the hotel obliged with cold Cruzcampo in a dimpled glass tankard. It was not John's first of the day. He was shirtless, sticky, and by the looks of the cherry-red skin beneath grey-brown chest hair, he'd dropped off during an afternoon siesta in the sun. A dark sweat stain showed below the elasticated waist of his baggy shorts. He was shoeless, and his feet were grubby. His eyes were bleary, and he looked ready to collapse at any second. Linda was tanned and neat in strappy sandals and a short cotton dress that showed the outline of a pale yellow bikini.

Timothy Middleton joined them, every inch the staid civil servant.

Michael felt that even he would like to suggest, "Some people might get rid of the jacket and tie, for once."

'Looking after you?' asked Middleton, after the usual pleasantries.

'Food's not up to much,' said John, 'but apart from that it's okay. You are paying the bill, aren't you? I mean, everything's included?'

Linda nudged him.

'Don't worry about the bill, Mr Harrington. It will be taken care of. Apparently, Inspector Fernandez has some news for us.'

Michael coughed. 'Ahem... er, yes. The Guardia Civil have arrested two Dutchmen on suspicion of abducting David and Alison.'

'Are they all right?' Linda grasped the arms of her chair.

Michael shuffled in his seat. 'I'm afraid I can't say for certain. You see, they've found bloodstains at an old finca – a farmhouse – near Orba, and they match David and Alison.'

'Oh, my God.' Linda gripped John's hand, though he sat as stiff as if he'd just been set in concrete. Even his eyes were frozen.

'Look,' said Michael, 'I know it sounds pretty awful, but there could be all sorts of explanations. There's no need to fear the worst at the moment. The Guardia Civil are making further inquiries.'

John suddenly moved. He took a gulp of beer, and wiped his lips.

'Don't give us "further inquiries" crap. Are they dead, or what?'

Michael was not surprised by the abruptness, and replied equally brusquely, 'They haven't found bodies, if that's what you mean.'

'These Dutch geezers, they've confessed, then?'

'They admitted meeting David at the finca, but not Alison. They were working a scam, pretending the place was theirs to sell and trying to get people to hand over a deposit. But they deny anything more. Oh, and the police found David's hire car in an old garage nearby.'

Linda gasped, a hand raised. Middleton passed her a handkerchief.

'Sounds like they're bang to rights,' John said, returning to the Cruzcampo. 'Did they get David to part with any money?'

'No, they say they just met him and showed him round, and then he left.'

'They would say that, wouldn't they. What do the police think?'

Michael sat back. 'Well, they seem pretty certain the two were involved, and I must admit there's circumstantial evidence...'

'You don't believe it was them, do you?' said Linda, hopefully.

'I know this sounds cold, but until there are bodies, it's impossible to be certain.' He realised how grave this sounded, and tried to recover. 'But of course, there's every chance they're alive. We have every reason to hope. It's just best to keep an open mind until the Guardia Civil finish their inquiries.' He recognised his police-speak and added, 'I've interviewed the suspects, and from my experience there's a great deal of room for doubt.'

'Sounds to me,' John broke in, 'like you're trying to get them off the hook. Typical of British police, soft on everything. The Guardia don't mess about. You've got bloodstains and the hire car and these two blokes admit they met David. They don't want to go down for murder, that's all. They're just trying to save their skins. Are the Guardia going to charge them?'

'If they have evidence,' said Michael.

'With murder?'

'If such turned out to be the case, I expect they would.'

'There you are. Told you the Guardia don't mess about, so why do you come here with this talk about further enquiries and reason to hope? If they're dead, I just hope those bastards are topped.'

'Capital punishment no longer exists in Spain, Mr Harrington.'

'More's the pity, then.'

Linda had been weeping into the handkerchief. She looked up at Michael with pink-rimmed eyes. 'Do you really think they're dead?'

'I just don't know, Mrs Harrington. I certainly hope not,' Michael said, trying to sound sincere. He would have reached forward to comfort her, but didn't think John would take kindly to the gesture.

John returned to the offensive. 'So where do we go from here?'

To Michael's surprise, Middleton decided to lend a hand, reciting helpfully, 'I think we shall all just have to await developments. I'm sure the Inspector will keep us informed, won't you Inspector?'

'Of course.'

'In the meantime, the Consulate will do everything it can.' Middleton smiled, and for a second Michael expected him to add, "to make your stay a pleasant and happy one."

'Just so long as you cover the bills here, Mr Middleton,' John said. He stood up. 'Where's the barman?'

He turned back to Michael. 'See those Dutch bastards get what they deserve.' He strode towards the bar.

Linda looked up. 'I'm sorry,' she said. 'He's really very upset.'

Michael felt like commenting, "He has a horrible way of showing it," but settled for, 'I'm sorry too, Mrs Harrington.'

Michael's next move was to call Jose Luis on his mobile phone, deliberately avoiding the office number.

'Can you talk?' he asked.

'What do you mean? Of course I can talk.'

'I mean the Colonel's not listening in, is he?'

'What do you want?'

'You don't think they're guilty, do you?'

'I have my doubts, about Hagemans at least.'

'Then what are you going to do about it?'

'What do you suggest I do, open the cells and let them out?'

'I'm serious. The Colonel's going to railroad them into court and he'll probably get a conviction. Two innocent men could go down.'

'That's for the courts to decide. It's not my problem.'

'You need to talk to Hagemans. He's the weak link. Find out if he was ever away from Van Doorn long enough for him to go back to the finca alone. And see if you can check the numbers called from Van Doorn's mobile. He could have contacted David Harrington again. Oh, and another thing – do your lab people have any idea how old the bloodstains are?'

'Didn't see anything in the report, just the DNA test results.'

'See if they can find out, will you?'

'Don't ask much, do you? Any idea how long all this will take?'

'I'm sure you can manage it, Jose Luis.'

'Well, I'll see what I can do. But if the Colonel finds out, I'll be in deep shit.'

'So be careful. And do me another favour? Let me know if you find anything at the garage in Denia. I'll call you in a couple of days.'

The next call was to Rosana. 'Are you free for dinner tonight?'

'I'm not sure.'

'Good, book somewhere nice. I'll be back about seven-thirty.'

An hour later he was explaining, 'No, thank you, Grandma, I'm having dinner with Rosana.'

'Oh, that's nice. By the way, Julio was looking for you today.'

'Was he?' Not hard to guess what that was about.

After several dress rehearsals, Michael settled for a pale yellow short-sleeved shirt with button-down collar, beige chinos and brown leather belt. He almost dispensed with socks, but couldn't quite bring himself to go through with it, so put on a pale brown pair, inside an almost new pair of tan loafers, which he buffed to a lustrous sheen.

Walking to Rosana's house, a curious sensation overcame him, of nervousness, excitement, anticipation. After a deep breath to bring him back to calm, he knocked at the door.

'Miguel-Ángel, come in.' Rosana's mother led him awkwardly into the house, dragging her left foot along the tiled hallway. Her cotton dress was covered by an apron, tied in a bow at the back. 'Rosana won't be long.'

'Thank you, Mrs Ferrando Moll,' he said uneasily.

'Please, if you will, call me Isabel. And this is Asunción, Rosana's grandmother. She and your grandmother are cousins, you know.'

'Pleased to meet you again... Mrs Asunción,' he said, hesitant to be informal. He shook the black-garbed old woman's hand.

Isabel gestured to a wooden chair, topped with a tapestry cushion. 'Please sit down.'

The chair typified the rest of the room, rustic and homely.

Nothing matched, but everything blended perfectly, and the smell of furniture polish mingled with the aroma of cooking.

But the tapestry cushion sagged as he sank into the chair, as if trapping him, and about to say, *'What are your intentions towards my daughter?'*

He was rescued by footsteps on the stairs, and turned to see a heavy velvet curtain pulled aside, as if the Queen were pulling a chord to reveal a plaque.

Rosana paused briefly on the final step like a model at the end of a catwalk. Her dark shiny hair flowed in carefully sculpted waves across one side of her face, and down onto her shoulders. A narrow gold chain hung around her neck and glistened against her olive skin.

She wore a simple khaki cotton dress that buttoned all the way from the rounded neck to the calf-length hem. It clung to her bust and hips and was gathered at her slender waist by a narrow black belt. Her shoes had thin straps around the ankles and toes, with a cut-out flower in black leather sitting on the top of each foot.

He returned his gaze to her face, conscious that he stared.

She met his smile with her own, and spoke through glossy lips.

'Well, Miguel-Ángel, will I do?'

'You look... ' He struggled to rise from the sagging chair.

'Don't say smashing,' she said with a grin, 'or I'll kill you.'

A few minutes later, at the Restaurant La Tasca on the edge of the village they were greeted in French by the waitress, Celine. She kissed Rosana before being introduced to Michael and took them through to a walled courtyard at the back.

A few tables were occupied, but Celine led them to a table shielded by night-scented jasmine, lit a candle in a small glass holder, and left the menus.

'The meal is pleasant; fresh ingredients neatly presented without over-elaboration, the conversation is easy and relaxed, and what are you doing in a place like Parcent?' Michael asked in the break between the main course and dessert.

'What's wrong with Parcent?'

'That's just a question cops use to find out what a person's doing.'

'I was born here.'

'Witness is being evasive.'

'Okay, I left for university, moved to Madrid, rented an apartment, took a job as a trainee account manager at Banco de Bilbao, became a branch manager and married Vicente, an investment broker. We lived a high life with posh cars, international travel, yacht in Barcelona. That was all very nice, and Vicente was nice, but I wanted a change.'

'Children, that sort of thing?'

'You're perceptive – all of a sudden.'

'It's my job, he said perceptively.'

'Anyway, father died, and then mother had a stroke. Grandmother is not at all strong, so I came back. I guess it gave me an excuse to end the marriage, but it was over for me, in any event. So here I am.'

'Happy?'

'Happy enough.'

'You don't find it quiet? After Madrid and Barcelona.'

'Sometimes you have to come to realise what's important. There's something that means more than any of that.'

'Like family?'

'Now you're being really perceptive.'

Michael realised where the conversation was heading, and anticipated the next question.

'And what about your family?' she said.

'I didn't realise I had one here,' he said, 'until recently.'

'And now? Are you evading the question?'

'Only because – this is dessert, I think.'

After placing dessert on the table, Celine paused. Customers were thinning out, and it seemed curiosity was getting the better of her.

'So you're the long lost grandson. I didn't know Maria Carmen had a grandson until this week. What suddenly brings you here?'

'Just visiting.'

'Oh, what do you – ' A shouted instruction from the kitchen pulled Celine away before she could finish her question.

'Is that true, then?' Rosana asked.

'What?'

'You're just visiting Parcent.'

'Maybe. I don't know. A few days ago I was an English policeman, now I'm in Spain with a family. I own a house, land, and problems.'

'And?' Rosana stroked her hair away from her face.

'And I've met this beautiful woman who seems to know my thoughts before I do, and who has a way of getting me to do things.'

'So tell me all about your life in England. How someone with so much Spanish blood became so bitter, is my first question.'

'You know most of it.'

'I know your father left Spain, rather than stay in Fontilles. I know your mother left with him, but I don't know about you, personally.'

'You want the whole story?'

Michael recounted what Maria Carmen had told him, but Rosana followed with, 'What about you, yourself? Your own story, please.'

Michael sighed.

'My childhood was no different to anyone else's, Rosana. But one afternoon I went to my best friend's house and his mother said Andy couldn't play, and I must never come to the house again. Mum said they were not nice people, and we should ignore it. A few weeks later, we moved. Mum transferred to another hospital.'

'And then?'

'A few years later, my mother told me what had happened, about this village, and Fontilles. She didn't blame anyone. She accepted that she and Dad could never live a normal life. But I worried I might have the disease, or I'd catch it from Dad. I could see how much she loved Dad, how close they were, but... well, once I stupidly told her they'd ruined my life.... Dad had no self-pity. But it hung over me. We moved a third time, to Derby, I left home to join the police. I studied part-time at University, then did a Master's. I met Aurora, we married in 1993. I should have told her about Dad, but she found out when he died. She thought I was deceitful. Which I was, in many ways. We were both relieved, I think, when the divorce came through. Mum died last year. That's about it.'

'Your father gave you a Spanish name and taught you Spanish, so why do you profess to hate Spain?'

'It was the language of my father, but not his country, as far as I'm concerned. That's why I learned it. He hated Spain for what it did to him, of course.'

'You don't know that, and the people in England were no better.'

'Some – but at least they didn't lock him up.'

'You think Fontilles is a prison?'

'It was, essentially, which is why my father ran away.'

'He was young. But Fontilles is not the place you make out.'

'How would you know?'

'I visit. The sanatorium's open. I'll take you tomorrow.'

'No.'

'Why not?'

'No, look, these are my problems, Rosana. It's not a good idea to force people into things. Let them take their own time. In the long run, this sort of thing never works out, where people are forced to do things before they're ready, in their own minds. That's my last word.'

'But...'

'No *buts*, Rosana, I mean it. And it's time we left.'

'*But* we haven't had coffee.'

Coffee came and went, and on the way back, the night air was still and warm and the sky was sprinkled with stars.

'Thank you for a nice evening,' Rosana said unconvincingly, at her door. 'Sorry if I spoiled things. It's just that, if we're going anywhere, you need to be sure of your feelings.'

'Going anywhere?'

'I mean, if we're going... '

The meaning was clear, and he moved to her, placed his hand around her back and pulled her close. She returned his kiss, her hand around the back of his head, her fingers running through his hair. Footsteps sounded on the other side of the door, and he started back.

'So?' Rosana said.

'What?'

'So are we going to Fontilles tomorrow?'

'Will you give that up? I can't go.'

'I'll see you in the morning,' said Rosana, drawing her door key from her purse. She lifted a hand, and touched his cheek. 'And file your prickles before you come.'

'Don't exaggerate.'

But she had manipulated him with great skill tonight. Either that, or he'd had too much wine.

Chapter Ten

'Ah – Michael, I was about to call you this morning, but you've beaten me to it.' Jose Luis sounded serious.

'Any news?'

'Yes, and it's all bad for our Dutch friends, especially Van Doorn.'

'What's happened?'

'We searched the garage in Denia and it was mostly junk. Some probably nicked in Holland, but nothing of any real value. But here's the best part. We found a metal toolbox amongst some car gear. The key to the box was on a keyring we'd confiscated from Van Doorn. In the box, we found almost ten thousand euros. Some of the notes had Van Doorn's prints, none of them had Hagemans'. But some had David Harrington's.'

'And you don't think it was Van Doorn's life savings, boosted by David Harrington out of sympathy for his predicament?'

'Don't let the Colonel hear you make a stupid joke. Anyway, it gets better. We interviewed them both again last night, separately. Hagemans seemed genuinely surprised and very scared when he realised the implications. He broke down again, and I tell you he was squealing. If he knew anything about the money I'm sure he'd have told us. Van Doorn was a different story, his usual defiant self to begin with, but when we pressed him, a little more pressingly, politely implying that David had told someone they'd met again, he came up with a different account. He says David Harrington contacted him a month ago and said he was interested in the place at Orba. He went there to meet him, on his own, and says Harrington paid him a deposit of ten thousand in cash. But he still says that he only took the money, then Harrington left. Van Doorn says he promised to get the paperwork to Harrington in a couple of days, but of course he never did.'

'What do you think?' asked Michael.

'It's looking pretty grim, at least for Van Doorn. I can believe that Hagemans might not have known about Van Doorn's last meeting with Harrington, otherwise I'm sure he'd have told us. He could have been doing the frightened rabbit thing, but when we told him about Van Doorn's story he was shocked, you could see it. He remembers Van Doorn disappearing for a day a few weeks ago, but he says he doesn't know where he went. Van Doorn just told him he had some business in Calpe.'

'I don't know, Jose Luis, Van Doorn's story doesn't add up. Surely no one would be so stupid as to hand over ten thousand to a stranger.'

'Round here, Michael, people do strange things. Who knows?'

'What's going to happen to them now?'

'We're very close to charging Van Doorn.'

'With murder?'

'What else? We've got the prints, the car and the bloodstains. Oh yes, I almost forgot. The lab boys say the bloodstains are at least ten days old, and could be six weeks. It's difficult to be more precise.'

'So they could date to when Van Doorn says Harrington met him?'

'Yes.'

Michael was still thinking. 'Like you say, it looks bad for Van Doorn. But if his story stacked up, you'd expect David Harrington to have reported the con when he realised he'd been had. But you still haven't heard from them, or found them... or their bodies.'

'We've widened the search area around the finca in Orba. It seems the most likely place to look.'

'Do you think they're dead?' Michael asked.

'It looks that way. Even if the Dutchmen have got them tucked away somewhere, we've had them in custody for four days now. Without food and water I dread to think what state the Harringtons would be in.'

'Surely the Dutchmen would say so, if they'd locked them away somewhere. It's better than going down for murder.'

'You'd think so, wouldn't you. But who knows?'

No. Something was wrong. The Dutchmen had been caught too easily, and they'd made no attempt to hide the evidence against them. Perhaps they'd thought the finca was too remote for anyone to find it. But leaving the prints, the car, the blood and money was just too inept, even for a couple of bunglers like Hagemans and Van Doorn.

'Any chance I could interview them again?' Michael asked.

'I don't think the Colonel would be too happy. And after last time, I'm not sure the Dutchmen would want to see you. Look Michael, I'm grateful for your help, but for the time being it's best if you stay away. If anything happens I'll let you know, and if you think of anything give me a call.'

Michael sat back. The evidence was stacked against Van Doorn, and even if they never found the Harringtons there was enough to charge him with murder. Michael had to admit that he would do the same if he were running the case in England.

'Michael,' called Maria Carmen, from the bottom of the stairs.

Rosana met him at the door with a questioning smile. 'All right?'

He'd been telling himself it was, and now he smiled in response.

'Come on, then.' Rosana held his arm on the way to her car. 'It's only about twenty minutes. I'll drive.'

In other circumstances Michael thought, he'd have approved of Rosana's jeans, the knife-edge crease that ran down her long slender legs, and her broad brown belt with a gold buckle. Her boots would have been less to his taste, but the blue silk blouse that revealed a hint of white bra beneath would have attracted his attention. As it was, if she was trying to take his mind off where they were going, he hadn't noticed a thing.

Up from Parcent, the road towards Orba swept over the mountains before plunging down a series of hairpin bends into the next valley. As green as the Jalon valley, it was dominated by orange groves and vineyards, and scarred by urbanisations that clung to every hillside.

They fringed Orba, then from a Val de Laguart signpost, the road climbed into pink and white blossoms which gradually became green.

Rosana explained that cherries were the main crop in this part of the valley. Normally, the blossom would have disappeared by now, but an unusually cold winter had held it back.

'Fontilles, straight ahead,' she said at last, looking up through the windscreen towards the top of a hill in the distance.

A cluster of yellow stone buildings stood on the summit. On a bright day, the scene might easily have evoked a hilltop castle. But the clouds had thickened, and they descended into a forest where pine trees clung to steep slopes and a steel-grey haze covered a long stone wall, about two metres high, that snaked its way up the mountainside.

Ahead, a pair of stone towers interrupted the line of the wall. This must flank the entrance – with its gate, barred and bolted.

But Rosana drove straight between the twin pillars and up into the complex, heading for a small car park. Opposite, a building of church-like design looked as if it housed the administration block.

Rosana turned off the engine and looked at Michael.

He knew his face must be white. Sweat trickled down his shirt.

'Perhaps this isn't a good idea,' she said.

'It's fine.' Michael tapped her hand. 'Thanks for bringing me.'

She nodded, and gripped his arm as they walked towards the building – a gesture that could have been to prevent him from bolting.

Through the mist, an old man in cardigan, jeans, and faded pink baseball cap, looked up from sweeping pine needles from the road.

Rosana clasped his arms, kissed him, and turned.

'Miguel-Ángel Fernandez, this is Juan Garcia.'

Juan propped his broom against a tree and offered his hand.

The man's fingers dug into Michael's palm, and he looked down. Juan's fingers were bent and truncated, his thumb was missing. Michael resisted an instinctive, almost overwhelming, urge to yank his hand away. He held firm. Juan released his grip. Their eyes met, and Juan grinned.

'Dr Santos is waiting in the reception wing,' he said.

Juan led the way through a hall and up to an office dominated by a window that overlooked a deep, tree-lined ravine.

Dr Santos sat away from the window, behind a low table.

A man determined to disguise the onset of middle age, Michael summed up, also known as a 'Two-Tone Button-Down' or 'right twat' in the force. In a high-collared dog-tooth two-tone grey suit and chisel-toed brown shoes, Santos represented the epitome of the epitome.

But Santos' tone was friendly. He came straight to the point.

'Welcome to Fontilles. I understand you want to know more about leprosy. In particular, what happened to your father.'

All right, this was not the force, and the man's fashions might have been chosen by his wife. In any case, Rosana had obviously given Santos some forewarning, and he was prepared, and he was obviously willing.

'Thank you, Dr Santos,' Michael said. 'I appreciate it.'

'Please call me Eduardo.' The doctor sat down.

'To start with,' he began, 'leprosy is still found in one hundred countries around the world, even the United States. More than twelve million have been cured in the last twenty years, but seven hundred thousand new cases are diagnosed each year, including two hundred and seventy last year in the USA.

'Theoretically we can eradicate it. The problem is stigma. Since Biblical times, lepers have been shunned – remember Ben Hur?'

'Well, the chariot race, Dr Santos. Not sure I remember the rest.' Michael gripped the chair, and loosened his collar. It was getting hot.

'Well, some people associate leprosy with dirt, and others still believe leprosy is a punishment from God. This means, in some parts of the world sufferers don't even see a doctor, though treatment is highly effective.'

Dr Santos got up, and went to his desk. He switched on an intercom and asked for coffee, then came back and sat down. 'Where were we? The bacillus Micobacterium Leprae, that Dr Armauer Hansen discovered in 1873 is what causes leprosy. So it's also called "Hansen's Disease."

'Leprosy is very difficult to transmit, and has a long incubation period,' Santos went on. 'Years. No one's sure how it's transmitted. The microbacterium's in the respiratory tract, so it's possible that it's passed through droplets in the air – but that's not proven. But the disease can be spread through prolonged contact, and the most common contact is family. For that reason, many believed leprosy was hereditary, though it's not. Most people, ninety-five percent, have an in-built resistance, so they're immune, even with prolonged contact – but this makes the disease difficult to research... We just don't have all the answers, I'm afraid.'

Michael sat forward.

'What about treatment? I'm afraid I'm abysmally ignorant.'

'That's all right. Just a minute.'

A young woman came in, with a tray holding cups and a pot of coffee. 'Just put it here, Maria, we'll pour – No, Rosana, I'll do it.'

As soon as the cups were handed out, Michael took a long sip. Rich, dark and aromatic. He hadn't realised how dry and tense he'd been. He glanced up at the doctor, then sat back on the soft cushions.

'Thank you,' he said. 'This is all extremely interesting and useful information. And thank you for the coffee.'

'Good.' Santos smiled. 'About being ignorant – so are most people, so don't worry about that. Basically, there are two categories of leprosy. The milder form is tuberculoid. Dry or discoloured skin, loss of sensitivity, particularly to the face, arms or legs, where it can cause enlargement and lesions on the skin. Seventy percent of patients suffer from this form. The more serious form is lepromatous leprosy. This is characterised by large lesions, all over the body. Sometimes it affects the eyes, nose and throat and can lead to blindness, voice change and mutilation of the nose.

'Both forms attack the nervous system. Untreated, it can cause neurological damage – sensory loss in the skin, and muscle weakness. People with long term leprosy often lose parts of their hands and feet, though usually because of absence of sensation, rather than disease.'

'I see,' Michael said. 'And treatment?'

'Treatment is highly effective. We use dapsone, rifampin and clofazimine. A cure takes six to twelve months. Occasionally, it needs repeating. Patients are non-contagious within a few months, but treatment can't reverse damage done before diagnosis.'

'What about my father? Was leprosy treatable in the early fifties?'

'Certainly. I've just been looking at his records.'

Michael nodded. He sat up, and took a long draught of his coffee.

'Your father suffered mild tuberculoid leprosy. Lesions on arms and legs, couple of smaller lesions on face and elsewhere. He also had muscle damage. I expect he had a slight limp.'

Michael nodded again. 'It didn't seem to hurt him.'

'No,they wouldn't. He was given multi-drug therapy. I see the drugs worked for him, were working when he left. He'd have been non-contagious, and if he continued treatment, he'd have been cured.'

Michael shifted in his chair. 'Yes, he continued treatment. But the disease recurred, and he was treated again. I think more than once.'

'Very possibly,' said the doctor. 'Especially with the earlier drugs. Still, he was unfortunate, to repeat.'

'My grandmother mentioned that he was locked up at Fontilles.'

The doctor looked uncomfortable now. 'There's nothing in his records, but it's possible. Even today, the key is immediate isolation and treatment. But attitudes were a lot different in the 1950s. The stigma was much worse, and practitioners tended to impose their will upon patients – well intentioned, but mistaken. Today we know so much more about it not being contagious. And we have better support and counselling.'

'I see.' Michael finished his coffee. 'Thank you, Doctor. But I'd better not keep you any longer.'

Rosana also put down her cup.

Dr Santos stood up and smiled, holding out his hand as they rose after him. He shook hands with Michael. 'Well, I've been very pleased to meet you. Thank you, Rosana, for bringing Miguel-Ángel to visit us. Now, Juan will show you around, and if you'd like to know anything else, I'll be in my office. Be sure to call in on your way back, if anything else occurs.'

'I will. And thank you, again.'

Juan conducted the tour of Fontilles, reciting, 'Sanatorio San Francisco de Borja was founded in 1902 by a Jesuit priest, Father Carlos Ferris, and a lawyer, Joaquin Ballester.' Juan stopped to pick a few leaves up and put them in a bin. 'In the late eighteenth century, leprosy hit the rural villages. This area was badly affected, though no one knew why. Over the years, patients found work to do, and the sanatorium grew into a village.

'The Sanatorio became self-sufficient. A bakery and a carpenter, cobbler and wine presses were set up. Once, Fontilles accommodated three hundred, but we now have sixty residents and one hundred and fifty out-patients. The main work these days is training and research. Doctors and nurses visit from all over the world. Fontilles runs programmes in China, Asia, and Latin America.'

The sanatorium could not have been more different from the picture Michael had had. Like the grounds of a vast country estate, its tree-lined groves were punctuated by small gardens. Tiny alcoves held statues of saints, or distinguished figures linked with Fontilles. Juan reeled off the names as if he knew them all personally.

The main building was a huge quadrangle of three storeys, a tower at each corner. Painted white, with a terracotta tiled roof, of castle-like proportions, it resembled Spanish Paradors Michael had seen on TV.

Inside, a marble-floored lobby was lit by a high, vaulted ceiling; and further on, a sunny courtyard featured a garden and a fountain.

A few people wandered around, others basked in the sunlight that had broken through the clouds. They all looked to be on holiday.

Michael asked Juan why no one looked ill.

'Fontilles is now home to the elderly or infirm, not just leprosy sufferers.' Juan hesitated, then went on. 'I was sorry to hear about your mother and father. I met your father, just before he left. I knew your mother, too. I had great respect for her.'

Michael hesitated, then said, 'Thank you for telling me.'

'Your father's contributions were, of course, greatly appreciated.'

'Sorry?'

'Your father – he was one of the most fervent supporters of Fontilles. His donations must have been thousands of pounds, over the years.'

'I see,' Michael said. 'Yes, I understand what you mean.' He shook Juan's hand again. 'I can't tell you how much I appreciate this.'

On the drive back down the mountain, Michael tried a cool summing up. For years he had known that his father had left Spain to escape incarceration. But far from a medieval dungeon-like place, the sanatorium was warm, cheerful, and clearly dedicated to providing treatment, care and understanding world-wide, and combating ignorance and prejudice.

No villagers had shunned his father. It had been an old priest.

Michael had used Fontilles' cruelty, and family and village rejection, to feed his resentment toward Spain. Much of his life had been wasted.

Everything he'd believed in, everything that had influenced his attitudes, his personality, his being, felt wiped away. Like someone with amnesia, it would be a struggle to discover who he was and where he came from. Most importantly, he now had to view the world without prejudice and partiality. But he felt a profound sense of pointlessness about his life.

'Shall we stop for coffee?' Rosana said.

'If you like.'

She stopped a minute later at a small cafe, went inside, and Michael headed for a shady corner of the terrace. Two boys and a girl played on a slide, their parents sat on the grass. Gentle sunshine filtered through the trees, as the children squealed and shouted.

Sunlight on a half-turned face, dappled branches in the shade... red soil, flushed cheeks... Michael pictured a young man at a window, looking up at the mountains, the sun setting through the smoke of burning leaves, warming the mist along a ravine. His thoughts turned to his childhood when he'd played happily with friends, before he knew about his father's illness. The father of the playing children was about the same age as Michael, and he contrasted the family with his own purposeless life.

He could suddenly find nothing worthwhile to raise his spirits; nothing to look forward to; nothing worth living for.

Rosana returned to the terrace, carrying two cups.

'Was I wrong to press you to go to Fontilles? It wasn't what you imagined, was it? But it's best to know the truth.'

'Sometimes it's easier to build your life on things you believe in.'

'But what if they're false?'

'Yes, even if they're false, it's easier – no, that doesn't make sense. I'll put it another way... As far as I was concerned, I may not have been aware of it, but the past was another country, psychologically – as well as physically... and I suppose I was not ready to visit it.'

'I see. So – where do you go from here?'

'Back to England. Looks like the case is as good as solved.'

'What about last night?' Rosana said, with a glance across at him.

His mobile phone rang, and as if distracted, Michael looked to one side. 'Last night,' he said, 'perhaps I got carried away.'

Rosana stared coldly as he spoke into the phone.

'Jose Luis... What?... Are they sure?... When will they know?... Where are you?... I'm coming over – no, I insist, I'll be there in twenty minutes.'

Michael switched off the phone and turned, as if entirely oblivious to the frustration on Rosanna's face. 'I need a lift to the finca. It's not far. They've found a body. I have to get there right away.'

He stood from the table without glancing at her, and moved towards the parked car. Rosana followed.

On the road to Orba, Michael talked – deliberately, and detachedly – about the latest development. 'This is the final nail in their coffin. It looks as if this is Mrs Harrington – they won't know until tomorrow – so that's it for the Dutchmen – at least for Van Doorn. If they find Mr Harrington, that will wrap things up... though I still don't get it, really. It's been too easy. But, as Jose Luis says, people do some strange and stupid things. I'll have to speak to John and Linda Harrington later on. I'm not looking forward to that – oh, I think it's over there somewhere,' he added, pointing to a track on the left, ahead. 'Yes, you can see the police cars. Turn in here.'

Rosana pulled into the track. Brambles scratched the roof as she negotiated potholes. About seventy-five metres down the track she was confronted by two Guardia Civil officers, and stopped.

'Just drop me here, thanks,' Michael said. 'I can make my own way back.'

He turned to Rosana as if to kiss her cheek – surely she saw he was in no condition to make decisions, let alone a commitment, and that this was for the best – and that he'd spent so long being self contained, ignorant and self deluding, he was no good to her – or to anyone, for that matter, even himself.

But Rosana stared straight ahead in silence, and a kiss could only be patronising and dismissive, so he got out of the car. Rosana crunched the gears, slammed into reverse, swung the car around, and headed back down the track.

Before she'd disappeared, Michael was trying to persuade the officers to let him pass on the strength of his civilian ID card, but it took Jose Luis being called over, to get him through. They walked past the dilapidated finca and continued along a track to a clump of almond trees and a roughly pitched tent. The forensics team in white overalls and latex gloves were busy. Two ambulancemen lifted a stretcher with a black plastic body bag.

'Can I have a look?' asked Michael.

'Sure you want to?' replied Jose Luis. 'She was wrapped in an oil groundsheet, so the body is supposed to be "well preserved", but if you ask me it's been buried a long while. Sure you want to look?'

'I think I need to.'

Jose Luis nodded to the men placing the stretcher on a trolley. One unzipped the front of the bag and pulled the seam apart to reveal remnants of skin over bone, and red earth. The blonde hair was tangled and matted, stuck to one side of the face by a clot of dry black blood. Michael winced. Then he saw the eyes. The soft doe eyes from the photographs were now set cold, staring into infinity.

Michael turned. 'Any sign of Mr Harrington?'

Jose Luis's face was pale. He looked nauseated. 'They're still looking,' he said, 'but there's a huge area to cover. It could take days, unless the suspects help us out. I'm heading back to Alicante now to talk to them.'

'Give me a lift? I need to pick up my things from Parcent.'

Jose Luis parked outside Bar Moll, and Michael asked him to wait.

As he walked past the bar, someone shouted, 'Hey!'

Julio, in overalls and boots splattered with paint and plaster, strode out, reeking of alcohol. 'I've been trying to talk to you. About the house, and the land.' Julio grabbed Michael by the arm.

'You don't come into it.' Michael pushed his hand away.

Blood rose in Julio's cheeks. 'I've been stuck here like a dog, and you turn up after your leper father disappears for fifty years – '

Michael displayed measured calm. 'When and if I decide what to do, I'll discuss my inheritance with your father.'

Julio grabbed Michael by the throat, shoving him against the wall.

Michael's knee slammed into Julio's groin. He screamed and crumpled to the ground.

Jose Luis joined the scene. 'Everything all right?'

'This is my little cousin, Julio.' Michael dusted off his hands. 'Julio, this is Captain Jose Luis Perez of the Guardia Civil. Tell him how you are.'

Julio uttered a long, low groan.

'Good, because I have to dash.'

His grandmother's house was empty. He had his suitcase packed in seconds, and was heading along the hall when Maria Carmen appeared in the doorway. Her eyes moved to the suitcase.

'I've got to get down to Alicante, Grandma. Something's just cropped up. Urgent.'

He kissed her cheek, and moved to one side for her to pass. 'It's business. If anyone asks for me, can you let them know?'

'When are you returning?'

'I'll phone.'

He stepped outside and walked on, not looking back.

On reaching Rosana's house he paused for a second, considering whether he could devise a useful message, then he continued straight on down to Jose Luis's car.

Back at police headquarters, the two Dutchmen were lined up for interviews in separate rooms. Colonel Cardells was strutting outside.

'Still think they're innocent, Fernandez?' he said in the corridor.

'Can I be there when you interview them?'

Cardells hesitated. 'You can sit in... but don't say a word. Ramirez will interpret and if you want to speak, ask first. Understood?'

In the interview room Van Doorn slouched back in his chair, as if nonchalant, but he looked less arrogant than he had earlier.

His solicitor, Erik Mohl, sat up straight beside him, crisp and business-like in cream shirt and paisley tie.

'What's that bastard doing here?' Van Doorn looked at Michael.

'He's here as an observer, nothing more,' said Ramirez.

Mohl nodded approval, and Michael sat down.

The Colonel slammed a photograph onto the table. 'Recognise her?'

Van Doorn glanced quickly at the picture. 'Means nothing to me.'

The Colonel smiled. 'It means you're going down for murder. That's Alison Harrington, and guess where we found her?'

He had Van Doorn's attention now. 'I have no idea.'

'A few metres from the finca in Orba, where you met David Harrington and he gave you ten thousand euros. The finca where we found the bloodstains and your fingerprints. Where is he buried?'

Van Doorn's face displayed anger and fear as he shoved the photograph back across the table and knocked the solicitor's file to the floor. 'Look, I conned Mr Harrington, all right, but I know *nothing* about any murder. I never even met Mrs Harrington.'

'That's your final word?' the Colonel asked, 'You're not going to tell us what you've done with Mr Harrington?'

The solicitor intervened, as if to appear useful. 'My client has denied murdering anybody, Colonel, and unless you've further questions I can really see no point in continuing this interview.'

'So we'll just have to keep digging around the finca until we find Mr Harrington, won't we? Then perhaps your client will talk to us.'

'Can I ask a question?' Michael looked at the Colonel, then Erik Mohl. The Colonel glowered but didn't object, and the solicitor nodded.

'Did Wil know about the money you got from Mr Harrington?'

'I never told him.'

'Could he have found out?'

'It's possible, but he never said anything.'

'Did Wil ever go to the finca alone? I mean, after you met Mr Harrington and he gave you the money?'

Van Doorn turned the possibility over. Suddenly he was interested and keen to talk. 'He could have done. We're not together all the time. He's had plenty of opportunity to go over there without me. What are you thinking? He might have gone there alone, and done them in?'

Mohl had just about caught up, and he interrupted. 'Wait a minute. What are you suggesting? That my, er, client, Hagemans, did this?'

'Of course, I forgot, you represent both suspects?' said Michael.

'Colonel Cardells, I must object to this,' said Mohl. 'Inspector Fernandez is trying to drive a wedge between my clients.'

'I'm sure he's only trying to get to the truth,' the Colonel said. 'Now, shall we talk to Mr Hagemans?'

Between interviews the Colonel pulled Michael to one side.

'I'm not sure what you're up to here, Fernandez. Of course they'll blame each other, but where will that lead us?'

'To the truth perhaps,' said Michael. 'Or not.'

Hagemans was nervous, and almost as straight-backed as the solicitor. The photograph of Mrs Harrington produced horror on his face. He once again pleaded whimpering ignorance.

This time, the Colonel picked up Michael's lead.

'Mr Van Doorn says you could have found out about the money and gone back to the finca. Perhaps you met Mr Harrington again? And you met Mrs Harrington, as well? We think you had an argument, and you killed them both.'

Mohl folded his arms, noting a hesitant reaction.

'An argument is no reason to kill people,' Hagemans said. After another second of hesitation, he went on – suddenly switching from timid and twitchy to angry and resolute, showing a side to his character previously hidden. He leaned forward, staring coldly at the Colonel. 'I see what Johan's trying. It won't work. He took the money from Harrington, not me. He had a motive to kill the Harringtons.'

'Can you account for your movements over the last two weeks?'

'What do you mean?'

'Well, you say you never went back to the finca, so perhaps you can prove it by telling us everywhere you've been?'

'How the hell can I remember where I've been the last two weeks?'

'I'm sure you can if you try, Mr Hagemans, and we'll be asking your friend to do the same. We'll leave you to think about it.'

The Colonel returned to his office, with Jose Luis, Ramirez and Michael in tow. 'Well, gentlemen, I'm not sure where that takes us, except that now they're blaming each other. I guess we'll have to charge them both with murder, then see if one squeals and gives us something against the other. In the meantime, they'll stew. Perhaps we'll know more after the post mortem, and forensics have finished. And we'll just keep digging at the finca until Harrington turns up. I'm sure he's buried round there somewhere. Anyway, thank you for your help, Michael. I expect you'll soon be on your way back home?'

'Oh, not for a while. As you say, there's the post mortem and forensics. Do John and Linda Harrington know about the body yet?'

'I was hoping you'd handle that,' the Colonel said, with a cool raising of an eyebrow. 'That's what you're here for, isn't it, liasing with the family, that sort of thing? Anyway,' he said, 'it's all coming to a conclusion, and when we find Mr Harrington's body it'll wrap things up nicely.'

The Colonel was a smug, detached sort of a bastard.

'Not so much for the Harringtons,' Michael said

'No... well, perhaps not, but at least we've got the culprits.'

'You're sure of that, Colonel?'

The Colonel bristled. 'Of course. What more do you want?'

Michael hesitated, but set his shoulders and pressed on. 'Bloodstains from Mr and Mrs Harrington were found in the finca, but there were only a couple of sets of their fingerprints. If the Dutchmen held the Harringtons, it certainly wasn't at the finca. So where was it?' Michael raced on. 'And if the Harringtons weren't abducted,' he said, 'but were killed more recently for their money – where were they hiding? Why? And what happened to that money? Harrington had a lot more than those ten thousand euros. Hagemans is not as stupid as he first appears. He may have known about Harrington meeting Van Doorn, and later phoned, saying he'd hand over the documents at the finca. So then he met Harrington, and his wife, or... and – there are just too many loose ends.'

The Colonel exploded. 'Don't muddy the waters now, Fernandez. This isn't England, where you have to cross all the T's and dot all the I's in case some judge throws the case out on a technicality. We've got all the evidence we need. In fact, I don't want you here again. Your involvement is at an end. You can speak to the Harringtons, then I suggest you get back to England.'

Michael opened his mouth to protest, but the Colonel cut him off.

'Goodbye, Inspector Fernandez. Thank you for your help. You can leave your ID card at the desk on your way out.'

The meeting with John and Linda Harrington went as expected.

He broke the news about the body, leading them to fear the worst about David. John was indifferent, or pretended to be (though he reddened, shivered, and got his handkerchief out to attend to a suddenly runny nose), to anything other than how long they should extend their visit to Spain. Linda was tearful, genuinely distressed. Even so, she agreed to identify Alison's body when John declined the responsibility, with another shiver, on the grounds that she was not his blood relative.

Michael made no mention of his doubts about the two suspects, allowing John and Linda the scant comfort of thinking the culprits had been caught.

Just after ten, Michael arrived back at his hotel and returned the phone call from Chief Superintendent Bowater.

'I hear you've been upsetting the Colonel again.'

Michael explained his reservations about the case, and found the Chief Super surprisingly sympathetic.

'All the same, Michael, I don't see what more you can do. And the Colonel's made it clear that he wants you off the case.'

'I'll just hang around for a while all the same, if that's okay with you. I'll take leave, if you'd prefer it that way. I want to see what the post mortem turns up, and if forensics can shed any light.'

'Stay on for a bit, then. No need to take any leave, but be careful. And if nothing occurs in the next few days, you'd better think about coming home.'

A couple of brandies failed to bring sleep. He tried to concentrate on the loose ends of the case but his mind drifted to Fontilles, and his grandmother's story. Had his father *ever* hated Spain? What about Maria Carmen, Uncle Pepito, Pedro?... The house, and the land?

He drifted back to the rooftop terrace, where he'd marvelled at the setting, with Rosana. Couldn't build a life on a kiss. Or... his senses when they touched... Drowsy thoughts gave way to the perpetually deep, dark dreams he could never clearly recall.

Chapter Eleven

Next morning, Michael killed time around the hotel, since it was too early to contact Jose Luis to see if there'd been any further developments. He strolled to a kiosk where he bought the Daily Telegraph, and found a small article on page four:

FEARS GROW FOR COUPLE MISSING IN SPAIN

Spanish police have discovered a body believed to be that of Alison Harrington, missing in the Alicante province of Spain for over four months.

Mrs Harrington and her husband David, from Nottingham, disappeared in January this year, failing to return from a trip to buy a home on the Costa Blanca. The body was found buried near a remote farmhouse on the outskirts of Orba. It had been the focus for police inquiries after the arrest last week of two men believed to be involved in property fraud. Mr Harrington is still missing and police are continuing to search the land near the farmhouse.

British Detective, Inspector Michael Fernandez from Nottingham CID, has been helping Spanish police with their search. He was unavailable for comment last night. Last year a British couple were murdered in the same area after travelling to Spain to look for a retirement home.

Back at the hotel, there was a message from the Daily Mail's reporter, another from a reporter for The Sun. He ignored both. He'd hoped for word from Jose Luis, and hoped there might be a message of some sort from Rosana. He was disappointed on both counts.

By six that evening he could wait no longer, and called Jose Luis.

'I've got some news, but I can't talk to you now,' said the Spanish detective in hushed tones. 'I'll call you back in an hour.'

For ninety minutes Michael stayed by the phone, wondering what further twists had emerged.

Perhaps they'd found David Harrington, or his body. Perhaps the Dutchmen had confessed. Perhaps the real killers had been found.

The news when it came was devastating.

Jose Luis gabbled excitedly, 'The post mortem confirms the body is Mrs Harrington. Killed several weeks ago, hard to be definitive about when she was killed, because she was protected by the oilskin. Killed by blows to the head – very deep gash on the back of the head. And,' Jose Luis rushed on. 'Listen to this. We *found the murder weapon*. A rusty old mattock, about eighty metres from the body. It has bloodstains, and we lifted prints from the stave – and guess what? We've matched them to the Dutchman.'

'*Jesus*. Looks like curtains for Van Doorn, then.'

'No, not Van Doorn, Hagemans. We lifted Hagemans' prints. Looks like your hunch was right.'

'What hunch?'

'You suggested he found out about the money Harrington gave Van Doorn. We think Hagemans tried for more and ended up killing them both. That explains why we can't find the rest of the money.'

'You still haven't found David Harrington?'

'No. We scoured every inch around the finca, but there's no sign.'

'So what happens now?'

'The Colonel plans to charge them both with murder tonight. He might reduce the charge for Van Doorn if he comes clean, but if not he'll try to make the murder charge stick for both of them. He's hoping one of them will crack and tell us where Mr Harrington is – or we'll have to go over the whole property. Oh, he's arranged a press conference for tomorrow morning.'

'Does he want me there?'

'What do you think, Michael? He's speaking to your Chief Superintendent tonight. He'll say there's no need for you to be there. He will acknowledge your assistance at the press briefing, but say there is no further need for your involvement. John and Linda Harrington have been invited, and Timothy Middleton will support them. Of course, he'll promise to keep searching for Mr Harrington for as long as it takes, but he'll hint that Harrington's presumed dead and the case is good as closed.'

'What do you think, Jose Luis?'

'Look Michael, I've tried to help as much as I can, but we've reached the end of the road. Even you will admit the evidence is overwhelming.'

'I guess so,' said Michael without conviction.

'What will you do now?'

'Go straight back to England. Look Jose Luis, thanks for your help. I mean it. I know we haven't always seen eye to eye, but I appreciate you've gone out on a limb for me a couple of times. I hope it all works out for you, and I hope I haven't marred your record too much with the Colonel.'

'Don't worry about me, Michael. The Colonel's just happy to have wrapped the case up. It's been good to work with you, and if you ever come back to this part of Spain, be sure to look me up.'

'That's kind of you, Jose Luis, but I doubt I'll be coming back.'

The first flight to East Midlands was on Sunday afternoon.

Today was Friday. For a moment he thought of spending Saturday in Alicante – after all, he'd hardly seen anything of the place, but... In the end, he made a call.

'Oh Miguel-Ángel, I'm so glad. Are you coming home?'

'I'm coming to Parcent, Grandma, but the case is over. I'm booked on a flight to Britain on Sunday afternoon. I thought I'd come up in the morning and stay the night. I need to talk to you and Pepito.'

'Of course. I just wish you could stay a bit longer.'

'Grandma, I have to get back to work. We'll talk in the morning.'

'Are you going to talk to Rosana? She asked about you.'

'I'll be back as soon as I can.'

The hotel booked him a hire car, to be delivered early on Saturday and returned to El Altet airport on Sunday afternoon. He rose early, breakfasted on the terrace, and checked out of the hotel with all his belongings. It was a warm spring day with only a few puffy clouds in the clear blue sky. The sun had gradually risen earlier and higher during his stay, the shade dwindling in the middle of the day.

The drive north took him once again past the distant skyscrapers of Benidorm. He never did get to visit the package tour centre of the universe, but somehow he wasn't bothered. He left the A7 at Benissa and followed the twisting road through Senija and the one-way chicken run in Lliber. Emerging into the flat bed of the Jalon valley, he glimpsed the church tower of Parcent and wondered if this was the last time he'd see it.

Uncle Pepito and Maria Carmen were waiting outside on the terrace. They greeted him with smiles but anxiety on their faces as he walked through. After sitting down, Michael decided to skip formalities.

'Grandma, Uncle Pepito, I've thought about what I should do. I understand the house is worth a sizeable sum for foreign buyers, but I don't want to sell. I would like to keep it, and visit from time to time. It needs repairs, and furnishing, I know, and I'd be grateful if Uncle Pepito could organise that work?'

Pepito nodded acceptance.

'As I understand it, this house passed to my father and Pepito when my grandfather died, and my father's share belongs to me. Of course you, Grandma, must live here. As for the land, I understand that nothing can be disposed of unless Pepito and I are in agreement. I'm happy to let Pepito decide.' Michael looked at Pepito. 'If you ever need it, you know you can sell some or all of the land. It's up to you.'

Pepito burst out, 'I'll never sell anything.'

'That's what I wanted to hear,' replied Michael. 'And I want Pedro to keep working the land and continue taking income from it. My share is his, for the time being at least.'

Pepito stepped forward suddenly, and clasped Michael in a hug.

Maria Carmen looked up from her weathered wicker chair. She lifted her gold-rimmed spectacles as Michael bent at her side.

'Grandma,I thought you would be happy with my decision.'

'I just wish you'd stay, my Miguel-Ángel.' She touched his hand softly. 'What do you have to go back to, in England?'

He wanted to say, I don't want to let anyone down, but I have to take possession of this new life at my own pace. He wanted to explain his feelings about his father, and Fontilles, the village, and the land. But words could not express the way he felt and, to his dismay, he simply maintained his steadfastness, knowing the pain it caused.

'Grandma, I've made up my mind. There are reasons.'

Silence fell, finally interrupted by Pepito. 'It's the people's dinner tonight. Everyone in the village. Will you come?'

He began to decline, but his grandmother's face made him wilt.

He wasn't sure why, or what he was going to say, but he decided to call at Rosana's house – and did so, only to discover she was working that morning at the insurance office in Jalon. He greeted the news with what he thought was relief, but turned out to be disappointment.

On the spur of the moment, he drove to Jalon.

The roadside verges, he noticed as he approached the bridge into town, were littered with abandoned cars.

Michael queued to cross the one-way bridge, but it was delayed by cars trying to get in and out of an unofficial car park on the far side. The weekly rastro market was in full swing.

Crawling along the riverside road he passed almost a kilometre of rickety tables and blankets set out on dusty ground.

Between trees that fringed the dried-up riverbed, ladies' underwear fluttered over cracked clay urns, tarnished brass, records, tables, chairs. The sound of a Venezuelan nose flute wafted through his open car window, accompanied by an aroma of hot dogs and fried onions and the sweet scent of churros sizzling in hot oil. The fish and chip shop was doing a roaring trade, and the Brits looked to be out in force, along with Dutch, Germans, and a few Spaniards.

A row of parked coaches slowed his progress, and just as he'd cleared the blockage a yellow-clad workman turned his table tennis bat from "go" to "stop." A construction crew had decided Saturday morning was the ideal time to lay the tarmac of a roundabout.

He waited at the head of the queue for ten minutes, watching the confusion of the market. A local policeman chatted to the yellow overalls, and pulled on a cigarette.

A Land Rover drove out of a rough patch of land, and Michael pulled in. As he stepped out of the car, cement dust puffed beneath his feet and covered him in fine white powder. By the time he neared the insurance office he was sticky, hot, smeared with half-set cement, and out of breath, having jogged 100 metres, concerned that it was approaching one o'clock. He pushed open the glass door and marched up to the counter.

Rosana sat talking on the telephone and tapping a computer keyboard. She glanced up when he came in, but returned to the screen without changing her expression.

Her soft white silk blouse hung loosely round her waist and shoulders, and her dark wavy hair brushed gently against her cheeks like – well, like a hairstyle on the cover of a magazine.

At the end of her call, she said, 'Do you want travel, health, or life?'

'Lunch.'

'I'm sorry, Michael, I don't feel like lunch today.'

'Do you recommend the local fish and chips? I'll get some.'

'No... but there's a little tapas bar... just around the corner.'

Bar Rull nestled nearby in the corner of a small square, and their seats were in the shade of a billowing jacaranda tree. Rosana ordered the tapas, which were quickly served.

As the condensation on a bottle of chilled rosado wine turned to droplets, Michael explained that the case was as good as over and he was booked to return to England tomorrow. He outlined his decision about the house and the land, and looked for signs of approval.

'But am I telling you something you already know?'

'Not at all,' replied Rosana with a nod. 'I'm just not sure why you're bothering to tell me any of it.'

If that was meant to sound dismissive, it hit the mark. 'I just thought you deserved an explanation, Rosana, that's all.'

'An explanation? You're a free agent. You don't have to justify yourself. So we met and – well, nothing. An emotional episode. As you said the other day, perhaps we got carried away. We're adults, we don't have to make excuses. Let's leave it that.'

'Yes...' Michael almost said, *that's fine by me*, but somehow he did not want that. It was just... that he couldn't think straight. And... he didn't like being rejected.

'This is how you really feel?' he asked, after a short pause.

'What do you care how I *really feel*? You've made up your mind, you're returning to England. Go home. It's clear I don't figure in your plans, so, as I said, why should you care about my feelings?'

'No, but as I said, I'll be coming back. That's why I asked Pepito to do some work on the old house.'

'Well, jolly good for you, *Michael*. A nice little holiday home for two weeks a year. See the old relatives, and admire your quaint little olives and oranges. You can take off your tie, and flap about in a straw hat. Won't that be fun? Only please, do not ever look *me* up.'

She turned, crossed her arms and raised her chin.

'Look here, Rosana, what do you expect of me? Two weeks ago I'd never set foot in this country. I never even knew my family here.'

Rosana swung round.

'And how did you reach the age of almost forty or whatever, without knowing your family?'

'You know why.'

'No, I do not.'

'Because of my father.'

Rosana's eyes narrowed, her voice hardened.

'So your father was a leper. But he wasn't rejected by his village as you believed, but by a stupid, nasty old priest. And he wasn't incarcerated in a dungeon. He chose to leave Spain, for his own reasons. Just like you.'

'What do you mean?'

'Face it, what happened to your father has been an excuse to deny your Spanish ancestry. What was it, really? Did kids pick on you because you have latin looks and a funny name? Is that why you call yourself Michael? Why you act and dress like some sort of superior English gentleman and look down your nose at everyone? Why did you reject your father? – not because of leprosy, but because he had made you half-Spanish.'

Michael sat up. 'Perhaps you have a point. But this is not the time or place. I just wanted to let you know my plans. Let's leave now.'

Rosana hesitated, then placed a hand on his. 'I'm sorry, Michael... I just wanted to get you to face a few misconceptions, and change – '

'I know, but let's leave it, Rosana. I can make up my own mind.'

Outside Maria Carmen's house, tables and chairs took up most of the street, and food was being passed out from every doorway, when

Michael came downstairs. Flat coca breads laden with peas, tomato paste or anchovies, were being torn apart by hand. Spicy sausages sizzled on a gas-fired barbecue, cold tortillas were carried out in heavy pans, and warm pasties of spinach and tuna were piled high on trays alongside mountains of bread, plate-loads of sliced serrano ham and chunks of hard cheese. Baskets of fruit lay in waiting, jugs of wine shot from one end of the table to the other. The village band played cheerful music that wafted through the warm night air.

He was late, tired and unenthusiastic, having spent the afternoon brooding in his room, and he wanted a quiet night before his early departure in the morning... but the hubbub from the street reminded him of expectations.

His emergence from the house seemed to go largely unnoticed, as all continued talking – though within seconds Maria Carmen had made space, Pepito thrust red wine into his hand, a plate arrived piled high, and cousin Pedro presented him a grin and a slap on the back.

Rosana, with her family further down the street, looked up briefly but gave only a cursory nod. Closer by, Julio offered a glare.

Everyone else looked happy – possibly too happy to be convincing. But eating, drinking, chatting with family and friends, they seemed to belong; from old people, revered by their youngers, to small children encouraged to join in the festivities. With the exception of Julio, warm greetings began to come from everyone around the table. This was, probably, friendship and fellowship beyond anything before in his life... like a celebration of life itself. A part of him wished he did belong here.

At one in the morning, the party began to wind down. The band retired, and revellers sauntered home through the narrow streets. A rocket lit the sky, sending a boom around the mountains. Michael used this as his excuse to retreat. Rosana had already left.

He should have made an effort to circulate in her direction – if only to pay his respects to her mother and grandmother – but the opportunity had passed.

Sleep evaded him. The noise from the street below gradually faded to silence, punctuated by occasional bursts of conversation or laughter.

Finally, he drifted into a vague dream, with images and scenes flashing like disjointed film clips. A loud crash disturbed the dream, followed by a thud and the tinkling of glass. He blinked, but saw only darkness. He turned on the lamp at his bedside, swept back the bed clothes, blinked again, and looked around the room. The windowpane at the side of the wardrobe was shattered. Splinters were spread over the bedside rug, and the surrounding wooden floor. A rock the size of his fist rested at the foot of the door, wrapped in white paper, tied with a knot of string. He reached for his shoes, shook them to release a few small splinters of glass, and slid them on. He crunched over more glass to reach the rock, and remove the paper. Even looking at it upside-down, the single word written in capitals with a heavy, black felt-tip pen was easy to decipher – LEPER.

He left early next morning, having swept the bedroom floor as best he could. He said his farewells to Maria Carmen, mentioning the rock but not the note. He kissed his grandmother on both cheeks, then picked up his case and stepped out of the door. He hated goodbyes, and there was no point in prolonging this one.

Most of the village was asleep, the streets silent, as he wound his way down to his parked car.

The sky was a clear sapphire blue, like most of the mornings since his arrival in Spain, and the temperature was rising. He walked in shade where he could, and looked up now and again at the swallows weaving in and out of rooftops. A cock crowed as the church bell rang out a 9.30 chime. Strings of plastic bunting fluttered as he passed along the painted road outside the town hall, beneath an ancient set of fairy lights, now dimmed, that formed the words, "Bones Festes."

He paused to look back, and raised his eyes to the white church tower, silhouetted against blue. That image could haunt his dreams, and he wondered if he'd ever see it again.

Slowly, he continued his walk to where his car was parked near a pollarded maple, one of twelve in front of the coopertiva bar. In the circle of dark shade under the tree, he made out a figure leaning against the trunk. He didn't need to look twice, to know who it was.

'You weren't going to leave without saying goodbye?'

Once again she confronted him, trying to get him to reflect on his behaviour. Why must she do this? Did she think she could flick a switch? Why couldn't she simply leave him alone to run his own life the way he wanted, instead of acting like an Auntie Nelly alter ego?

Defence strategy. Answer a question with a question.

'Would you care if I did?'

'Yes, I would.'

'What?'

'I would have cared, if you hadn't said goodbye.'

He walked up to her. 'Okay, I'll say goodbye.'

'Oh, this is stupid. I couldn't let you leave without saying goodbye. I know I've pushed you – but I never meant to hurt you.'

'You're not going to ask me to stay, are you?'

'Would there be any point?'

'No.'

'Then I won't.'

Michael was almost disappointed. Almost.

'Rosana, you know I can't stay. I don't belong here.'

'I said I wasn't asking you.'

'I know, but I wanted you to understand.'

'It's all right. I do understand.'

'We're still friends, then?'

'Always.' She leaned up and kissed him softly on the lips.

He moved back, resisting the temptation to pull her in.

'Would you like me to come to the airport, to see you off?'

'It's kind of you, but I hate protracted goodbyes. I'm glad you came, and glad we're still friends. Let's leave it at that, for now, and I'll keep in touch.'

'I'd like that.'

Michael glanced in the rear view mirror and returned Rosana's waves until he reached the junction at the edge of the village. He looked for a smile from her, but didn't see one.

The afternoon ValuJet flight to East Midlands was only three-quarters full and Michael found a window seat with no one at his side. Someone on the in-bound flight had left a Daily Mail in the pocket in front of him, and he browsed the pages as the plane taxied. It was an abrupt reintroduction to England and English politics.

The front page was dominated by: BROWN TAX. Page two proclaimed RECORD VIOLENT CRIME. The Prime Minister warranted only page four with: SPIN SPINS OUT OF CONTROL AGAIN.

By the time he reached page six the plane was beginning to level off. Michael felt his eyes grow heavy. His head slumped to his chest.

The newspaper fell to his lap and he briefly awakened. He was about to return the paper to the pocket when page six caught his eye: SPANISH POLICE CHARGE COSTA MURDERERS.

Three full columns spelled out the case against Hagemans and Van Doorn, and reported the continuing search for David Harrington. Photographs of David and Alison appeared beneath the headline.

Lower down the page, there was an interview with John Harrington – announcing his return to Britain, and full of vitriol about Spain and the Spanish police, who'd refused to investigate the case for so long, although they had their good points compared to the British police. No mention of Michael Fernandez, thank God. At least he'd be spared Ironic Celebrity Status when he got back to the office.

According to John Harrington, it wasn't safe to buy a house in the Costa Blanca because you would probably get murdered in the process of looking.

The story was a God-send to the feature writers, always on the lookout for easy copy to fill the inside pages.

Page seven reported the results of a hastily conducted survey of Brits in the Costa Blanca, complete with photographs of the eager participants under the banner: WOULD YOU BUY A HOUSE IN THE COSTA BLANCA? Views ranged from: 'It's shocking, it would definitely put me off buying a house here,' to: 'We love it here and it's much safer than in England.' Michael folded the paper and returned it to the pocket in front.

For a moment he thought about Hagemans and Van Doorn sweating it out in Alicante prison and awaiting their trial.

At least the villains had been apprehended. As for the newspapers, it was already yesterday's story and he doubted there would be much more coverage. Unless, of course, David Harrington was found.

Chapter Twelve

A charcoal grey sky and heavy rain greeted Michael's arrival at East Midlands airport. After Spain, he almost loved it. The colours were drab and dismal, but there was freshness in the air and a smell of damp earth as he descended from the plane. Even the taxi driver's predictable, half-hearted, and enormously boring rant about asylum-seekers and the health service made him want to laugh – or would have, if he had the energy.

He climbed the steps of the small apartment block where he owned a flat and had to think for a second, to remember the entry code for the security system. A patch of fresh graffiti was posted at the side of the door – a multi-coloured tag that must have taken at least twenty minutes to complete. Scorch marks at the foot of the metal door suggested someone had set a small fire, as if the vandals had needed to keep warm. He unlocked the box and collected his post – mostly unsolicited brochures, and bills – and climbed the stairs to his front door. Inside, the room was cold and uninviting, illuminated by the phosphorescent glow of street lamps outside the window. It didn't look much better with the lights on, but he dropped his case, removed his soggy jacket, and kicked off his shoes before slumping, completely relaxed, into the leather recliner in front of the lifeless television. Within five minutes he was asleep.

He woke just before seven, and the idea of getting back to work was suddenly exciting.

He showered and shaved, noticing a bit of a tan. An image of his father flashed across the mirror. It made him think of the ribbing he was likely to face when he re-entered the tight-knit domain of the official Criminal Investigation Division jokers.

In fact, when he went in, the jibes were gentle and good-natured, and he took them without retort. His desk was surprisingly clear apart from memos, bulletins, and 'The Job' – the police magazine. A yellow post-it note attached to the phone said: 'Please see the Chief Super.'

Penny Edwardes seemed to turn slightly pink when he entered the outer office, and even to slightly suppress her usual frivolity.

'Welcome back, Michael. Chief Super's waiting. Go right in.'

Michael tapped on the door and stepped inside, to a smell of paint and wallpaper paste. He stumbled on the new beige carpet. The desk was the same, but in a different position, and a new coffee table with couch seating occupied the corner where a bookcase had stood. Everything else was pretty much the same, including the family photos and the bravery award.

'Welcome back, Michael, take a seat.' Bowater gestured towards the chair by the desk. This was not going to be a coffee table chat. He was in full uniform with three shiny crowns attached to the epaulettes of his jacket and a row of coloured ribbons sewn above the breast pocket. His peaked cap with chequered band rested on a pair of brown leather gloves on the corner of the desk. Michael sat down and crossed his legs.

'Been a few changes since you left. What do you think?' Bowater scanned the new décor.

'Very nice. Glad the budget stretched to it.'

'Just thought you ought to see this – it arrived yesterday by fax.'

He handed a sheet of white paper to Michael, who spotted the crest of the Guardia Civil.

'It's from Colonel Cardells. You'll understand better than me, but it's clear he's grateful for your help in solving the case. Says something about tact and diplomacy, doesn't it? Anyway, I've passed a copy to the Chief Constable. Thought he ought to know. What do you say?'

'Just doing my job, sir.'

'You're too modest, Michael. I know you were thrust into a potentially tricky situation over there. You handled it very well. Pity about Mrs Harrington, but at least they got to the bottom of it. Things would have been much more difficult if they hadn't arrested the killers. It's just a shame they haven't found Mr Harrington yet. What do you think?'

'They might never find him.'

'What, they've hidden him better than they hid his wife?'

'He's certainly well hidden, that's for sure.'

'What about the two Dutchmen, do you think they'll go down?'

'All the evidence points that way.'

'But you're not so sure?' Bowater frowned slightly.

'There's just something not quite right. Oh, the evidence is pretty overwhelming, but there are still too many loose ends.'

'That's typical of you Michael, always want things neat and tidy. I thought you'd realise by now that life isn't like that where the criminal fraternity is concerned. Anyway, it's all done and dusted and it's good to have you back. We've got a new assignment for you.'

Michael straightened, curiosity mixed with suspicion.

'Don't look so worried, Michael, we're not sending you back to Spain. A new team's being set up as part of the Community Safety Partnership, to tackle youth crime and anti-social behaviour. Vandalism, graffiti, yobbism, truanting, glue sniffing, that sort of stuff. You see, the Council's research boffins have been talking to Youth Offending, and they reckon there are twenty to thirty young yobs, "prominent nominals" I think they call them, the key players responsible for most of the trouble. Council elections are next year and the politicians know this kind of crime is top of the voters' concerns, hence the new team. What do you think?'

Michael tried not to let his scepticism show. 'What is this team supposed to do?'

'Well, everyone says the right hand doesn't know what the left is doing. You know, we catch 'em, the Courts let 'em go, or refer them to Social Services, then we catch 'em again. It's a merry-go-round, and the little buggers know it. So this new team, did I tell you it's called "The Frequent Young Offenders Forum"? will bring all the agencies together to co-ordinate their efforts.'

Michael cringed at "co-ordinate," an excuse to swap stories, discuss strategies and argue over responsibility. A recipe for inertia.

'Who exactly will be involved?' he asked.

'Just about everyone – the police, that new woman the council have just appointed as Community Safety Officer, social services, magistrates, probation staff, housing associations, and environmental services, education welfare officers – the whole shooting match.'

Such as endless hours in fruitless meetings, piles of paper passing backwards and forwards, pointless debates about supporting young people rather than punishing them. He'd need excuses for not being able to get to meetings. He'd send a sergeant or a constable instead. This was not criminal investigation, but an exercise in petty politics designed to show that everyone was pulling together, when they were going in opposite directions. It would look good in the Force's Annual Report, and in the politicians' election literature, but the yobs would still be creating havoc out on the streets.

'And what's my role?' Michael tried to sound interested.

'You're in charge, Michael. You will be Chairman – or should I say "Chair" – of the Forum. You'll report directly to the Community Safety Partnership, through me of course. And, as Chairman – sorry "Chair" – of the Partnership, the Council's Chief Executive will be taking a personal interest. You've met Colin Deakin, I think.'

'I have.'

Ruthless, self-seeking egomaniac who'd stop at nothing to please his political masters, since his knighthood depended on it.

'It's a great opportunity, Michael, and very high profile. This is the future of crime reduction. Catch them young, divert them from crime, and steer them towards more productive forms of recreation.'

Michael recognised the words, from the latest Home Office research.

'Any questions?' Bowater asked.

Michael thought for a moment.

'Good,' said Bowater, 'I know you'll make a good job of this. I have every confidence in you. Penny's got all the details, and you'll find a few dates pencilled in your diary already. I have to dash now – I'm standing in for the Chief Constable at an award ceremony for cadets. Keep me posted, and remember this is very high priority. We need results, and fast.'

Penny handed him a pile of papers and files, topped by a glossy 100 page document: Home Office Crime Reduction Manual, Supplement 23 - New Strategies for Tackling Youth Crime and Disorder.

The enthusiasm he'd felt at returning to work evaporated.

Catching murderers, robbers, rapists, and thieves was what he did best, not heading up a talking shop to deal with a few petty yobs.

Worse was to come.

A meeting had been arranged with Colin Deakin and Adrienne Forrester, the Community Safety Officer, for six o'clock that evening.

There would be a presentation to councillors on Thursday night, and weekly meetings of the Frequent Young Offenders Forum had been scheduled for every Wednesday morning. There was a file on each of 23 named young offenders, with patchy details from all agencies involved. None of it amounted to a solid case against anyone.

He tired of the paper in half an hour, and did not read beyond the executive summary of the Home Office blurb.

He leant back in his chair, laced his fingers behind his head, and gazed from the window across the roof of the nearby shopping centre, glistening in the rain.

Traffic crawled along the Broadway, being overtaken by empty buses cruising along the bus priority lane.

He could make out St. Martin's church spire, blurred by drizzle and merging with the drab, cold dark clouds. He snapped forward in his chair and re-shuffled the files on his desk.

At the meeting with the Council Chief Executive Deakin remained three minutes, after which caramel-complexioned, sleek-haired Adrienne Forrester, Community Safety Officer, arranged and re-arranged her legs while throwing words like 'cycles of deprivation' and 'latent potential' round the room.

The first hour of the first meeting of the Frequent Young Offenders Forum was spent pouring coffee for late arrivals amid jokes slotted into arguments between agencies, and refusals to divulge confidential information.

Thursday night's presentation in the Council Chamber was a slick affair, though only half the councillors had bothered to put in an appearance. Deakin and Ms Forrester put on polished performances, backed by a Powerpoint slide show with elaborate graphics full of bar charts, statistics and key phrases. The word 'partnership' was repeated ad nauseum.

Michael was introduced, from the background.

As he left the Town Hall, a uniformed attendant wished him goodnight. He turned to respond, and a notice board caught his eye.

Amongst the clutter of department names and direction arrows something stood out: PRINTING DEPARTMENT, ROOM 317.

'Who's in charge of Printing these days?'

'That's Mr Brooks,' the attendant replied. 'Alan Brooks.'

'Has he been here long?'

'Long as I can remember. He took over when Mr Harrington left. Have you heard about him? He went to Spain to look for a house and now they say he's dead.'

'Yes, I read about it.'

When he arrived next morning, the Printing Department was not what Michael expected. No darkroom, with metal plates clanking around drums, and rollers spreading ink. Instead, a pair of giant Xerox Docutecs almost five metres long stood in tandem, each with its own computer console. They purred quietly, spitting out printed pages. A machine in the far corner eschewed paper at a slower pace, in colour.

'It's all changed since Harrington was here,' said Alan Brooks with pride. 'We're all digital, directly linked through the Council's Wide Area Network, and to the Graphic Studio upstairs. Our work all comes straight down the line. We farm out the wet printing to specialist companies. We just couldn't compete, with our old fashioned presses. Now we concentrate on short-run work – rapid turn-round, straight to the post room and out.'

'Very impressive,' Michael said.

'Anyway, you didn't come here to talk to me about printing, did you? Let's go into the office.'

The small glazed cabin in the corner of the printroom mirrored the high-tech appearance of the print operation. The only exception was the notice board, littered with bulletins, fire drill procedures, a leave chart, bits of paper and photographs, mostly curling at the edges and gathering dust.

Alan Brooks adjusted the blind to deflect the sun, and sat down behind the gleaming desk. He removed thick-lensed glasses and rubbed his eyes. Michael took a seat on the other side of the desk.

'You were out in Spain, weren't you? Do you really think that David is dead?' asked Brooks, now fiddling with his bushy brown eyebrows as if to straighten them. 'That's what's the papers claim.'

'The evidence seems to point that way,' replied Michael. 'Though we can't be sure. I'm afraid we won't be, until we find him or his body. The Spanish police are still looking. Can you just tell me, what was he like, when he worked here?'

'As a person or as a boss?'

'Both.'

'As a boss he was very pleasant, perhaps even – too pleasant. He hated confrontation. He was from the old school, in terms of printing. There was nothing he didn't know about the insides of a Heidelberg print press. They're the Rolls Royce of small presses, you know. We had three, about ten years old but good for another ten. Although he was the manager, he was never happier than when he was on the machines, and if anything went wrong, more often than not he'd roll his sleeves up and fix it. I imagine that's why he resisted the latest digital equipment for so long. Oh, he could run the machines all right, but if anything goes wrong – and it does – you have to call out an engineer and wait. I think it was like losing control to David, you just punch a few buttons and the computer does the rest. A lot of the traditional skills disappear with digital machines. Camera work, plate making, ink mixing, fine tuning the machines, it's all defunct.'

'You said he hated confrontation?'

'Yes. Well, you see – David worked his way up from the shop floor, so to speak. He was never really cut out for management. He was a good organiser, but he'd never put the staff under pressure. He hated having to say no. Some of the staff knew it and took advantage. Not in a big way, but if you know your way round a print workshop there are all sorts of dodges to get out of doing some of the – let's say – less interesting work. David knew them all, but still he let some of the staff get away with it. You'd think the staff would respect him for it, but it doesn't work that way.'

'Were you surprised when he took the offer of redundancy?'

'I'll say. Don't get me wrong, I wasn't unhappy when he left. Not because I didn't like him, I did, but it gave me the opportunity for promotion. And it gave the Department a chance to modernise, which might never have happened under David.'

'So why were you so surprised?'

'Well, that he could afford it, that's all. Okay, he got a nice redundancy package, but no pension. He was just forty-eight, you see, and under the Local Government Pension Scheme, if you're redundant before fifty, you don't get your pension until sixty. That's a long wait, unless you have a job, or plenty of savings. I was surprised he didn't hang on for a couple of years, then look for redundancy. That's the deal everyone's looking for. Early retirement, redundancy package, lump sum and immediate pension.'

Michael looked at the frayed cuffs of Brooks's pin-striped shirt. His greying hair and moustache suggested mid-forties, and Michael wondered if he was working towards his own early retirement.

'Did he have plenty of savings, do you think?'

Brooks scratched his chin, and paused a moment. 'Never given it much thought... He was careful. Not tight, just careful. But he had good suits, and did like expensive shoes.'

Michael's ears pricked.

'What do you mean by expensive shoes?'

'I don't know, exactly. Leather brogues, that kind of thing. Handmade, I think. A bit old fashioned for my taste.'

Michael looked down at Brooks's cut-price rubber-soled shoes.

'I see. Anything else he liked to spend his money on?'

'Holidays in France. He was a bit of a wine connoisseur, by all accounts. Not in a big way, I don't think he could afford it, but he knew what he liked.'

'France, then, regularly?'

'Definitely France, every year for as long as I can remember. Tell you the truth, we were all a bit dumbfounded when we heard he was looking at houses in Spain. I thought perhaps property was cheaper.'

'Would it surprise you that he and Mrs Harrington were looking at houses in Spain that cost more than two hundred thousand pounds?'

Brooks shot forward. 'My God. I never imagined he had that sort of money. Perhaps he had a windfall, old uncle died or something...'

'What part of France did he visit, do you know?'

Brooks was still wondering about the two hundred thousand price tag. 'Er, sorry. Erm... Gascony, I think. He and Alison used to tour.

Just set off in the car. Sometimes they went camping, sometimes they stayed in those little country places, what do they call them?'

'Gites?'

'Gites, yes that the word.'

'Did you know Alison?'

'Not really. Met her at a couple of Christmas parties. That's about it.' He glanced around the room, fiddled with his tie and stretched the muscles in his neck. 'Cracking bit of... Have you met her?'

Only in a body bag. 'No, but I've seen photographs.'

Brooks seemed to be losing interest in the discussion.

He moved back from his desk, and turned to look behind him. 'Bit stuffy in here, isn't it. Shall I open the window?'

Brooks lifted the aluminium window frame to slide it open a couple of inches, and the blinds fluttered in the draught.

Michael continued, as Brooks returned to his seat.

'Did David have any special workmates he was particularly friendly with?'

Brooks fingered his moustache.

'Not that I know of. He'd chat with lots of people, especially some of the office girls who used to bring down work for their bosses. But then we all did. There was a bit of a game we played, if the girls had an urgent job and we were busy. Some of them flirted a bit to get the work done quickly, though we'd have done it, anyway.'

'Anyone in particular?'

'No. Like I say, we all did it, and more often than not David was tucked away in his office.'

'Did he meet friends after work? – beer on Friday night, that sort of thing?'

'Not to my recollection. He just packed up work, got on his bike and cycled home.'

'He cycled to work?'

'More often than not, yes. They only had the one car, a beat up old Honda, and I think Alison used it most days.'

'Perhaps he was a saver after all,' Michael mused.

'You could be right. You hear of these people, don't you. Live like paupers, then die and leave a fortune to the cats' home.'

The discussion was coming to an end, and Michael was not sure it had been of much use.

'Well, thank you for your time, Mr Brooks. If you think of anything else, please get in touch.'

They rose and shook hands across the desk, and Michael moved towards the door.

As it opened, the breeze from the window lifted the papers on the notice board, and Michael glanced in that direction.

Something caught his eye. A photocopy of a lottery ticket, with six rows of numbers. A similar sheet was pinned to the wall in the Crime Prevention Office back at the police station.

The old boys in the office, mostly ageing constables waiting for retirement, had often joked with him about what they'd do when they won the jackpot. Then he remembered the lottery ticket found in David Harrington's jacket at Gleeson's storage depot.

'Office syndicate?' Michael fingered the corner of the sheet.

'Oh, er – yes. Been doing it for years.'

'Ever win anything?'

Brooks pursed his lips and let out a short puff of air.

'Couple of ten pound wins – oh, and four numbers one time, just over a hundred pounds. Waste of time really, we'd be better off putting the money in a box and having a good party at Christmas.'

'Do you always use the same numbers?'

'Yes. Sometimes we do a lucky dip, as well.'

Michael thought for a moment, mulling a remote possibility.

'Do you mind if I have a copy of this?'

Brooks looked bemused.

'Not at all, I suppose not, but...'

'Don't worry, I'm not going to use your numbers. Doesn't sound like they've been very lucky, anyway. Who keeps the ticket?'

'I do, in my wallet. Wouldn't be safe, leaving it around the office.'

'And before you?'

'What? Oh, see what you mean. David kept it. But there's no way anyone could fiddle it. I always take a copy of the ticket and pin it on the board. Someone, usually Andy, checks it first thing Monday morning. He brings his newspaper in and goes through the numbers.

You'd hear the shout from here to the police station if we ever won any serious money.'

'Andy?'

'Andy Fielding, operates one of the big Xerox machines. Been here years. He's on leave this week, otherwise you could talk to him.'

'Would he remember all the numbers, do you think?'

'What? Andy, I doubt it. He has a job remembering what day it is sometimes. Look, you don't think...?'

'I don't think anything, just covering the angles, that's all.'

Alan Brooks placed the sheet on the small desk-top copier in the corner and waited until the copy slowly emerged.

He passed it to Michael.

As he crossed the floor of the CID office an inspector shouted.

'Hey, Michael.'

He waved a large manila envelope, about two inches thick. 'Pretty little thing from the Council brought this over and insisted she handed it to you personally, but I persuaded her it would be safe in CID. I suppose we can expect a few visitors from the town hall, now you're moving in higher circles. What's that new Community Safety Officer like, Adrienne someone-or-other?'

'She'd eat you for dinner.'

Michael took the envelope to his desk, and noticed the heavy red letters: PRIVATE AND CONFIDENTIAL. He tore it open and pulled out a sheath of papers: FREQUENT YOUNG OFFENDERS FORUM: AGENDA. Beneath it was another bundle of paper, stapled at the corner: COMMUNITY SAFETY PARTNERSHIP: INFORMATION SHARING PROTOCOL – FIRST DRAFT. He thumbed through the 32 pages, shoved them back into the envelope, and slid it into a bottom desk drawer. He had other things on his mind.

Michael found the website for the National Lottery Organisers and searched through previous results for the main draw. Now he hit a problem. The results on the website went back only six months, and he doubted that was long enough for his purposes.

He reached for the phone.

An hour later, all he'd got was the run around.

He decided to pull rank, quoted the Chief Superintendent's name and mentioned a murder enquiry.

It did the trick, and he finally got through to Jeremy Catterall, Head of the Claims Department. Michael explained his suspicion, not mentioning that it was nothing more than a hunch, and outlined the information he needed.

'So...' said Catterall. 'You want me to check a series of numbers for the main draw to see if any won over the last twelve months?'

'Exactly. Can you do that?'

'Not personally, but I do know a man who can. One of our statistics and records staff should be able to run the numbers through the computer.'

'Great. Thanks. How long will it take?'

'It's urgent, you say?'

'It's of the utmost urgency. A man's life may depend upon it.' This was a bit melodramatic, but tended to get results.

'Give me the numbers. I'll call you back in about half an hour.'

Michael could have used the time to read the INFORMATION SHARING PROTOCOL, but his thoughts were on how you'd swindle your mates when the numbers were pinned on the board every week. He stared at the sheet of paper Alan Brooks had provided – a copy of a copy of an original lottery ticket. Then he looked at the ticket Sergeant Rawlinson had recovered from the jacket at Gleeson's. It was dated for the draw on Saturday 13th July last year.

Both tickets contained six lines of six numbers, but on David Harrington's ticket, one line was different. Michael recalled two weeks as a constable in the Registry, filing records, extracting information, photocopying reports.

It took him about five minutes to figure out the answer.

The phone had barely completed its first ring before Michael snatched it from the cradle.

'Jeremy Catterall here, about those numbers you gave me.'

'Any luck?' Michael said, excitement rising in his voice.

'Well, it's interesting. We ran over the past eighteen months, to see if we could match any winning sets of six numbers. Nothing came up.'

'I see.' Damn.

'Then we did a more selective search to see if just some of the numbers had been drawn, and we found one of the sets of numbers matched four out of the six numbers drawn on 8th May last year.'

Michael sat up. 'How much would that have won?'

'One hundred and eleven pounds.'

'I see.' Dead end.

'But here's the really interesting bit,' Catterall said with a sense of satisfaction, 'We added in the Bonus Ball and came up trumps. On 13th July last year there were eleven winners with five correct numbers plus the Bonus Ball, including one of your sets of numbers.'

'And...?' And, and – *and?*

'Oh, sorry, you want to know how much, of course. Three hundred and fifty thousand pounds.'

'*Each?*' Michael asked incredulously.

'Each.'

'Tell me, are the winning numbers – 12 14 21 33 40 and 49?'

'Yes, that's right. They all came out of the draw except 33, and that was the Bonus Ball. But how did you know?'

'A lucky guess,' said Michael, smiling as he looked at the line of numbers he'd highlighted on the photocopy Alan Brooks had provided. He took a moment to consider the implications. £350,000. A lot of money for one man, but split six ways, about 58 grand apiece.

Well worth ripping your mates off for. Worth killing for? People had died for much less.

'Can you give me the names of the winners?'

'I thought that might be your next question, Inspector,' said Catterall. 'There's no problem with nine of the names, they didn't ask for anonymity, so I can release them, subject to an official request.'

'And the other two?'

'When winners ask for anonymity, we protect their privacy. That means we won't disclose details to the media or in response to casual inquiries. But there's a precedent, where there's suspicion of fraud.'

'Tell me about it?'

'Well, if we get an official request, explaining the grounds for suspicion, then the powers that be will at least consider it.'

'What sort of official request are we talking about?'

'I don't wish to appear rude, Inspector, but I think it would need at least a letter from your Chief Constable.'

The meeting in Bowater's office began cordially. Michael outlined his progress with the Young Offenders Forum. Bowater was impressed.

'I knew we had the right man. Succeed with this project, Michael, and you could be set for stardom. Anyway, you asked to see me?'

Michael coughed. 'Well, it's about David Harrington. It's just...'

'What?' Bowater exploded. 'That's over. Case closed. The Young Offenders is your number one priority. You haven't got time to rake over the Harrington case. Let it drop. Is that clear?'

'Yes.' Michael outlined his discussion with Alan Brooks, pressing on through several attempts to pull him up short. Finally he explained what Jeremy Catterall had told him about the winning numbers.

'All very interesting, but it proves nothing. Maybe the syndicate in the print department just forgot to check their numbers that week.'

'No sir, Catterall has confirmed that all prizes were claimed. So – don't you see? It means that someone, almost certainly David Harrington, took the winnings and did a runner. It puts a whole new perspective on the case. It means the Harringtons didn't disappear, they went into hiding. No wonder they were looking at property that seemed way out of their price range. They had three hundred and fifty grand that no one knew about.'

Bowater looked to be fighting his instincts, dreading the thought of reopening the case and upsetting Colonel Cardells.

'Still doesn't prove anything. Maybe they just got robbed of more than we knew about. That would be poetic justice, don't you think?'

'It would, but what if they weren't robbed? What if they set up Hagemans and Van Doorn to make it look as if they were abducted?'

Bowater looked up, incredulous. 'And Mrs Harrington happened to get killed along the way? It still doesn't make sense.'

'But what if it was all part of David Harrington's plan? Suppose he wanted to get rid of his wife? What better way to cover your tracks than fake your own death as well, and set up Hagemans and Van Doorn to take the rap?'

Bowater was finally beginning to consider the possibilities.

'So where would we go, from here? We still have no proof.'

'I need a letter from the Chief Constable to get the National Lottery list of winners' names, including the two who asked to remain anonymous. I'll bet you anything Harrington's name turns up. Then we have to reopen the investigation because the whole basis of the disappearance has changed.'

'I don't know... '

'Sir, the kudos. The British police solve the real crime, get one over on the Guardia Civil. Even the Foreign Secretary would be impressed.'

The Chief hesitated. 'Something still baffles me, Michael. How could Harrington fool his colleagues? You say a copy of the ticket was pinned on the notice board, and someone always checked it.'

Michael took a sheet of paper from his folder and passed it over. 'What do you think that is?'

Bowater gave the sheet a cursory glance, as if reluctant to take part in a guessing game. 'It's a photocopy of a lottery ticket.'

'Actually, sir, it's a photocopy of a photocopy of a lottery ticket with six rows of numbers for this Saturday's draw, to be precise.'

Michael reached into the folder and removed another sheet of paper, which he thrust across the desk. 'And what's that?'

Bowater was becoming irritated at being treated like a trainee detective. His eyes focused on the date of the ticket.

'Same thing.' He tossed both sheets back in Michael's direction.

Michael pushed them back. 'Look again, sir.'

This time Bowater studied the sheets thoroughly, but refused to look puzzled. 'So one line is different. So you bought two tickets.'

'But how would I know which line to change, before the draw was made?'

Bowater's frustration boiled over. 'Get to the point, would you?'

'The first sheet I gave you,' Michael continued with a flourish, 'is a copy of an original ticket for this Saturday's draw. It contains six lines of six numbers including, in the fourth line, the numbers 12 14 21 33 40 and 49. As it happens, those were the numbers that won last July. The second sheet's a copy of two different tickets which I cut, then stuck together. Or rather, I copied them. I cut the copies, then pasted them together, then copied the pasted sheet. The top half is from the original ticket, with this Saturday's date. The bottom half is from a different ticket – and you'll see that the fourth line is completely different. If you look carefully, you can just about see the join, but it's imperceptible unless you're looking for it.'

Bowater fiddled with his spectacles and took a closer look.

Michael produced another photocopied sheet of paper.

'This is the sheet Alan Brooks gave me with all their regular numbers. And this is the ticket we found in Harrington's jacket for the draw on 20th July last year. They're identical, except for one line.'

Bowater compared the two and found the line that was missing from Harrington's ticket – 12 14 21 33 40 49.

'Mmm... I see what you mean.'

Now Bowater had to demonstrate that the penny had finally dropped, and he launched into an explanation. 'So after the draw on Saturday night, Harrington or someone bought an almost identical ticket for the next draw, with a different set of numbers substituted for the winning line.' He paused, for this to sink in. 'Then he put the two together, keeping the original date, to make a composite copy without the winning line. Next he switched the sheets on the notice board, some time before Monday morning. So long as no one remembers the numbers, he's got the winning ticket in his pocket, and off he goes to claim the prize, asking for anonymity – '

'And if all this happens just as you're offered a redundancy package, you can see why he'd be tempted,' Michael added.

Bowater took on a superior air. 'Leave this with me, Michael. I'll speak to the Chief Constable. You pay full attention to the Young Offenders. If anything comes of this, we'll inform the Guardia, and let them handle it.'

'But, sir –'

'No buts, Michael. Get on with the project. After all, you've made such a good start, we can't possibly take you off it now. Can we?'

Waiting for news, Michael sat through another Frequent Young Offenders Forum meeting, this time dominated by squabbles about the content of the Draft Information Sharing Protocol. Apart from that, he simply read and re-read the file on David Harrington – at one point spreading across his desk all the photographs of Harrington they'd acquired. What a curious collection of contradictions. Mr Reliable, bachelor until late 30s, marries "painted princess" ten years younger. Steady plodder at work, suddenly packs it in to start new life. Loves France, goes to live in Spain. Careful, even miserly, he cycles to work but splashes out on expensive handmade shoes – more than one pair, at that, Michael noticed from the photographs. And now, it seemed, Mr Trustworthy had swindled his workmates.

On Wednesday afternoon Michael received the call.

'Chief Super wants to see you. Soon as,' said Penny. 'Sounds grumpy. What have you been up to, then?'

Bowater was back in civvies: crisp pink shirt, patterned silk tie and pale grey suit. 'Well, Michael, here's the list you asked for, but there's no sign of Harrington's name.'

He passed the faxed sheet of paper across his desk.

Michael nodded. 'Yes... Well, it was probably too risky for him to use his own name.'

'So he – ?'

'Either he used a false name, which isn't too easy given that you need to produce some proof of identity in order to claim a prize.'

'Or?'

'He claimed through someone else.'

'Someone he trusted,' added Bowater firmly.

'Yes, sir, with his life. And it has to be someone on this list, because we know that someone claimed that prize.'

'So where do we go from here?'

'Can I keep the list a few days, for more inquiries? My guess is, it's one of these last two names. The two who asked for anonymity.'

'All right, on no account are you to neglect the Young Offenders' stuff. Understood?'

Stuff the young offenders. This was real police work.

'Understood.'

Back at his desk, Michael focussed his attention on the last two names: Paul Makin with an address in St. Ives, Cornwall, and Sandra Marlowe with an address nearer home, in Derby.

Makin checked out. He was on the St. Ives Electoral Register and registered to pay Council Tax.

Sandra Marlowe was a different story. She'd been registered at the address in Derby until late last year. A one-bed flat in a converted house. But a new name now appeared on the Register of Electors, which meant that Sandra Marlowe had moved some time before 10th October last year when the new register was compiled.

Michael's nose twitched for a moment, but then he thought again.

It was hardly surprising that she'd left a one-bed flat if she'd just claimed three hundred fifty grand from the lottery.

He doodled on a writing pad as he tried to assemble his thoughts.

13th July – syndicate wins lottery.

August – David and Alison Harrington visit Benidorm.

Late October – Harrington's house sold.

Late November – David Harrington takes redundancy, leaves job.

7th January – David and Alison leave for Spain.

It all seemed to fit together like a timetable, but something was missing. Michael's next call was to Alan Brooks.

'Thanks for seeing me the other day, it was very helpful. I'd just like to ask, when was Mr Harrington first offered redundancy?'

Brooks thought for a moment. 'Let's see, he left at the end of November and they had to give him three month's notice, so I guess it was around the beginning of September.'

'But it didn't just come out of the blue, it would have been talked about before that. Am I right?'

'Oh, yes, sorry. It had been on the cards for a while.'

'Since when?'

'Let me think. I believe... some time around June. We were all called to a meeting with Dave Richardson. He's the Assistant Chief Executive who has overall control of the printing department. He said that the Best Value Team would be carrying out a review of the department, and he doubted the results would be very favourable unless we modernised and focused on – "our core activities" were his words. He mentioned slimming down, and we all knew what he meant. I think David spoke to him privately after the meeting because he sensed the writing was on the wall.'

'And this was June, you say?'

'Hang on a minute. I've got last year's diary here, I can check.'

Michael listened to the pages being flicked.

'Yes, here we are. The meeting was on 27th June. Of course there were formalities to go through. They had to call for volunteers for redundancy in the first instance. Anyone who was interested was given an estimate of their redundancy entitlement, before they made up their mind. I think they made the decision some time in August and the formal period of notice started at the beginning of September.'

'Did anyone else volunteer?'

'Besides David, you mean? Well, there was only Steve Boynton. He was fifty-eight, one of the old print machine operators. It came as a godsend to him. He couldn't wait to get out, and he took his pension at the same time.'

Now it all made sense.

When David Harrington realised they'd won the lottery, he'd already guessed he was redundant. The redundancy money and the money from the sale of the house, plus his savings, wouldn't be enough to live off for long. But an extra three hundred fifty grand...

'Is that all, Inspector?'

'Yes – oh, does the name Sandra Marlowe mean anything to you?'

'Sandra? Yes, of course. She used to work here, in the Housing Department. Secretary to the Director. She was always popping down with rush jobs at the end of the day, especially Fridays.'

'You said "used to work here"?'

'That's right, she left last year.'

'When exactly? Do you know?'

'October or November I think, but I can't be sure.'

'How old was she?'

'Now you're asking. Difficult to say. She was *very* attractive, very efficient, and – well, slim, elegant, and a bit superior. If I was to hazard a guess I'd say late twenties, but perhaps a bit older.'

'Would you say that she was riendly with Mr Harrington?'

'What?... You don't think...'

'No, I don't think anything. Really. Just... did she know David Harrington?'

'Well, of course she knew him. Like I said, she was often bringing work down. But I never saw anything out of the ordinary between David, of all people, and her, if that's what you're getting at.'

'I'm not getting at anything. And do me an important favour, would you? Don't mention a word about this conversation to anyone. It wouldn't do to talk about police business. And I'll be wanting to get in touch again.'

'Mum's the word. I'll stand by then, Inspector.'

'Thank you very much.'

It took the best part of an hour on the phone to persuade the Council's personnel manager to reveal information about Sandra Marlowe. Aged 29, she'd worked as Secretary to the Director of Housing for the last five and a half years. She left on 12th October last year, saying she was taking up a job in the private sector. A photograph on file was taken last year for the ID card that operated the automatic entry system installed at the offices.

Michael asked for a copy of the photograph, and asked to borrow another photograph that the manager mentioned was still on the cork board – one that showed her, and everyone else, at an office party.

The address on the file was the same flat in Derby given by Sandra Marlowe when she claimed the lottery prize.

The flat, number 3A, was on the top floor of a converted Victorian villa on the outskirts of Derby. The house had recently been painted, and the small front garden was planted with pansies and cabbage-like shrubs. A column of doorbells was attached to the wall inside the porch. Michael pressed all the bells and came up with two responses.

A male student in 2B looked nervous at the sight of Michael's warrant card and made no move to invite Michael in. He thought he knew the lady in the top floor flat, but that was about all he knew. They'd spoken only briefly on a couple of occasions and he had no idea why she had left, or where she'd gone.

The old lady in Flat 1A, Mrs Montgomery, was considerably more helpful, and only too happy to give Michael, over tepid tea and chaff-like digestives, the benefit of her observations.

Yes, Sandra Marlowe, it turned out, had lived in the flat for two years. Mrs Montgomery had known her quite well, just to speak to. Most unusually, Sandra Marlowe had beautiful greeny-blue eyes, with those dark lashes you see sometimes. She was a model tenant, clean, smart, professional and very quiet, and she always kept regular hours, leaving and returning at the same times every day for her job with the Council in Nottingham. She didn't go out much, perhaps Saturday night and sometimes Sunday, but she was was never late back home.

Visitors? Oh yes, a man sometimes dropped her off in a beige-ish car, but never went up to the flat. The description was gathered from behind curtains, but yes, he used to kiss her goodbye as she got out of the car.

Probably her boyfriend, surmised Mrs Montgomery, and he seemed a very nice man, though quite a bit older than she.

So where was Sandra Marlowe now?

Mrs Montgomery didn't quite know for sure. Sandra had left rather abruptly, but there'd been quite a flurry of post just before she left and (it being left on a table in the vestibule) Mrs Montgomery had noticed some of the mail was from Spanish property companies. In fact, post had continued to arrive after Sandra left, and Mrs Montgomery had thoughtfully kept it, in case Miss Marlowe came back. It was handy somewhere.

'Did you ever get a clear view of the man in the car?'

'Well, he generally dropped Sandra off after dark... '

'Do you recognise anyone here?'

Michael took out various photographs, and the office party photograph with Sandra Marlowe in the back of the middle row.

'In this one, for instance?'

'Oh... Though normally Sandra wouldn't look like that. I'd describe her as elegant. You could just imagine her running an office, though those people might be *quite* different, away from work. She trained to be a nurse, she told me, before she went into office work, but she'd found the long hours and work very hard. I'd never really imagined her in a party hat.'

'I suppose party hats are compulsory at these functions. There's nobody else you recognise, is there? The man in this photograph in the grey suit, wearing these black brogues, or here in brown brogues, and on the left here, for example.'

She brought one of the photographs up to her eyes. 'No, I'm afraid not... He doesn't look as if he's having a very good time, does he?'

'That's another thing about office parties, I suppose.'

Back in the office, Michael opened the post, full of brochures offering properties in Spain. One letter was of particular interest.

It began: "Further to your recent interest in renting a holiday villa in the Costa Blanca, we have pleasure in enclosing our latest brochure and price lists." The letter was signed: Susan Shaw of Saunders & Shaw, Spanish Villa Rentals.

A little later, Michael trudged through drizzle along Nottingham's Broadway, his scarf and raincoat collar up, heading in the direction of Saunders and Shaw.

It was a mid-June afternoon and the pavement glistened in murky light. He passed the latest piece of civic architecture, a water feature in grey marble and steel.

Detergent foam rippled over the pool, formed clouds, and broke off to roll down the street like clumps of tumbleweed.

At the side of the fountain, under a canopy over the entrance to a shopping mall, a gang of youngsters in school uniform congregated.

One of the girls shouted at the shopping mall security guard, who watched from the sliding doors, 'What you fucking staring at? Fucking paedophile.'

Michael shivered and hurried on.

Five minutes later he hit the jackpot at the office of Saunders & Shaw. Susan Shaw, ostentatious as ever, explained carefully that Sandra Marlowe had rented – was still there, almost certainly, since she had paid in advance – a villa in Altea Hills between Benidorm and Calpe in the northern Costa Blanca.

'What?' exclaimed Chief Superintendent Bowater.

'I'm going back to Spain.'

'You're bloody not, Inspector, you're staying right here. You're getting on with this Young Offenders project.'

'But sir, David Harrington and Sandra Marlowe conspired to claim the lottery money, then ran off to Spain.'

'So pass the details to the Guardia Civil and leave it to them. There's no need for you to go rushing off to Spain again. They can handle it.'

'I can't sit round waiting for the Guardia Civil to mess things up.'

'And what if I order you to stay here?'

'You may have my resignation, if you need it.'

Bowater's eyes flashed, and his face turned a deep, angry crimson.

Michael jumped back as Bowater's fist slammed the desk, making the new Royal Worcester cup rattle in its saucer.

'If you defy me, Fernandez, it won't be resignation. I'll have you fired. If you go to Spain – you might as well stay there.'

Hoping to appear strangely calm, Michael met Bowater's stare.

He closed the folder on his lap.

'I might just do that,' he said quietly.

He rose from his chair, and walked out of the office.

Chapter Thirteen

The ValuJet website had availability on the flight scheduled out of East Midlands at 4.30 the following afternoon. Michael paid with his credit card and arranged to collect the ticket at the airport. Next he made a call to Spain, and then to Jeremy Catterall at the National Lottery. The prize had been paid to Sandra Marlowe by cheque, and Catterall was sure it had been cleared or he would have heard about it.

'Is there any way you can find out where the cheque was paid in?' asked Michael. 'It must have gone into a bank account somewhere.'

'It's a bit unusual, but I expect our bankers will be able to tell us,' Catterall replied. 'It could take a couple of days, though. I'll need to get authority from someone senior in our accounts branch.'

'That's fine. I understand. Just see what you can do. Oh, by the way, if you get the answer, don't call me. I'll contact you in a couple of days.'

Michael landed at El Altet in the middle of a fierce electrical storm that left a torrent of water rushing along the road in front of the arrivals hall. Jose Luis was there to meet him, a raincoat casually slung over his shoulders.

'I thought we'd seen the last of you,' he said with disdain and a huge grin. 'Never give up, do you?'

By the time they reached the A7, the sun was shining, and steam was rising from the road as the patches of moisture shrank to nothing.

'We've had her under surveillance since you called yesterday, but there's been no sign of Mr Harrington,' Jose Luis announced as they sped northwards past Benidorm once more. 'But there is a man with her, and they seem to be very friendly.'

'What do you mean by friendly?' asked Michael.

'They've been sunbathing by the pool, rubbing sun cream on each other, and there's been an occasional kiss. Of course we can't see what's going on inside the villa, but it's safe to assume he's not her brother.'

'Any idea who he could be?'

'No, but he looks Spanish, though it's difficult to be certain.'

'Age?'

'Difficult, again. Younger than her, perhaps in his early twenties, quite a physique, skimpy swimming trunks, gold chain. He could be a beach bum.'

'What do you mean?'

'Come off it, Michael, don't tell me you don't have them in Britain. Young men with deep tans, hanging around the beaches, preying on single women who want a little holiday romance... Age no barrier, so long as they have money. They move in for a couple of weeks, enjoy spending the ladies' money, show them a good time while the holiday lasts. Then it's back to the beach to find another willing victim.'

'That wouldn't work in British weather, but a gigolo, you mean?'

'Well, not exactly, but you're on the right track. Anyway, this is all supposition until we talk to the guy, and find out who he is.'

They left Benidorm behind them and rounded a long curve as the mountains rose up from the narrow coastal plain. The old town of Altea was on the right, with ancient colour-washed houses engulfing the mound of rock that overlooked the bay and once offered protection from pirates.

On their left, a jagged ridge rose into the sky. This was peppered with villas, huddled together and clinging precariously to the side of the slope. The once-barren mountainside, home to little more than a few drought-resistant trees and bushes, now accommodated a vast collection of houses, fighting for space and a glimpse of the Mediterranean.

'Welcome to Altea Hills,' said Jose Luis as they left the motorway.

They zigzagged their way through the warren of almost identical villas until they reached Villa Catharina about half-way up the slope.

'We were lucky,' said Jose Luis. 'We found an empty villa above Casa Emelia, the place Sandra Marlowe is renting. It's not perfect, but there's a good view of the terrace and pool. Come on, I'll show you.'

They descended rock-edged steps from the road, and walked through Villa Catharina. The villa was cool, spacious and light, but had floor tiles the same grey as the weathered rocks that lined the steps outside. The walls were white. Furniture and curtains added spots of bright colour, but failed to combat the mortuary-like atmosphere. On the terrace, Sergeant Ricardo Ruiz sat beneath a rickety-looking canvas pergola with curtained sides that shielded him from prying eyes above and below, right and left.

Michael was introduced to the sergeant and enquired about recent developments. There were none.

Sandra Marlowe and her boyfriend had spent the whole afternoon by the pool. Sandra had been reading, the man had listened to a stereo through headphones. They'd talked at intervals, and Sandra had brought drinks from inside: a beer for the man, and a long clear drink for herself. They had remained on the terrace until half an hour ago. It was now almost eight, and they were still indoors.

The sergeant's radio crackled and he listened to the message.

'Mariela says they're leaving the house,' he reported to Jose Luis.

'Tell her to stick with them, and keep us posted.'

As the sergeant relayed the instructions, Michael prepared to move. 'Who's Mariela?' he asked.

'Officer Poquet,' said Jose Luis. 'She's been keeping watch outside the villa for two days now.'

'Shouldn't we be there, too?'

'Relax Michael, let Officer Poquet do her job. There's no need for us to go tearing after them. Pour yourself a drink, and have something to eat. The fridge is fully stocked, courtesy of the letting agent.'

Michael took a cold Coca-Cola for himself and poured a beer for Jose Luis. Sergeant Ruiz was released for the night, and they sat in the naya watching the sun slowly sink. The Mediterranean gradually turned from turquoise to indigo, and then to black.

Officer Poquet reported by radio that Marlowe and friend had taken a table outside Cafe Mozart on the Altea sea front. Mariela, in a nearby restaurant, had ordered dinner so as not to appear conspicuous.

'So, Michael, what do you think happened?' asked Jose Luis as he relaxed in a padded armchair and sipped his beer.

'To the Harringtons? Well, let's assume David Harrington was having an affair with Sandra Marlowe. When the office syndicate came up on the lottery, he saw his opportunity. He knew he could be offered redundancy, and he took his chance. Sandra claimed the money, then came to Spain to wait for Harrington. David and Alison Harrington arrived later, but we still don't know where they stayed after they left the hotel in Benidorm while they were supposedly looking for a house to buy.'

'So what do you think happened to Mrs Harrington?'

'Well, Harrington might have planned to buy a house with his wife and keep his mistress handy nearby. Then – perhaps he decided his wife was getting in the way, so he'd get rid of her...'

'Because she was getting in the way? Like a big table, you mean?'

'No, but let's just say he killed her – maybe money came into it. When their disappearance, which he hadn't planned, became headline news, he knew he'd be hunted so he had to fake his own death. Now, I still think the Duchmen are a couple of small time crooks – amateurs – but let's just imagine Harrington saw an opportunity. He planted evidence to prove they did it, and made sure her body would be found, and then he planted enough evidence to convince everybody that he was dead as well, though his body would never be found.'

'A spectacularly mercenary and complicated plot,' mused Jose Luis. 'Clobber your wife on an impulse, though partly for money, then realise you might be hunted down, so cover it up, set someone else up for no particular reason, and watch them go down for life. Apart from that, he hardly made sure the body would be found. We were lucky.'

'Where there's money and a woman involved, some men are capable of anything.' Michael took a long drink, and gasped. 'That's the stuff – jeez, that's cold. I *was* joking, you know. Harrington could have killed purely for money. Or for his mistress.'

'Which is all well and good, Michael, but it doesn't square with what we have now. Sandra Marlowe's living it up with her toy boy, and there's no sign of Harrington.'

'That's why we need to talk to her. When do you plan to go in?'

'What's the rush? The moment we go in, we blow our advantage. We should just keep a quiet eye on her for a few more days, and see what turns up.'

'What? And what if nothing turns up?'

'We can go and have a chat with them. In the meantime, we're doing a few background checks on Ms Marlowe. Let's see what we find out.'

'I think we should go straight in now, or first thing tomorrow. We're just wasting time.'

'You sound as if you're in a slight hurry, Michael, but I can't see why. From what I've heard, you don't have a job to go back to.'

Michael sat forward and cocked his head to one side. 'Oh?'

'Your Chief Super was on the phone to the Colonel this morning. Something about your return being unofficial. Against his orders.'

Michael sat back again. 'Things will sort themselves out. I just want to get to the bottom of this, as soon as possible. What did Cardells have to say? I don't suppose he was too happy about having me back on the scene.'

'He didn't seem too bothered. I guess he'd rather get to the truth, than have the conviction of two innocent men on his conscience.'

'I didn't know he had a conscience.'

'You've got the Colonel wrong, Michael. Oh, I know he comes across as a bit of a tyrant, but he's a good cop. He built his reputation on one of the best investigative records in the force. He's feared but respected, and no one will be happier if we find out what's really happened here. Besides, it will look much better for the authorities if it turns out the Harringtons weren't abducted, tortured or killed by a band of local gangsters. Better for the property market and tourism, if you see what I mean.'

'That's a bit cynical, isn't it?'

'Perhaps, but in this case it's the truth. Anyway, like I said, there's no rush for the moment. I thought you might want to pop back up to Parcent for a while. I gather you're a big landowner in those parts.'

'No... ' Michael tried to hide his surprise. 'It's just an old house and a bit of land. It's not spoiling for me.'

A glint lit Jose Luis's eyes as he asked the next question.

'I thought there might be another reason for you to get back...?'

Michael raised his eyes to meet Jose Luis's expectant glance.

'No.' He returned his gaze to the horizon.

The hiss of the radio interrupted the silence.

'They're leaving now,' said Officer Poquet. 'I'm on their tail.'

Fifteen minutes later the lights went on at Casa Emelia. Soon after, Sandra Marlowe and friend were relaxing on a swinging seat, with coffee and glasses of brandy on the table in front of them.

They sat, swung, talked, and drank for the next half-hour before locking in a long kiss. Michael watched through the binoculars feeling like a peeping tom as they writhed, touching each other into arousal, constantly readjusting in a search for the right position. He was relieved when they finally ran, giggling, into the house.

Jose Luis dismissed Mariela, and announced his own departure.

'There's no point in my staying, Michael. I might as well get home to the wife. You'll be all right alone, won't you? Looks like our friends have gone to bed for the night, so it should be quiet until morning. No need for you to stay up. I suggest you get some sleep. I'll be back first thing in the morning.'

'Fine,' Michael said, though he'd have preferred some company.

'Just remember, don't do anything stupid. This time, you're not an honorary Guardia Civil official. If anything happens, call me.'

'Right.' Michael finished his drink. 'I'll get onto it.'

Nothing did happen.

Michael sat on the terrace watching the villa below. The outdoor light had been left on, but the rest of the house was in darkness. His eyes grew heavy and, half asleep, his thoughts drifted to Pedro's necktie, booming fireworks, and Rosana... until sleep took over.

Jose Luis returned next morning to resume the watch. Officer Poquet was back outside Casa Emelia. The morning passed without incident, and at Michael's suggestion, Mariela joined them for lunch.

Thick, black-rimmed reflective sunglasses dominated her appearance and gave her an air of mystery as she entered the house. The remainder of her face was perfectly proportioned, with high, protruding cheekbones, a narrow nose and soft pouting lips. Long, shiny blonde hair, parted in the centre, framed her features. Without seeing her eyes, Michael reserved judgement. But the sunglasses remained firmly in place for the whole of her short visit, and her conversation was confined to the briefest of pleasantries until she returned to the car.

Casa Emelia was quiet, until Sandra appeared on the terrace at four, to give her boyfriend (if that was what he was) a wave through the window, as she headed towards the car parked in the road above the villa. Presumed boyfriend emerged, and stretched out on one of the sun beds by the pool.

Mariela was in pursuit, and reported the details when Sandra Marlowe returned about forty-five minutes later. This time officer Poquet removed the sunglasses that had veiled her features as effectively as the Lone Ranger's mask. It confirmed what Michael already knew: this was a very attractive young woman with an approachability factor of zero. She delivered her report without excitement or emotion.

Sandra Marlowe had parked in the underground car park by Altea's railway station. Her first call had been to the tobacconists on Calle St. Carlos, from where she'd emerged with a carrier bag appearing to hold two cartons of king-sized cigarettes. Her second destination, which she reached on foot from the tobacconists, was the CAM Bank on Calle Vicente. She had used the ATM in the entrance lobby to withdraw an unknown amount of cash. Mariela had watched her insert a card into the machine, punch in some numbers, then remove cash and a printed slip of paper. Miss Marlowe had driven directly back to Casa Emelia where she was now enjoying a poolside drink with the boyfriend.

Jose Luis was already on the phone.

'The CAM Bank, are you sure?'

There was a pause before he continued. 'How much?'

Another pause.

'Okay, thanks.'

Jose Luis flipped the cover of the mobile phone.

'That was HQ. Sandra Marlowe had an account set up in January with the CAM Bank, Altea Branch. Current balance is forty-two thousand, six hundred fifty euros. Opening balance, seven thousand euros. Another deposit was made on 14th April – fifty thousand euros – in cash.'

'Mmm,' Michael said, 'good, but we still haven't found the lottery money.'

'Perhaps she has another account,' said Mariela.

'Then why haven't your people at HQ found it?'

'Perhaps they will, given time. But the account could be in a different name, in which case we might never find it.'

Michael thought for a moment.

'I need to make a call to England. Is the phone here connected?'

'Sorry, no house phone,' said Jose Luis. 'It's standard practice in rental villas. Prevents abuse. You have a mobile, don't you?'

'Yes, but I don't get expenses on this trip.'

He made the call, but kept it brief.

'Damn!' he said. 'That was my contact at the National Lottery. Sandra Marlowe paid the winner's cheque into an off-shore branch of the National Westminster Bank in the Isle of Man.'

'So?' said Jose Luis. 'Phone them up then, and see if the money's still there.'

'I wish it was that simple. These off-shore banks are extremely reluctant to give details of their clients' accounts.'

'But I thought there were new rules, to say that they had to.'

'Well, yes, but only if there's a suspicion of a crime or fraud.'

'So, what's the problem with that?' Jose Luis asked.

'The problem, my friend, is that I don't have any authority, and I can't really ask Chief Superintendent Bowater for his help, can I?'

'Perhaps we can ask. I could speak to the Colonel, if you want.'

Jesus.

'That could take forever. I know you mean well, Jose Luis, but why don't we just go down and have a chat with Miss Marlowe?'

It was Jose Luis's turn to show irritation. 'Look, Michael, we still don't have much to go on here. All we have is your suspicion that the Marlowe woman claimed a lottery prize that didn't belong to her.'

'It's more than just a suspicion.'

'Even so, the real crime is the murder of Mrs Harrington, and we're no nearer to solving that. We hold the cards, and we should sit tight for a while. We've only been watching them a couple of days.'

Michael was in no position to argue. 'Okay, but I hope we're not wasting our time. And could someone *please* check whether the CAM Bank registered the withdrawal Sandra Marlowe made this afternoon.'

Mariela didn't wait for instructions. 'I'll get on to it right away, but the banks will close soon, so we'll have to wait until morning.'

'Spain!'

Jose Luis forsook his family that evening and remained with Michael. Sergeant Ruiz kept watch, until he was dismissed at ten. Michael and Jose Luis chatted on the terrace, whilst keeping an eye on the villa below.

At nine-thirty next morning, Officer Poquet, still hiding behind the dark glasses and icy as ever, returned.

'Any news from the bank?' Michael washed a stale croissant down with the last of a cup of coffee.

'They don't open until ten-thirty,' Mariela said, 'and we'll have to wait for someone in the bank to authorise release of the information.'

Michael's eyes flicked skyward for the merest fraction of a second, and she flicked her blonde locks behind her shoulders,.

'I'm sure it would take just as long in England, Inspector Fernandez.'

Sandra Marlowe rose first at Casa Emilia. She drove to a bakery on the outskirts of Altea, returning with a long thin carrier bag. She breakfasted alone on the terrace. Her companion emerged then, and plunged gracefully into the deep end of the pool. He came out after two lengths and joined her on one of the white chairs at the table. After a brief conversation, Sandra removed her bathrobe to reveal a bright yellow bikini, the top of which she removed as she stretched out on her back to lie on the cushioned sunbed.

It was past midday when Mariela took the call from HQ.

At 5.07pm the previous day, 600 euros had been withdrawn from the ATM at the Altea Branch of the CAM Bank on the account of Sandra J Marlowe.

'Damn,' said Michael.

'I gather you hoped the withdrawal was from another account?'

'Exactly. The rest of the money must be somewhere, and I hoped the withdrawal would show that – but we're no further forward. I still think we're wasting time, Jose Luis. Why don't we have a look round?

I'll do it myself, if you want. I can wait until they go out, then find a way to get in.'

'You've been watching too much television,' said Jose Luis. 'We don't do that in Spain, and I'd hate to arrest you for housebreaking.'

Michael sat back and folded his arms, and Jose Luis looked at Mariela and shrugged.

'Okay, Michael. If nothing happens tonight, we'll go in first thing in the morning. But remember, it will just be for a chat. We won't be arresting them, and we've not got a warrant to search the place.'

'About time.' Michael sat up, and poured another coffee.

Delivery of a pizza to Casa Emelia was the highlight of the evening.

Michael slept well and rose early for the action.

Jose Luis turned up at ten-thirty with Mariela, who still emitted a frosty edge behind her shades, but was wearing a short denim shirt that revealed slim, tanned legs.

'Thought you said first thing?' Michael said, not looking at the legs.

'What?' Jose Luis said. 'You couldn't expect us to charge in at the crack of dawn, and rouse our two lovebirds in their nest. Are they up?'

'No signs of life, as yet.'

'Good. Let's have coffee, then we'll take a stroll down there.'

They walked the short distance down to Casa Emelia, and opened a wrought-iron gate to enter from the road, descending precariously steep terracotta steps edged by rocks. Two lemon trees, either side of the base of the steps, sparkled with small green fruits. A short, crazy-paved terrace led to the front door of the villa.

Sandra Marlowe's head appeared around the door after a second push on the bell.

Her wispy blonde and brown hair was ruffled and damp as if she'd just climbed out of the shower, her green-blue eyes were half-closed under thick lashes. She restrained a yawn as Michael began to speak.

'Sandra Marlowe?'

'Yes?' Her eyes widened and seemed to sparkle blue, green and gold. Behind her, a phone began to ring.

'Detective Inspector Fernandez of Nottingham CID. I'm helping the Guardia Civil with inquiries into the death of Alison Harrington and the disappearance of her husband. This is Captain Perez, and Officer Poquet of the Guardia Civil. I wonder if we could ask you a few questions?'

Now fully alert, Sandra opened the door wider, pulled up the collar of her bathrobe to cover any cleavage, and tightened the dangling belt, knotting it firmly around her waist.

Michael looked for signs of panic, but saw only concentration as she hesitated before speaking.

'Yes, of course, Inspector. Come through to the back terrace.' She stepped aside and led them along a hall, across the lounge, and through double doors to the terrace, now bathed in bright sunlight.

'Over here.' She pointed to a hardwood table and chairs beneath a vast canvas parasol. 'You'll be cooler in the shade.'

She turned back to the house, and a few seconds later the phone stopped ringing.

As they walked toward the table, a ripple of water signalled Miss Marlowe's companion emerging from the pool. He grabbed a towel from a sunbed and vigorously rubbed away droplets of water from his deeply tanned body. After wrapping the towel around his neck he approached the table with an inquisitive look.

'Good morning,' Armando said, in a rich baritone, in English.

Sandra swept back out of the house – adjusting her hair with one hand, clutching something small, silvery-pink (latest thing in Spanish mobile phones?) in the other.

She jammed the phone into the pocket of her robe, and announced firmly, 'I'd like you to meet Armando Bertomeu. Armando, this is Inspector Fernandez from England, and his colleagues from the Guardia Civil.' She smiled around the group and added, 'Coffee?'

'That would be very nice,' Michael said quickly. 'Perhaps Mr Bertomeu could make it – and Officer Poquet, here, could help.'

Mariela looked up icily, but responded to a nod and glare Jose Luis directed toward her as if to imply that it *might* not be *purely* her coffee making skills, this time, that were being called upon, although she had better not complain if it was.

'We'll let you know when we're ready for coffee,' Michael added. 'We'll have a chat out here first, Miss Marlowe, if that's all right?'

Sandra gave a nod.

Armando smoothed his hair back, looked over Officer Poquet's head as if he didn't see anyone, and headed for the house.

'So how can I help you?' Sandra said.

Michael opened questions, leaning forward slightly.

'Miss Marlowe – '

'You can call me Sandra.'

'Sandra – we'd like you to tell us about the Harringtons.'

Sandra lit a cigarette. She sat stiffly for a moment, then suddenly her shoulders relaxed and she slipped back in the chair, physically letting go as she came clean, at last.

'I've been expecting someone to come round. To be honest, it's a relief. I know I should really have come forward before now. I've been agonising over it for a couple of weeks... but it's very difficult.'

'In what way, difficult?' Michael asked.

She frowned and hesitated. '...David and I were having an affair...'

'Were you?'

'Well – why else would you be here?'

'Ah – yes. I see what you mean.' Michael smiled. 'And it's certainly a difficult situation. But after all, Mrs Harrington was found dead. So if you can tell us about your relationship, and anything else you know about the Harringtons, it'll be very helpful at this point.'

'Yes, I see.' She took a hard pull on her cigarette. 'Well, David and I had been seeing each other for about eighteen months... We met at work. I saw him in the office, when I took papers down to be printed. He was nice – everyone thought so. He went to extra trouble for people, and he had a lot of patience, even when things were needed in a rush.

'One day, he asked to meet me outside, for coffee and a chat. I was quite surprised, but he was easy to talk to. We met quite regularly after that, just for a meal.'

'You knew he was married, of course?'

'Yes. He didn't go on about Alison, just said they didn't have much in common. He's a serious person. Well-read, and thoughtful.

He likes eating out at special places, going to the theatre, that kind of thing – which I do myself – but Alison wasn't interested.'

'She didn't like going out?'

'It wasn't that. She was – well, if she stayed in it was for beer and television, and if she went out, she liked a noisy pub, or dancing. Gradually, he told me this. At first, mostly, we talked about work, and – well, news, and books, and other topics. I got the impression he didn't have anyone much to talk to. The men at work couldn't much be bothered with him, and the girls were a bit dismissive as well. You know, he was quiet, rather shy, and he had a bicycle, and so on. Careful, cautious type.'

'Not the trendiest person, then.'

'No. Thoroughly nice, but not really noticed, I'd say.'

'You did meet him for more than just a few meals out, though?'

'To begin with, that was all. But I liked his company, and I knew – I sensed – that he liked me, and was attracted. To be honest, he was a bit too – well, unsophisticated for me to be interested in beyond friendship, at first. A bit boyish, and earnest. But we met a couple of nights a week, and I was lonely. We had fun. He laughed at my jokes. And I'd broken up with someone a short time earlier, and it had been hard.'

'Someone otherwise committed?'

'Yes. I just had my moments when I felt down, and I really appreciated company, and the respect and attention David gave me. He even gave me ridiculous little gifts, and – thinking about it recently, I think I found it reassuring. Then he asked me to go with him to a conference in Harrogate. I made no promises, but he was never an aggressive sort of person, so I wasn't worried, and I thought it would be a nice few days with someone who – well, hung onto my every word, and, as I said, laughed at my jokes, and I laughed at his. I'd got used to him, and... that's when it began to get more serious between us. He talked about leaving Alison, but to be honest, I think he was frightened of her. And then of course, there was the money.'

'Money?' asked Michael.

'Yes, David was concerned about the cost of a divorce and having to give her a share of the house and their savings.'

'I see. Go on – I interrupted you,' said Michael.

'Oh, well, the offer of redundancy came through, and that changed everything. At first I thought David would be more decisive about leaving Alison, but it had the opposite effect. He was worried she'd claim half his redundancy money, and hurt him even more. To be honest, it almost broke us up... If he was fully committed, that was one thing. I wanted us to be together. He was nothing like my – well, my usual type, either, who I couldn't trust at all.'

'You'd had some trouble?'

'I liked excitement, I suppose. Like an idiot.'

'Like a lot of people.'

'I know. We like *never* to know what someone will say or do, in advance. Makes for an exciting life. But I found something else with David. He was unpredictable and witty enough to interest me, but I trusted him, respected him, and I felt secure... A big change for me.'

Sandra stubbed out her cigarette, picked up the packet, and pressed the corners carefully together with her fingers.

'I'd finally got something I wanted. Even now, I know I was right about David, to respect and trust him. But here I was, living like his bit on the side. I mean, it wasn't really like that, he wasn't that type, and she had him desperate to get away just find someone to talk to, which is all there was between the two of us for a long time – I knew all that. But he just wasn't, finally, making that commitment to me, and it didn't suit me. I was getting discouraged.'

'So how did you come to be in Spain?'

'Well, Alison had wanted to live in Spain since they came on holiday last year. David preferred France, but thought they could move over here, and he could move again later. He gave me enough funds, and I gave up my job and rented this place. The idea was that after a decent period of time he'd leave Alison, then we'd go to France. In the meantime, we'd see each other. That's why he rented the villa down the road in Altea la Vella.'

'Can I ask, then, why David and Alison spent so many weeks looking at houses together – why did he look at so many properties?'

'It was just strategy. He took Alison to see quite a few houses – even properties they clearly couldn't afford, telling her they had to understand the market before making a decision. When she got tired of it, he said he was checking properties, but most of the time he was here with me.'

'I see... But... then why didn't he contact his family? He must have realised that suddenly losing touch would raise an alarm?'

Sandra reached for a cigarette. 'Just a minute.' Her cheeks hollowed as she sucked the flame of the pink lighter. 'I don't usually smoke so much.' She pursed her lips and exhaled. 'Alison found out. Well, in the few weeks they'd been at their villa David was always making excuses for not buying property, and going off alone. Then on the 10th of April, a Tuesday, David left his phone in the car when he went into the supermarket – she'd been checking his mobile whenever she could get hold of it, he said, and he always cleared it of messages from me. But that time she found one...'

'What happened?'

'Alison rowed with him, back at their villa. She said she was going back to England, and she demanded half his redundancy money. She was a very controlling person, and David just went out onto the terrace. I know David, he'd never touch anyone, but she followed him, tried to push him back inside, from the edge of the terrace...' Sandra shivered, and hesitated.

'Yes?'

'*She fell back...* You know how the gardens here have all these rocks? She landed badly and hit her head. He took her inside and tried to resuscitate her, but... there was nothing he could do. She was dead.' Sandra shivered again. 'Killed outright. He came straight here.'

'With the *body?*'

'No - no, of course not. But I told David immediately that he had to go to the police. It was an accident, so obviously it would be all right. These villas are not only isolated, but with all the unrailed terraces, open steps and nasty rocks they're dangerous. It's easy to slip by the pool, too. The police must have seen it happen many times before. But David said that, considering the two of us, it would look suspicious, and he had no witnesses to confirm it was an accident. He was totally terrified, was my impression. He just sat there. Then... after a while, he suddenly said it could all be for the best...'

Sandra drew on her cigarette, her hand shaking.

'He calmed right down, very quickly. He sat there for a while, then said he could get rid of the body at an old property in Orba. He'd already visited the place. It was a bargain – but unsellable.'

Michael said quietly, 'I'm sorry, could you explain?'

'It was a rough old finca. Cheap, though not cheap to the locals. Anyway, David went down to put Alison into the boot of his car and take her out to Orba. He came back afterwards, and said he'd buried her and put her belongings out with trash somewhere, and he'd set things up so if she was ever found, police would think she'd been killed by the sales agents – and he must be dead himself, as well.'

'Did this seem like a sound plan to you, Sandra?'

'*No*, it did *not*. At that point. David was... so cold about some things. He frightened me, once.'

Sandra's wiped her eyes. Her voice trembled. 'I said we should have told the police the whole story in the first place, and...'

'What happened?'

'This was a side of David I hadn't seen – he spoke to me as if I was an enemy. Perhaps he was in a sort of panic, because later on he softened, and reassured me that it wasn't so bad. But then he said, very calmly, that I must never say anything to anyone. He said if we went to the police now, I'd be implicated as well.'

'Fair comment, I suppose, although you were right in principle.'

'I *was*. But I *said* we had to report it to the police. It was only an accident.' Sandra began really crying now. 'I *said* they'd understand. But he wouldn't listen – as if he had something else he was worried about – and I even started wondering about Alison...' Sandra drew a long, shuddering breath. 'Though I knew it was an accident.'

'What happened after that?'

'Just a minute.' She gasped, and wiped her eyes again.

'He said he had to leave Spain, but he stayed. I think he got nervous about leaving. He'd dumped his car at the finca, so he was walking or using my car. He was starting to think he was safe, and of course the body was safely buried, and he was about to go to the bank to get the money – but then the search started, with articles in the papers, and not long afterwards we heard you'd arrived in Spain.

'Finally, the police found Alison's body. When that happened, it was too much. He turned up one night and said he really was leaving.'

'What did he mean? – he was leaving at once?'

She sniffed, reaching for the cigarettes. 'Yes, going to France, and he'd send for me when everything died down. I wondered about that, because surely it was dangerous for me to go to France? – Actually, I thought it might be safer to just stay in Spain and get a job, or go home. But I said, let me know where you are, and I'll come if I can.'

'When exactly did he go, Sandra??'

'On the 28th of May.'

'So that is where he is now, in France? – did he say where, in France, he was heading for?'

'Gascony – he's been before, on holidays.'

'Have you heard from him recently?'

'Not for a few days.'

'But you've heard regularly since he left?'

'Yes, but he never gives me any number to call. He phoned just after he left, then about... ten days ago. Then again last week, and a few days ago – he'd read about the two men being arrested, and he assumed you were still here, of course. I told him the papers here say he's probably dead, too.'

'Those are the only times he's contacted you, since leaving?'

'Yes. I think so... He's called four or five times.'

'You didn't actually promise you'd join him in France, later?'

'*No*, and that's not just because I was scared. I had nothing to do with Alison's death, but there was the thing about me being implicated – and he seemed to become all ruthless and icy, as if protecting his money was all that mattered. And he even looked different, with that ridiculous beard.'

'He'd grown a beard?'

'Yes, a hideous goatee thing, but it looked stupid because it was pure grey and his hair is sandy.'

Michael looked at Jose Luis. He appeared to be have been keeping up with the conversation, and he said something now in Spanish.

'Ah, yes – Captain Perez just reminded me. The money.'

Sandra's head lifted wonderingly. She stared at Jose Luis.

Michael continued. 'Mr Harrington had quite a lot of money, as we understand it. His redundancy payment, but also the money from his house in England. We know he drew most of it out in cash. Do you know anything about what happened to that?'

'He took that with him to France.' She hesitated, and continued. 'But not all of it. He gave me fifty thousand euros before he went. It's in my bank account, what's left. You can check, if you like?'

'We've done that.' Michael studied Sandra's face, looking for, and finding, apprehension. 'So some time after hiding Alison's body, David went to France, saying you could go and join him, though he knew you had misgivings. And he gave you fifty thousand euros – to keep you going?'

Sandra lowered her eyes, then looked up.

'Oh, it doesn't matter, I might as well tell you. Actually, I did ask him for more. I need funds. But he has promised to send money through – any day, now.'

'He sees it as a payment, perhaps, to keep quiet?'

'No, no, it isn't like that.' Her hand shook as she lit another cigarette. 'Not at all. He *knows* I'm stuck in Spain, I gave up my job. I can't even afford to move from this villa. The rent's paid for another two months, so I've just been staying here, trying to figure out what to do. I'll have to go back to home, eventually, I know, but I thought that perhaps I could even get a job here... Anyway, he said he'd send more... Not that anything's arrived, yet.'

'You realise, Sandra, that you could be in serious trouble.'

'I've told you, though,' She looked up, tearful again, and indignant. 'I had nothing to do with Alison's death. I didn't even know her.'

'I mean, for holding back information, or stymieing an enquiry.' Michael leaned forward again, and lowered his voice. 'Think for a minute. Is there anything else? Something about David? No matter how small or insignificant you think the information is, it could help us – and help you.'

It was Sandra's turn to study Michael's face, as if to look for a hidden purpose to the question.

'The lottery money... you mean?'

'Yes.' Michael sat back. 'Anything you can tell us about David's actions and lottery money will be regarded as very useful co-operation on your part.'

Sandra gave him a shocked stare.

'However...' Michael said, not sure whether he'd seemed to imply she should blame David to save her own skin. 'All we want to know is, did David let you know at once, when he won the lottery? And when was that?'

'Oh, it was just at the time he was offered redundancy. He didn't want Alison to know, whatever happened, so he asked me to claim it for him, actually.'

'How much are we talking about? A big win?'

'Yes, very big... Three hundred and fifty thousand pounds... '

Michael sailed on. 'Did he tell you it wasn't entirely his to claim?'

'No, he did not.' She looked up, her mouth tight. 'Not *then*. But since you know,' she sighed, 'I might as well tell you. He somehow fiddled it, I don't know how. He said so later, quite pleased about it, but I knew I'd be in trouble if I ever talked, so I wasn't going to tell you – I mean, that's a lot of money.'

'So what happened to that money?'

'We... I paid it into an off-shore account in the Isle of Man. Soon after David came to Spain, he had me transfer it to a Spanish bank. '

'Whose account was it?'

'David's. You don't think he'd trust me with his money forever, do you?' The bitterness in her voice was obvious.

'I should tell you, Sandra, that we've traced only one Spanish bank account for David Harrington, and there's no sign of the lottery money.'

'So?' She looked more angry than perplexed.

'So what bank account did you transfer the lottery money to?'

Now she went on the offensive. 'I only wish I knew. I was given no information. David arranged it all himself. I just signed some papers and they were faxed off to the Isle of Man. That's the last I heard of it.'

Michael sat back and folded his arms. 'Another question, then. Two men were locked up in Alicante prison for a murder they didn't commit. Did either David, or you, think of any way to help them?'

Sandra focused on the far distance. 'I had enough to deal with. I knew they were criminals, but frankly, they'd get off, being innocent.'

'One would hope so, certainly. Now, just one more thing, Sandra. 'Your companion, the young man making our coffee. Who is he?'

'Armando,' she answered. 'He's a friend of mine.'

'What's Armando's part in all this?'

'He's just a friend. Listen, he knows nothing about this. I'd much rather you don't tell him anything at all about it, if that's all right.'

'How long have you known each other?'

There was hesitation in her voice. 'He's been here for a few days.'

'He's a closer friend than that, isn't he? I think you can tell me.'

Her eyes fell to the ground. 'We met last year.'

'During the affair with David?'

Sandra tensed. 'Don't read anything into it, Inspector. I met Armando on holiday in Fuengirola last year. That's all. But when David left, I was stuck, with not enough money to get out. I was just waiting around – and I was lonely, and anxious, and actually I thought it was dangerous to be here alone. I needed protection. So I called him. Nothing wrong with that, is there?'

There was a lot wrong, but it would have to wait.

'When exactly did Armando come here?'

'About two weeks ago. A week last Sunday. From the 3rd, I think.'

'Thank you, Sandra,' Michael said. 'That's very helpful. Perhaps the coffee's ready now.'

Jose Luis took his cue. He went into the house, returning a minute later with Armando, who was carrying a tray with glasses, a jug of iced water, and a box of tissues. Mariela held another tray, with a coffee pot and mugs. Sandra helped herself to a glass of water and a fresh tissue, and blew her nose with one vigorous blast, followed by a second, more refined effort.

Armando had changed into white jeans, white slip-ons, a pale blue T-shirt. He glanced at Sandra curiously, then began to pour coffee.

Michael pulled out a chair. 'Why don't you join us, Mr Bertomeu? Miss Marlowe has been telling us about you.'

Armando sat down, said nothing, but smiled helpfully.

Michael said. 'You came here – when?'

'I think... two weeks, maybe... '

Michael drained his coffee. 'So tell me, what do you know about the Harringtons?'

Sandra placed her glass on the table.

'Armando knows nothing about either David or Alison Harrington. I have never mentioned them to him.'

Very convenient. Now, if Bertomeu didn't know anything, or if Sandra said he didn't know anything, he couldn't contradict her. On the other hand, Michael should have interviewed Bertomeu separately.

'If that's the case, I think we're finished here.'

Michael rose, then sat again as Jose Luis spoke in Spanish.

'Captain Perez reminds me you need to go to the police station in Alicante to make a formal statement. Now would seem as good a time as any. And we'll need a statement from Mr Bertomeu, as well, and,' he turned to a slightly less nonchalant Armando, 'we'll need your address in Fuengirola.'

'Actually, I live in Malaga,' replied Armando, as if that were somehow better than Fuengirola.

'Oh, and you may want to contact the British Consulate, Sandra.'

The comment was designed to cause alarm, and it succeeded.

'Is that really necessary, Inspector?'

'I'm afraid the Spanish police tend to take murder quite seriously.'

'But as I've explained to you – it was an accident.'

'I realise that, but we only have your word for it at the moment.'

'Well, I only have someone *else's* word.'

'In any case, it being a potential murder enquiry, the Spanish Police would like to ask a few questions, and get your formal statement.'

'I'd better pack some warm socks, then,' she said, struggling for bravado. 'And dig out my Spanish dictionary.'

'Do that – and before you leave here, you'd better give us the address where David Harrington stayed. The villa where the accident occurred.'

Jose Luis spoke, and Michael turned back to Sandra.

'The Captain has pointed out that we need to search this house. He can get a warrant, of course, but that's unnecessary in the circumstances, don't you think? I can do it now, with Officer Poquet.'

'Yes.' Sandra straightened. 'I'll just get dressed first, though I'm afraid it's a waste of time, Inspector. You need to find David, and –'

'All in good time.'

'Decent coffee.' Jose Luis drained his cup. 'Not a bad set up all round.'

'Like a movie setting for the lovely lady.' Michael looked toward the pool, and stood up.

'Did you think Armando looked nervous? I didn't.'

'No...' Michael shrugged. 'He looked like the cat who swallowed the cream. Come on, let's walk around the front. We've got to inspect the premises, and it's hot under this parasol.'

At the front of the house, Jose Luis led the way to the front steps and sat down in the shade on the terrace.

Michael followed him, stepping carefully over a trickle from an irrigation pipe. 'It surprises me,' he said, 'that in such a dry climate, there's enough water to irrigate gardens like this – it seems sort of wasteful and extravagant, as we like to say in England.'

'That's what everyone's here for, I suppose.' Jose Luis wiped his forehead with a handkerchief. 'To be wasteful and extravagant. But seriously, the gardens are set up to conserve water – even the rocks and gravel around the plants help to retain moisture.'

In the garden of lemon and orange trees, each tree was set in a circular bed, edged with pale-apricot terracotta tiles. The soil was covered with creamy-beige gravel.

'All very neat.'

Michael's stomach rumbled. He released a silent burp.

'Hungry, Michael?'

'I missed breakfast.'

Jose Luis smiled. 'Why don't you ask Mariela to make you a bocadillo, or perhaps she could pop out and get you a pizza?'

Michael considered the possibility and said, 'I think I'll wait. But... I still don't know how this part of Spain can be so prolific, when it's so dry.' He wouldn't mention that he wanted help to explain the prolific growth in Parcent.

'Would it surprise you to know this area gets the same rainfall as south England, all in a couple of months in winter? Sink a bore anywhere around here, and you'll hit water. In the hills, it runs down from the top. Springs are everywhere.'

'I see. Thank you.' Michael nodded at a tree with withered leaves, at the other end of the terrace. 'It didn't help that poor specimen.'

'Appearances deceive the naive...' Jose Luis sighed. He sat back. 'Michael, that looks like a nice, expensive, newly-planted mature lime tree which is having a hard time between seasons, but then again it could just be blight, or lack of water... or too much water. There is an ancient agricultural secret which is common knowledge to Spaniards like myself who never do gardening, leaving that to the prolific casual labourers of Alicante, and the wife.'

'And that secret is?' Michael stood up.

'There have been a few storms but otherwise no rain for months, so everything's dry, no matter what you do. That happens, in Spain.'

Jose Luis smiled innocently as he eased himself up.

'Springs or no springs, drought can hit foreigners, even lucky new rich Parcent landowners.'

'Oh?' Michael shrugged. 'I don't know what all that scientific jargon's supposed to mean. Come on. We'd better go and see if Miss Marlowe's packed her socks.'

'Make sure they're in separate cars,' Michael said, watching Sandra float down the path, toting a wispy summer jacket and a large handbag. Mariela hurried behind, her sunglasses glinting like headlights.

'We can hold Sandra and Armando for how long?' he asked quietly. 'Ten days, right?'

'Ten days without charge,' Jose Luis said. 'If we really have to.'

'Should I bring along some mineral water, Inspector?' Sandra asked as she neared. 'And a sandwich?'

'The police station water is perfectly drinkable,' Mariela said. 'And we have a cafeteria, which provides meals. '

'Let her get some mineral water, at least,' Michael said, nodding. 'Or even some of her own coffee. We don't want anyone dying on us.'

Sandra glided back up the path, and Michael turned to Mariela.

'Oh, and in case we want her to stay a while, you'd better get her to pack a few T-shirts.'

He added quietly to Jose Luis, 'Can you take her back to the station, and get her statement typed and signed, but don't confiscate her phone. Get a listening device into it. Settle her in one of the detention rooms, give her bag back, and pick up and record any calls, if you can do that?'

'We *can*, but – '

'It can't be used as evidence, I know. Never mind, we might get a lead if she gets a call. Oh, and can you question Bertomeu? I want to hear his side of the story, see if he really is Sandra's toyboy.'

'Looks like it to me.' Jose Luis grinned.

'I mean, *just* her toyboy.'

'Ah, then all pertinent facts shall be uncovered. After that?'

'Keep them there tonight at least, let them stew. Officer Poquet and I will search this villa, then we'll look over the one Harrington rented. In the meantime – there are a few things I want checked out. We'll need the forensics boys.'

'Actually,' Mariela said, finally turning to follow Sandra, 'our chief forensic scientist is a woman.'

'So, er – we'll need her, as well.'

The Casa Emelia search turned up little of interest, at first. A few statements for Sandra's CAM Bank account were on a sideboard, along with a three-day-old Daily Express and last week's Costa Blanca News.

The kitchen looked hardly used. At one end of the worktop a dry chopping board stood in front of a block holding steak knives. At the other end, a pink plastic basket contained utensils. A bottle of 'Lemony Soft' dishwashing liquid glittered peacefully on the sill and, in a musty cupboard under the sink, a dust-pan and brush lay on a sheet of old newspaper next to a small rubbish bin. A few Mediterranean cookery books were stacked on the dresser.

The fridge was empty but for a large carton of skimmed milk, one of orange juice, half a dozen eggs, a bunch of wilting parsley and a pair of plastic-wrapped steaks. Perhaps, Michael thought, Mariela could... He dismissed the idea. An electric percolator sat, as if banished from the kitchen, on a living room corner table next to the television.

Two of the three bedrooms appeared entirely unused. The wardrobes contained only a couple of half-empty suitcases, and folded bed linen.

In the main bedroom, the queen-sized double bed was rumpled. Four pillows were scattered over a duvet cover that rested on the floor, to one side of the bed.

Michael approached the dressing table. Hairbrush, nail varnish ('Luminous Peach'), cleansing lotion, and perfume – Anaïs Anaïs.

He opened a drawer and found underwear; some items white, some red, many black, and all of it extremely skimpy.

'Officer Poquet – I think you had better continue over here.'

Mariela looked inside the drawer, withdrew a pair of black thong-like panties, and held them stretched in front of her hips.

'Not embarrassed, are you, Inspector?' she said, with a slight smile that revealed, for the first time, perfectly even, perfectly white teeth. For a second, Michael couldn't help staring, imagining the panties underneath her mini skirt, instead of outside...

He looked away, his face reddening. 'I just think they look very uncomfortable.'

'Appearances can be deceiving.' Her smile broadened to a grin.

Michael turned his attention to the en-suite bathroom.

His and her toothbrushes, Adidas after-shave, a twin-blade razor, some Spanish toothpaste, and Eucryl Smokers Toothpowder. In the medicine cabinet, Ibuprofen for headaches, and a half-full Spanish prescription bottle of 'Zolpidem' for sleeping – made out to Ronald Fletcher. He slipped a paper tissue around the bottle, pocketed it, and returned to the bedroom.

Mariela tossed a foil strip in his direction. 'Contraceptives.'

'You don't say?' He tossed the strip back. 'Anything more revealing?' he asked, immediately realising his mistake.

'Like this?' She held a short see-through negligée against her body.

'Yes, well – it takes one to know one.'

Mariela's smile disappeared. 'What does that mean?'

'I don't know.'

Michael opened the first louvre-doored wardrobe and slid garments along the rail – light-weight summer dresses, tops, skirts, and a woollen jacket. The base of the wardrobe was home to five pairs of shoes, mainly high-heeled, leather and elegant. All very tasteful in the shoe department, though everything was covered in a fine layer of the dust he'd noticed settled quickly in Spain. He had to dust his own shoes off, each morning.

The adjoining wardrobe was obviously Armando's, though there was barely enough to fill a hold-all, let alone a suitcase: two pairs of jeans, three short sleeved shirts, five T-shirts (assorted colours) one pair of shorts and several pairs of Calvin Klein Y-fronts. For a second he thought of holding them up for Mariela, but only for a second.

On the floor of the wardrobe a pair of leather loafers sat. Michael checked the size, and replaced them.

Over on the other side of the wardrobe he spotted some dusty brown leather brogues. He picked them up to examine the leather-lined inners and found a gold embossed stamp inside each heel: LOAKE SHOEMAKERS ENGLAND. He turned them over, to see the hard leather, hardly worn soles, were stamped with a figure 8.

'Don't suppose you know the European shoe size for an English size eight, do you?' he asked, not really expecting an answer.

'Common knowledge, Inspector. It's a size forty-two.'

Michael was replacing the brogues when he noticed an almost dust-free spot where another pair of shoes must have stood until very recently. He set the brogues down very carefully and precisely within the outline, and closed the wardrobe door.

As they left the villa and began up the steps between the lemon trees, something caused Michael to halt. Something in the air? Halfway up, he turned to look back. A few small, jagged rocks at the edge of the steps, set amongst smooth slate-grey rocks, were as red as the soil, and oddly lopsided, almost as if someone had been sneaking in to play with them – and some of those trees had more than a few fruit missing, if he wasn't mistaken... But a powerful whiff of lemon distracted him, underpinned by another scent (*perfume?* – surely Mariela wouldn't have helped herself to...?), Mariela started the car, and he hurried up to the road.

By the time Michael and Mariela arrived at the villa used by David and Alison Harrington, the forensic team was crawling over every inch.

Mariela had contacted the letting agent, who'd confirmed the villa was rented from 17th January to 26th May by a Ronald Fletcher. (No, he hadn't checked the man's identity. Why should he? The rent was paid monthly in advance, in cash, and a sizeable deposit was paid – which had not yet been reclaimed; people forgot this from time to time. The agent had checked the inventory. Nothing was missing. It was hard to say if Fletcher had left early. No doubt he'd be in touch when he finally remembered his deposit.)

There had been two lets after Mr Fletcher. No neighbours overlooked the villa, which was surrounded (Mariela discovered) by holiday homes; some vacant, the occupants of the others there for only a week or so. Mr Fletcher had used the maid service for a week, then cancelled it.

Michael opened the door of the villa, and stepped inside.

'Where do you think you're going?' The voice came from a cotton-suited figure in a white facemask and a hood.

Mariela intervened. 'Sorry, Alicia. This is Detective Inspector Michael Fernandez. Inspector, this is Alicia-Marie Llopis, chief forensic scientist.'

The facemask was removed to reveal unsmiling, glossy red lips.

'So this is our meddling English detective.'

The hood was pushed back, and boyish, glossy, spiky brown hair sprang to attention.

Michael got straight down to business. 'Found anything useful?'

'Too early to say just yet. Usual stuff. Fingerprints everywhere, hair in the plugholes, pubic hair in the bottom of the shower. No sign of blood, if that's what you're hoping.'

'I'm not sure what I'm hoping.' Michael looked around. 'What about the garden? It's where we planned to concentrate.'

'That's next, but have you seen it? There must be almost eight hundred square metres. It's going to take a while.'

'Miss Marlowe's hire car? Have you been over that yet?'

'It's down in Alicante, but there's a problem. It was rented ten days ago. She changed it from the original car she hired. She's given Jose Luis some excuse about wanting an automatic.'

'Are you…?'

'Looking for the first car? No, actually, Inspector, we're hoping someone will just pop it into the police station, save us the bother.'

Michael and Mariela found Jose Luis in a dingy office at Alicante Police HQ where a small shaft of sunlight illuminated a swirl of smoke. Jose Luis stubbed out his cigarette in the overflowing ashtray.

'There's a sweet named after you two.' He beamed. 'M and M's.'

Mariela gave a sardonic smile in response. 'I assume you've found the car, then, Captain?'

'Yes, I have, actually. On its way here now, on a trailer. It was hired to a German couple in Alfaz del Pi. They were none too pleased when we took it away.'

'And forensics?' Michael asked, sitting down.

'Going to take a while, I'm afraid… Couple of days, at least.'

Michael frowned. 'What did Armando have to say?'

'More of the same, and it checks out. He lives in Malaga, where he's a part-time singer in a nightclub in Fuengirola. He met Sandra last summer, after which she phoned now and again. He came here two weeks ago when she phoned him and said she wanted company.'

'Have you got Sandra's statement?'

'It's being typed up now… Oh, and I asked her how Harrington went to France. She drove him to the centre of Benidorm where he was going to hire a car. It must be Spanish registered, so it shouldn't be too hard to find – in France, I mean. We're asking around, to see where he hired it from…'

'So what do you think, Officer Poquet?' asked Michael.

'About Miss Marlowe, or Armando?' Mariela sat back.

'Both.'

'Sandra Marlowe is plausible,' Mariela said slowly. 'Very convincing, as she went along. I can see how she could be drawn in, lured by someone she totally believed in – and attracted by money, and a secure, luxurious life abroad. It would be a huge contrast to what she was used to, I gather.'

'Even with Mrs Harrington on the scene?'

'Well, if her lover was everything to her...' Mareila looked up. 'Have you ever been in love, Inspector? Be honest now. Tell the truth. Have you ever been deeply, truly – and blindly – in love?'

'Question's a bit vague. What if I had?'

'You would know such love can all destroy rational thought, change your personality, alter your views and overrule your conscience.'

'I see.'

Mariela continued. 'All I'm saying is, if Miss Marlowe truly loved David Harrington, I can easily believe she'd come here – to be near him, in the hope, however unrealistic, that they'd have a life together.'

'And when the accident happened, and Alison died?'

'She'd be shocked. But... inside, she'd possibly be relieved, in a way. After all, it opened the door for her and David to be together.'

'So why didn't she go with him when he went to France, or wherever he's hiding?'

'Perhaps, as she said, she saw a different side when he was cold and calculating. She became put off, perhaps? Or afraid of him.'

'Or both. And what about Armando, Mariela? What's your opinion of him?'

'He'd go back to Malaga when the money dried up. I wouldn't touch him with a barge pole. So – tell me, what do you think, yourself, Inspector?'

'I think we need those forensic reports. Right now, on the double.'

'You should be tearing off to La Belle France, Michael,' said Jose Luis. 'Harrington has quite a head start on you.'

'This is true, but I have an important question to ask Sandra, first.'

If Michael had planned an intimidating interview, he would have been disappointed The interview room was bright and airy, with a large south-facing window at one end. Only the narrow bars at the window, criss-crossing the outer frame, gave a hint the room was for detention.

Jose Luis seated himself in a corner, behind Sandra Marlowe who sat on a hard grey metal chair that matched the desk in front of her.

'Did you find anything?' Sandra pulled a cigarette from the packet.

'In a manner of speaking.'

Michael pulled up a chair on the opposite side of the desk.

'That pair of hand-crafted brogues in your wardrobe interested me. Can you tell me about them?'

'Yes – they're not Armando's, Inspector. David left them.'

'When was that?'

'It was... just before the accident.' She sent a ring of smoke drifting. 'One evening he told Alison he was going for a walk.' She glanced up. 'He sometimes said that, but he came up to see me. Anyway, when he arrived, he took a swim and changed into flip-flops, and didn't change back when he left. He had other shoes, the same – '

'The same?'

'Yes, the same style, different colour.' She shrugged. 'It's surprising he forgot, because he has a thing about good shoes – some people are like that. It's a sort of pillar of the establishment thing, I suppose. But he was under stress, later, so he changed quite a lot...'

Jose Luis leaned forward, speaking in Spanish.

Michael sat up.

'That's all for now,' he said, 'but Captain Perez needs your passport. Just a precaution, but you aren't going anywhere, are you?'

'No, but is it really necessary?'

'Yes, I'm afraid so. You have it, don't you? Only we didn't see it back at the house.'

For the second time since they'd met, Michael thought he detected faint panic in her eyes, as they flashed before she regained control.

'Yes, I have it here.'

She picked up the canvas shoulder bag from the floor by the desk, lifted it onto her lap, and began to rummage inside, lifting out items and putting them back.

Compact, cigarettes, lighter, hairbrush, lipstick.

She appeared to locate something and plunged both hands deep inside, fiddling to extract a sheet of paper from the passport before producing it.

'Can I have a look at that, Miss Marlowe?' Michael said.

'What?' She dropped the passport onto the desk.

'The piece of paper you just withdrew from your passport.'

'Oh, that. It's just a photocopy.'

She thrust the folded paper forward across the table, next to the passport on the table.

Michael examined the worn sheet, unfolded it, and turned it around to study the details. His eyes were drawn to the photograph – black-and-white, but identifiably clear. He picked up the maroon passport to compare the inside back page with the photocopy, then checked indistinct areas across the folds, confirming it was a copy of the original. Next he examined the stamp at the edge of the page, AYUNTAMIENTO DE ALTEA, with its indecipherable signature.

'What's this?' He looked at Sandra.

'A stamp from the town hall, to certify the copy. It's a service they provide so you don't have to carry the original all the time. There's a big racket in stolen passports out here, you know, so I usually carry only the copy and leave the original at home. It's much safer.'

'Thank you, Miss Marlowe, you've been very helpful.'

'You're welcome – does that mean I can go now?'

'We're going to have to ask you to remain here for a little while.'

'All right.' Sandra picked up the cigarettes. 'I'll wait.'

He said casually, 'Sure you wouldn't like us to contact a lawyer?'

Sandra met his eyes with a slight frown of puzzlement.

'Do I need to have a lawyer?'

'No, not really.'

Hell of a lot better if she didn't – and the refusal of a lawyer could indicate overconfidence, and a chance to worm out the truth... if it didn't mean thorough rehearsal. Or innocence. It also meant he could invent a few witnesses – if he could figure out, witnesses to what.

In Jose Luis's office, the mood was sombre.

'No progress, then,' he said.

'That's not right at all,' said Michael. 'We're obviously a great deal further forward.'

'Apart from the obvious, in what way?'

'Look, we've been told how Alison died, where the Harringtons lived, that David grew a beard – and we've also tracked some of the money.'

'The money's tracked,' Jose Luis said, 'Not one other thing has been proven, yet.'

Michael folded his arms. '*Obviously*. But we do know that Sandra lied about one thing. Or else David did...'

'How do we know that?' Jose Luis raised an eyebrow.

'You've never owned a pair of Loakes handmade brogues, Jose Luis, have you?'

Chapter Fourteen

The money was the key. Find the money, you'll find the answers. Right. David Harrington had taken all the cash from his Spanish bank account. Perhaps he'd indeed taken it all through to France... And that would account for the redundancy money, and the proceeds of his house sale. Sandra Marlowe's account held the remainder of the 50,000 euros she said David gave her, but that still left more than 150,000 euros unaccounted for. And what about the lottery money – another 500,000 euros, still missing?

The lottery money had been paid into the account in Sandra Marlowe's name in the Isle of Man. If Sandra Marlowe had told the truth, it had since been transferred to an account in Spain. But whose? The Spanish police had found nothing in her name, or in the name of David Harrington.

Michael's attempts at careful, rational analysis were, for once, defeating him. The equation grew more complicated with each element he introduced. He was, as he'd once accused Sergeant Rawlinson, going round in ever-decreasing circles, assembling a bottomless jigsaw puzzle.

For a second he thought of asking Superintendent Bowater to track the money from the Isle of Man account, but quickly dismissed the idea. No, he'd call Brian Small. He could do with a decent meal, and Brian's knowledge would be cheap at the price, and a chance to relax over lunch.

Brian suggested Parcent, but Michael made an excuse, saying he had little time, and they settled for a return to the Calpe seafood restaurant.

'I heard you'd returned to England,' Brian announced next day.

'I did.' Michael signalled the waiter to bring the wine.

'So to what do I owe the pleasure today?' Brian beamed across an array of salads and seafood, and undid two buttons of his cardigan.

'Brian, it's sweltering.'

'Ah – you don't have my experiences on the lower slopes of the African uplands with the black rhino and the leopard. You're too soft.'

'Perhaps,' Michael turned their glasses up, 'but do you remember last time we met, you explained how a person might open a bank account in Spain, or get someone to open it for them?'

'Aha. Thinking of buying a little place over here, after all?'

'I have a little place here, now – '

'What?' Brian sat back. 'And you didn't buy through me?'

'Long story, tell you later. Now, what about the bank account?'

'All business today.' Brian sighed. 'Okay, the bank account's easy, as I told you. You fill in a form, present your passport, register for an NIE number, then you can just open a bank account.'

'I think you told me a photocopy of a passport is good enough?'

'Yes, it's quite usual, especially when people are buying a house in Spain and they've returned to the UK. They fill in the forms, return them by post with a copy of their passport, and their asesoria does the rest for them.'

'And when the account's been opened by the asesoria, you can transfer money over from another account, say in the UK?'

'Or pay cash or a cheque into the account – or electronically.'

'What about withdrawing cash from the account?'

'You just go along to the bank, or use your card in one of those machines, if it's only a small amount.' Brian sliced a piece of fish.

'No, before that happens, I was told that you'd have to present your passport.'

'Sorry, I was rushing ahead.' Waving a forkful of fish and salad, Brian said cheerfully, 'Look, is there a point to any this?'

'I'll come to that in a minute. You were saying?'

'You'd have to present your passport at the bank the first time you went, to get yourself a cheque book and cards, before you could withdraw cash.'

'The actual passport, not a photocopy?'

'Yes, yes, the actual passport. Are you going to tell me what this is all about?' Brian stabbed another piece of fish. 'The excitement's killing me.'

Michael pushed his plate to one side and distributed the last of the white wine. 'You'll have to keep this strictly to yourself. Nothing official has been released yet. David Harrington had a great deal of money, a lot of it not his.'

'*Strewth.*' Brian looked up. 'He robbed a bank or something?'

'Not exactly. But let's say it wasn't his to spend.'

'Well, he won't be spending it now, will he? According to the papers, like as not he's dead,' said Brian.

'Perhaps – but right now, we need to account for the money.'

'Hence the questions about bank accounts. You think it's banked?'

'All we know is, it's not in Harrington's bank account.'

Brian took a sip of wine.

'So what's all this about you having a place, then? I thought you didn't like poor old Spain. What changed your mind?'

'I never said I disliked everything about Spain. I've just found out I've inherited a house in Parcent, that's all. And some land.'

'What sort of house? How much land?'

'A modest town house. The land's mainly oranges, olives and almonds. Oh, and there's a vineyard. Don't know how much, but a good few acres.'

'Jesus, Michael.' Brian looked ready to burst. 'Do you have any idea what that little lot's worth, especially around Parcent? The house alone must be worth a couple of hundred thousand.'

'Who says it's for sale?' Michael said. He picked up a knife and firmly cut into a tomato.

'Sorry... It's the property agent in me, think in terms of values all the time. So are you thinking of moving in?' His tone was hopeful. 'Yes, you *are* thinking about it – I can tell.'

Brian leaned forward, clutching his glass.

'I tell you, Michael, you won't regret it. Spain is a wonderful country, and the Jalon Valley is really special. I just hope you're coming here because you want to.'

'What do you mean?'

'I told you, some people are just fed up with Britain. They miss the best of it, here. But you speak the language already, and you're half-Spanish.'

'Yes... ' Even now, *half-Spanish* rankled, as if he was carrying it round like a placard at the airport. But this time he didn't protest.

Brian went on. 'So what will you do? You could take up farming, I suppose, if you're not going to become a property speculator.'

'No – this is all in the realms of fantasy, Brian.'

'Exactly. Just my point. This place is Fantasy Island. You can make of it just what you want. The opportunities are boundless, and like I say, you have an advantage over most people.'

'You're getting a bit carried away here. All I want to do is clear up the mess this case is in. And right now, I'm a long way from that.'

Fresh pineapple arrived, coffee followed, then the bill. Michael picked it up. 'Strange... They haven't added the wine, or the dessert or coffee, to the bill.'

Brian smiled. 'I think you'll find it's all included. Like I said, Michael, Fantasy Island.'

Michael set down a generous tip, and pushed back his chair.

'Where are you staying?' Brian asked, standing up.

'For now, in a rented villa in Altea Hills, but I'll probably have to move out before long if the case isn't solved quickly.'

'What do you think of it? Altea Hills, I mean.'

'Nice villa, but it's all too built up for me. Actually, it reminds me of a seventies housing estate in Britain, except that the sun shines.'

'Altea's not like Parcent, is it?' Brian added with a grin. 'Matter of fact, I'm going to Altea Hills tomorrow myself, to pick up a couple of prospective purchasers, a Mr and Mrs Jaines. No, not Jaines... *Haines*. That's it, James Haines. Funny name – easy to get mixed up.'

Michael's eyes widened, and his expression froze for a moment.

'You all right, Michael?' Brian asked. 'What on earth is it?'

'Brian,' Michael said, his face melting into a beam. 'In policeman's terms, you're a missing link to a hopeless puzzle. But I have to go now.'

'Any time. It's been a pleasure.' Brian looked bewildered.

'Believe me,' Michael called back, 'the pleasure's all mine.'

Michael sped towards Alicante, thoughts on anything but driving. All he could think of was Harrington – Carrington. He went through the alphabet – Barrington (possible) Farrington (possible) Larrington (doubtful) Marrington (doubtful) Warrington (possible). He was breathless when he entered the police station, to be greeted by a startled Mariela.

'Where's Jose Luis?'

'What?'

'I need you to get in touch with him right now.'

'What's the problem?' Mariela asked, spinning her chair.

'I said *now*, Officer Poquet. This is *urgent*.'

At eight-thirty in the evening they were still awaiting news.

'So what makes you think we'll find the money in another name?' Jose Luis asked, picking up his coffee cup and swirling the dregs.

'It's just a hunch,' said Michael. 'When I first looked at the interview notes with Hagemans and Van Doorn, they said that the man they met at the finca in Orba called himself Carrington. At first we thought it was just a typing error or even a mix up in pronunciation – you know how guttural Dutch is – but do you remember, Jose Luis, they confirmed it when I spoke to them later? He used the name Carrington, not Harrington. Something Brian Small said to me this afternoon set me thinking. If you are going to use a false name, why use one so close to your real name?'

'And the answer is?' prompted Jose Luis.

'David Harrington needed to open a bank account to get the lottery money over here. A professional might have arranged forged documents, but Harrington's not in that league, so he had to do the next best thing.'

'Which was?' Mariela asked.

'A subtle alteration to his name. You remember the copy of Sandra Marlowe's passport? It looked very official, stamped by the town hall. As Harrington knows, a photocopy is very easy to alter. All he does is alter the initial letter of his surname and he's got a document good enough open a bank account in a different name. No one would know what to look for.'

'But surely you'd need to produce some original documentation at the bank in order to withdraw money?' Mariela said.

'Of course. The bank would ask to see your passport, not a copy.'

'So how could he get away with it?' asked Jose Luis. 'Assuming you're right, of course.'

'What's the first thing you look at in someone's passport?' Michael said. 'Picture yourself doing it.'

'I don't know. Photograph, I suppose.'

'Exactly. You look at the photo, then at the person presenting it. If the photograph matches, that's usually enough. Even if you glance at the name you might not notice the initial letter of the surname is different. It takes some nerve, I know – but if it all went wrong you could bluster your way out of it by saying someone at the bank had made a mistake.'

When the phone rang, they all froze. Michael tried to make sense of the muffled words, as Jose Luis scribbled in his notebook.

'Damn!' Jose Luis ended the call.

'Well?' Michael asked.

'They've found it – that is, they've found an account in the name of David Warrington at the Javea branch of the Banco de Valencia. It was set up on the 2nd of February this year with 510,000 euros, transferred from the National Westminster Bank in the Isle of Man. It has to be our man.'

Jose Luis's voice told Michael that this was not a breakthrough.

'So what's the problem?' he asked.

'The problem is, Michael – we're too late. The money was withdrawn yesterday – all of it, except a few euros. The bank received a faxed request last week, and they needed five days' notice. Someone, presumably David Harrington, called in yesterday and walked out with the lot.'

'Where did the fax come from?' Michael asked.

'They're checking now, we should know in a few minutes.'

The call came, and they were no further forward. The fax was sent by a busy Benidorm newspaper and stationery store. An assistant remembered a fax to the bank, but had no record of who paid the one euro charge.'

'We've got to interview the bank clerk in Javea,' said Michael.

'I agree,' said Jose Luis. 'Though it'll have to wait till morning.'

'This is where I mutter something unintelligible,' Michael said.

'Go ahead,' Mariela said, 'But do you think it was David Harrington?'

'I think it was David Harrington,' said Jose Luis. 'And I think that after all this searching... we've missed him by just one day.'

'At least he's still around,' said Mariela, sounding hopeful. 'Still in Spain. At least – 'Her optimism evaporated ' – he was yesterday.'

Teresa Carreres looked up nervously when Michael and Jose Luis entered the private office in the Javea branch of the Banco de Valencia.

The assistant branch manager, she was dressed in impeccable black patent leather loafers and charcoal grey trousers, and she had a dazzling, precisely knotted fuchsia pink silk scarf tucked down the front of her bright white shirt – but an awkward, rather shy crimson flush rose to her cheeks as they browsed the documents on the desk.

The Branch Manager, Señor Alvarez, hovered, catching glances she threw in his direction through her designer spectacles, as if trying to assess his mood.

The signatures of "D. Warrington" on the fax and the receipt for the cash were more or less identical, but David Harrington's signature H was vaguely adjusted to appear like a W.

'Tell me,' said Michael, 'You checked Mr Warrington's passport?'

'Yes, of course. It's standard procedure.'

'And did the man resemble the photograph in the passport?'

'Well, yes. But you know what passport photographs are like. They're very small and often out of date. Put it this way, there was sufficient resemblance for me to be satisfied.'

'And did you check the name on the passport?'

'I'm sure I would have done. Again, it's standard practice.'

'Could you miss a discrepancy between Warrington and Harrington?'

'Well – it's possible.'

Teresa looked anxiously towards Señor Alvarez, who felt obliged to assist his junior colleague.

'You must understand Inspector,' he said, 'we probably handle around ten large cash withdrawals a week. They're quite routine at this branch. Normally a faxed request and production of a passport is enough to confirm someone's identity. I don't think we can blame Miss Carreres if she failed to spot a very subtle deception.'

It was Michael's turn to reassure. 'No one's blaming you, Miss Carreres. But what did he look like? I know you checked his passport photograph, but can you describe him?'

Teresa hesitated. 'He was middle-aged... I see so many people...'

'Perhaps this will help,' said Michael, placing a photograph of David Harrington on the desk. 'It was just yesterday, so perhaps – ?'

Teresa studied it. 'Yes... Only... his hair was longer. I think...'

'You didn't happen to notice what was he wearing?'

'Yes, I noticed his clothes. In fact, I spotted him sitting in the waiting area in the foyer. He looked out of place, because most customers were tourists in shorts and T-shirts. Before he came to my desk, I was thinking he must be a businessman. He had on a blue shirt and a nice blue striped tie. And he wore an expensive-looking summer suit, pale grey.'

'What about demeanour? Did he seem nervous or anxious at all?'

'He was sweating a bit, but I put that down to the suit and tie, though he didn't have his arms in the sleeves – he had his jacket over his shoulders. He seemed quite relaxed in his manner.'

'Anything else?' Michael asked. 'About his clothing?'

'I just remember he looked immaculate. When he came to my desk, I was surprised he was English.'

'I understand what you mean, but tell me, did he have a beard?'

'No, definitely not. He was smoothly shaven.'

'And what about the money, then? How was it packaged?'

'It was all five hundred euro notes, as requested in the fax, wrapped into bundles of ten thousand euros, and sealed in polythene.'

'Ms Carreres, what does 510,000 euros look like?'

'The bundle? About the size of a large briefcase, I'd say.'

'Did he count it?'

'No, it was sealed in polythene and initialled by one of the clerks. Most people accept it like that without counting.'

'And what did he do with it?'

'He signed the receipt, I handed it over, and... oh, I remember he asked for bags. It's not uncommon. You'd be surprised how many people come unprepared. I found him two of our Banco de Valencia carrier bags. We put the money into the bags behind the counter, then he left. He was very polite. He shook my hand, and thanked me for my assistance.'

Michael stood up. 'Thank you, Miss Carreres, you've been very helpful. Is there a phone I could use? I need to call England.'

'Of course,' Alvarez replied. 'You can use the one in my office.'

As they followed Senor Alvarez along the corridor, Jose Luis tapped Michael on the shoulder.

'Where do you think he's gone? France?'

Michael walked on. 'No, I don't think David Harrington's gone anywhere.'

Alvarez left the two detectives in the privacy of his office and Michael made the call, ignoring Jose Luis's pleas for an explanation.

At the mention of Penny Edwardes' name Jose Luis glanced away. Michael talked rapidly, then hung on in silence as he waited.

The response came after a few minutes. Michael asked another quick question then replaced the receiver with a satisfied smile.

'We're going to the airport, and we need to get our skates on.'

'What's going on?' said Jose Luis. 'I didn't understand a word.'

'Come on, I'll explain on the way.'

Jose Luis raced southwards along the A7, flashing lights to clear the outside lane. The horn was blaring so loudly that Penny's return call to Michael's mobile phone was barely audible, but he got what he wanted.

The car screeched to a halt in front of the departure point at El Altet airport. Michael leapt out and ran towards the automatic doors.

Inside the hall, hundreds of people were scurrying across the wide space. Others were lined up at check-in desks, going through the security scanner, standing around the duty free counters, or waiting by the departure gates.

Michael glanced up at the electronic notice board.

He looked at the three lines of people, trolleys and bags shuffling up to check-in desks. Uniformed ladies issued standard questions before labelling suitcases, tapped on the keyboard and handed out boarding cards. He thought about rushing to the front of a queue and demanding a halt to the check-in process.

Instead, he took a deep breath. No need to panic – yet.

From one side he scanned the three dwindling queues advancing on the desks handling the 15.20 ValuJet to East Midlands Airport.

These were the last few stragglers for the flight.

Jose Luis caught up, panting.

'I expect he's gone through,' Michael said. 'Can you check?'

'I'll try,' Jose Luis said.

The handling agents were Spanish, and he soon returned.

'You're right, Michael, he's gone through. But there's no need to worry, the flight won't be boarding for half an hour.'

Jose Luis flashed his Guardia Civil ID card at the security point to get them through to the departure lounge, and began to rush forward.

'Wait,' Michael said. 'If he sees us wandering round he'll do a runner. Think this through. What departure gate are they using?'

'Fourteen.'

'Let's get down there, see if we can find somewhere to watch.'

They found a position beside a coffee kiosk overlooking the seating area at gate fourteen. A few passengers were gathered, though the first call had only just been announced.

From here they could view passengers as they arrived after the long walk down the concourse.

Jose Luis studied the backs of heads as if wondering how he'd recognise their man.

Michael looked for something else, and it wasn't long before he spotted it. Amidst the steady shuffle of passengers' feet heading for the gate, the shiny black brogues stood out a mile. He tapped Jose Luis on the arm and nodded. They approached from behind.

'Mr Harrington?' Michael asked.

The man froze and his knees seemed to buckle slightly.

'Hello, Mr Harrington. You know Captain Perez, don't you. Jose Luis, you remember John Harrington?'

Chapter Fifteen

'So,' Jose Luis said, driving back to Alicante police headquarters, 'how on earth did you guess it was John we had to look for?'

'I did not guess, Jose Luis. It's a long story, but – well, I couldn't help thinking David Harrington would only skip the country without the lottery money if he was afraid. If he was afraid, why come back? Why not get someone to act for him? Also, Teresa said the man had longer hair.'

Jose Luis sighed.

'Hair grows, Michael. People change...'

'And then there was the jacket. Do you remember Teresa saying the man had the jacket of his suit around his shoulders, and his arms weren't in the sleeves?'

'So?'

'It may be quite a normal thing in Spain for a man to wear a jacket like that, but it's virtually unheard of in England. Unusual, anyway.'

'Even so, what does that tell us?'

'It tells me the jacket didn't fit well, it was too large.'

'That's a little flimsy, Inspector.'

'But you're forgetting the shoes,' Michael replied. 'That's the key. When Teresa at the bank described who collected the cash, it could have been David Harrington, especially when she said how immaculately dressed he was – suit, shirt and tie – but *she never mentioned the shoes.*'

'So?'

'If someone so immaculately dressed had been wearing a pair of scruffy trainers, I think she'd have mentioned it, don't you?'

'Possibly... But so what? So the man at the bank was tidily dressed. Teresa Carreras told you that.'

'Well, when Mariela and I searched Sandra's villa, I found two pairs of shoes in the wardrobe. Now, one pair belonged to Armando, but the others were a pair of size eight brown brogues, handmade by Loakes of England. Those brogues were obviously David's, and Sandra confirmed that. But they were slightly dusty, and there was an outline of dust where another pair of shoes had been until recently. I placed the brogues in that space. They fitted *exactly*.'

Michael paused dramatically, and looked at Jose Luis.

'Dusty shoes, a dusty outline. Michael, how on earth can you measure dust in terms of time? – and what does that tell us?'

'That there was recently another pair of brogues in that spot – and they were now *missing*,' Michael said with an air of triumph.

Still Jose Luis looked stumped.

'How could you know what's missing from a space?'

'As I said, I tested the shoes still there – they fitted the dust outline perfectly. Look, Jose Luis, you remember those photos we have of David Harrington? In almost every photograph he wore brogues – they're his trademark. And one pair was black, the other brogues were brown.'

'Do you really notice such things, Michael? You need to get a life. But I still don't understand what made you think of *John* Harrington.'

Michael shot a glance at Jose Luis and smiled.

'It's obvious. Someone posed as David Harrington. That person had to look like David, but they needed to borrow one of his suits and a pair of good shoes – black shoes, of course – you'd never wear brown shoes with a grey suit, would you? So I considered those facts, and that I'd never seen John in anything but shabby clothes – and trainers.'

'And that's why you phoned Penny?'

'Exactly. I asked her to find out if John Harrington was in England. She spoke to Linda Harrington, who said John came back to Spain six days ago and was to return this evening. Hence the rush for us to get to the airport. I also asked Penny to find out where John was staying, and see if he'd checked out. She called back just before we got to the airport. John was at a hotel in Albir, just down the coast from Altea. But he *hadn't checked out*. The receptionist told Penny his clothes were still in the room. So I figured he spent last night somewhere else, which meant *he would still be wearing the outfit that he wore to the bank.* '

'Including the shoes?'

'Of course, including the shoes.'

'You and shoes,' sighed Jose Luis. 'You just made a lucky guess.'

'No, listen, it's simple. You can fake Calvin Klein jeans, or Lacoste shirts. You can buy a passable fake Rolex, but you can't fake good shoes. And shoes say more about a man than anything else he wears.'

Jose Luis looked around vaguely. 'I'm quite sure that's true in some cases.'

'But of course, all this begs the question,' Michael said, 'Why did David Harrington leave Spain without his passport – and even more importantly, *why did he leave without his best shoes?*'

'That's two questions.'

John Harrington and Sandra Marlowe were in separate cells at Alicante Police headquarters. The money from the bank – recovered from John Harrington's suitcase – was in safe custody.

Sandra was willing to talk, but John insisted on the presence of Timothy Middleton from the Consulate, and a lawyer, and an interpreter.

Michael was in no hurry. He needed results from forensics, and Alicia-Marie Llopis of the white overalls was on her way.

When she arrived, she was taller in high heels and looked quite different as she breezed across the office in a navy blue trouser suit with a bolero jacket over a stiff-collared green shirt. She joined Michael, Jose Luis and Mariela at the long conference table, and slapped down a bulky file.

Michael offered a hand in a greeting and, unsure of his ground, opted for safety. 'Señora Llopis,' he said carefully, 'thank you for coming.'

Alicia-Marie nodded toward his hand, and took a seat. 'There's more to do, but we have the basics. DNA will take a little longer.'

She placed half-moon spectacles on the end of her nose, tossed a cursory glance in Michael's direction, and opened the file.

'No conclusive finds. We took samples from inside the villa, but have to wait for DNA results to confirm whether any belong to David or Alison Harrington. Even then, it would prove only that they stayed in the villa. We've been over the garden, paying particular attention to the rocks. Fortunately, there were just a handful, in a rockery at the edge of the terrace. There were no significant finds, no blood. It's possible, of course, that the area was hosed, even scrubbed, and it's possible that a rock has been removed, but that particular villa has massive rocks, too weighty for one man to lift, and they're set into the earth, so it seems unlikely.'

Jose Luis intervened. 'So there's no evidence to support the story that Alison Harrington died after hitting her head on a rock in the garden?'

'None we could find.'

'But if the area had been thoroughly cleaned?' Mariela asked.

'Highly unlikely. People tend to underestimate just how thorough they'd have to be to wash away every particle of blood, especially from a porous material like rock. And even then, some residual evidence would turn up in the surrounding earth. We could even expect bloody hands to leave fingerprints, something else people don't realise.'

Michael nodded, vaguely working on a different theory, which he thought he'd better keep quiet about, for now.

'Shall I continue?' Alicia-Marie asked.

'Please,' Jose Luis replied quickly, as if to show he was in charge.

'Yes,' Michael added.

'We've reviewed all the evidence collected from the finca in Orba, especially the wound to Mrs Harrington's head and the blood stains found on the mattock previously assumed to be the murder weapon. It's inconclusive. There's grime, earth, bits of rock, and evidence to prove the mattock was indeed in contact with Mrs Harrington's skull. But there's nothing to prove initial contact with another object, such as a rock.'

This was not getting to the point, and it was wasting time.

'Can we move on?' Michael asked. 'Sandra Marlowe's car?'

'I'm coming to that. Much more interesting. But I'm intrigued, Inspector Fernandez, as to why you asked us to examine her car?'

Michael felt a smug twitch coming on, but suppressed it.

'Oh, it was just that Sandra Marlowe told us that after Alison had died – in the accident at the villa – David Harrington took her body in his hire car to the place in Orba. In the original forensic reports, there was no evidence of blood in his car. Not surprising at the time, since we were working on the theory that Alison was killed at the finca. But Sandra's version made me wonder.' He paused. 'We found David Harrington's car in an old garage near the finca, so how did he get back from Orba to Altea? It must be forty kilometres, and I imagine there's no bus service in those parts.'

Alicia-Marie looked across at him with what could be interpreted, Michael thought, as appreciative admiration, or irritation.

'Well, your hunch was right. Sandra's first car had been washed, inside and out. The hire company had even valetted it for the next hire. But, as I said, it's not easy to obliterate evidence. We found blood samples in fibres of the boot lining. We're still waiting for DNA, but we've matched the blood type to Alison Harrington, and that's not all we found, Inspector.'

Michael stared at her, as did Jose Luis and Mariela.

'We found David Harrington's blood type, as well. Just a little.'

The ensuing silence was broken by Mariela. 'Harrington's dead...?'

'Remember, he's faked his death once already,' Jose Luis said quickly. 'I think. So my response would be, we'd better have another word with Miss Marlowe.'

'I think you've nailed it, Jose Luis,' Michael said. 'But Señora Llopis,' he added, still erring on the side of caution, 'apologies for the imposition, there are a few things I'd like you to check on as quickly as possible, please, if you wouldn't mind.'

That Sandra had lied, Michael knew, but he was still a long way from the truth, or... else he was too close to it. He spent the rest of the day and much of the night ruminating, trying to fit together the pieces of an increasingly bizarre puzzle. If he was right, Alicia-Marie Llopis would find the answers.

When, late the next evening, the chief forensic scientist reported back, those pieces were uncovered.

Now... all he had to do was fit the pieces together...

In the meantime, he looked up 'Zolpidem' on the internet, and found it was a highly effective sleeping 'hypnotic' for short time use. Some possible side effects of Zolpidem included amnesia, tolerance (with the accompanying danger, naturally, that someone might forget what they had taken, and overdose), dependence, and changes in behaviour and thinking. It was also noted that alcohol should never be consumed with Zolpidem or other sleeping tablets, since alcohol could significantly increase the side effects. All common sense, really, but it could be worth asking the doctor how long David had been taking the medication.

Surprisingly, early next morning Colonel Cardells indicated he didn't want to be involved in the interviews. They decided, then, to start with Ms Marlowe. Mariela joined Michael, the theory being that a female officer could help to draw out information.

Sandra was waiting. Her face was white, and she looked tired.

Michael sat down. 'Guess who we found with the lottery money?'

Sandra shook her head and blinked. 'David's lottery money?'

'We found it on John Harrington.'

'On John...? You mean – David gave it to him?'

'Well, John knew he'd find it in an account at the Banco de Valencia.' Michael watched for any sign of intense concentration. 'You know about this, Sandra? You told us that David had you sign some papers to transfer the money from the Isle of Man, but you didn't know what account that was. Isn't that right?'

'I can't remember, now.' She shook her head. 'I'm confused.'

'Something else odd, Sandra, is that John had David's passport with him when he went to the bank. I wondered where he'd got it.'

'Did David give it to him?'

'John doesn't deny that either you or David gave him the passport.' In fact, John had said nothing at all, about anything.

Sandra shook her head slowly, her eyes wide.

'And Sandra, I wondered where John got David's handmade black brogues, that until a few days ago were next to the brown pair in your wardrobe.'

Her eyes opened even wider. 'John took David's shoes?'

Mariela said carefully, 'Sandra, the woman in the stationery shop in Benidorm was shown your photograph. She remembers the fax you sent to the bank, to set a precise time for the cash withdrawal. The woman is willing to testify in court that she remembers who your fax was sent to.'

This rehearsed statement omitted the fact that the woman had not recognised the photograph, but Sandra sat slowly forward and sighed.

'All right....' She folded her hands together. 'I didn't say anything, in case you'd picked up David too, but actually he did ask John to get the money. You see... David was nervous about being recognised, even with the beard. He was afraid he might be questioned at the bank. It was silly, and I told him he wouldn't be, but with all the police around, he was nervous. John, on the other hand, was not being searched for, and the account was in another name, and they look enough alike.'

'So when John visited my villa, when he was over here, he and David discussed it. It seemed perfectly safe. He'd just use David's passport, and pick up the money. If he was questioned, he'd just say the passport and instructions were posted to him, and he assumed he'd have to pay off some kidnappers for David, and he was doing his bit. Nobody could prosecute him for that. In fact, of course, David was going to be outside the bank.'

Sandra sat back and gripped the arms of her chair. '*But*, after Alison's body was discovered, David wanted to go through to France, which John agreed with, so I had to arrange everything. Which I did. When it was set up, John came over. I took the passport, and an outfit left here for him – David chose clothing to make John look well off – down to his hotel in Albir. I was supposed to wait outside, while John picked up the funds – and I was meant to be there before he went in, as well. But you turned up, and I was brought here, and I couldn't get to the bank at all... so I didn't know what happened, if he'd been able to get the money, or not...'

'I see. What about Armando's involvement?'

'No, no, he's not involved in any way at all. And I've told him I have my own money.'

'I see, yes. So now we go on to – '

'Just... ' Sandra crushed her cigarette packet. 'I'm sorry, I'm a bit overwhelmed by all this. Could we take a break for just a second?'

'Of course we can. And Officer Poquet might find you some more cigarettes, perhaps...'

Mariela left the room, returning seconds later. 'Fortuna Lights with menthol filters,' she announced, before adding, as if remembering to be kindly, 'and here's some coffee for you.' She deposited a cup.

Sandra took out a cigarette, fingers trembling.

Michael turned pages in a file. 'This is your earlier statement,' he said. 'Regarding Alison. David told you that she fell and hit her head on a rock in the garden at their villa?'

'Yes.' Sandra lifted the plastic cup of coffee. 'That's right.'

'The forensic team found no evidence.'

'Well, they wouldn't. David cleaned it all up.'

'But I noticed that elsewhere, a lot of rocks edge very steep, unrailed steps that lead down from the road. And it struck me when I was at your villa,' Michael said, 'that some were upside-down.'

'Some of the steps were upside-down?'

'No, I mean most rocks in your garden are smooth, weathered and grey, while a few by the steps are sharp, and red from the soil – indicating they've recently been turned over, or half-turned. Underneath, they're grey and smooth. The forensic team have found in the soil what we believe will prove to be Alison's blood.' Michael paused, to give Sandra time to offer information. 'Therefore,' he said finally, we conclude that the incident took place at your villa.'

Sandra quietly sipped her coffee, then looked up with a fierce frown, holding back tears. 'I *didn't want to be implicated* in her death, is all. It wasn't fair. And I thought if you knew it happened at my house you might hold me up asking questions, so I wouldn't get to the bank in time to pick up the funds from John. So I just said that it happened at David's villa.'

'I see. So let's look at what happened after the accident. You told us David put Alison in his hire car, and took her to the finca in Orba?'

Sandra nodded. She pulled on her cigarette, and took another sip.

'Yes, that's right.'

'But we found David's car in the garage near the finca in Orba. Which made us wonder – how did he get back to Altea? We thought someone had helped him, so we did a luminol test of your car.'

Sandra twisted in her seat, watching Michael turn a page in the file. 'Not your current hire, Sandra, but the car you used until a couple of weeks ago. It had traces of Alison's blood. You helped him, then?'

Sandra's eyes glistened.

'Just a minute.' She swallowed some more coffee.

'You need to tell us the whole truth, now,' Mariela said in a calm, quiet voice. 'It makes all the difference if we can say you co-operated, and it'll be much better for you. It'll be off your shoulders.'

Sandra nodded vigorously.

'I know – I *know* that, it's just that Alison followed him to my villa, after finding my message on his phone. It was the usual thing, just a joke. I'd forgotten I wasn't supposed to call him at that time, when he and Alison went to the supermarket on Tuesdays. We realised what must have happened, later... I'd just got up from resting, and didn't think. He went into the supermarket, and Alison waited in the car, and he always left his phone – it would look odd if he took it in. Waiting in the car, she could have seen the message when it came through. Anyhow, he got back and found her reading a magazine, and he assumed she'd missed it...'

Sandra took a deep breath.

'Then he headed up to me, after she'd gone for a walk down to the shops – you know the import shops they have near all the tourist areas. When I opened the door he showed me the message, saying it was pure luck she hadn't seen it – and I suddenly saw her behind him, coming down the steps... We figured it out, later.'

Sandra sat back, and looked at Michael. 'She'd been waiting in a taxi – they have taxies lined up, down by the shops – and followed him. I could see the top of the taxi. Anyway, she started running down the steps and she slipped – it had been raining, the steps were wet. She fell back, straight onto the rocks.' Sandra spread her hands out, and stared at them. 'I ran up. The rocks had split her skull. I could see it, at once.'

'What did David do?'

'He just stood there...'

'Did she have any pulse when you checked?'

'Only a tremble – then it stopped'

'What did you do? What did David say?'

'I nodded she was all right, and I told him quietly to see to the taxi, go up and pay the driver off. But when he came back... I had to tell him that Alison was dead.'

'He was shocked?'

'Terribly. We both were. Of course... I fetched a waterproof sheet. He lay it over Alison, but he seemed faint. We went inside, I made tea, and we talked.' Sandra shivered. 'Obviously, David couldn't report it, as he said, because how could we prove it was an accident? And he had all that money in bank accounts, and then there was me... If my name came up in investigations, the lottery people might see it and think they had to tell the police something...'

'If the taxi driver hadn't left, he could have been a witness?'

'To her arriving, that's all.' Sandra looked at Michael. 'We simply had to cover it up – what else could we do? Then David got his idea. He called the man from the old finca and said he wanted to pay a deposit, then drove out there, me following. He put Alison into the boot of my car, under the boot carpet. That night, he used a metal thing he'd seen one of the Dutchmen pick up, got some blood on it, and scattered it. He cut himself a little, and scattered that blood as well. Then he buried her, tidied up the boot of my car, put his car in the garage, and we both went back in my car.'

'Why did he want to prove his own death? Rather than disappear?'

'No, he didn't. Really. It was just insurance. He never imagined Alison's body would be found – at least, not so soon.' Sandra shivered. 'He said we *had* to get everything covered up, since he hadn't yet withdrawn the funds.'

'Sandra, how long did it take to tell David to pay off the taxi?'

'Not long. He just ducked across the garden and up the drive.'

'Does nobody use the steps?'

'Well, we never do. They're too narrow and steep, I suppose. They're fiddly, and there's a gate.'

'Later, at the finca, when David hit his wife. Did he ask you to do that for him?'

'What... what do you mean?'

'It's difficult to brutalise the body of someone close. It's not something a person can normally do, unless he hates someone.'

'He *didn't* hate her. He was deeply, deeply shocked she was dead.' Sandra sat back, appalled. 'He hardly touched her – just smeared blood across – and I can tell you now, we were both traumatised.'

'I see. But it was necessary to be practical, because of the lottery money... he was already hiding his name. Oh, what reason did he give his wife for that? Using a different name to rent his villa, for example?'

'Property agents – and they can really be relentless. When David and Alison were at hotels, agents would call up night and day, and that's typical. David told her they could have dangerous connections, actually, because he wanted to lay it on to scare her, a little.'

'But he never told her anything about the lottery money?'

'Of course not. We had plans for that ourselves – she'd just have wasted it. But keep in mind, Inspector, that he did plan to buy a flat for her, and provide her with living money, you know. That's all he wanted – to be fair.'

'Did David say why he was first interested in the finca, Sandra?'

Sandra lifted her coffee, thinking back.

'He said it could be developed, and resold. But the two agents didn't seem to know what they were doing, and then he suspected the land wasn't registered. There's a lot of warnings in the papers about scams like that. Anyway, he met Van someone out at the finca, the day of the accident.'

'Why did he want to pay a deposit, if it was a scam?'

'Well...' Sandra glanced up. 'To be sure the man showed. David thinks of everything. He told the man he wanted the keys to the house and the garage so he could get a builder in, to do an estimate for reforming the place. But he also wanted one of the men to sign a receipt. He's very clever, really.'

'He got the keys, then?'

'Yes, of course. He was sure the man would give him the keys even though the place was not actually sold. And once he'd paid, he knew the men would never come near the place again for fear of being caught.'

'If it was a scam, you mean?'

'Well, if it wasn't, and David never contacted them again, they'd just hold onto the money, wouldn't they. They got it for nothing... But you see, he was even more certain it was a scam, when the man signed the receipt without making a note of the purpose of the deposit or even having a contact for David apart from a mobile phone number – which was no longer even used. He'd got rid of that phone weeks ago.'

'What if the men did go ahead and sell the land elsewhere?'

'David was quite sure the land would never sell, if those two were selling – or even if they did, not likely to anyone who'd develop it.'

'Where were you, Sandra, while this meeting was taking place?'

'Just waiting in my car – down the road about half a mile.'

'I see. And so – what happened, later?'

'We waited until dark. Then we went in.'

'You and David buried the body together, at the finca?'

'He buried it. I wouldn't touch it.'

'You helped with the digging, though?'

'Well, I was actually too slow, as he pointed out – but I did help fill the hole.'

'I see. So... another thing... John had David's passport – ?'

'Of course he had,' Sandra said abruptly. 'John needed it for the bank, Inspector. Proof of identity. David always plans things *very* carefully. He posted the passport to me from France, to give to John.'

'So when did David go to France, and send the passport?'

'He left early on the 28th of May. I drove him down to Benidorm. He planned to take a taxi, then buy an old car for cash in another town. A couple of days later, he called from France and said the passport was posted – it reached me on the 4th of June.'

'Did he send it registered?'

'No, just ordinary post. They don't deliver here, and I had to collect it from the post office in Altea. I went three days running, come to think of it, so they'll possibly remember me doing that – can you ask them?'

'We will. How were you going to get it back to him?'

'That's the strangest thing. I'm supposed to drive through to take the money to him, whether I decided to stay in France or not – but that's the problem. He's given me no details of his location yet. I have my phone here. He was supposed to call and check that the pick-up went smoothly, straight after John went to the bank. *Why* hasn't he called?'

'Could he have called John?'

Sandra looked up sharply. 'Yes! Can you ask him?'

'Er – we can and will. Good thinking.' Except that they'd confiscated John's phone and found nothing on it. 'Just one last point, Sandra.'

Chapter Sixteen

'Can you run through the afternoon John came up to your villa?'

Sandra sighed, and fixed her eyes on the wall.

'Yes, well... John and Linda were brought over, and the next thing we knew, the press conference was on TV. When David saw that, he was really worried, as you can imagine. That evening, he got me to phone John at his hotel in Benidorm, and he spoke to him.'

She glanced at Michael.

'John was expecting the call. You realise John had been in touch with David all along?'

'He knew Alison was dead?' Michael met her eyes.

'Yes – I mean, we didn't just suddenly call John at his hotel, out of the blue. David had already phoned John in the UK, just after the accident. He didn't say anything had happened to Alison, just told him he'd decided to lay low for a while, because – well, he had to say something – he said he'd helped himself to some funds from Nottingham, without being specific.'

Sandra nodded, and leaned her arms on the table.

'I have to explain something, first. David had been planning to give John a share of that money, which he hadn't got from the bank yet, and thought he'd better not for a while, as he told John. The fact is, the only reason David couldn't call when Linda was home was because she'd want to speak to Alison and, you know, he was too nervous to deal with that – besides, excuses could only be made once or twice. It's such a simple little thing, but he had to deal with it, and worked something out. He planned to say later that Alison had been ill, to explain away not phoning, and say she'd then died – mind you, John didn't know all that. There was no need to tell him.

'Anyway, what happened was, John promised not to say anything to his wife about the money. Playing the big protecting-Linda role, I suppose. David said he's inclined to make out she's helpless. In any case, when the phone calls seemed to stop, Linda got it into her head that they were in trouble. John dismissed her worries, but he can't have done a very good job, because she went off to the police. John tried to quiet things down, but next thing we knew there were all these articles in the papers...

'After that, David often phoned John in the UK when Linda was out at her bingo, but none of us ever expected the police would take this search to the extent they did... And David couldn't suddenly jump up then, saying, "Sorry, Alison had an accident and I buried her." But what could we do? The papers kept building up the story, and finally John and Linda came to Spain. John was waiting at his hotel for David to phone...'

Sandra looked up with earnest intensity.

'You have to understand the brothers, Inspector. For one thing, David planned long *before* he went to Spain to help John out financially. David's always saying, what would John say if he could see this, he'd be green, or he'd love this, or that... They might seem competitive on the surface, but in fact they're close, and loyal, and keep in close touch.'

She sighed. 'Next day I went to get John from near the hotel. I recognised him, of course. I'd seen photographs, and knew he looked like David. So I picked him up, and took him to the villa.'

'He and David talked things over, then?'

'Yes. David told John about the accident, though not saying it happened at my villa. They came up with the idea that John could possibly pick up the money from the bank, in place of David – with a cover story in case there were questions. Then David would go to France until things settled down. Eventually they'd tell Linda, as David had planned, that Alison had fallen ill and died, and it had to be kept quiet. Linda would understand, especially when John explained about the money David had taken from Nottingham.'

'John did agree at once to this?'

'Well – to be honest, I think he thought it was a bit exciting – but as I said, despite what people may think, they are close, and of course David always planned to give him some funds.'

Sandra hesitated, before going on. 'But then, you see... Alison's body turned up, totally unexpectedly, so it looked like an even better idea they'd come up with, for John to pick up the money from the bank...'

'How did the idea of John picking up the money come about?'

'I think John suggested it, first. But in any case, it was decided. Then from the day he came up to the villa, John was waiting at the pool or bar every afternoon in case we called – and when the news came about a body being found, David confirmed the plan at once with John, but said John should go back to the UK and wait to hear it was all set up. He was going to France, himself – it was important he should get out, rather than wait.'

'Yes,' Michael said thoughtfully, before continuing. 'Just one thing, Sandra. Do you have another phone?'

Sandra hesitated. '...No.'

'We do need to check this one.'

'But... ' Sandra reached inside her bag. 'What if David calls?'

'We'll switch it off while we check it, then get it back to you. But if there's any call, we will be listening in, I have to tell you.'

Chapter Seventeen

'Great, so now we have another mobile phone,' Jose Luis said as soon as they returned to his office. 'How the hell does that help us?'

'Well…' Michael said. 'I just thought, perhaps… I don't know.' He raised his cup of coffee, put it down as his fingers began to burn, and picked up the phone again and stared at it.

Mariela snatched the phone from Michael's hand, pressed a few buttons, and worked through the menu.

'Give me a couple of hours,' she said, striding to to the door.

'Right,' Michael said, staring at his empty hand. 'That settles that – which is probably just as well. I know nothing about Spanish phones, and I think it's time for a nice chat with our obnoxious John Harrington, who – '

'– still awaits his lawyer, his interpreter, and his consulate staff.'

Michael lifted the cup again and took a sip. 'This is disgusting.' He replaced the cup and blew on his fingers. 'Let's barge in anyway, and see what happens. I can show you how British cops use certain questions to assess nonverbal behavior and unconscious verbal clues. It's our catch-them-off-guard technique.'

'I thought you lot used deerstalkers, hunches and intuition?'

'Jose Luis.' Michael held out a tray. 'What general knowledge. You're a genius. Let me carry your coffee in for you.'

As Michael and Jose Luis entered the interview room, toting the tray loaded with coffee cups and a stack of files, John Harrington stubbed out a cigarette in an overflowing ashtray. He exhaled the last drag and began to stand up but sat down again, scattering pages of the Daily Mail.

Today, John was dressed in his own suit. The old jacket was draped over the back of his chair, he'd rolled up his shirtsleeves and loosened his tie, and he looked hot, red-faced, and defiant. An all-round obnoxious, miserable specimen.

Michael sat down. 'Hello.' He nodded toward Jose Luis. 'The Spanish inspector won't stay. Just the two of us will have a chat.'

John Harrington loosened his tie further, as Jose Luis left the room to watch through the two-way mirror and record the interview.

John crossed his arms, and looked up at the far wall with glassy eyes, as if in a trance.

Michael lowered his voice. 'You've been in Spain several days?'

'Ah – what?..Yes.' John's gaze drifted to Michael's tie.

'In Albir.' Michael nodded. 'You were staying there. Anything much to do down there, John?'

'Not really...' This sparked: 'I walked about. Read the papers.'

Michael leaned forward. 'Mr Harrington, John, you know what we're here to talk about? Your brother, David. I now understand that when I first visited you in Nottingham, David had phoned you recently.'

John gazed up at the ceiling as if looking for cracks.

'And I believe you saw him, when you were last in Spain?'

'Yes.' Now John turned his attention to Michael. He nodded. 'Yes, I did. It won't do David any good if I keep quiet, I've decided, though he told me to clam up if I had any trouble. Anyway...' John's eyes, flat, unblinking and bloodshot, met Michael's. 'I'm involved in all this. I got a call at the hotel and spoke to David, when I came over for the press thing. David's friend Sandra met me down the road, and drove me up to see him, the next day. Up at her Spanish villa.'

'How did you feel going up there, John?'

'I was worried we might be followed by the police – but I lay across the back seat, and Sandra kept an eye out while she drove.'

Michael pulled out a notebook, pretended to scribble. 'And at the villa, when you arrived?'

'David was waiting.' John paused for a sip of coffee.

'How did he seem to you?'

'He had a beard, and it made him look older. But to tell the truth he'd just slowed down a lot, was my impression.' John refolded his arms firmly. 'Probably tired out. He looked a bit spaced out, too. Sandra said he took tranquillisers of some sort, so that could account for it. But he'd fallen apart from all his problems, that's what I'd say.'

'When exactly did you go up to the villa, John?'

'The day after the press conference. '

'Did David tell you what had happened to Alison?'

'Yes... she'd fallen down some steps, taken a crack on her head.' He frowned and rubbed his forehead. 'And, well, that was it, you see. He couldn't report it because he'd stolen – not exactly stolen, but embezzled – some money, from the place he worked. And he'd transferred it to Spain.'

'You said to me once, at your home, that David was miserly?'

'Yes. David asked me to find out as much as I could about the investigation, and put the police off by being negative and hostile.'

'You did a very good job of that, then. Go on.'

'Well, it started like this. When Alison had the accident David couldn't tell anyone, in case they started checking his background because of the money he'd taken, and he hadn't wanted to worry us. So he thought he'd just keep out of contact for a while, then he could say Alison had been ill and died in Spain. But what happened was, Linda went to the police, and he couldn't come forward at all – because of the big search starting up.'

'How much money was involved, John?'

'*Thousands.*' John shook his head. 'And that was on top of the redundancy and the house money. Another three hundred and fifty thousand... pounds.'

'Did he offer you any funds at all, when he told you about Alison's accident?'

'He did say, yes, that he'd give me thirty-five thousand pounds – but you see, he'd already told me he was going to help me out a bit financially, before they went to Spain, so,' John reached for his cup, 'I know he wasn't just telling me about the embezzled money after I got over here, to get me to help him, over the accident business.'

John took a great gulp of coffee.

'I mean, there was no reason for him to tell me anything at all about the accident, as a matter of fact. He'd buried the body at the finca place, and he could have just said Alison had gone off, and she was keeping out of sight to make trouble for him. Wouldn't have surprised me, her doing that.'

John rubbed his left arm with his right, staring back at the table.

'But he'd phoned me at home, and said it would be best to seem to be out of touch for a while, in case anyone in Nottingham got wind of the money he'd embezzled, and in case they asked me and Linda any questions, but...'

John sat forward, leaned his elbows on the table and clasped his hands together, looking at them.

'We didn't realise how concerned Linda really was, or how excited the newspapers and the police would get when she reported Alison and David might be missing. I mean, people go missing all the time, don't they? – often, they don't want to be found. I never expected anything to come of it, nor did David. But it all blew up into a huge headline thing. But anyway,' he looked up sharply. 'About the money. I hadn't told Linda a word about getting any financial assistance from him in the first place, because it was meant to be a surprise when it came through.'

'But all this was before the police discovered Alison's body?'

'Yes, yes. When that happened, David realised he had to go to France, and leave the money business completely to me and Sandra. He was in a real panic, himself.'

'When did you know he'd gone to France?'

John thought for a second. 'When he phoned and said he was going.'

'When exactly was that?'

'Just before we left Spain, so I was at the hotel. That would have been the day previous to the day before we left, I think.'

'Two days before?'

'That sounds right. Oh, and he phoned later at home on the 23rd, to say he was leaving in a few days and he'd send his passport back, and he'd leave a good suit and things for me. And then just a word on the evening of the 27th to say he was all packed and he was off to France. Next day, I think.'

'I see... And, er, after that?'

'Sandra called me at home a few days later to confirm everything. She was to set it all up, for me to come and collect the money.'

'You'd agreed to do that already, though, to help out, hadn't you?'

'Yes. Well, it seemed quite straightforward.'

'That was your idea?'

'No, but David was relying on me – he needed the money. And he'd do it for me, if I was the lucky one, if you're wondering. He's helped me in the past. Anyway, it was the least I could do. He was in no state.'

'When did you last speak to Sandra, John?'

'On the morning I went to the bank – on the phone.'

'Sandra is here now, actually. Upstairs.'

'Is she? Oh, all right, then – she can tell you – '

'Can you first just sum up for me, what happened?'

'I think so... Yes.' John sat back. 'Well, see, David had the money, the illegal money, in a Spanish account, and he wanted that out of the bank in case it was ever traced by the police, being illegally obtained and so on. So David wanted me to withdraw the money from the bank, which wasn't in the name of Harrington, so I'd be all right, and I look quite like him, and similar build – and he'd already decided on my thirty-five thousand pounds, but he couldn't get at it. Later on, when it was sorted, I'd tell Linda I'd tracked him down in Spain, and tell her about the accident, and why we'd had to keep it from her, her not being too good with secrets and already stressed, and so on.'

'So what happened, then?'

'Well, I came to Spain last week. Sandra had booked and paid for a hotel – she's a fully qualified secretary, used to work with David, upstairs – and she brought down the suit which was a bit big, and a good shirt and a special tie and some of David's good shoes, a bit on the big side because I'm a half a size smaller, but quite comfortable. She'd set things up with the bank, but then I had to wait around a few days until the money was due to be collected.'

'And David's passport?'

'Yes, she brought that, too.'

'About the other night – why didn't you go back to your hotel?'

'Something was wrong.' John sat bolt upright. 'I phoned Sandra in the morning to confirm what time we'd meet outside the bank before I went in, but there was no reply. Half an hour later, she phoned me back.'

Damn. 'What did she say?' Sandra must have made the call the minute she went back inside the villa to get dressed.

'She said she might not be able to make it, and if she didn't I should keep out of sight as much as possible, then go straight home with the money. She might not be available to answer a call from me, she said, but she'd get in touch after I got home. She didn't turn up at the bank and I got worried, so that night I slept in the hire car.'

'All right.' Michael stood up. 'You'll have to stay here for now, John. We'll get you to sign a statement to confirm everything you've said in this interview constitutes the facts as you remember them.'

'All right. I'll stay here, then.' John picked up his empty cup. 'Any chance of another coffee? This is good.'

'Of course.' The man had to have a cast-iron constitution. 'Oh, and we'll find that lawyer, too – I'm sorry, I forgot about that.'

'No, that's all right. So long as David's in the clear – even if he doesn't have all his money, it's better this way – and Sandra's told you about Alison's accident, so those men in prison are cleared.'

'Sandra's adamant about the accident, that the men were not involved, and we're looking for David now... But I'd feel more comfortable if you did have a lawyer. It is standard procedure.'

John nodded. 'Right, then.' He nodded again, smiled faintly, and reached into his pocket. 'Half an hour without a smoke.'

'Do you want to phone your wife?'

He froze. 'Could someone call her?'

Michael nodded. 'I'll explain you're helping us. She's not to worry.'

Mariela was in the office with Jose Luis, when Michael returned. She stopped leafing through a wad of paper, and looked up smugly.

'You first,' she insisted, waving an arm toward a chair.

Michael joined them at the table.

'John's story is pretty much what we knew already,' he said.

'Does he know where David is?'

'If he does, he isn't saying. What about Sandra's phone?'

'Interesting...' Mariela said, as if waiting to be prompted. She smiled, her white teeth flashing.

Michael widened his eyes, then rubbed them with the flat of his hand. 'Do you have something of relevance to say, Mariela, or is it just the price tag that's impressive?'

'What does that mean?'

'I don't know.'

Mariela picked up Sandra's phone from the table.

'*This*,' she said, 'is a Motorola 2120 mobile phone on a standard UK contract with Orange. It has an international SIM card, which means you can make and receive calls virtually anywhere in the world. Details of the last twenty calls received are stored in the call register embedded in the chip – unless they are deleted.'

'Right.' Michael looked up at the ceiling. 'So... ?'

'Now,' Mariela said emphatically, 'here's the clever bit. Listen... ' She paused again. '...If someone calls this phone from abroad, a part of the call cost is charged to the account of the person receiving the call – in this case Sandra's account. It's done that way so that the service provider can recover the cost of foreign "air time".'

Michael sat forward, working through the implications. 'Which means – we need to get hold of a copy of the account?'

Mariela smiled again.

She pushed the wad of papers across the table.

'You were about to mutter something disparaging about Spain?'

Michael opened his mouth, but Mariela interrupted.

'You need to say thank you to Colonel Cardells when you see him... and thank your Chief Superintendent Bowater, as well.'

'Okay, I will, but spare me their telephone numbers.'

'All right. Now, the account shows calls Sandra made, including to John Harrington's hotel in Benidorm when he was there, and to his home in Nottingham, presumably when she arranged for him to come back to collect the money. No incomings are listed, apart from charges for two "calls received while roaming." These are calls that came in from abroad.'

She thrust the page in front of Michael who studied it carefully, noting the highlighted items.

'But this doesn't record the numbers from which the calls were made,' he said. 'We're no further forward.'

'Patience, Inspector.' Mariela flipped to another sheet of paper. 'So we know from the account that two calls were received from abroad, but the account doesn't give details. Next, I checked the call register on the phone. This showed two calls received from abroad, and it listed the numbers.'

'And?'

Mariela continued. 'One call is from John Harrington's phone in Nottingham. The other is from the National Westminster Bank in the Isle of Man. Presumably they phoned Sandra to confirm the content of her fax, when she asked to transfer the money to the account in Spain. Banks often do this as a double check.'

'It shows no calls from France?'

'Exactly.' Mariela, tapped the papers together, placed them in a neat bundle, and sat back. 'God knows where those calls came from.'

Mariela stared at Michael, as if demanding an answer.

After staring back for a moment, Michael stood up. 'Forget that. Come on, Jose Luis, we're going to do some real work.'

'And just who is "*we*"?' Mariela asked crisply.

'Me, he and you. I suppose the Guardia Civil have no official issue wellingtons?'

'Never heard of them. Anything else?'

'Three large lunch boxes, and a flask of *percolated* coffee.'

Six hours later, Michael opened the door of the interview room. He'd removed his tie, and the armpits of his pale blue shirt were wet with sweat, though he'd had his shirt off until half an hour ago. He should have showered, but he wasn't going to stop now. This piece of the puzzle should only take a few minutes.

He crossed the room and adjusted the blinds to cut off the sunlight flashing across the table.

Sitting down quickly opposite Sandra, he nodded an instruction to Mariela, who'd come in behind him. She rolled her eyes, placed her coffee on the table, and went to sit by the door.

'Sorry to call you back, Sandra, but just a couple of questions.'

Michael passed Sandra a cup of coffee from the tray, and took one himself, holding it carefully by the rim. 'Comfortable here?'

'Yes, strangely enough.'

Dimples dented Sandra's cheeks. She lifted a frond of silky fair hair from her face, and took the cup.

'They brought me the Daily Mail and a property magazine, Inspector.' She looked up with an almost mischevious smile. 'On the basis that they'll come in useful if I win the lottery, I suppose – although I have to say, I don't care much any longer, for lotteries.'

'That's good. I...' Michael smiled slightly and lifted his coffee, taking a sip and then recoiling as it scalded his tongue. 'Ouch.'

Sandra sipped, seemingly unaffected by the heat of the steaming coffee. 'You need to slow down, too, Inspector. Smell a few roses.'

'Yes – yes, well, the fact is that it's been urgent we try to find David, Sandra, as you've pointed out.' He paused. 'To that end... it's important to know exactly what David told you he *had in mind* when he left. Has his behaviour puzzled you?'

'Well, that's the understatement of the year...' She hesitated for a second, then looked up. 'But no. I was wrong about him, that's all.'

'Meaning – you feel yourself taken in by him, in some way?'

'I've been trying to figure it all out. It's probably been good for me, to be here, strange as it may seem. Because it suddenly struck me, the last few weeks were more relaxed than any of the time I spent with David. It was just one problem after another, trying to get – that perfect life, I suppose. But David is not so different, I think now...'

'From?'

'Some other men. Oh, he always presents himself immaculately, as the gentleman – has quite a fixation about it. That should have told me something.'

She hesitated thoughtfully, and took another sip of coffee. 'But... he can never stand anyone touching his things, for example... And I think, possibly, he's been following an obsession, and I couldn't see it. I got some of that fever, myself, I suppose, thinking I'd have a decent partner, a secure life.' She gave a slight shrug. 'But at heart, I think now, he was always looking for the perfect-looking image. To impress everyone, for a change.'

'You're thinking that's why he... '

'Well, I'm wondering now, if that even explains why he was attracted to me in the first place. You see, he seemed to think his wife was a bit beneath him – she didn't impress his family, or the friends he thought he'd make, after he made his new life.' She looked up sharply. 'You know, don't repeat this but I think he's even been making use of being missing, in a way, trying to glorify himself, like some sort of martyr. He might not even know he's doing it. Or care.'

'What do you mean?'

'Oh – ' She held her coffee up. 'Even when he told his brother about the accident, he made out he was doing everything, taking money, for example, to help the family, and the reason he's had to keep hiding out is to help John and Linda, as much as himself.'

'You think it's a bit of acting?'

'It never occurred to me, but... as I said, I now think if he wants the perfect image, can't stand anything that might mar it. That's why,' Sandra glanced at Mariela, 'there's been such terrible stress.'

'Stress...?'

'Well, for me, of course, and also others.' Sandra nodded. 'It's felt endless. As I said, I haven't just been resting here. I've been thinking. It seems to me that he was afraid of going to the bank, himself, but not of anyone else getting into trouble. He's been letting everyone else to take the risks.'

'Yes, I see. And how do you feel about all that, now?'

'I realise that the money didn't really matter... neither did David's great plans. I just want to... but anyway, it's too late.'

'Too late to – ?'

'Make amends. David taking the money had nothing to do with me, but Alison's death should have been reported.'

'Are you sure he didn't want to report it?'

Sandra glanced up.

'Well, there was nothing to damn well stop him, so why didn't he? – I just got caught up with protecting his money.'

'I know, but...' Michael twirled his coffee cup thoughtfully, trying to think. 'Perhaps he had trouble deciding. He wasn't thinking clearly.'

'He was thinking clearly enough to get out to France.'

'But he was weak, and indecisive, sometimes? – or confused?'

Sandra sighed.

'Yes... I know you're right. But the result was making everything unnecessarily complicated. Going all the way out to Orba to bury Alision, and trying to prove he was dead, too, just in case anyone found her – ridiculous. He just had to be clever, I started to realise, show how much smarter he was than everyone, and he seemed to be angry with those two idiots at the finca, as if he wanted some kind of revenge on them for trying to trick him. Just to be clever. He could have buried Alison at his villa, as I told him at the time.'

'He didn't *seem* to listen, or...?'

'No he really didn't listen, I'm sure I made no sense to him. I failed to get him to see reason. He should have just picked up the money himself in the first place, but he didn't have the nerve. He'd get up to a certain point, then he was always backing out of everything.'

She was close to tears.

'How did David sound when he called you first, from France?'

'He was just asking about the money.'

'Did you ask him for any money for yourself, at any time?'

'Only what he promised, for living costs.'

'Did you believe his promise to send you that?'

'I had no reason not to, so... yes. It would be best for him, too. Besides, how can I get to France without at least enough for that?'

'He said he would send you funds to tide you over?'

'Yes.'

'But you didn't actually promise to live in France?'

'I said I'd take him his money. After that, I'd think about it.'

'What was to stop you just taking as much as you needed, from the funds withdrawn from the bank by John?'

'Well... ' She drew back, shocked.'I hardly think... It would be all packed up, in any case. It's a set amount.'

'It's a very large amount. I would expect you to consider that.'

'Yes, but – ' Sandra waved a hand. 'You have to understand that I don't care. I don't *want* any of his money, after all the trouble. I've felt released here, once I knew he'd gone. Even if he offered a large amount there'd be strings attached – that's the problem.'

'He was intent on getting it, though? – Did you think it possible he might turn up, if you didn't take his money through at once?'

'Probably not, but – well, yes.'

'How would Armando feel about that?'

'My concern is frankly about David, not Armando.'

'You'd feel some resentment toward David, if he turned up, or fear? How did you feel about meeting him to hand over the money?'

'I just simply wanted to get rid of it. So long as he didn't come back here, that's all. I've had enough.'

'Did David say what kind of car he was driving in France?'

'He might have, but mainly he just wanted to talk money.'

'You don't remember anything about what car he was driving?'

'No.' Sandra sighed heavily, and reached for the cigarettes. 'Well, I don't. I suppose I didn't really want to know. I'm sorry.'

'And now you feel you've left him behind, in a sense?'

'Yes.'

'Your phone records show no calls ever came through your phone from France.'

'Oh...?' Sandra frowned. 'What do you mean?'

'We are arresting you today, Sandra, for the most grave of offences.' Michael went on, 'There has been a major development this morning. David has been found.'

Sandra's hand, holding the unlit cigarette, froze in the air. 'You know where he is?'

'David is dead.'

'What?'

'And his death automatically implicates you.'

Sandra replaced the cigarette on the table.

'What do you do you mean? – you've been to Gascony?'

'David Harrington was found under a lime tree in your garden, his luggage with him. He had a skewer in his back, through to his heart.'

'*David?*...' Sandra whispered, her eyes wide.

'The pathologist's preliminary finding is that David has been dead for at least three weeks. Armando was not at your villa at that time, and John was in Nottingham. You were alone.'

Sandra shook her head. 'I don't understand. I suppose I could have been alone at that time...'

'You were, if David left for France on the 28th, as you said.'

'He did.'

'Can you account for there being no phone calls from France?'

Sandra shook her head again. 'He *told* me he was in France ...'

'You said the passport came from France, too,' Michael went on quickly. 'The post office said they thought they'd seen you at some time, when we showed them your photograph, but they didn't remember any specific mail from France.'

'Well, I do think that would be asking a bit much.'

'You didn't keep the packaging, then?'

'No – well, nobody keeps old packaging.'

'Can you tell us why you felt you had to do this?'

'What do you mean...?'

'To David. He was not your type until he came up with the lottery scheme, was he?' Michael nodded. 'He was agreeable and impressed by you, however, and best of all – he had a great scheme. But as you explained, so scathingly, he was a pillar of the establishment. Stolid, boring, and self important. On the other hand, Armando is attractive to you, isn't he? Very much your type?'

Sandra lifted her eyes. 'I suppose, but David was...'

'A bit naive? Not love exactly, then. But why did you have to kill him? Some sudden emergency?'

'No.' Sandra blinked slowly, and looked down. Her voice was soft. 'Of course I did nothing to him... It wasn't like that. After the accident – he was cracking up. He was taking sleeping tablets, but they did no good. Those two men were arrested for Alison's murder. He'd planned it, but it was on his conscience. Then he said he was going to tell the police about the accident. I told him he couldn't do that – and he agreed, but he was depressed, and then – he did that. I found him, in the kitchen.'

'You found him with the skewer in his back?'

'Yes – yes, I don't know how he did it, but I found him on the floor of the kitchen, like that. I was sorry then, of course, that I'd told him we couldn't go to the police – but at that point, what could I do? If I told anyone, let alone the police, it would have been the end of everything.'

'Everything?'

Sandra shook her head and sighed. 'Everything we'd planned.'

'Your plans, Sandra. All right, let's say that David was cracking – though he did not reveal any such concerns of conscience about the two men to John. I rather think your first explanation that he was contemptuous of them, and annoyed, would be nearer the truth. And let's forget the story that David killed himself, since it's ludicrous to imagine he thrust a skewer into his own back, neatly into his heart. So let's just say you killed him – when he was asleep, we assume, since he was found in pyjamas, and I have no doubt we'll find traces of sleeping medication. There was all that lottery money sitting in the bank – over half a million euros. And you could now get that money for yourself, since David had asked John to pick it up. John had no way of knowing his brother would be killed by you.'

'Me?'

'All right – exactly when did you find David dead, then?'

'On the 27th.'

'You're sure?'

'Of course.'

'Sandra, on the 24th of May you asked two labourers to come and dig a hole below the terrace on the morning of the 28th. Mario and Manolo had been working two doors down from your villa. They look after gardens for absentee owners, and do odd jobs as a one-off, for cash. They remember you clearly coming up to their truck, explaining the size and depth of the hole you wanted for a large shade tree...'

Sandra sat back. She shook her head slowly.

'They made a mistake. I said I wanted a hole dug for a small tree.'

'What did you tell them, when they dug it too deep?'

'Nothing.'

'Quite. You gestured and used your dictionary to explain it was perfect, and said you'd have someone else plant the tree and replace the soil. It's unfortunate that they remember you so clearly – one drawback of having such striking good looks, perhaps. The assistant in the garden centre remembers you, also. She advised you against transplanting a lime at this time of year, but you wanted something quite light and small, with shallow roots and an attractive appearance. However, even with regular watering, disturbing the roots in the dry season isn't a good idea.'

'I just wanted a small tree.'

'A small tree, and for that you needed a deep hole?'

'That was a mistake.'

'On the evening of the 27th, we assume a few hours before he was killed, David phoned John to say he was leaving next day. But I don't think the Guardia Civil need look for anyone else who could have killed David and dropped him into that deep hole, do you?'

Sandra glanced quickly at Mariela beside the door, then met Michael's eyes.

In a fierce, fast whisper that only he could hear, she said, 'You know nothing. *Nothing.* David was sabotaging everything, all the way. I was simply determined not to let him take me down with him. I couldn't let him go to the police.'

She glanced coolly over toward the door again, before continuing, 'He was going to tell some stupid story to the police about the accident. And he wanted to send me to France, first. I could not let him do that.'

'No, you couldn't.' Michael said. 'Because before you thought of exactly how you could get all the money for yourself and get rid of David, encouraging his nervousness over the bank and planting the idea that ignorant John could stand in for him – and well before you killed David – there was another obstacle.'

'What do you mean?'

'Alison.' Michael kept his steady tone. 'You sent that text deliberately, knowing she'd see it... and it's all right, that sort of thing happens a lot.'

'What sort of thing... ?'

'And we have a witness.'

'What?'

'The taxi driver.'

'Who?'

'Why did you not tell us you spoke to Alison on the steps?'

Sandra's face suddenly flushed. She sat back. 'I don't know what you mean. I'd like to see a lawyer, please.'

'The driver didn't pay particular attention to Alison when he was driving her up,' Michael said, 'but remembered the man with the beard coming up to pay the fare, and the location of the villa. What would you say if I told you that when Alison left the car, telling him to wait, the driver moved to look down and he saw Alison sit down on the steps, you came up and spoke to her – he could see you.'

'Nobody could, I – I spoke to her only for a second, when she was getting up. She pushed me, and she fell – '

'Nobody could overlook you from the road, is that what you were going to say? But from a certain angle, they can. We now know this.'

'She *pushed* me. Then she fell again.'

'When David went up to the road, we believe you took advantage of the situation. You pushed Alison's face down quickly into the dirt, and struck the back of her head with a rock. Then you told David she had fallen, when trying to push you. No doubt you were suitably shocked, and he believed you. He wanted to cover the matter up, naturally, but if the police had investigated, if David had reported it later – finally having doubts about keeping quiet, thinking that since it was an accident, it could all be proved and sorted – the police would have found evidence. Only you knew there was evidence.'

Sandra stretched a hand out suddenly toward Mariela's cup of coffee, as if reaching for a knife.

'Sandra, the small rocks lining the steps at your villa were mostly flat and grey, weathered smooth over the years. But as I mentioned earlier, we found some of them were not in their usual positions. They had obviously been moved. They now exposed their sharp underside, and they were stained red from the soil in which they'd been set.'

'I had to clean up.' Sandra said. She kept her eyes on the table. 'In the dry weather, the earth was loose, so I couldn't get the rocks back into their original positions. Is this important?'

'I have to tell you that we found traces of blood on the sharp, red side of one of the rocks. That rock and several others had been washed, evidently with washing-up liquid, but blood is not easy to get rid of, especially from porous material. On inspection, we ascertained that the blood on the sharp side of one particular rock proves it was lifted and used on Alison. It was that sharp under-side which struck Alison's head, which proves Alison was murdered.'

'Which proves *bloody nothing*.' Sandra's cheeks burned red. She shot a glance across the table, picked up Mariela's cup and hissed, 'So you can wipe that *stupid* smirk off your face.'

'We also suspect that you enjoyed all your plotting, deceit and subterfuge – and the manipulation. The killing of two people who got in your way was satisfying to you, no doubt. It's certainly very satisfying to us to have a water-tight case to put you away and protect any more victims from you.'

'So I'm Jack the bloody Ripper now?' She half rose.

'I hope not,' Michael said, a second before Mariela's cold coffee landed in his face.

Chapter Eighteen

'Michael,' Jose Luis said in the office a moment later, 'What made you decide to look for David in Sandra's garden, of all places?'

'Hang on. I thought she was going to kill me.' Michael wiped a towel over his face. 'Just a minute.'

'Here, have some water.' Jose Luis passed a glass across the table.

'Thanks... So, let's see. The phone records showed no calls from France. So where was David? If he was in Spain, why didn't he organise the bank visit, instead of Sandra? Why did he say he was going to France? ...Having no answers, I began to think he might be dead. Who had a motive? *Obviously* Sandra, as we know.'

'So, okay, yes, David might be dead, and obviously Sandra might have killed him for money – '

'Or to hide her actual role in Alison's death,' Mariela added. 'For once and for all, knowing the police might investigate more carefully and ask a few more questions than David had.'

'Or not. But both, actually,' added Michael. 'Which is my point.'

'What?'

'But I mean,' said Jose Luis, 'Why think of the *lime tree?*'

'Oh, that – just your simple detective work, as we say in Nottingham. David's villa rental finished on the 26th. It seemed certain he was at Sandra's villa, before supposedly taking off for France. So, *if* he was dead, it's likely he was killed at one of those two places.'

'But he phoned John *after* he left his villa, so...'

'Quite – so, er, if Sandra killed him at her villa, she'd have to dispose of the body. The obvious place was the garden. You said the lime tree looked newly planted. And I thought, well, why plant an expensive mature lime? It's not as if she owned the place. The position was right. She could just drag the body out, then roll it off the terrace into the hole. I couldn't see her digging a deep enough hole, so I thought of the labourers. Two and two, as we say in Nottingham elementary schools. Elementary, as another famous detective said.'

Mariela crossed her eyes and sighed. 'He didn't actually. But I suppose I did quite like,' she went on, 'the way you suggested that the taxi driver had seen something, without actually lying about it.'

'Well, of course he did remember everything just as I said – I only invented the part about him looking down and seeing Alison on the steps. I was absolutely positive that if Alison had been seriously injured David would not have casually walked up and paid off the taxi, and given no impression of anxiety to the driver. But someone very cool and quick-thinking, a practiced, convincing liar, someone used to blood and who knew what was needed to kill, a calculating narcissist, could have – '

'Yes, very clever, Michael,' said Jose Luis. 'And lucky. But one more question. I was always expecting you to rush off to France at any minute, and you never did. Why not?'

'I thought you might all be wondering about that... ' Michael looked expansively around the office, as if to address the world. 'Shoes.'

'*Shoes?*'

'Now, listen.' Michael folded his arms. 'You need to know this. David Harrington might, going to France, have had the the foresight to leave a pair of shoes for John. But let me tell you, Jose Luis – someone like David Harrington would never, *never*, leave behind *two* pairs of Loakes handmade calfskin brogues.'

Initial paperwork out of the way, Michael, Jose Luis and Mariela sat down to coffee and bocadillos in the staff canteen.

Suddenly ravenous, Michael ground his jaws on the dry bread, then put up a hand as three long strands of stringy ham dangled down his chin.

Mariela smiled primly. 'I think someone needs a sharp slap.'

'Or a napkin,' Jose Luis added. 'I have a grubby one.'

'Ha, ha.' Michael swallowed the ham, and brushed crumbs from his face. 'Very nice, but I could starve at this rate. How's John doing, Mariela, by the way?'

'You wouldn't believe it,' Mariela said, 'but he lay down and went straight to sleep when he got back inside. We'll tell him about David after we've got DNA confirmation – procedure, and all that.'

Jose Luis said suddenly, 'You know, John will get David's money, eventually – what's left of it.'

'Apart from the lottery winnings,' Michael said, picking up his roll again. 'What's left of that, will go to the original winners.'

'I wonder,' Mariela said, 'whether David's original share remains his, after it's returned to the lottery. What's the law in England?'

Michael and Jose Luis stared at her.

'If so, David's share would go to John and Linda, as well as his other money... ' She gazed dreamily into space. 'I think I could really go for that John Harrington, if he brushed himself up.'

Michael nearly choked on a bite.

'He's fixed up very nicely with his wife, Linda, I'll have you know. Although... if *you* ran off with *John*...'

'Sorry to interrupt the happy gathering,' Sergeant Ramirez said from the door, 'But the Colonel would like to see you, Michael. Right away?'

'Ah, Fernandez, nice to see you again. Take a seat.'

Colonel Cardells was in full uniform, three silver shields glistening on the epaulettes of a rumpled white shirt.

A large oil on the wall, of the Capitan General of the Guardia Civil, King Juan Carlos, in uniform, seemed to frame his head.

The massive oak desk made the Colonel look smaller, but the scowl had been replaced by a benign smile, making him look almost jolly. He smiled for about two seconds, then sat down and leaned forward, elbows on desk, flabby chin resting on intertwined fingers.

'Now then, Detective Inspector. I hear you're in a bit of trouble?'

The tone was light, but Michael didn't answer.

'I've just been talking to Chief Superintendent Bowater,' Cardells went on smoothly. 'He tells me you resigned, just before you came back to Spain.'

'In a manner of speaking.' Michael straightened his back.

'It's all sorted.' Cardells nodded. 'I've told him how helpful you've been and what a brilliant detective you are. He should be proud of you.'

Michael nodded. 'May I ask what Superintendent Bowater said?'

'Well, I won't go into the detail, but he said your job is waiting for you, and that you've nothing to worry about.'

'I see, sir. Thank you.'

'But...' Cardells leaned forward and lowered his voice. 'But how would you like to work for the Guardia Civil, instead?'

'The Guardia – sir?'

Cardells stood up and marched over to a map on the wall.

'Something like four hundred thousand ex-patriots live permanently on the Costa Blanca – most of them British – and literally millions more come every year for their holidays. Sadly, there's a corresponding crime wave out here. Much of it involves the British, either as victims or villains. For some time now we've been thinking it would be useful to have a fluent English and Spanish speaking detective on the force.'

He crossed back to the desk and sat down, beaming.

'The job is yours, if you want it. We wouldrank you as a captain and help with relocation expenses, all that sort of thing. What do you think, Inspector Fernandez?'

'I'm honoured... truly honoured. But it's a big decision.'

'Of course it is. But we'd love you to join us. I'd like you to think it over.' Cardells stood up. 'Take as long as you like, but get back to me and let me know.'

'Thank you, Colonel,' Michael said, standing for his hand to be vigorously shaken. 'I will, sir – I certainly will do that – sir.'

Cardells added, 'If you took the job, we'd assign Officer Poquet to work alongside you.' An ominous twinkle lit the Colonel's eyes.

Back in the canteen, Jose Luis and Mariela looked up, grinning.

'Bastards. You knew all along what that meeting was about.'

'What did you say?' Jose Luis asked impatiently.

'Said I'd think about it.' Michael sat down and reached for coffee.

'What's to think about?'

'Don't know. It's just me, I suppose. I have to think, before I do any thinking.'

Standing up, Michael took the hand offered by Jose Luis, knowing they might never work together again, and squeezed it.

When he saluted, Jose Luis laughed, clapped him on the shoulder, and saluted back.

Michael walked over to the door, where Mariela was waiting.

She held out her hand, and as he shook it, her hazel eyes filmed over in what he thought could be tears, if not watery film – then she reached up to kiss him lightly on the cheek. Her lips felt softly moist.

'We could have dinner tonight,' she whispered.

He opened his mouth and found himself saying, 'Mariela – you're absolutely not going to believe this, I can hardly believe it myself, but there's something I've simply got to do.'

Chapter Nineteen

Michael's destination was about an hour and a half away. He knew that if he didn't go now he might never go. He thought about confirming his return flight to England, but that could wait.

With a few belongings in a suitcase in the back of a hire car, he hit the A7 in familiar territory. At Benissa he left the motorway, paid the toll, and took the turning for Senija.

The sun was starting its westward descent, and he headed directly towards the shallow beams of light that radiated from yet another cloudless sky.

Shadows began to lengthen as he neared the traffic lights at the approach to Lliber.

Green changed to red. He thought about following the three drivers in front of him who jumped the signal, but didn't.

Instead he stopped, waited, and admired the scenery.

The soft pastel-painted walls of the houses indicated life had been little changed by the tide of development in this part of the Jalon Valley, or by any influx of foreign residents.

But who could really know what went on behind the closed front doors of houses that, within living memory, had echoed to the slow clip-clop of over-burdened mules and the creaking of wooden cart wheels?

On the one hand, mechanisation in the form of chugging, rattling, smoking diesel engines had changed the resonance, as well as the volume... but perhaps had not greatly increased the pace of life or changed the values people held.

Just as the images of yesteryear were crystallising in his mind, as he drafted a report on the matter, a convoy approached in the distance, lead by a German-registered Audi.

Michael studied the cars as they filed past, noting their registrations. After the Audi came a line of cars registered in Britain, Britain, Holland, France – Spain – Holland, Britain, and Belgium.

Where else in the world, even in capital cities, could you see such a multi-national collection of vehicle registrations? Yet here it was, streaming through a two-donkey pueblo in the middle of nowhere.

As he passed between the houses, two lurid lilac walls stood out from the neighbouring beige-painted houses, as if to announce foreign ownership.

Not that he was involved in, or should even be worried about any of this ostensible destruction, of course: "He Who Hated Spain." And perhaps, in some way, it was all for the best.

He shrugged, and drove on.

A lone pursuer in a white van emblazoned with the letters, "STEVE JONES – PLUMBER," overtook him as he left the village.

The wide open space of the valley unfolded and Jalon came into view. Parcent stood in the far distance.

Along the road, vines stretched out at angles, their leaves maturing in the heat of early summer. Tight bunches of tiny, pale green grapes were just beginning to swell.

Approaching Jalon, his eyes were drawn to the vast urbanisation of Almazara that loomed high on the northern mountain like a giant, concrete crater. It seemed to have expanded horrifically since his last visit... But why should he care?

The riverbed, as he fringed the town, looked as dry as ever.

The bodegas were doing good business, as usual. Day trippers lugged heavy plastic flagons across the road, and staggered towards their coaches. The fish and chip shop was doing a roaringly British trade, serving tourists happy to eat within inches of passing traffic.

He began to speculate about the forces at work in the valley that had brought about such changes in just a few years.

Economic necessity?

Subsidising of a struggling rural way of life?

Greed? – and why should he care?

He crossed the bridge, left Jalon behind, and pressed on for Alcalalí.

The direction sign had been amended in dribbling black paint to read: ALCANALÍ. It seemed that the Valenciano protesters were concerned about more than the demise of their regional language.

The landscape changed as the valley narrowed, and vineyards were replaced by orange groves.

The blossoms he'd seen wilting on his last visit had given way to tiny oranges, barely visible within the deep green foliage of sculptured trees. Already the fruit was beginning to swell, absorbing the warm sun as if storing it up for winter harvest.

But here and there, builders' rubble lay discarded by the side of the road. At the edge of a neat orange grove, an abandoned car sat, its windows smashed, bodywork disintegrating, as rust ate into metal.

Sofas, chairs, refrigerators and other discarded household items were lined up alongside a row of rubbish bins as if hoping that one day they'd be noticed.

Michael pulled over near the bins. He'd been drifting off to sleep.

He blinked, stretched, and lay back in the seat.

A silver-haired old man trudged by in ragged clothes, rope-soled shoes laced around his ankles. His back was bent under a canvas sack, a tattered straw hat shielded his eyes from the amber glare of the sun.

He passed the unsightly tip apparently without regard, and continued on his way, tracing steps he'd probably taken for most of his life – as if to say, "This is not the Cotswolds or the Lake District, you know, where order and tidiness are essential ingredients of life – and where conservation is of paramount importance and it's easier to buy a scarf from Taiwan than a loaf of bread. This is Spain. Life is more important than order, and tidiness. What does it matter if perfection is marred by progress? Life continues. The sun rises and sets, seasons come and go. Life is not about neatness and congruity. Life is friends, fellowship, family, and food on the table."

Michael sat up and stretched.

The old man had long gone. Nobody was on the road ahead.

He turned the key, pulled out, and a few corners later Parcent came into view – with its narrow streets of houses huddled around a knoll, watched over by the fretwork church tower.

He parked on tree-lined Avenida de la Constitución and climbed the hill. The Placa del Ploble was crowded with vans and cars.

Bar Moll was packed, the buzz of conversation as difficult to pierce as the smoke-filled atmosphere.